ALLEN STROUD

RESILIENT

Book Two of the *Fractal* Series,
Following *Fearless*

This is **FLAME TREE PRESS** book

FLAME TREE PRESS
6 Melbray Mews, London, SW6 3NS, UK
flametreepress.com

US sales, distribution and warehouse:
Simon & Schuster
simonandschuster.biz

UK distribution and warehouse:
Marston Book Services Ltd
marston.co.uk

Publisher's Note: This is a work of fiction. Names, characters, places, and
incidents are a product of the author's imagination. Locales and public names
are sometimes used for atmospheric purposes. Any resemblance to actual
people, living or dead, or to businesses, companies, events, institutions, or
locales is completely coincidental.

Thanks to the Flame Tree Press team, including:
Taylor Bentley, Frances Bodiam, Federica Ciaravella, Don D'Auria,
Chris Herbert, Josie Karani, Molly Rosevear, Will Rough, Mike Spender,
Cat Taylor, Maria Tissot, Nick Wells, Gillian Whitaker.

The cover is created by Flame Tree Studio with
thanks to Nik Keevil and Shutterstock.com.
The font families used are Avenir and Bembo.

Flame Tree Press is an imprint of Flame Tree Publishing Ltd

flametreepublishing.com

A copy of the CIP data for this book is available from the British Library
and the Library of Congress.

HB ISBN: 978-1-78758-715-1
US PB ISBN: 978-1-78758-713-7
UK PB ISBN: 978-1-78758-714-4
ebook ISBN: 978-1-78758-716-8

Printed and bound in Great Britain by Clays Ltd, Elcograf S.p.A

ALLEN STROUD

RESILIENT

Book Two of the *Fractal* Series,
Following *Fearless*

FLAME TREE PRESS
London & New York

FOREWORD

Back in 2015, I was attending the Science Fiction Foundation masterclasses at the Royal Observatory in Greenwich. Pat Cadigan was the guest tutor for the afternoon and the text she asked the gathered group of Ph.D. students and other researchers to analyse was a short story by Alfred Bester.

As part of the discussion, Pat gave an account of Bester's difficulties in getting some of his content past his editors. A close analysis of the writing revealed he was describing non-white characters, a fact that wasn't immediately obvious on first reading as it was subtly done.

This moment resonated for me. As did another moment at Eastercon the next year when I attended a panel discussing non-white male protagonists in Fantasy and heard the speakers discuss how, as young readers, they had created their own images of different heroic characters, editing out the gender or ethnicity descriptions even as they read them to preserve the sense of identification they felt with those characters as being female or gay or Black or Asian.

Fearless, the first book in the series, is a product of my thinking along those lines. The opening chapter is a barometer. Captain Ellisa Shann's physical disability is part of who she is. The opening introduction to her in the book is purposefully designed to be hard hitting and to linger in the mind of the reader. When it was first read at Fantasycon 2017, I could feel the audience were a little uncomfortable, and felt perhaps the fourth wall break, and her casual accusatory tone, were aimed at them.

I was born in 2080, with no legs. Perhaps that gives you an image of me? An image that defines who I am to you as a person?

Maybe you get a sense of who someone is by their limitations? Do you think who we are is determined by what we look like? What we can't do? Or what we don't have? The world doesn't work that way anymore.

In a way, the accusation is levelled at the reader, but also in a way, it isn't. This isn't about feeling guilty over some specific action or wrongly accused of prejudice. Instead, I wanted to banish the default of considering her as a person with two arms and two legs. I wanted to make sure the reader would not slip into seeing her that way as some of Bester's readers, including his editor, had slipped into accepting a white western default. I judged that our genres have moved on sufficiently to accommodate a physically disabled protagonist who is not restricted by her body in the environment she lives and works in. The accusation is blunt and abrupt. That's the point. It is made that way, so we all remember who Shann is and what she represents. The image of her lingers, because of the jolt.

It is also a massive risk, gambling with the identification and empathy of readers on the very first page of chapter one, introducing the main character. But then, as writers, we have to take risks. This was the first time I chose to do so right from the beginning.

The fourth wall is broken again right at the end of the book, with Shann talking to us about her dilemma and her feelings. To me, it was important to do this for a couple of different reasons. Firstly, less importantly, there's a symmetry to it, providing a sense of finality. Secondly, more importantly, it prioritises the second key theme of the book on an equal footing to the first. Shann is suffering from a mental illness brought about by the stress of her situation. The onset of this illness has been shown in the narrative of the story and the way she is compartmentalising her emotional reactions right up until the moment they overwhelm her, and she cannot control herself.

As a writer, I have come to believe that a book is a partnership between two imaginations – the writer and the reader. There is room for both, and for a story to stay with us, both have to be given space to work. I welcome you, the reader, to imagine the scenes I describe in ways that are personal to you. Beyond the words on the page, the story is yours to shape and visualise as you wish. But in these specific elements, I wanted to be clear and unequivocal. This is Shann. This is who she is, at the beginning and at the end.

PROLOGUE

2017

'Oumuamua, the first known interstellar asteroid, may contain water, scientists say, and if it does, that means it's water from another star system.

First detected by deep space telescopes on October 19th, the asteroid's velocity and approach vector do indicate that it originated from one of our neighbouring solar systems. Although, at this stage, no researcher is prepared to go on record and say which one.

When it was first detected, 'Oumuamua's strange elongated shape provoked widespread speculation that it might be an artificial body, or 'spaceship', but that excitement quickly died down when the body showed no signs of 'outgassing' or course correction when it approached the Sun. However, the race to investigate this possibility did demonstrate to the wider public the limitations of our telescopes and tracking systems to accurately determine the shape of an object travelling through space.

But the latest findings suggest water might be trapped under a thick, carbon-rich coating on its surface.

'Oumuamua is scheduled to leave the range of Earth's telescopes by the end of the year. Given its highly unusual orbit, it is likely we will never see it again.

CHAPTER ONE

Holder

"Name and Employee ID please?"

I sigh, wipe my sweaty forehead with the back of my arm and hold up my badge, right in front of the camera.

The guy on the screen leans forward, squinting at it. "Sorry, I can't read that. Can you tell me where you're from?"

"Natalie Holder, Amalgamated Solutions?"

There's a delay, latency on the connection to his remote access terminal somewhere else in the world. The guy glances down at some paperwork in front of him. "Yes, okay, I have you. Employee ID number?"

"AK667AB1E8."

The same pause. "Great, yes, that's fine." He looks up at me again. "You been here before?"

"No, it's my first time."

"All right. Before you go through, the regs state I need to advise you to make sure you're hydrated and that you have supplies. The Hub is one of the least hospitable places on Earth. Your pass entitles you to a two-hour stay, but after that, it'll expire and if you stay on premises for too long, you will too."

"Sure, understood."

"Great, then let's get you moving."

A beam lances out from beneath the screen, bathing me in red light. I hold my breath, expecting the worst, but the worst doesn't come. Instead, the scan completes and a buzzer sounds. The door in front of me unlocks and starts to swing open. I'm keen to get moving, but

I don't touch the moving panel. The last thing I want is unnecessary attention. These people need to think I'm legit.

I need to do my part. Nothing more, nothing less.

I'm through the door and inside. The temperature is a couple of degrees cooler here; forty-two Celsius, as opposed to forty-four or forty-five. I can feel the heat coming off the painted concrete walls. It's like an assault, all targeted at me, the only person here.

Out in the middle of nowhere at the entrance to the eighth wonder of the world.

The Atacama Desert, in the former republic of Chile, is home to the largest energy tile farm on Earth. The reflective glow from the massive solar array can be seen from space, even as far as the Luna colony at times. The accompanying underground hydro-battery and distribution network make this one of the most sensitive facilities on the planet.

It's also unstaffed. The whole complex is unsafe for human habitation, owing to the extreme heat generated by the system. Rather than waste money on expensive coolant processes, everything has been designed to tolerate fierce temperatures. The technology in here is the same as the stuff they use on Ceres and in the asteroid mining stations.

Seven thousand multinational corporations rely on these arrays for their day-to-day electricity. Supply companies beneath them pay regular rates for their power, and beneath them are the eight billion individual citizens of Earth. The whole system is a corporate control web. Two hundred years ago, who would have thought access to electricity would become the way the powerful keep the rest of us in line?

According to the schematic I've seen, mobile autonomous security units patrol the interior. They're maintained and monitored by different commercial contractors across the globe. Each of them has a territory. Whilst I stay on the authorised route for my visit, they won't be a problem. As soon as I'm detected deviating, the nearest unit will be tasked to intercept me, but there's latency there too, I'll have a few seconds.

So, when I make my move, I need to do it carefully.

I start down the path. I grew up in Nigeria, so the heat is something I can tolerate, but the reflection of light bouncing off all the tiles is like looking at the sun in all directions. Three steps in and the brightness is hurting my eyes. I've no choice but to keep my gaze fixed on my feet and the scoured gravel underfoot. The instructions specified the distance I need to walk in metres, so I've been practising to keep my stride in a regular pattern. However, now I'm here, I can't help but worry I've mis-stepped in some way and I'll end up lost.

Sixteen metres to the first turn. Go right.

I make the turn. Any outward sign of hesitation might be observed, so I can't second-guess myself or the directions. *Eight metres, then left. Twelve metres, then right again. Four metres, then you're there.*

There's a shadow over the ground where I stop as instructed. I glance to my left and see the control panel; the reason I'm supposed to be here, according to the authorities. I kneel down in front of it. The location is a small blind spot in the camera coverage. I'm to work on the system using the panel, diagnose the error that was detected, and apply a bespoke software patch, so there's no need for the security monitoring to be alerted to a deviation.

Not for a while.

My gaze falls to the metal section beneath the control panel. There's a ventilation grille big enough to fit through. Behind it should be a powerful electrical fan. I reach out and brush my fingers against the metal, but there's no breeze. Either the fan is switched off, or….

I take out my powered screwdriver, fit the correct socket and start undoing the bolts. There's eight of them, but they come away pretty easily and the grille lifts off without resistance. Underneath, there's no fan, but an open space into darkness, out of the sun.

I sit on the ground and lower myself in. About three feet below, my boots meet a step, then another immediately below that. I turn around and begin climbing down.

Into darkness.

Six or seven steps down my eyes begin to adjust. I'm in a concrete box. The shadows of objects clutter the floor. I take out a small pen torch and carefully flick it on.

The extractor unit has been disassembled and left here in a pile, as they said it would be. The chamber has been excavated too. There's a hole in the far wall where someone's managed to break through to the next room.

I step off the ladder and walk towards the hole. I shine my torch into the empty space. If I crouch or get on my hands and knees, I'll be able to get in here, but I need to be careful. The equipment I'm carrying is fragile.

Very fragile.

I crawl into the hole, shuffling over broken stones and mud. It's much cooler down here where the sunlight can't reach. I'm shivering a little. Maybe I got too used to the blazing heat outside.

Well, it'll be hot enough in here pretty soon.

The tunnel ends abruptly. I have to trust we're in the right place. Whoever dug this out had a job to do, just like me.

I turn and lie flat on my back in the dark. The little pen torch has a corded loop. I drape it over a hanging rock, and it illuminates the space above me, so I can see my hands and work.

The three containers I've been given are in my pockets. I pull them out and connect them together, as I was shown. The device is a reaction explosive, powerful enough to obliterate me and everything around me in a two-kilometre radius, once it's activated. The tunnel is right above an underground regulator too. Once I press the ignition switch, this whole place will be wrecked. The damage will be catastrophic.

Everything has been carefully arranged. That's how it works. You fail when you try to overcomplicate your job. So, instead, everyone does a part. The security clearance was forged, the security scanner was hacked. The ventilation system removed, the hole dug. All of it planned and patiently put together over months by different people.

I'm the last piece in the puzzle.

My hands are shaking, either from the cold or from nerves. I take a moment, steady my breathing. These will be my last minutes alive. I have a purpose. I always wanted a purpose. This is my purpose. This is what I was put here to do, so others can live better and break the chains of slavery. I am what they used to call a martyr, a sacrifice to the cause.

The tears come then, and the sobs. Great body-racking heaves that make me feel sick. I try to fight them in the enclosed space, clinging desperately to the tube in my hands. This little three-sectioned thing that is the key to humanity's future.

Then I go calm. They tell you about this when you train. There's a moment of acceptance, a moment when everything becomes clear. The world becomes small and nothing matters apart from you and the trigger. You and the bomb.

That's the moment you have to seize. Otherwise, you panic, and it all goes to shit.

I press the trigger.

2019

Scientists have confirmed the detection of a second interstellar wanderer into our solar system. This time, though, they've managed to find it much earlier in its journey, so there's substantial excitement over what we can learn.

2I/Borisov is named after Crimean amateur astronomer Gennadiy Borisov, who discovered the comet with his homemade telescope. '2I' stands for 'Second Interstellar'. According to the International Astronomical Union (IAU), the comet is 'unambiguously' interstellar in origin. The race is now on to find out as much as possible before the object leaves our solar system.

The comet is currently inbound towards the Sun, and will reach its closest approach (perihelion) on the 8th of December at a distance of approximately three hundred million kilometres (one hundred and ninety million miles) — about twice the average distance of the Earth from the Sun.

The comet is approaching the planetary orbital plane at an angle of around forty degrees and is travelling at more than 150,000 kilometres per hour. It's between two and sixteen kilometres (1.2 and 10 miles) in diameter, and current observations note signs of outgassing and the sort of debris tail we've learned to expect from comets ever since they were first observed more than a thousand years ago.

Two recent analyses of the comet's colour and spectra have revealed its suspected material composition. It appears to be similar to the solar system's long-period comets that originate in the distant Oort Cloud, rather than the short-period comets that come from nearer to the Sun.

Scientists are currently attempting to use their recorded data on the comet's velocity and trajectory to trace its path back to its point of origin, far outside our solar system. We can only speculate what it may have been a part of, or been a witness to, on its travels.

CHAPTER TWO

Drake

Start of the week is always a bitch in Jezero.

I round the corner to see the queue at card registration stretching out the door. They're all hard-working civilians like me; the requisitioned Mars workforce, kept that way under CorpGov contract. That's how the game works.

I need to renew my pass, we all do, every few days. If you don't, it reverts to its basic code. That's enough to get you into a public facility, but not much else. Everyone in that line is a specialist like me, working with specialist equipment in a specialist area of the colonial dome. That's the reason they got a ride up here from Earth. There's always a long line to get to the reader.

But today, on this particularly Martian morning, it's particularly long.

I stop in the street, the grips of my boots digging into the rubberised grid designed to slow down anyone running too fast in thirty-eight-percent gravity. I've got just under three hours left on my card. I can come back later, but that'll mean hoping I get a break in my shift, otherwise I'll end up locked in surgery, or depending on the kindness of others.

Well, I guess they depend on me often enough.

Ahead of me, two people are arguing in the street: a man and a woman. They're speaking in an Eastern European language I don't recognise. Both of them wear the grey one-piece uniform of the maintenance division. Workers in that department monitor critical base systems and communication relays. MarsCol needs people who can sit in chairs waiting for something to break down and who have the technical expertise to fix it or work around it when it does.

The three interconnected Jezero domes sit in the crater of the same name on a flatbed of clay. The exterior of our home is continually buffeted by dust storms and solar radiation. Despite our perfect shield against the outside, the average life expectancy of manufactured technology on Mars is half that of anything made and operated on Earth. To compensate, all the people who live up here have to be able to improvise and make use of redundancies, otherwise we're all screwed.

"Doctor Drake? Are you all right?"

I glance in the direction of the question and smile. "Fine, Antonio, fine. Just intimidated by the queue this morning."

Antonio Sammatri lives in my apartment block. He's in his forties, going bald gracefully, and works in the Colonial engineering office. I'm pretty sure he's just come from the registration point too. "Might be the one on Saturn Street is less busy?" he suggests.

"Might be," I say. "Any idea why we're so busy today?"

"No. Sorry."

"When did you get here?"

"About two hours ago."

I sigh. "Well, I can't wait in that line. I have patients to see. I guess I'll have to come back when things die down."

"You got enough time left on your card?"

"Probably not."

Sammatri stares at me, then grunts and shrugs. "Be seeing you, Doc," he says and wanders off.

I stare at the queue for a few more minutes, then turn around and begin walking to the hospital.

★   ★   ★

"Doctor Drake? There's a call for you on channel six."

I'm just inside the door of Jezero Main, the hospital where I work. The place is busy with the walking wounded and ill. The DuraGlas walls ensure all manner of human suffering is on display as people wait for assistance. Mars is unforgiving. Working here is hard on the body, mind, and soul.

The receptionist has called me over. I can't remember her name. I think it's Ulanda, but....

"Thanks, I'll take it in the booth."

There's a private comms unit for employees. It doesn't require credit to connect; as it's an official communication, the hospital will pick up the tab. I get inside and sit down on the plastic chair. The system recognises a presence in the room and the retina scan starts up, quickly identifying me. "Employee ID 376-0C. Welcome, Doctor Drake. Connecting you with central requisitions."

The screen lights up. The picture is distorted, but quickly coalesces into a coherent image. I recognise the face immediately. Most people around here would.

"What can I do for you, Deputy Governor?"

"Emerson, we have an emergency call from Phobos Station. The mining shuttle *Chronos* is due to dock six hours from now, and according to the last transmission, they're bringing in a whole crew of injured miners from the moon's surface. Looks like there's been some kind of seismic event down there. We're requisitioning a team of medical operatives to report to the station. That includes you."

Augustine Boipelo has been in post for the last three years. She's from Botswana and an appointed official under the elected governor, Joachim Dramms. Of course, voting in that election is limited to Martian citizens, those carefully selected individuals who don't need to renew their passes every twenty-four hours.

Boipelo is one of Dramms's three deputies. Her area of responsibility is in managing space traffic and import/export logistics. A personal call from her indicates this situation is serious.

"I'll head to the ferry straight away," I reply. "There is a small issue though."

Boipelo's brow pinches into a frown. "What's the problem?"

"My temporary pass runs out in a couple of hours. I've not been able to renew it. I'd planned to do that later this morning, but if I'm heading to the station, I won't have a chance."

"That I can sort." Boipelo leans back from the screen. "I'll arrange for your clearance to be renewed under the emergency protocol for the duration. Then you can concentrate on helping people." I hear a murmured voice off screen and Boipelo looks up at someone behind the camera. "I need to go. Good luck, Doctor."

"Thanks, I—"

The line goes dead.

I stare at the screen for a few stolen, contemplative moments. Going off planet is an uncommon requirement of my work. This will be the first time in three years I've been requisitioned for a job like this. Mining is an inherently dangerous activity in any environment. Phobos is an unstable moon. Despite the low gravity, shifting wrong can trap anyone who isn't prepared. I know what sort of injuries to expect; limbs crushed and immobilised for transit. We don't get as much of that down here, but I can certainly prepare. The station will have all the necessary supplies, but there are a couple of things I could take with me.

I leave the communications booth and head for my office. The ID scanner recognises me as I approach, and the door slides open.

There's a man sat in my chair. He stands up as I enter. He's wearing a Fleet dress uniform and I'm instantly worried. "Are you Doctor Emerson Drake?" he asks.

"I am. What's the problem, Lieutenant...?"

"Rivers, Doctor."

"Lieutenant Rivers. What can I do for you?"

My guest looks awkward. He's young, probably just out of the academy and set up here on his first commission. He still has the bootcamp haircut, buzzed right back to the scalp. He clearly has authorisation to be in the room, but he's not happy about being here. "I've been sent to inform you that we lost contact with the *Khidr*. Your brother is on board, I wasn't sure if you—"

"Yes, I know where he is."

I stare at the officer, then, when I have his eye, look meaningfully at the door. He gets the hint and nods, producing a metal chit which he holds out to me. "We're doing our best to re-establish contact. Should you want to get in touch and get updates, you can reach me directly with this."

I stare at the card in his hand. Then, on impulse, decide to take it. "Thank you," I say. "Now, if you don't mind?"

"Of course." Rivers leaves and the door slides shut behind him.

I turn to my terminal on the desk. There's no sign that it's been tampered with. Of course, if Rivers is any good at being a snoop, he won't leave any traces. I still don't like the idea of some stranger being in here without me, or one of my team. Fleet are usually okay, but on Mars you have to be careful. There are all sorts of corporate agendas at work, all the time.

Hydroponics Technician Jonathan Drake. Born in 2082, three years after me. He graduated from Ontario University and followed me into space. Our parents died in 2095, in a road traffic accident, so there was never much of a life left for us on Earth. Jonathan went military, enlisting in Fleet straight out of high school, so most of his tuition was paid for. By then, I'd already taken an offer from Mediventure, one of six companies who were subcontracted to run MarsCol's hospitals. They made me a good offer to come here. There's no better fresh start than a new planet. I journeyed up like everyone else, hoping to complete my contract and then freelance, charging top rate for my services once I'd become a citizen.

That was how it was sold to us. The reality was a little different.

According to legend, at the end of the first millennia in the old Christian calendar, Eric Thorsvaldson, known as Eric the Red, came back from discovering Greenland and sold it to his people as a bright and fertile country where they could make a fresh start. The stories worked, and he led a colonial mission of ships which founded two settlements on the shores of the new land which lasted nearly five hundred years.

Eric the Red – the Red Planet. Both using propaganda, both being careful with the truth. *Red* – there's an irony in there that I can't quite explain.

Most new arrivals on Mars found their contracts had been *reasonably modified* as soon as they got off the shuttle. There are good reasons, of course. The colonies have to become self-sustaining. That agenda is higher priority than honouring any individual agreement.

Sure.

The terminal powers up, the retinal scan logs me in. The screen displays an update to my citizenship status. Boipelo is true to her word. The emergency requisition means an extra set of privileges. Not quite as good as being a full citizen, but I'll take what I can get.

In addition to the renewal, a seat on the next transport from Jezero to Phobos Station – the *Angelus,* departing in just under an hour. A ground car is due to pick me up in four minutes from outside the front of the building. No time for anything but to comply.

Well, almost no time.

I key up the communication records, using my new emergency privileges to access whatever I can. I'm looking for anything sent from the *Khidr,* anything that'll give me more than I've already been told.

A list of comms packages scrolls up the page. This is a list of verified transmitter packages since the *Khidr* launched. All standard procedure. Up here we're supposed to be one big happy family, with everyone staying in contact. I can't read any of the contents, but I can see the logs and the file sizes. According to this, the ship's locator beacon has been transmitting constantly since it left Phobos five days ago. It went dark four hours ago.

Four hours? That's pretty quick time for notifying close kin. Maybe I'm being overly suspicious, but….

An alert flashes on the screen. The ground car is here. I key the log-out sequence and leave the room, heading back out to the lobby.

"Leaving so soon, Doctor?" Ulanda calls out from the front desk.

"Yes, so it seems." I smile and shrug. "Been requisitioned. Back later."

"You'd like your appointment list cancelled then?"

I stop dead in the middle of the hall and walk over to her, lowering my voice. "That should be done automatically, it's got a priority clearance." I nod towards the entrance. "They've sent a car for me."

Ulanda's eyebrows shoot up and I realise I'm going to be the talk of the building for at least the next hour. "You had one personal appointment request, a Mister Jacob Rocher? I added an appointment just before lunch."

"Well, I'm sure he'll be notified."

"I guess so."

I glance out of the DuraGlas doors. An automated ground car has just pulled up. "That'll be for me," I say. "Thanks for your help."

"I didn't do anything."

"Well, thanks anyway."

Outside, the back door of the ground car opens when I press my thumb against the lock plate. I get in, and as soon as I do, the vehicle begins to pull away. I'm alone inside the vehicle; the automated driving system, designed for Earth's packed streets, is more than capable of handling the 'barely there' traffic of Jezero and our destination, Hera spaceport.

I have a little time while I'm in the car. My mobile screen is keyed into the office system, so I can access *Khidr*'s communication log. I think Lieutenant Rivers was just doing his job. He's young and clearly didn't want to be there. Someone up to something more nefarious would have...I don't know...seemed calmer and more polished?

The logs have file sizes against them. The last transmission from *Khidr* was a small one, probably an automated position signal. Before that, a larger transmission looks like it might actually contain a written report. I don't have clearance to get access to these, but someone on Phobos Station might.

Plus, a favour for the Deputy Governor keeps you in her mind. Who knows? Maybe that elusive citizenship request will go somewhere if I'm a good little employee and help out these poor miners. Maybe if I—

"There is a priority news alert from Earth on channel one. Would you like to see the broadcast?"

I glance up. The measured female voice of the computer driving the car is familiar to anyone on MarsCol. The same voice is used for most public voice-activated systems. Any news from Earth will have been relayed via the open media channel. That means a delay of around fifteen minutes. News channels have got used to managing this. All interviews conducted between different colonies, ships and stations are pre-recorded. However, that does raise the question: what could possibly be a priority news alert for us all the way out here? It has to be something serious....

"Sure, display broadcast, please."

A screen on the back of the driver's seat comes on. There's a woman talking and a blue ticker scrolling across the bottom of the screen – *Catastrophic explosion in the Atacama power array. One casualty, thought to be the perpetrator.*

"...authorities on the scene have reported that damage is still being assessed. However, independent sources have claimed that the array will need to be almost completely rebuilt, a task that could take decades...."

Okay, yes that's serious. The broadcast cuts to an aerial view of the site, probably from a drone camera. Looks like some opportunist got there, recorded something and got away before the corporate military could shoot down his flyer and arrest him. The barren ground is blackened and there are fires, with thick black smoke pouring into the sky.

I'm leaning forward, my hands gripping the seat as I watch the camera pan around. It's strange. I haven't been to Earth for ten years or more but seeing this...it makes you care.

Shit....

The car wobbles a little and the automated driver makes a sharp turn to the left, jolting me back to the present. There are people spilling out of buildings onto the streets. It's clear the news is out there, and nobody likes it. Anything that's bad for Earth will be bad for us. All those corporations and governments relying on the array will be less likely to send supplies and shipments out here, or out even further to the mining stations.

Yeah, this is going to have an effect, a big effect.

I'm still thinking about all that and watching the news when we pull up to the departure point at Hera dock. There's a figure waiting for me on the steps as I get out. I don't recognise him, and he looks confused when he realises I don't have any bags apart from my work satchel. However, he does lead the way through the entrance, down the corridor and into the transport module. When I'm set, it pulls away from the port, taking us the final three kilometres to the launch pad.

A few minutes later I'm all strapped in, along with six other people they've requisitioned for this emergency. I don't have time to speak to anyone or see who they are.

Then blast off, high g's, and we're on our way.

★   ★   ★

The presence of 'stretch marks' on the surface of Phobos is an indication of its decline. The computer-projected orbital track for the little moon suggests it will eventually collide with Mars, which will be a world changing event, causing earthquakes and altering the planet's orbit.

"Our commercial planning needs to factor in all the likely scenarios we will face when establishing a colony," Hajyan Alkini, Chef de Mission for the newly formed Mars Corporation, explained at the organisation's first news conference this morning. "This research is not new. We've known about it since the initial planning phase of our project. Phobos is a clear and present danger to our work, but it is also an opportunity."

Alkini and his colleagues went on to outline this opportunity. The unique situation of the moon's declining orbit means it lies outside the preservation treaty terms written into the corporation's charter and mandate for colonisation, making it a resource that can be mined and exploited without concern for maintaining its surface condition.

"We have a chance to use Phobos as a resource. Its proximity to Mars and the unique gravitational flux it is experiencing as it degrades provides us with a chance for mining, which is unprecedented in human history. There is also definite need. By breaking up Phobos, we would be acting to preserve Mars."

Phobos is a small moon that follows an orbit closer to its planet than any other in the solar system. That orbit is doomed to fail. Every year, Phobos inches closer to Mars, which increases the gravitational pull between the two objects.

Report in the *Oceanic Times*, dated 15th of September 2101.

2029

The replacement proposal to the 1967 Outer Space Treaty was finally ratified at a special session of the United Nations Congress this evening.

Named the Solar System Treaty, the new agreement has been hailed by scientists and industry leaders as being a much more rational approach to the exploration and utilisation of 'local space' – the inner planetary territory around our sun.

"The twentieth-century agreements were made at a time when we really didn't know that much about our neighbourhood," Doctor Bryalla Kanchowa, leader of the Chilean Space Exploration Association, said just before the formal vote. "Getting out of Earth's orbit was a task only achievable by two nations at that time. The Outer Space Treaty was designed as much to hold them in check and prevent the development of a new theatre of war as it was an agreement to be cautious with how we explore and utilise the resources around our planet and beyond."

The new treaty paves the way for commercial missions beyond Earth's immediate vicinity and clarifies the rights and ownership rules for corporations looking out to the various planets, moons, and asteroids that might be mined for profit. Whilst there were some objections to any proposal that endorsed this kind of activity, the majority of the scientific community appears to be behind the move and accepting of the new treaty.

"It's about time," said Michael Fradoli, the appointed representative from SEACO – the organisation that co-ordinates research and safety standards between private industry partners who are working or looking to work in space. "The moment is now. If we wait any longer, people are going to start making up the rules for themselves. With the United Nations taking an interest and making this move, we have a framework we can work with."

CHAPTER THREE

Johansson

"Captain Shann, under article four of the Fleet commissionary code, I need to inform you that we, the senior officers of your crew, are relieving you of your command."

Major Le Garre says the words and I watch Captain Ellisa Shann crumple. She's pushed herself to the edge and beyond. We're alive because of her, but it's been too much, the cost is more than any one person should bear.

She drifts back toward the corner, using her hands to lower herself down into a sitting position, below the rest of us, drifting in zero gravity here on the bridge of the *Gallowglass*, the ship we have captured. We're looking down at her now, and suddenly, I'm very aware of her lack of legs. To me, she's always been a larger presence than this.

She's broken. I can see it.

I'm part of this decision. As the third ranking officer left amongst the surviving crew, I have to endorse any action to remove her from her position made by my superiors. Now, seeing her reaction, in a way I'm relieved. She's too exhausted to argue and too ashamed of herself to disagree. Thank God. None of us has any fight left.

Breathing is hard; it puts strain on the staples holding my stomach together. Talking is worse. Most of the drugs I was given have worn off. The pain is like the bullet is still in me. It's hard to think about anything else.

"We have to talk about Duggins," I manage to say through clenched teeth. "I think he's alive."

"Yes, you said," Le Garre replies. "We need to monitor the anomaly and get as much data as we can. I'm not ruling out any action at this stage."

"But you don't want to mount a rescue?"

"Not yet, we're in no shape to help him."

"What about Chiu? What do we do with her?" Arkov asks.

"What we already agreed," Travers says. "She's sedated for now. We prep a cryopod for her and put her in storage for the trip back to Phobos."

"You want me to get on that?"

"When you've rested. I think you should take a few hours off first." Le Garre looks around the room, catching the eye of anyone she can. "Anything else?"

She's stupidly calm. I know it's a projection, to try and keep all of us calm, but it's not working for me. The meeting is over, but no one wants to leave. We're all sat mourning the death of our captain, who's right there, mourning alongside us. The image of her, the unbreakably strong leader who kept us alive under impossible circumstances, is dead. It never really existed. I probably believed in it more than anyone else. I built her up into a gigantic character who could do no wrong.

Ellisa Shann is a human being. I see that now. I started to see cracks the moment I defied her orders and risked my life to EVA out of our ship and hack the computers of this ship, the *Gallowglass*, which led to us capturing it and surviving when the *Khidr* was destroyed, but I thought she was looking after me, trying to protect her crew.

Maybe she was, maybe she wasn't. We made it, defying the odds and defeating the *Gallowglass* crew when they should have killed us all out there. After seeing her reaction to Sellis, our technician, being murdered right at the end, I think she was holding it all in, losing a little bit of herself every time one of us took a hit.

"April, you okay?"

Quartermaster Sam Chase asked the question. He is looking at me, his expression carefully neutral. As a sergeant, he doesn't get a say over who's in charge. I nod to him but push off from where I'm settled. "Time for some more meds I think," I announce. "As your acting chief medical officer, I'm prescribing some enforced downtime. I'll see you all in six hours."

"That's a good idea, Ensign," Le Garre says. She glances at Travers, who nods. "Light duties I think for a little while. Chase, Arkov, and I will familiarise ourselves with the ship. Johansson, you and Travers take a break…you too, Shann."

The silence is awkward. I can't look at her. Instead, I concentrate on breathing and getting to the door. When I'm out and in the corridor, I feel a little better. At least I don't have to look at Shann whilst she's going through the worst. She can't be left alone, though. Le Garre will realise, she'll take care of that, won't she?

I have to be sure.

I'm back in the medical room. Ensign Chiu is still there, unconscious on oxygen as before. Looking at her reminds me of everything we've been through – a distress call, an ambush, a battle with an unidentified ship, an attempted mutiny, another battle. Each time the situation arose, we worked the problem and didn't think about the odds.

After the first fight between the *Khidr* and the *Gallowglass*, when a Rocher clone boarded the ship, Chiu was blackmailed into siding with the mutineers. To think I wanted her dead for betraying us. I feel pretty ashamed about that. She must have been bleeding for most of the time she was in EVA getting here. Her career is over, but she still fought to survive.

Helping her helps me. In a strange way, I feel lighter, as if it's some kind of penance. No, maybe it's not so strange. Over the centuries, plenty of people have become better human beings after they've done something wrong.

I check the screen displaying Chiu's information. The synthesised plasma is starting to bring her blood pressure back up. The Rocher clones are universal donors – they would be; it makes sense to manufacture humans who can be fixed easily.

The computer has identified a nick in the artery in Chiu's right thigh as being the cause. Looks like it was a piece of shrapnel that tore through her suit during the ship-to-ship transfer or before. Her face is sweaty and smudged with dirt, but otherwise she could be asleep.

I reach out to stroke her leg with my right hand. I only remember it isn't there when I see the socketed end with no prosthetic attachment. The mistake is embarrassing. Thankfully there's no one here. I'm not used to operating like this. I don't feel myself. I've been wearing a mechanical unit for as long as I can remember.

Damn it!

I move to the other bed, the one I was in only a little while ago. A fresh ampule of mambalgin is plugged into the injector, waiting for me to use it when I need to, but that's not yet, despite the pain. I need to be sharp.

The terminal is near the end of the bed. I touch the screen and reactivate it. The communications log is still active, just as I left it. *Gallowglass* is further away from the compacted wreckage of our old ship, *Khidr*, but our active sensors are still picking up transmissions. I pick through them, looking at the visual representations of the noises. The same whistling and oscillations that I heard before. Nothing like the one time I thought I heard Duggins calling my name.

I flick back through the files, pick out that one and replay it.

"Johansson...."

Yeah, it's faint, but it's him. I'm not wishfully imagining a word into that noise. I key up the ship's main dish and instruct it to rotate so we can get a better signal. The system reports that the hydraulics are damaged, but they work well enough to complete the manoeuvre. *Awesome. Now what do I do?*

I set up a folder for recording as much data as possible and activate the high-resolution camera too. Still images and video feed, all useful information I can study later.

I pull myself up onto the bed, pick up the injector, and position it firmly against the muscle in my thigh. There's a hiss as I press the trigger and the synthesised snake venom is delivered. The numbing sensation hits me after a minute or two. It's lovely after all that pain.

"April?"

I glance over. Chiu is looking at me. She's awake, her voice muffled by the oxygen mask. I nod and try to smile. I'm not sure it comes out too well. Then I give her a thumbs up.

Chiu awkwardly returns the gesture. Then she shuts her eyes again. *Well, that's a good sign.*

The safety straps deploy as I settle back on the mattress. The scorch-marked ceiling of the room bears witness to what we did before we captured this ship. The battle, it all seems like it was a long time ago, almost like it happened to someone else. Did I really pack myself into a torpedo and....

Yeah, the drugs are kicking in, this is *nice....*

"Ensign?"

I know the voice and instantly I'm out of the dreamy trance back into reality. *She* is here. She has come here to find me.

"Captain? What can I—"

"It's not Captain anymore, Ensign, you know that."

Shann is by the door, still wearing the same beaten expression. Again, I look at her and notice the lack of legs, seeing them as something missing.

"Ensign, can I talk to you, please? Sorry, I didn't want to stop you getting a break."

I fumble with the strap release, find it, disengage them and sit up. "Sure, Captain, how can I help?"

I'm still calling her Captain. That's a conscious choice. It's her rank. She still deserves it. The *Khidr* was her commission and it's been destroyed, and she's been stripped of command, but for me, that's how I know her. It's a little act of loyalty, I guess. I hope she sees it that way.

"Travers and I had a quick chat after the...meeting. He suggested you might prescribe me something?"

"Of course, is it your shoulder or an injury you haven't—"

"No, nothing like that. I just need to sleep and not think about it. Something that'll knock me out for six hours."

I remember the sedative Bogdanovic loaded us all up with during the mutiny. I find myself smiling at the thought, then quickly school my expression. There was nothing funny about what happened. Damn these drugs.

"I can give you something, no problem." I get up and move to the dispenser. It's already set up with my new authorisation code. I key that in and pass her the two ampules that it drops into my hand. "You shouldn't be alone, Captain. You know that, right?"

Shann gives me a weary grimace. "Yeah, psych evaluation, post trauma protocols. I guess all of us are going to struggle for a while after what we've been through."

"You more than most of us, Captain."

"Maybe."

She looks at me then, and there's something of the old Shann in her eyes. Her expression hardens. "You need to watch her. You might be the best chance we have."

I frown. "Watch who? I'm sorry but—"

"Watch Le Garre. She's going to fuck it up. Sooner or later, it'll happen. Be careful." That stare is cold. Her eyes are like chips of ice. "When she makes a mistake, I won't be able to do anything."

"Captain, are you suggesting we shouldn't have—"

"No, not at all. You were dead right. I'm not fit to be in charge. Le Garre's the right choice. Travers will back her up, but you…. You need to be the extra. The eyes that see what they can't see. Sooner or later, that's going to be needed." She takes the pills, swallows them, then turns away. "Thanks for the meds, Doc."

"Captain, can I ask you a question?"

Shann stops and turns back. "Of course, anything you want."

"Why did they do it? I mean, why did they attack the *Hercules* and then attack us?"

"I'm not sure," Shann says. "But you remember what we found in the cargo? Aside from the containers for the gravity anomalies, we found colony equipment – automated pollenisers. There's no reason why any of the existing colonies would need that kind of equipment. They already have the ability to manufacture all the replacements they would need."

At the mention of the anomalies, my thoughts stray to them. The impossibly black shapes we found that we released into space and that took control of the wreckage of the *Khidr*. They are still out there, packed under all the debris of our old ship.

Shan is still looking at me. I flinch and bring my thoughts back to the conversation at hand. "So, you think the *Hercules* was supplying an unauthorised colony?"

"Possibly. That would give a clear reason for the *Gallowglass* being sent to intercept the ship."

"But it doesn't explain how the situation escalated and they murdered the crew."

"Look around you. This ship isn't equipped to take prisoners. Someone wanted the *Hercules* stopped and their operation shut down without any survivors or any public scrutiny."

"So, they were always going to kill them?"

"Yes, and us. We got in the way."

"I see. Thank you, Captain."

"Don't mention it," Shann says. A moment later she's gone.

I glance at Chiu. Her eyes are closed. Did she hear any of that?

★   ★   ★

2048

With the launch of the Avensis probe, project leader Doctor Malcolm Palgrave of the European Space Alliance has finally published his papers on the theory of Einstein's Well.

Writing in the Astrophysical Journal, *Palgrave explains the concept behind the Avensis mission – to search for the cause of the gravitational anomaly that has baffled scientists for more than a century.*

"The planetary orbits, asteroids, comets, everything that goes around the Sun behaves as if there's another mass out there in the furthest part of the solar system. Most of the effect is countered, on the inner planets, by Jupiter, but it's there as a tiny tilt on Earth's orbit. For a long time, we've assumed the mass has to be a planet, but it could be something else. Instead, Einstein's Well might be out there. It's a miniature black hole, the size of a football or a beachball, with an equivalent density to a large planet. Something with those kinds of properties could definitely affect the orbital paths of all objects in the solar system, including the Earth.

"*The Avensis probe is being sent out on a wide-angle orbit in increasing elliptical loops. Our hope is that we can detect and analyse the gravitational effect on the probe, compare it with our observations of the effect here on Earth, and pinpoint the location of the object causing the effect. Then we can send a probe out there to take pictures.*"

If the Avensis mission is successful, scientists hope to be able to use the acquired data to help plot ship navigation trajectories to the outer solar system with less risk of errors.

CHAPTER FOUR

Holder

"Data transfer complete. Okay, Natalie, can you open your eyes for me please?"

The man's voice isn't familiar, but some kind of instinct makes me follow instructions. I'm in a clean white room, strapped to a chair. The man is wearing a red plastic suit, plastic gloves and full-face cover with a see-thru window in the front, the kind of thing I've seen in films involving some kind of mass plague.

"Do you know where you are?"

I look around. It's a different voice, coming from a speaker in the floor or the roof. I shake my head.

"What's the last thing you remember?"

I close my eyes. I can see the tunnel hacked out of the concrete. I remember crawling inside, holding the bomb in my hands...pressing the trigger. "I...I...died."

"Excellent. Doctor Summers, could you come out here and join us, please?"

The man in the red suit nods. He goes to a door, opens it and stands in a small room. Jets of gas envelop him, then another door opens, and he exits out of sight.

Carefully, I test the straps holding me to the seat. They are adaptive restraints, tightening a little as I push at them. I swallow and try to slow down my breathing and my racing heart. Something is wrong. Something is very wrong.

I died!

I don't know these people. I don't know where I am! All I remember is the Atacama complex – the Hub. It was hot, I got through security and down into the ventilation chamber and—

The door to the room opens. There is a man dressed a white jacket, trousers, shirt and tie. He is even wearing white shoes.. He's large and brown skinned. I'd guess Samoan or Fijian, from somewhere like that. Trailing after him is Doctor Summers, his plastic mask removed to reveal a thin garrulous Caucasian face dominated by a thick pair of old-fashioned glasses.

"Well done, Natalie," the man in white says. He was the voice on the speaker. "What you've achieved is remarkable. Truly remarkable. You're a pioneer of biotechnological innovation."

"How am I alive?" I ask.

"You were transferred out," Summers explains. He's trying to smile, but all he does is show me a set of yellow and uneven teeth. "We maintained a direct link between your brain and a conveyance nodule. At the right moment, your consciousness was copied— Well no, not exactly. The base plate of your consciousness had already been duplicated onto the backup, the new memories and experiences, the last ones you had, they were transmitted to the nodule. After that, all we had to do was retrieve it and upload another copy of the brain image to your new host body, this body."

"So, you brought me back to life."

"In a manner of speaking, yes."

"Why? I...I wanted to die."

The man nods. "Best if you leave me with this, Summers," he says.

Summers gives him a look of relief and scampers back through the door. When we're alone, the suit moves towards me. He's smiling now, his teeth also huge and bright white.

"You don't remember me, do you, Natalie?" he says softly. "You have no memory of who I am."

I blink slowly. My eyelids are the only defence I have from him – a pathetic defence. I'm trying to remember something about his face or his voice, but there's nothing, just a blank. I can't even associate him with people I do remember. My mind refuses to connect him to anyone at all. It's like he's some kind of alien.

"People underestimate me. I'm big and strong. They think that defines me. They assume strength is my identity, that a big man like me can't be clever, can't be intelligent. It's a mistake. You should never judge on appearance."

He turns away from me and walks over to a table near the door. He picks up something and comes back, holding it out. It's a mirror. In it, I can see the reflection of my face.

That's not my face.

My hands twitch involuntarily. I'm bald. My face is drawn and pale under the harsh artificial lights. I want to reach up and touch the skin of my cheeks and feel the bones and muscles underneath. They don't look like me. They don't look like the me I remember.

"A good host. The best money can buy. Tailored specifically to our needs here on Earth. When you are here, this will be you, this will always be you. Get used to it. Get used to everything about what you are now, because this will be your life. Your existence will be unique and incredible, but you will never be stable or secure. Everything about you is constructed, tailored and designed for whatever purpose we need."

The mirror is only a few inches from me. His face behind it, his breath hot in this sterile room. I can see his teeth, white and sculpted, a perfect display, clearly bought and paid for. There's a faint musky smell. I can't identify it. My mind is scrambled in his presence as information slips away even as I experience it.

"Your memories have been altered. New knowledge and experiences added to the imprint before it is uploaded to this brain. Every single thing that you remember could be real or it could be something we constructed using our neural network simulators. So, you say you wanted to die. I say, we wanted you to plant that bomb. By carefully conditioning your mind, your goal was achieved and our objective, also achieved."

The words make sense to me. I understand them. I know I should be horrified. If what this man is saying to me is true, I am an instrument, a tool. I have no free will. Any freedom I believe I have will always be an illusion.

"How many...."

"Like you? None. You are unique, the first of your kind and probably the last. If we lose you, we will make another, but it is extremely hard for anyone to finish you off. Oh, you'll die, you'll die a hundred times, a thousand times or more, but it will never truly be over."

He moves away from me then and suddenly it is easier to breathe, easier to think. He's walking to the door.

"This conversation will fade from your mind, as if it isn't important. After that, Doctor Summers will remove the last traces of whatever you remember from being here, whatever you remember about me."

I hear the words and bite down the anger that swells within me in reply. I want to hold on to this, I swear to myself that I will, trying to visualise and picture the room, keeping an image of it in mind even as I close my eyes. "Are you going to leave me like this?" I ask.

"That'll be up to Doctor Summers. He'll be re-joining you shortly to prepare you for your next mission. Everything about this place, about me and all of your previous life, will be erased. Goodbye, Natalie."

The door closes. There's a hiss of gas. The atmospheric mix is being altered. I can taste the air. Some sort of sedative has been injected into the room. I try to hold my breath, but after two minutes I'm forced to inhale, and almost immediately, my arms and legs become heavy and weak.

The door opens again. I see the red plastic mask and coat of Doctor Summers. Something sharp presses against my neck. "Sweet dreams," he says.

I clench my teeth and struggle, trying to force—

*   *   *

It's dark. I'm staring at my watch. It's 0300 hours, I'm in Port Sudan in a dinghy. I can see the water glittering in the darkness. I feel disorientated for a moment, like I've been daydreaming or having some kind of out-of-body experience, but now I'm back. I'm here and ready to do my job.

This is a boat deployment, using soft tops. We have reason to believe this freighter, registered as *The Zanzinar*, is carrying arms to supply the Sudanese government, which is fighting a civil war. This is in contravention of a United Nations arms embargo. It gives us a mandate to go in and investigate.

We cut our engines around five hundred metres out and paddled the final approach. This is a busy port, there's lots of noise even at this hour, but there's no point in drawing attention when you don't want to draw attention.

We're one team of six, with a secondary support unit waiting in helicopters and an extra man left in the boat. We have a fifteen-minute window and two objectives.

Primary objective: Discover, document and neutralise the weapons shipment.

Secondary objective: Secure the merchant ledger.

★   ★   ★

Both targets have been located.

The Intelligence assessment of this tub says there's minimal security – four mercenaries, armed with assault weapons. Any one of them could be a problem. The rest of the crew have gone ashore, but they will return before dawn to unload the shipment onto trucks.

We have to be quick, quiet and sure.

The metal rungs up the side of the ship are wet. I'm in soft-soled shoes to lessen the noise. My thick gloves grip the rungs as my teammates cover me going up.

Just before the top, I slow down and take a quick spot. Deck looks clear. Time to move. I'm up and over the side in one movement, crawling towards cover. When I'm there, I unsling my assault rifle, flick off the safety, and take up position covering the right.

Behind me, Echo-Two will have done exactly the same to cover the left.

"Echo-Six to control. We're on board."

"Good work. You are cleared to proceed."

We move in a flow across the deck. Overwatch discipline is maintained at all times. This unit might be international, but special forces training has been standardised across a range of countries for decades. In some ways, it was another successful American export before their country fell apart.

I reach a corner, the designated turn point of the first guard. He's a moment or two behind where we'd thought he'd be. The flickering flame of a pocket lighter indicates why; he's trying to smoke a roll-up and is looking down, concentrating on that.

I raise my rifle and fire twice. The silenced rounds are spat out and the guard drops with a muffled thud. I move forward, crouch beside him and check his chest, feeling the last beats of his heart.

One in the throat, one in the top of the head. Both fatal.

"Echo-One to Control. First hostile is down."

As I'm talking, the team is moving past me. There's a brief flash as another rifle spits out quiet death.

"Echo-Three here, second is down."

I'm moving forward on the overlap, up the stairs into the steerage. This room is full of windows. The port floodlights illuminate the whole space, but it also provides a good vantage point. We need to know it's clear, quickly, and then move on.

"Echo-Five, third is out."

One guard left. He'll be below deck, along with our targets and any other surprises. I check my watch. "Thirteen minutes left. Steerage is secure. Three and Four, move up to here and set up. Five and Six enter on the starboard side. We'll go in on port."

"Copy that."

The staircase on the far side descends into the bowels of the ship. There's a touch on my shoulder; Echo-Two is right behind me, ready to move. I reach up and pull down my night-vision goggles. The world changes into a mix of green shades against black as we start down the steps.

Jack. Pot.

"Control, we have confirmed discovery of the primary target. I'm looking at a crate of twelve AT-505 Razorback missiles."

"Confirmed, Echo-One. Time check on window. We're reading nine minutes."

"Nine minutes, agreed."

Echo-Two moves in front of me, camera in hand. As I open boxes, he takes pictures. Time, date and location are stamped on each image.

The system is the same used by internationally authorised weapons inspectors to verify equipment they've checked. The pictures will be uploaded directly to a secure operations server and received by Control in seconds.

"Control, request permission to move to demolition?"

"Confirmed, Echo-One."

The det-cord is in my backpack. I pull it out and start attaching it to the crates, along with a set of C4 cubes and timers. The rigs we run with are modular and pre-assembled. We've rehearsed in a warehouse with a similar arrangement of crates half a dozen times, and before that, simulated tactical insertion missions just like this one in training, dozens and dozens of times.

"Seven minutes, Echo-One."

There's a noise. I stop and ready my rifle. Echo-Two does the same. A flicker of green confirms contact. Two's rifle spits once, a man grunts and falls to the deck.

"Fourth is down."

I push up my goggles, Two does the same. "Another day in a terrorist paradise," I say.

"Amen, sister," he replies.

Thirty seconds of work completes the demolition rig. "We need to complete the sweep," I tell Two. "Make sure there aren't any more of them."

"We should move on the ledger," Two says. "We have time."

I look at my watch again. There's five minutes left in the safe window assessment.

"One to Three?"

"Receiving."

"What are things looking like up there?"

"All clear at the moment."

The secondary target is under my operational discretion. The merchant ledger will be on the deck below in the captain's cabin. If I think we have time to grab it, I can authorise a go. If not, we withdraw.

Four minutes, forty-five seconds.

"All right, Five, Six, complete the sweep and demolition set up. We're going for the secondary objective."

"Confirmed."

"Let's do this."

Two moves ahead of me to the staircase. I reach forward and tap his shoulder, indicating that I'm following right behind him.

"Control to One."

"Receiving."

"The analysts are going over the images you sent us. There's some discrepancies."

"Do you want me to go back and take some more?"

"No, the images are clear, but these aren't Russian-made anti-tank missiles. Analysis has requested additional material."

"Understood, Control." These are the kind of orders I hate. We're on a fixed time limit and the specialists are asking me to find additional material to support their theory on who the supplier might be. That means we may have to take more photos, looking for maker marks.

It's dark. Examining missiles in detail will take longer than we have. But the ledger might be able to corroborate their reports. *Risking lives to cover someone's ass?*

I'm counting down the time; it's a habit, carefully perfected over twenty years of missions like this. We reach the deck. Two opens the door as I cover the entrance. I move inside and turn to the right. Two follows and covers the left.

Four minutes.

We sweep the rooms; bedroom/office and en-suite toilet shower. There's no one here. Two shoulders his weapon and heads for the desk. He tries the handle – locked. He pulls out a combat knife and jams it into the wood. The drawer splinters and papers spill across the floor.

"Fuck!"

"One, this is Three. We have incoming. There are trucks on the dock. Mission time is reduced by ninety seconds."

I make the mental calculation. *Two minutes left.* "Quickly! Pick up what you can. We need to move!"

Two kneels down and gathers up the paperwork, tucking the bundle under his arm. I lead the way back up the stairs.

"One, this is Five and Six, we are done. Moving to extraction."

"Confirmed."

We're back on the top deck in under a minute. I can hear the truck engines and shouts from the jetty. There's no reply from the dead guards.

"Echo-One and Two. Job done, moving to extraction."

Our signal releases Echo-Three and Four from their fire support position. They'll be the last to leave the ship, so risk to them is the highest.

I'm shouldering my rifle and on the first steps of the ladder as they begin to move. There's more shouting and gunfire. I stop and start to turn around, but then reconsider. I don't know Three and Four, but they're on this mission; that means they're professionally trained.

"Move faster!" shouts Two.

I step off the rungs, press my feet to the sides of the ladder, and let myself slide. As I reach the bottom, I raise my foot and push off from the side of the freighter, letting go of the rails at the same time.

I land in the soft top and overbalance. The boat pitches, someone swears, and hands grab at my arms. "One is secure!" Five shouts.

The pattering of automatic weapons echoes out in the night. There's more shouting and I hear people on the ladder above us. "One to Control, twenty seconds and we're moving. We have secured primary and secondary targets. Requesting air support to cover our withdrawal."

"You have it, One. UAV is inbound to your location."

I can hear the buzzing sound of a prop-driven plane, except that it isn't a plane in the conventional sense. An RQ-18 – Ravage air support drone, deployed to cover our escape.

Tracer fire from the drone illuminates the sky. I get a quick glimpse of the aircraft's silhouette in the darkness as it skips towards the freighter, firing its belly-mounted machine gun. We don't need precision targeting here, just enough ordnance to keep the enemy from firing back.

"Three and Four are on board."

"Let's go!"

★   ★   ★

Atacama Investigation Report Summary – Date 20.11.2118

An analysis of the incident suggests a high level of funding and co-ordination. Whilst we might presume this to be the work of a small aggressor cell, I believe that is what they want us to believe. These are not isolated agitators; there is a movement against us, a movement to destabilise our arrangements with Rep. Chile and Atacama Local Corp.

Our extrapolation of possible strategies indicates that by provoking a power shortage on Earth, the consequence is a reduced international focus on the Corp Colonial Initiative (CCI) as subsidiary companies move to take advantage of an opportunity in the supply chain. Energy costs will rise globally, meaning a reduction in launches as profit margins to Luna and Mars are subsequently reduced. The colonies will suffer shortages, but they will also start to look outwards and towards their own assets to fill in the necessary gaps. Whilst such a drive towards self-sufficiency might be good for them in one respect, it is not a net gain for us at this stage. Our phased transition will not be complete for another five years, so we are not in a position to take advantage of a development switch.

At this stage, I would recommend activating a retaliatory strategy. Something suitably effective that demonstrates equivalence to our unknown foe. Assets are in place for several potential strikes. The plans are included. I'll leave it to you to determine which of these you wish to implement. When you are sure, contact me by the usual means.

CHAPTER FIVE

Drake

After the burn, the transit is fast. Then we decelerate and manoeuvre towards Phobos Station. This bit, the last few kilometres where we need to line up and match velocity with their orbit, always takes the most time.

The passenger cabin is dark, lit only by the flickering lights of people's personal screens. We're all strapped in, facing away from each other with plenty of spare seats. My guess is that *Angelus* will act as an emergency evacuation shuttle if we need to get anyone down to Hera from Phobos for specialist medical attention.

This is my sixteenth trip into space, my first emergency response. The seat straps have relaxed a bit, but they aren't letting us roam around as they might on a standard journey. The pilot is cutting a few corners, using a bit more fuel to get us into dock as quickly as possible. That means a few more g's on the way in.

The personal screen in front of me is showing the trajectory plot as a graphic. They won't show the actual exterior view from the ship's cameras whilst we're on final approach. The twists and turns can add to the sense of disorientation some passengers feel, particularly when it comes to matching the station's rotation to generate gravity.

What we don't get to see is the engineering marvel that is Phobos Station, officially designated *Phobos Alpha*. Three rings rotate around a central pole, the entire structure built in orbit, with the top and bottom rings added whilst the main ring continued to rotate and provide a home for the station's crew.

The trajectory plot has us, the station and the mining shuttle marked out against the graphic of Phobos and Mars beyond it. The ship is approaching the station on a different path. The computer has marked out their ETA, about fifteen minutes after ours. Clearly, they were able to report the emergency ahead of takeoff.

I did my zero-gravity medical training on Earth Station 4. It was six or seven years ago. I key up the basic summary provided in the mission briefing. I remember the main issues related to circulation and open wounds, but there are a few details that are always worth remembering. Phobos Station has gravity, but we're out in a constructed environment. Who knows what might happen? The auto-medics are programmed for this eventuality, but there's no harm in being prepared.

I look through the rest of the documentation. Phobos Station. Date of manufacture: 2072. Date of completion: 2088. Number of crew: eighty-three. Most of those are Fleet with a mix of commercial contractors and civilian specialists. The station governor is one of the few Mars citizens. A perk of the job, I guess.

I'm glancing around, trying to see the other passengers. There are four people in here other than me. I'm guessing they're all medical specialists, probably people I've heard of or met. I turn back to the screen and key up the roster. The names start scrolling.

Doctor Jennifer Bremner – Fleet Medical Officer.

Doctor Emerson Drake – Civilian Medical Officer.

Andrew Olajima – Fleet Medic.

Ulla Magin – Civilian Medic.

Thomas Liu – Fleet Security Specialist.

Ulla and I have worked together before at Jezero. She transferred out to Syrtis a couple of years ago. She's a little older than me, from Turkey originally and excellent at her job. The others…well, if this is a Fleet operation, we are here to provide extra hands. I don't need to worry about organising things. The military can deal with the logistics.

One issue stands out. Why do we need a security detail? We're travelling from Hera to one of humanity's key transport nodes. Phobos Station manages traffic from all across the solar system. Are the people who organised this trip expecting trouble?

My hand strays to the chit in my pocket. My fingers brush the metal surface of it, and I relax a little. Lieutenant Rivers gave me a secure link application to get hold of him should I need to. I've seen these before. The chit will go into any terminal and override the local access network, providing me with a direct line to the person I'm trying to contact. They are used a lot by essential personnel working on extended assignment, just in case they can't renew their access privileges. They aren't rare, but they aren't common either. Someone in Fleet is clearly looking out for Jon, or for me.

The ship shifts and suddenly I'm not weightless anymore and being pressed into the back of my chair. The pilot is attempting to match our speed with the station's rotation. The sensation is unmistakably strange as gradually the force on me changes from pushing me back to pushing me down, so I am pressed down in my seat in the same familiar way I would be on Mars or Earth.

It's not exactly the same. Phobos Station generates 0.7 g. Enough for human physiology to maintain itself without being onerous but twice what we have on Mars. I've always found the sensation notably different. There's a kind of unsteadiness, like something is constantly moving, which it is.

There's a deep *clunk*, the lights flicker and then brighten. We've docked. The safety straps automatically disengage, letting me stand up from my chair. The other passengers do the same and I wave at Ulla, then nod absently at the others who I don't know. The acknowledgement is returned and then I'm quickly ignored as the military types fall into procedure. Doctor Bremner is listening to the security guy, Liu. She seems to be deferring to his judgement, probably best for now, but still another thing slowing us down.

"Docking checks complete. Passengers prepare for pressure test and departure."

Magnetic locks and clamps engage, making the ship shudder as it's grasped and secured by the station. I'm up with my satchel over my shoulder and moving towards the exit. Liu is in front of me, in front of all of us. He holds up a hand, indicating we should stand back.

The hatch opens, there's a little breeze as the two atmospheres join and mix. Liu steps out, through the airlock and into the station. There's no one in the hall.

Everyone else hesitates. I sigh and step forward, following him onto the dock promenade.

The whole place is empty. Weird. I'm looking around, trying to work out why, and then I see a banner hung from the roof – 'Happy Thirtieth Birthday Phobos Alpha!' it says in English, with an Arabic and Mandarin translation underneath. Some sort of celebration, I guess.

"Looks like we're missing a party," Olajima says, smiling. "That'd be why there's no one here at the dock."

"And potentially why they wanted extra personnel," Ulla adds. "A medical emergency when you've been drinking…well…."

"I'm sure they'll have followed procedure and kept people on duty," Samner says. Her frown indicates she has little time for small talk. "We're here to back them up, so let's back them up. Liu?"

Our security man nods and leads the way up a set of stairs to the access tube. There's a small, powered conveyer waiting for us. "*Chronos* will be docking on the far side, near to the medical quarters." He glances at the digital strip on his wrist. "We should arrive just after they get in. Everyone aboard."

"Aren't our pilots going to join us?" I ask, drawing the attention of everyone. It's the first time I've spoken, and I guess they're all trying to work out what to make of me.

"Doctor Drake, isn't it?" Liu says. There's a patronising edge to his words, softened a little by his broad smile. "*Angelus* flight crew need to stay prepped, in case we have to make an emergency evac. They're staying put until station control gives them clearance to disembark."

I shrug, swallow any further questions and take a seat on the conveyer and put my bag on my lap. The vehicle is little more than a metal box with seats running along a chain track. The chain runs continuously, counterclockwise to the station. The conveyer will move out of the park under its own power, then latch on to the links and take us around the station's main ring.

When everyone's settled, we pull away. There's no driver; the whole system is automated and designed with energy efficiency in mind. Any human settlement away from Earth has to be.

Ulla is sat next to me. I nudge her. "Did you see the news about Earth and the Atacama hub?" I ask.

Ulla nods. "It'll be a nasty, slow death. Corporations rationing power, switching off civilian districts in favour of heavy industry. I'd hate to be living there right now."

"It'll affect things up here too."

"Oh yes, I don't doubt it. Tough times ahead."

I gesture around, indicating the station. "Pretty shit news to get while you're having a party."

"Indeed, and then to be followed up with this mining incident. I hope no one is too seriously injured."

"I guess we'll find out."

We lapse into silence. I'm looking around and trying to take in as much as I can. The conveyer is heading around the interior of the station's main habitat ring, a huge torus that contains two levels. The orientation means the ring is immediately below us, flashing by as we pick up speed. Again, we're in a metal box, there's no opportunity to look out and gaze at the stars for the same reason as before. The spinning swirling vista would encourage plenty of people to vomit. On the wall there's a map of the ring with all the sectors subdivided. We're travelling through green (hydroponics) and orange (administration) to yellow (medical). Other regions on this torus are red (security) and blue (command).

"Three minutes, people," Liu says just as I feel the conveyer beginning to slow. A moment later, we come off the chain track and our little conveyer powers itself into a siding. Doors open to my right and I get out with the others.

Immediately, things are different. I can hear voices below – the sound of human activity is reassuring, even if it means injured people to deal with. There's another banner over the walkway and more signs of celebration with ribbons and posters on the walls. Station life, where you have to recycle everything, encourages people to be tidy, so there's little mess.

At the top of the walkway I get my first glimpse of the station crew. There are six or seven people below us getting organised. Liu leads the way down the stairs, Bremner right behind him.

"You folks the emergency team?" a man says. He's American. The drawl sounds like Tennessee or somewhere around that part of the world. He holds out a hand to Liu, who salutes and then takes it, shaking it warmly. "Major Gann, I'm in charge of the watch shift. You people missed the party. Sounds like we're going to need all hands to the pump down here." There's something in his hand. He holds it up. "Bio-monitors. Please take one, everybody. These are already keyed into the station's network. They'll help us to keep track of you."

"When are they due in, Major?" Ulla asks, taking one of the devices.

"Right about now," Gann says, turning towards the airlock doors.

As if on cue, a loud metallic *thump* indicates the arrival of *Chronos*. As I get to the bottom of the stairs, all conversations cease, and people turn towards the airlock doors. The sound of magnetic locks securing seems louder in here than it was inside our ship. I accept my bio-monitor and turn away from the spectacle, letting the first responders get to the front. Instead, I make my way into the emergency ward. I've never been here before, but these places are usually the same. Twelve beds, with auto-medics all on standby to receive patients. Two station doctors, Bremner and me. That'll mean three beds each, unless we get into emergency surgery, when we may have to double up.

"You okay, Doctor?" Ulla asks. She's standing by the doorway. I turn around and nod.

"Any idea what we're getting yet?"

Ulla shakes her head. "The major says they haven't filed any diagnostic reports beyond the emergency request."

"That's a bit odd. Surely the shuttle auto-medic should have transmitted—"

I'm interrupted as the world catches fire.

The blast is a visceral shock to my eyes and my ears. I'm thrown backwards and crash into one of the beds. I roll across the mattress and onto the floor, tipping the bed over on top of me. The hard metal floor smacks me in the chest and all the breath goes out of me, leaving me gasping for air.

My eyes are shut. The heat is intense. The air mix is oxygen rich, and the flames consume whatever they can before burning themselves out a moment later. The roaring in my ears continues. I open my eyes a little, squinting through the grit to try to make sense of the world.

Everything around me is blackened, pitted and scorched. The pristine ward has become the aftermath of a terrible incident.

I push the mattress off of me and get to my knees, coughing as I try to breathe the smoke-filled air. The back of the mattress is still burning. The bed is a twisted mess of broken aluminium and plastic. It saved my life.

A klaxon sounds, water jets fire from the roof, soaking me and everything in the room. Foam comes next, bathing the floor and the walls. The automated system is working. Hopefully, station security will have been notified and an emergency team will already be on the way.

An emergency team to rescue the emergency team. Yeah…that doesn't sound great.

"Hello?" My voice is crackly and hoarse. The word comes out as little more than a whisper. I try again louder. "Hello!"

There is no reply. I stand up and stagger across the room. I can't see anyone. None of the emergency team I came in with and none of the Phobos medical staff. The roaring in my ears is fading away, but I have a pounding headache. Bits of burned plastic and polymer drift through the air. The aftermath of a disaster is a weird place to be.

Amidst the gory remains of people there's a hand on the floor by the entrance to the emergency ward. A severed hand, burned and broken. I know instinctively that it's Ulla's. She was standing right there.

Then I see something move. The airlock door to the *Chronos* is closed. The metal is black and dented, but there's someone in there, someone alive inside the connecting passageway between the ship and the station.

I'm up and moving, all my aches and pains forgotten. I race back up the stairs to the walkway and the conveyor. As I get to the top, I turn, crouch down behind a low wall, and get my first proper look at the devastation.

The entire reception room has been blown apart. The emergency ward wrecked. It's a miracle the explosion hasn't blown a hole in the compartment, caused it to decompress and sucked us all out into space.

There is nothing left alive in those rooms. Twelve people are dead. I'm the only survivor, unless....

The airlock door opens and a figure in a pressure suit and body armour moves through. He's carrying a rifle.

In that moment, I realise, we've been duped. This isn't a medical emergency. It's an invasion.

★ ★ ★

ABOUT SETI – The Search for Extra-Terrestrial Intelligence

This organisation has been with us for more than a century. Born from the ramblings of the sharpest and most enthusiastic minds, much of its earliest and best work has been done through populism and innovation. Crowdsourced computing technology back when such things were in their infancy, algorithmic tracking and active database management, all devised and maintained by an enthusiastic community of individuals who wanted to do their part in helping to prove we are not alone in this universe.

There have been setbacks and false dawns. The greatest scientific minds can be fallible when presented with evidence that confirms their greatest desire or wish. Every conspiracy theory, fame-chasing wannabe and worse, has found there are ways to manipulate a community engaged in a positive-minded search for something by attempting to offer 'an answer'. The myth of the unexplained can provide clues, and it doesn't take much to stitch these together into some sort of convincing narrative.

In 2084, after one hundred years of SETI, The United Fleet Consortium approached the institute with an offer that would benefit both parties. SETI would become an official part of humanity's mission to the stars. Fleet would assign equipment and officers on every station, spaceship and off-Earth colony to work on the search and provide data for its community. In exchange, Fleet got a public relations boost that lifted it out of a mire of media investigations into corporate contracts and insider trading. Instead, Fleet became a beacon for public-private partnership. The largest human endeavour committed to the profit-progress strategy outlined by celebrated economist Horante Morovi back in the 2030s.

These days, SETI duties are incorporated directly into the work of technicians, specialists, and officers on board all Fleet assets. These are generally referred to as 'tertiary priority tasks' and form a day-to-day part of most crew assignments. The effect of this collaboration between space worker professionals and amateur scientists of all ages has been transformative. Whilst we have yet to uncover definitive proof of sentient extra-terrestrial life, our knowledge of our solar system and the stars beyond has been advanced by this partnership of discovery and open-source data analysis.

CHAPTER SIX

Johansson

Back when I was in orbital orientation, I remember one of the instructors trying to 'be friendly' – or at least, that's what he thought he was doing.

"We get a lot of people like you up here."

"What? Norwegians?"

"No…. It doesn't matter. Forget about it."

The instructor in question was unscrupulously fair. I never felt singled out or favoured, but the comment piqued my interest and made me look into what it might mean.

Writing an illegal data filter algorithm that could access private records of Fleet personnel and compile the relevant data didn't take me long. It turns out there was an unofficial programme in Fleet to recruit people born with physical disabilities. Ever since the construction of the first orbital space dock around Earth, there has been a high proportion of individuals selected from the different training schemes who had been born with some sort of physical impairment.

I couldn't find any evidence of this being a co-ordinated scheme. It appeared to be random, with trainees starting careers in all sorts of different departments and succeeding or failing at much the same rate as any other group category I constructed with the information, but there was definitely a higher proportion of recruitment when compared to other Earth-bound industries.

There seemed to be no distinction between those who had opted for corrective surgery like me, and those that hadn't, like Captain Shann.

Growing up, I didn't suffer much abuse. I guess mostly because the prosthetic 'plug-in' was so good, most children didn't realise that I was different. When the nerve hook-ups were added, even I came to forget I was different, until I had to take my hand off to recharge at night. Then I felt like I was weaker, more vulnerable. In my dreams, I'd be a person with two hands. That's always been the subconscious image I have of myself, for as long as I can remember.

I don't sleep for the full six hours. The drugs wear off after three and the pain starts to return. I prescribe myself some lower-level painkillers and the auto-medic dispenses them. I need to hydrate, eat some food and use the facilities, all the usual stuff that takes a lot more time to sort out in zero gravity. While I have something to do, my mind has focus. The minute I stop and try to rest, the guilt and the second-guessing come back. We broke Shann. I was part of that. I disobeyed orders and recklessly risked my life in a mad EVA plan to disable this ship's computer systems. It worked and we saved the crew, but could I have done something different? Should I have done something different?

I can't settle. I get up and move to the terminal to start doing some work.

We're in trouble. The three hours I've been unconscious hasn't changed that situation. To start with, the *Gallowglass* wasn't designed for this crew or for this number of people. The ship is a predator, with minimal life support facilities. During transit, half the crew is supposed to remain in cryo, with the other half supervising the automated systems. There's no exercise area, no rotating section to help the human body maintain its muscle mass and bone density on long trips. That means, ultimately, a long and slow death wasting away.

We have to get to Phobos Station before that happens, but there's also the matter of the *Khidr* wreck and Duggins being in there. If there's a chance he's alive....

My backdoor access lets me go through all the computer logs. The on-shift team have been busy. There's a host of diagnostic commands, error returns, and course inputs. We've changed position, lining up for a straight run to Phobos and Mars. Le Garre has plotted a course too, but they haven't keyed it in, yet.

According to this data, we'll get to the station in three weeks on conventional thrust. If we can use the resonance drive, that time is cut to forty-eight hours. The problem is, the drive was damaged during the first battle between the *Khidr* and the *Gallowglass*. It looks like there was a repair task issued to the crew, but no one updated it. I don't know whether it got repaired or not.

I frown and stare at the data. Le Garre knows I want us to try and rescue Duggins. That conversation was tabled when she took command and sent me for a rest. Was she planning launch us towards Phobos while I was asleep? Looking at this, I can't tell. Maybe she was going to talk to all of us after the six-hour shift? Technically she's in command and entitled to act like this, but after all we've been through, surely she'd see we need to be included?

Shann's words come back to me. *She's going to fuck up.*

The access code I got from the Fleet documents means I can undercut the entire computer system. I've already used it to set up temporary logins and user permissions for the others, overriding all the security *Gallowglass* was programmed with, but I can do more than that. I can disable the ship's engines so that they will only activate when I input the correct command. I can do the same with the whole ship, reserving control of key processes and functions to ensure whoever makes the decisions around here makes the decisions I want them to make.

If I do this and anyone finds out about it, I'll be court-martialled, plain and simple.

I spend the next half an hour rewriting the hacked code I used to set up access for the others, making it better and distracting myself from the choice.

When I've done all the little jobs, I return to the screen with the lock-out instructions. A whole page of programming is right there. All I need to do is finalise the last line and execute it.

I type out the last line. My finger hovers over the final command. I think back to what I wanted before this all started. April Johansson, studying for her lieutenant exam, needing a recommendation from the ship's captain and a senior officer before sitting the final paper. That person was desperate to fit in, desperate to impress and get ahead. That

April Johansson wasn't comfortable in her own skin and saw promotion and achievement as a way to get comfortable. When you're the one making the decisions, you're in control, right? Surely that's an easier place to be than following the orders of people who aren't as smart as you are and don't appreciate what you can do?

No. That's not how it works. When you're in charge, you have to make the life-or-death calls and you have to live with the responsibility of it. That's where Shann is right now. That's what's eating away at her on the inside.

I'm staring at my right arm again and my absent hand. Was my desire to have the surgery and my using an artificial limb an attempt to fit in socially? No, I don't think it was. Maybe I was conditioned by my parents when they encouraged me to wear and use the automated prosthetics? Unpacking all of that just isn't worth it now. As far back as I can remember, I've always seen myself as a person with two hands; that's why I feel so awkward with only one.

"Ensign, are you awake?"

I look around. Le Garre is in the doorway. I push myself up and away from the terminal. "Something you need, Captain?"

She tries to smile, but it's forced and covers a wince. "Major will do. It saves any confusion."

I nod, thinking back to how I addressed Shann earlier. This arrangement works for me. "Okay, Major. How can I help?"

"I want to talk to the prisoner."

The reference makes me flinch. I'd been counting eight people but not really thinking about who the eighth person was. The last time I saw Rocher, he stabbed me in the gut.

I nod towards the corridor. "He's in the airlock, where we left him. I disabled all the access controls and Sam welded some steel across the hatch. He's got air and a tube to piss in. That's more than his people would have given us."

"Is the two-way speaker unit working? Can I talk to him from outside?"

"It should be, unless he's disabled it." I turn back to the screen and bring up the security feed for the airlock. Rocher is floating in the middle of the room with his eyes closed, seemingly asleep. "Even so, I wouldn't talk to him alone if I were you, Major."

"I'd hoped that you'd come with me."

My fingers freeze in front of the screen. I chew my lip and there's a twinge of pain as I bite through the raw skin, drawing blood. I wipe the blood away on the back of my sleeve, leaving a stain.

"I'm not sure if I can do that, Major," I say.

"Johansson. The worst is over. We're going to be on this ship with the clone for the entire journey back to Phobos. You can't avoid him. Best to face him now." Le Garre's soft tone with a hint of her French accent belies the steel behind what she is saying. If I don't do this, she'll have to make other arrangements and I'll go down in her estimation. It's a calculated risk. She needs me. Of all the surviving crew from the *Khidr*, my skills with computer systems and my hack of the *Gallowglass* controls make me the most indispensable. She's also playing to my sense of ambition and pride, pushing me a little, a tactic that would have worked on the old Johansson, before all this happened, before we wrecked our ship and ourselves in the process.

"Okay, I'll do it," I say.

Le Garre tries to smile again and fails again. "I hoped you would," she says.

We move into the corridor towards the airlock. I go to the little window in the door. The thick glass is scratched on the other side. What has Rocher been trying to do? Inside, he's floating motionless in the middle of the room, just as I saw him on the camera.

I move across to the speaker and press the button. The green light indicates it's working. "All good," I say to Le Garre. "Go ahead and wake him up."

"If he's actually sleeping," Le Garre replies. She presses the button. "Okay, Rocher, we need to talk."

I've brought a portable screen with me. On it, I can see Rocher move in response to the noise. He's clearly awake. His lips stretch into a broad smile and, a moment later, he turns in the air, reaching out for the wall, grabbing something that allows him to pull himself closer to the door. He presses the speaker switch.

"Major Le Garre? Now, why are you here. Did the captain send you down here to do the dirty work?"

"I'm in charge now, Rocher. That means you're not being indulged. As far as I'm concerned, you're deadweight to us and no one will miss you when you're gone. I want clear answers, or I space you."

"That's pretty straightforward."

"The anomalies. What was your mission? To pick them up?"

"Yes, that's right. We were sent to collect them."

"What for?"

"I wasn't told."

Le Garre sighs and glances around at me. I shrug. Her approach is different, but she's already given away a fair amount of information and only confirmed what we already knew. She turns back. "What do you know about the anomalies?" she asks.

"Only that they've been around a long time. NASA detected them back in the nineteen-sixties, but they didn't know what they'd found. They have very interesting properties. At one point, *Gallowglass* was struggling to contain them."

"They have a gravitational effect."

"Yes, one that fluctuates, as if they're alive, with a purpose and agenda all of their own."

I reach forward and flick the switch on the speaker, turning off the transmission. "Major, he's being very helpful."

Le Garre frowns, then nods as she realises my point. "Don't worry, I'm not suckered in. I know what he's capable of."

"Okay."

Le Garre turns the speaker on again. "Was that why you attacked the freighter, *Hercules*, for the anomalies?"

Rocher stares at her through the scratched glass, then he backs away and looks at the camera, quite deliberately staring at me.

He winks.

He moves back to the speaker and presses the button. "Yes, that's the reason," he says.

"What were you supposed to do with the anomalies when you collected them all?" Le Garre asks.

"We were to return to Phobos Station. A shuttle transfer had been arranged."

"Okay." Le Garre takes a minute to think. Then she flicks off the speaker and turns to me. "All right, that'll be all for now." She nods towards Rocher. "No one comes here to talk with him without my express permission. If I come to you about it, you don't let me down here alone. Understood?"

I nod. "I think we should take further security precautions, Major. If he gets out...."

"Yes, it doesn't bear thinking about." Le Garre is moving away back up the corridor. "Talk with Arkov after the next muster, he knows all about airlocks. Between you, sort out whatever you think you need. For now, we keep him in there, conscious and alive."

"That'll be a drain on our resources."

"We'll make it work. We need to."

We are back in the medical room. Chiu is still there in bed. Le Garre loiters at the door as I go inside. "Thank you for your help, Ensign," she says softly as I pass.

I shrug. "What are you going to do now?"

"Call a meeting of the crew and figure out what we're doing." Le Garre nods towards Chiu. "Is she well enough to join us?"

"I'll find out." I move into the room, about to call out to Chiu, but then I notice her eyes. They are open, her pupils rolled back, displaying the whites. "Major I think she's having some kind of—"

Suddenly Chiu starts to spasm, straining at the straps that are holding her. A moment later the auto-medic alarms start to go off. Her blood pressure and temperature are rising fast, her heart is beating erratically. I'm by her side, looking at the readings and trying to instruct the auto-medic with one hand as I turn in zero gravity and steady myself with my feet. "Chiu, can you hear me? Chiu!"

Her face pinches with concentration, her pupils come back and focus on me. "April! Not Chiu, it's…me…. April, help me…."

"Duggins?" I know it's him even as I say his name. I lean in close. "Are you alive? Are you over there?"

"Yes! Trapped…changed…."

As quickly as it started, the spasms cease. Chiu's body relaxes, her eyes close, the readings fall. The logs indicate she's been given a large dose of dopamine. That seems to have calmed her.

"Duggins?"

There's no answer. I glance around at Le Garre, who is staring at Chiu in disbelief.

"You saw that, right? You heard what she said? It wasn't her talking to us. He's alive over there."

"I…." Le Garre swallows and pushes herself backwards. "Full muster briefing in tweny minutes. Make sure she's sedated. We'll discuss everything then."

Then she's gone and I'm left with the mess.

CHAPTER SEVEN

Holder

Remember his face!

Remember!

Whitewallswhitewallswhitewallswhitewalls....

What?

I open my eyes. I'm sat in the lobby of a hotel. This place is corporate boring; all clean lines of glass and concrete. The couches are dark leather with metal frames. You perch here, you don't relax.

I'm waiting here for someone. I glance at my watch. I've been waiting here for an hour or so.

I hate waiting.

I've never been a fan of hanging around. Either I'm doing something or I'm shutting down. Bed or bike works for me; asleep or out with the wind on my face whilst breaking traffic laws and speed limits. Loitering around here is like hell.

But I do it, because that's the job.

Today, I'm Alice Winters, bike messenger, in between deliveries having just dropped a package off with the concierge. I get to wait ten minutes or so before moving on. Of course, in that time, the person I'm really here to see will come downstairs from his executive suite and get into a waiting limousine, provided he sticks to time, like he has every day for the past week.

At that moment, the real mission starts.

Dark bike leathers blend in with the furniture. I'm breathing carefully, so I don't fidget and draw unnecessary attention to myself. The target has extensive security. Three members of his team are already here, but I bet there's more keeping watch on the building and the street outside. They'll be using body cameras, recording everyone going in and out. I will be picked up, but if all goes to plan, the operation will be over before they are able to identify me as a threat.

Gloves stay on, communicator remains in hand. I'm looking at the screen as it plays a streaming show rerun. The images move, but I'm not really seeing them. This part of the mission requires me to be under a complete communications blackout. The target's people will take every precaution. They've been here for a week, so the hotel will be packed with monitoring devices. Every person in here will be having their data access checked and recorded. My people might be able to get around that, but why bother when we don't need to?

This is a risk, but it's a calculated risk. I'm on my own if this goes bad, but we're in a fairly public place.

My attention is not really on the phone screen. Instead I'm concentrating on the lift door and the stairs, which I can see out of the corner of my eye.

Movement.

Training helps you resist the urge to look. People register people if they make eye contact. There's a high chance of that right in the moment someone enters a room. Don't look then, wait three seconds, then look, but without moving your head, just with your eyes. If you wait, the other person will have focused their attention on something else. That's the moment you get visual confirmation. Then, you wait some more, tracking them by listening and concentrating, not by watching. That's how it works.

Yeah…. It's definitely him.

The target's back is to me and he is wearing a dark suit. The hair is greyer than I remember from the photographs and has been left to grow a little. But it's him. I know it's him. Hours of studying video recordings of his walk and the almost imperceptible limp, favouring his left leg, give him away. That was a permanent reminder of his last altercation with another dangerous organisation.

David Hannington is a war criminal. He also claims to be retired.

But no one really retires in this game. He stays alive by throwing money at the problem and moving around, living in high society hotels, on rented yachts, all the best places where you can't nail him down, arrest him or put a bullet in his skull. Forty years ago, he was a Fleet special forces commando who disappeared after the rest of his unit was found dead in the Syrtis crater on Mars.

Thirty years ago, Earth First separatists tried to assassinate him in the backstreets of Paris.

Twenty years ago, there were rumours of him leading hijacking in the Red Sea.

Now, he's an old man and past his best, but even now, he's very rich and very dangerous.

Hannington passes behind me, his entourage flanking him, left, right and behind. The man loitering by the revolving doors steps in front of the group, completing the protective gauntlet. These men will be his personal guards, ex-military who've moved into 'consultancy' and 'private contracting'. They'll be special forces trained with reputations of their own, no doubt.

I wait until they are through the entrance and outside. Then I start to move, walking quickly to the same exit. Hannington is on the kerb, getting into the back of his car. My bike is a few yards down the street. I climb on, put on my helmet and start up.

Immediately, I'm in another world as the data overlays and communications links re-establish themselves. Their activation signals I'm back in the loop.

I put the bike in gear, kick the stand closed and drive away.

In the opposite direction to the limousine.

"Holder to Control?"

"Receiving."

"Target confirmed. Am establishing pursuit as planned."

"Acknowledged. Any trouble?"

"No, he didn't recognise me."

"I told you he wouldn't."

"Yeah."

I take the first left, then left again, and again. The limousine passes in front of me and I swing in to follow, with three cars between us. If Hannington planned to have a tail of his own security detail, I should be tracking behind them.

Three days ago, I was at home. I moved back to Interlaken after being discharged from active duty. I was walking to the local shop for bread and milk when a car drew up beside me. A man got out and handed me a thin brown envelope. Inside were my new orders and set-up resources to get me here, to Munich, under a false passport.

As soon as I read the letter, I was back in.

"Target acquired. Looks like they have a sweeper car in operation." The blood-red 4x4 ahead of me is hugging the back of the limousine like an eager child. The windows are tinted. I bet there's at least four more individuals in there, fully armed fanatics, ready to defend their employer at a moment's notice.

"We're on the move," Control says in my ear.

"Make sure you hang back," I warn. "These people know their business."

"Acknowledged. We're sticking with the plan. We'll stay ninety seconds away."

"Confirmed."

Ninety seconds without support. Again, this is a calculated risk. I can handle myself in an altercation, but I'm outnumbered. If they spot me, I'll need to act fast and hit hard. These people will not go easy on anyone who gets in their way.

A run at Hannington, though. That was too tempting to pass up.

I'm riding an old Sindler 88. A typical electro-motor courier bike. Not what I'd prefer to run with. However, this model's been modified, and includes some extra tricks. Two FN P216s are built into the front engine housing with a linked trigger under the handlebars. There's a third P216 in the messenger box on the back in case I need it. These little machine guns are short-range, anti-personnel weapons. I'll need something with more punch if we get into an exchange between vehicles. Besides, discharging a firearm on a city street in Germany will bring a lot of unwanted attention, so it's definitely not part of the plan.

I'm weaving between lanes. The mid-morning traffic is thick, but not impassable. I maintain the gap between me and the limousine, checking the road signs as we pass.

"Control, they're making for the autobahn. Looks like this meeting's going to be outside the city."

"Makes sense. Any idea which way?"

"Route eight to Augsburg, I think."

"Okay, when you confirm, we'll have the aerial team set down en route."

This isn't a small operation. We have twenty highly trained military specialists working to close the net on Hannington and whoever he's meeting. Most of them, for purposes of operational secrecy, I don't know or haven't met. Our target doesn't come out of hiding for a social call, so this must be important. The current geopolitical climate is heating up again. The proxy actors working across the globe to sow dissent and conflict in sovereign nations are reappearing. That's why people like me have been called back in. Hannington is part of that historical landscape too. Someone wants to meet with an old master and pick his brains or recruit him to a new cause. Anything that flushes out this new criminal contact is useful to us.

We're on the outskirts of the city now. The through road gains lanes and lifts over the local intersections. The limousine is gradually increasing speed and the red 4x4 does the same. To my right, I spot a police patrol car, pulling on from a junction ahead. The digital display in my helmet picks out the number plate and pings a request to the Munich police database.

There's no match.

"Control, you there?"

"Yep, receiving. What's up?"

"Do you have a trace on all local law enforcement vehicles in the city?"

"Not at the moment."

"Can you pull one up? We have a patrol car joining the party and my system says it isn't registered."

"Okay, checking." The portable data centre available to my support team is more advanced than I have available while driving. Munich police vehicles have GPS transponders and are linked into a central co-ordination centre. My handler can make an authorised request for their tactical plot of vehicles and quickly determine if any officers have decided to take a trip onto route eight. "Nothing nearby," Control says. "Looks like we have a rogue actor in the game."

I'm thinking about how this will play out. A limousine with escort is a very obvious mode of transport. If Hannington wanted to be discreet, this isn't the way to do it. "They know we're watching," I say out loud.

"What?" Control sounds surprised.

"This is too easy. Hannington is better than this. He knows someone is watching." We're picking up speed and getting into the suburbs now; the high-rise office blocks and apartments are fading into the background. "They'll switch cars when they're clear of the city. They'll pick somewhere under cover."

"Like under a bridge."

"Yes, exactly."

There's a pause at the other end. Control is talking to someone. "We need eyes on the transfer vehicle. Can you get to it?"

"It'll look obvious if I do," I reply. "We're going to need a secondary pursuit operative or a change of transport for me."

A switch-switch could also be happening. If Hannington dummies a change to the patrol car, or some other random vehicle and actually stays in the limousine, we'll lose him. We need more eyes. That means more people and that means more risk of discovery.

"Control, you need to make the call."

Another pause and more murmuring voices. My handler clearly isn't the one making the decisions. "Holder, you're authorised to continue pursuit of the limousine. If it pulls over, you ride by and give a visual report on the situation. We'll update your instructions after that."

"Understood." Clear orders can be hard to come by sometimes. I'm not adverse to using my initiative, but I shouldn't need to with these people. They're supposed to be the best.

The patrol car accelerates to join the outside lane. I keep an eye on him in my wing mirror. He pulls out, overtakes and slows down alongside the 4x4, which gives way, letting him in behind the limousine. Then, the patrol car activates its lights, giving the signal for the limo to pull over.

We're nearing a bridge. All three vehicles are slowing down. I pull out and around them, keeping my eyes on the road. "Control, looks like we were right, they're making a switch under the interchange. I'm overtaking."

"Understood. Is it the patrol car?"

"Yes, appears to be." I resist the urge to turn my head and look into the opaque limousine window. I wouldn't see anything anyway. "Whoever your secondary operative is, they better get here fast."

"We're on it."

There's movement behind me. In the wing mirror. The 4x4 matches my move, switching lanes and accelerating past the limousine. They're right behind me now. I can see the driver's face. He's glaring at me, concentrating on getting as close as he can.

I've been made.

"Update, they're on to me. The escort is not stopping. It's following me."

"Okay, what do you need?"

"Some of that ninety-second support you promised would be appreciated."

"That might be complicated to arrange. I'm not sure we can—"

The communication link cuts out. I flinch at the familiar sound of interference. This is a set up. Looks like I'm on my own.

Time to take extreme measures.

I put my foot down, *hard*.

There will be a minimum of four people in the 4x4. They will have no scruples about starting a firefight. Civilian casualties are like career achievements to them. The only thing that may give them pause is the loss of their own lives. Hannington doesn't have hundreds of fanatics willing to die for him. He'll want to keep his people alive.

Right now, they'll be weighing up how much advantage murdering me gets them.

There's another bridge ahead. I swerve to the right into the runoff section and pull a hard turn, dragging the bike over me as I crash towards the impact barrier. My leg scrapes along the tarmac and the gravel-lined verge. The stones cut into my plastic armour and the neoprene undersuit, scraping through both into the flesh of my legs. The pain is a familiar memory. Hundreds of corners on dozens of racing circuits, all those days when you push too hard, too fast, lose it and slide across the track into the traps.

My leg is burning agony, but I grit my teeth and hang on, keeping my head off the road. The wheels slam into the metal barrier, grip and tear through the boards. At the last moment, I twist the bike under me and the rear tyre grips on the mud and grass of the verge. The bike rights itself, the engine whines in protest and I'm away.

To anyone on the road, it'll look like an accident, that I lost control, but I suspect my pursuers won't be convinced.

A moment later, my suspicions are confirmed. A splintering crash and the 4x4 is through the barrier too. I glance around to see it charging up the hill towards me. Clearly, the engine has been souped up, because I can't pull away. One of Hannington's mercs leans out of the passenger window. He has an old semi-automatic in his hand. I catch sight of his face and gasp. He's identical to the driver, as if they are twins or....

He opens fire and bullets slap into the grass between us. I flinch, twist and turn, pulling the bike around, onto the driver's side, making the passenger's aim more difficult. But we both know it won't be long before they run me down.

I slam on the brakes, wheel the bike around, kick out the parking stand and leap off on the far side. The dual P216 pivots around in my right hand and I flip open the courier box with my left, grabbing for its contents; the extra gun and a belt of grenades.

The P216 in my hand. The grenades clatter to the ground at my feet.

I rest the gun against the bike seat and squeeze both triggers.

The 4x4 has reinforced glass and a reinforced chassis. These weapons aren't made for this, but they are what I have. Full auto, directed fire, straight into the radiator might do something.

It doesn't. The vehicle just keeps on coming.

Bullets slam into the bike, splintering the engine casing, shredding the tires and bouncing off the metal frame. I duck down behind it and snatch up the grenade belt, pulling all the pins. I hurl the lot over the top and throw myself out of the way.

The 4x4 crashes into the bike. The grenades detonate. Something slams into me and—

"Hello, Natalie."

The white-walled room. The man in the red plastic suit, Doctor Summers. I remember this even as the memories of Munich slip away. "Was I—"

"You did well, Natalie." The man smiles. I can see his expression through the plastic faceplate. It's not an attractive smile. He's not an attractive man.

I try to move my head, but it's restrained. I can feel something behind my right ear. It's some sort of cable, plugged directly into my skull – into my brain.

A plastic-gloved hand touches my cheek. "Just stay calm, Natalie. Take a rest. Let it go."

Whitewallswhitewallswhitewallswhite....

*　　*　　*

RECORDING...

Voice 1:

Hello, Jonathan. Sorry to wake you.

Voice 2:

Petra? Is that you? Jeez, what time is it?

Voice 1:

Four-seventeen where you are, I believe. Toyko, yes?

Voice 2:

If you're calling me, you know the answer to that.

Voice 1:

The scrambler encryption on your communicator ID is pretty thorough, but yes, we have your location. I wanted you to know that.

Voice 2:

You woke me up to threaten me?

Voice: 1

Not really. We both know the consequences of a direct attack. Just because we're on opposite sides in this, doesn't mean I don't regard you as a friend.

Voice 2:

So, the détente remains?

Voice 1:

Jonathan, we found the shipment manifests for the freighters. One of your people in Sudan got careless. We know what's going on and we're going to act. It's all starting to spiral. Pretty soon we're both going to be irrelevant in this.

Voice 2:

Are you sure this line is secure?

Voice 1:

I can't be completely sure. But it's secure as anything can be these days. Jonathan, this is your warning. Gavrilo, Jonathan, remember Gavrilo. I owed you. Now, consider our debt paid.

END OF RECORD....

CHAPTER EIGHT

Drake

I'm moving back up the passageway to the conveyor. I reach it as I start to hear the murmuring voices of the *Chronos*'s crew. I can't make out what they're saying, but there's definitely more than one person down there.

I hesitate beside the conveyor. If I activate it, the little transport will take me out into the tube and away from the carnage. However, the invaders might hear me. The moment they do, they'll know someone survived the explosion.

I also don't know if the conveyor will go back to the dock where *Angelus* is located. The chain runs counter to the station's rotation. I can't tell if there's a reverse, so it might take me right past the place I've just run away from.

The station security *need* to be warned. They'll have been alerted to the explosion, but they'll have thought it was an accident, so they won't be ready for a firefight. Who is ever ready for a firefight? Earth has had its wars, but up here? We're all supposed to be on the same side, trying to survive and thrive on worlds that were never made for us.

What are these people doing? What do they want? *This is madness!*

The portable screen I had before is gone, forgotten and lost in the explosion. There has to be a terminal around here somewhere, something I can use to make contact with the station crew.

Movement on the staircase. I crouch down, trying to hide behind the low wall beside the conveyor entrance. I see a figure coming up the stairs carrying a weapon. It could be the same man I saw before, or someone else. He's going to find me. I need to get out of here.

I make my way through to the conveyor. Instead of climbing aboard, I walk quickly to the rear of the platform and climb down into the tunnel. A few metres along is the parking entrance. The chain is still running along the main passageway.

I reach up and grab hold of the chain. The links are moving fast, and I'm pulled off my feet and dragged along by it, bumping into the side of the tube. I manage to hang on, lever myself up so my legs are locked around the links as well, and it pulls me into the tunnel.

Within seconds, I'm passing alongside the ruined medical compartments. I get a last look at the chamber below through a transparent DuraGlas window. It's just a glimpse, but I can see the burned and blackened interior where people died. Then I'm past it and moving on to the other sections of the station. The next zone is blue – the command compartments. Hopefully, there will be someone there. Someone I can warn.

The conveyor port is coming up fast. At the last moment, I let go, dropping towards the entrance. I bounce off the wall and skin my arm, slamming the back of my head against metal before coming to a stop in the middle of the empty tube.

I lie there a minute and try to catch my breath. Listening. I can't hear much over the sound of my own breathing and the pounding of my heart. There has to be someone here. Wherever they were holding the anniversary party, they can't have abandoned command and control.

I climb out of the conveyor tube and onto the parkway. The space is almost identical to the one I just left. I'm walking quickly but carefully, checking around corners when there are corners, moving towards the staircase down to the other levels.

The layout at the top of the stairs is different. There isn't a docking point here. Instead, I'm descending into a central plaza with different offices, technical administration and control rooms connected from this open space.

There are more anniversary banners and there's more evidence of a party, but now all of that seems like some kind of bitter joke. This tiny metal world, in orbit around an unforgiving moon, is in danger. It's being invaded by ruthless people who must have an agenda.

I remember the explosion on Earth at the solar array in Atacama that was all over the news as I was leaving Jezero. Could this be connected?

As I start down the stairs, I spot a workstation in one of the nearby offices. A flickering screen indicates it's switched on. I glance around and, seeing no one about, make my way there. I sit in front of the screen and press my thumb to the login pad.

The screen goes dark and then loads a version of my desktop from the medical centre on Jezero. Immediately, I touch the comms window and a selection of contacts opens up. I hesitate a moment before selecting MarsCol security. The situation up here needs reporting, but knowing which part of the colonial bureaucracy to contact first is tricky.

Still, once the information is out, I can always message more people.

I touch the video call activation button, the screen changes and the light for the camera on top winks on. I can see my own face in a picture window. The main display is black with the word 'connecting' written across it in an attractive italic serif font.

I'm waiting. Anyone who has ever experienced waiting for a computer to sort itself out and perform the task you asked for will know the feeling. In this case, knowing what I know, knowing what has happened and what is about to happen, the nervous tension and frustration at having to wait makes it all the more difficult to bear.

Time seems to slow down as the screen tries to make the call. One of those moments between moments when you're waiting for the technology to do its job. The frustration intensifies and I'm second-guessing myself. How long should this take?

Then the screen times out. The system has failed to connect.

I ball my hands into fists but force myself to stay calm. There could be any number of reasons why the call didn't go through. The Mars orbital satellite network is nowhere near as crowded as Earth's. The communication relays can be unreliable at times. If Phobos is between the station and a satellite relay, then connections are likely to be down.

I realise that it might have been intentional. The people attacking the station probably planned for this, determining the best moment to begin their assault right in the middle of an anniversary celebration and when the station's ability to contact anyone was at its weakest.

"Stand up and step away from the screen."

The voice is behind me and a complete surprise. Something is pushed against the back of my head. A gun, I guess. I raise my hands and do as I'm told, stepping to the right and turning around.

My captor is wearing the dark grey work suit of a technician. He's Caucasian, with brown hair and dark eyes. There's a hint of Slavic ancestry in his face.

He's wearing a station name badge with the word 'Rocher' written on it.

"Who are you?" my captor says.

I decide to be honest. "Doctor Emerson Drake. I was sent up here as part of the emergency medical team. I survived the explosion."

"Good to meet you, Doctor." The man taps his name badge with his left hand. "I'm Technician Gabriel Rocher. What happened to you?"

"I was over in the medical section. The *Chronos* docked and the people inside threw out some sort of demolition charge. It killed everyone in the room, apart from me. They aren't here for medical assistance. This is an attack, an invasion. They want to take over the station." I nod towards the doors. Rocher glances that way, but the gun doesn't waver. "They've started exploring. It won't take them long to reach here."

"Yeah. We better move then." Rocher smiles at me. The expression doesn't reach his eyes. It's like he's in shock and not quite processing the danger of all this. I guess I might be in the same state. "Were you trying to contact the authorities?"

"Yes; and raise the alarm here. Station security need to know they're walking into a trap."

"Good plan, same as mine. Comm beads are out, so I was trying to find a station too." Rocher lowers his weapon and slips past me into the seat. He pulls up the internal communication system and selects 'security', activating the call in the same way I did before. The screen does exactly the same thing, trying to connect before failing and timing out. "Damn, they must already be in the system, locking out the comms."

"What do we do?" I ask.

Rocher stands up. "We'll have to go there. If we're quick, we'll reach the security detail before the *Chronos* people do." He moves away from me, taking a chit from his pocket and jamming it into a slot on a wall panel. The panel slides back, and I can see a rack of weapons. He pulls out a second low-velocity pistol and holds it out to me. "Know what you're doing with this?"

I take the weapon. "Whether I do or I don't, I'd rather have it with me than not. From what I've seen, I don't think the people we're dealing with take prisoners."

Rocher nods. "We'll need to make our way through the corridors and hatchways. That means eyes open, trusting each other around every corner. I need to know you've got my back."

"Sure, I understand. I'm with you."

"Great."

Rocher moves away, gun in hand. He's walking on the balls of his feet in a way that suggests he's had military training. I follow a few steps behind.

My fingers go to the metal chit in my pocket. I glance back at the workstation. I could use it, override the system and send out the message. But if I do, I'll reveal to Rocher that I have it.

I'm not sure I trust him, yet.

We move into an unlit corridor. As we walk, lighting strips on the floor and the ceiling begin to glow, illuminating the path ahead. There's a T-junction at the end. Rocher slows down and raises his weapon. He gestures towards the passage to the left. I angle that way, keeping my weapon trained on the floor.

I edge to the corner, trying to see around it, into the shadows ahead. The strips begin to glow. The corridor is empty.

"This way," Rocher says. "Keep your eyes open."

We're moving down the right-hand passageway. I'm walking sideways, covering the route behind us as Rocher leads. My finger is on the trigger of the gun, my hands are trembling. For some reason, just holding a weapon makes this whole situation more real, more intense. I'm worried about my finger slipping, about shooting someone accidentally or giving away our position.

I've never been comfortable around guns. When I was nine or ten years old, I went on a school trip to a firing range. They gave us some of those old air guns. Some of the older kids started taking the piss out of me while it was my turn to shoot. I turned around, gun in hand, not even thinking about what I was doing. Everyone went quiet after that, even the teachers.

I didn't realise I'd been aiming the gun at my classmates, not until years later.

It's hard to keep up with Rocher. He's moving so carefully, but with impressive speed. I cannot match his pace and stay quiet. I'm falling behind. After a few minutes he notices and waits for me to catch up.

We take another right, then a left. There's a hatch at the end of the corridor. Rocher waits beside it, urging me forward. I reach him, a question forming in my mind.

"Where is everyone? Where was the party?" I ask, trying to keep my voice low.

"The anniversary? They're all up in hydroponics. The gardens are the best place for any kind of celebration. Going up there is a real treat, especially when you're stuck in a place like this for six months at a time."

I frown, trying to remember the colours. "Is that where we're going?"

"No, we're heading straight to security. This is a shortcut. At the other end is the main intersection. We should meet the duty team right there."

I nod and level my weapon into the darkened space through the hatch. I step through and hear an electrical hum, the same as I heard when the lights came on in the corridors, but this time, there is no glow or illumination, as if something isn't working.

"It's dark in here, we should—"

There's a hiss as the hatch behind me closes. I turn just as it seals shut.

I hear bolts lock and a light comes on in the corridor outside, revealing Rocher's face.

He's smiling at me.

"Hey, what are you doing?" I shout.

Rocher's smile widens. He taps his ear, indicating he can't hear me. Then the light goes out and I'm left alone in the darkness.

CHAPTER NINE

Johansson

We're back in the meeting room. Everyone apart from Chiu and the Rocher clone is here. Sam looks tired; Shann looks tired. We all look tired, I guess. Only Arkov seems to have got a decent amount of sleep.

"We need to get out of here," Le Garre says.

I clench my fist and gnash my teeth, fighting to stay calm. This isn't going to be a discussion, or if it is, it isn't going to go well when the ranking officer has already made up her mind.

"There's enough fuel in the tanks to get us to Phobos. It's going to take a while and it's not going to be easy. We'll need to replicate how the crew of this ship operated, some of us in cryo, while others work. That'll mean extended shifts, but it's the only way to make the supplies stretch for all eight of us on board."

"You've done the numbers then?" Shann asks. I look at her; the crumpled look of defeat is still there, writ large across her face, but something is making her engage and follow Le Garre's reasoning.

"I have," Le Garre replies. She glances at Travers, who nods. I know instinctively what that means. He's the one who did the calculations. They probably decided all this before she went to meet Rocher, while I was asleep. "We can make it if we run two shifts. As we become more familiar with the ship and effect repairs, more of us can go into cryo if needs be. We'll make it, but it's going to be tight."

"You need to tell them," I mutter, staring at the floor.

"Sorry, Ensign Johansson, what did you say?"

I raise my head, glance around at the faces. "I said, Major, you need to tell them. They need to know what happened to Chiu and what Rocher told you."

Le Garre eyes me for a moment, then nods. "Okay. Cards on the table. *Gallowglass* was heading to Phobos. They had a pre-arranged rendezvous with someone to pick up the anomalies. If we go instead, we may be able to turn the tables and find out who Rocher is working for."

"That's a pretty good reason to go," Sam says.

"That's not all of it," I say. "We had an incident with Chiu. Duggins made contact. He spoke to me through her. He's alive over there in the wreckage. Something's happening to him. We have to.... We should go and rescue him."

There's silence. No one knows how to follow my outburst. I'm stretching the line, pushing against Le Garre's authority, but I know I have to. *She's going to fuck up.* That's what Shann told me. I can't let that happen. We can't lose anyone else.

"Ensign, we can't get over there," Travers says. His voice is calm and gentle. He's speaking carefully, trying to talk me down. "The gravity effect of those anomalies is a lot less than it was, but if we get any closer, it could escalate again, and we'll be using up fuel. We barely have enough to make it back."

"Have you thought about how ridiculously impossible that is?" I'm angry now and some of it slips through in my voice. Travers doesn't deserve abuse, but he's being frustratingly ignorant. "Whatever those objects are, they shouldn't be able to change their density and mass. The gravitational properties of the anomalies should be constant. There's no explanation for the increase and sudden drop off. All we do know is that one of our own is in the middle of all that, asking for help."

"Once we make contact with Fleet, they'll send a ship to investigate and help."

"He might not have that long. We're here, right now. If we're going to abandon him, we need to acknowledge it and accept what we've done."

There's silence and I feel like I've dropped a bomb in the room. That's the crux of it. That's the bit Le Garre doesn't seem to get. She's responsible for people's lives. I want to try and rescue Duggins, but it'll mean risking all of us. Le Garre is in charge; she has to make that call and accept the burden that comes with it.

Similarly, we're all on the edge. We have to know she's going to lead us in a direction that gives us the best chance of survival. Otherwise, well…soldiers desert for reasons like that.

"Major, could I add something?" Arkov is speaking. His question is softly delivered, a nice mix of formal and informal. Le Garre nods and gestures for him to proceed.

"We are all very fortunate to be alive. That is owing in no small part to the efforts of everyone here. We are witnesses to a phenomenon that cannot be explained by our understanding of science. We are inadequate in the face of the mysteries of the universe."

"But if not us, who else?"

"Ensign Johansson wishes us to act. She is motivated by the instinctive desire to protect one of her tribe. A desire we all understand, particularly as we've lost so many friends." Arkov pauses and nods sadly. "Johansson asks us to risk ourselves one more time to save our friend. It is a noble idea. However, there is no record of what we have seen. No means by which we can relay it back to Earth or Mars, or Ceres. Our species will not advance if it does not learn from what we have experienced. The individual, over the species. It is a dilemma."

"There's the Rocher stuff to consider too," Sam adds. He's not looking at me. I don't think he can. Instead, he's staring into the middle of the room. "*Gallowglass* is not a Fleet registered ship. These people are part of something, some kind of conspiracy against everything we know. Someone needs to be told."

So that's that. This isn't a democracy, but even if it was, I'm out of allies.

"There is something else we can do," Shann says.

All eyes in the room go to her. She's still the captain, the real captain. I'm desperately hoping she can save my choice, save Duggins. She looks at me.

"Thanks to Johansson disabling the ship's weapons, there's still a number of torpedoes on board. We could modify one with some kind of sensor package and send it over, into range of the anomalies. We might get a clearer signal from it and we might be able to send a message to Duggins, if he's alive, to let him know what's going on."

"That sounds like a lot of work," Le Garre says. "We have a lot to do acclimatising to this ship and repairing the damage. I'm not sure we can manage jury-rigging a probe as well."

"I can do it," Shann says. "Leave it to me."

"Are you sure? Does that mean—"

Shann holds up a hand. "It doesn't mean anything more than what it is. I took some pills and got some sleep. I can work and you're going to need as many of us as possible to put in a shift." She looks at me, then at Sam and Travers before continuing, addressing Le Garre directly. "You made the right call. It's still the right call, but let me do this. It'll help."

"Okay," Le Garre says. She turns to Travers. "Lieutenant, I need this ship prepped and ready to depart. Can you do it?"

Travers nods. He looks pointedly at me. "I'll need Johansson's help, but yes, we can get it done."

"Then, the ship is yours," Le Garre says. "Time for me, Sam and Vasiliy to get a rest." She glances at Arkov. "Before you turn in, Ensign Johansson may need some help securing our prison."

Arkov nods. "Understood, Major."

★   ★   ★

"We need to talk, Ensign."

The bridge of the *Gallowglass* is only partially functional. The emergency lighting illuminates the room, and the three control chairs aren't currently functional, but at least the bodies of the Rocher clones are gone. It's just me and Bill Travers. He looks tired and serious, those dark eyes flashing in the half-light.

"You can't keep pushing Le Garre like that," he says. "We have to be a team."

I can feel my face going red. I flinch and look away, trying to hide it. There's nothing to say in response to his words. Again, this isn't going to be a discussion. He's used my rank for a reason, to remind me we're in the military.

"I need to know you're going to be a part of this crew."

I bite my lip, but I can't keep it all in. "I'd like to think I've proved how much I care, sir."

"That's not in dispute. You have to know when to contribute and when to trust others. Le Garre's in command. That means she makes the decisions." Travers rubs his face. "I think disobeying orders and going solo in that torpedo did something to you. Maybe it was the right call, but that doesn't mean you get to throw out the chain of command."

"I get that, sir."

"Do you? Do you really?"

I frown, thinking about it. "Maybe I see things a little differently to you, sir."

"That doesn't matter. We need your skills. We won't survive without them."

This conversation isn't getting us anywhere. I move around the room to the back of the first control chair. When we moved the ship, I used one of the terminals to hack into *Gallowglass*. We don't currently have operable control from here. To get that up and running is going to require some work. "The Major trusts you, sir. You can discuss things with her before she makes a decision."

"Of course, I'm the XO."

I open the panel on the back of the chair with a powered bolt driver. The fittings are the same as those on *Khidr*, but working on them with my left hand is difficult. "Shouldn't I be part of that process too?"

"Do you think a senior officer has to explain how she works to a junior officer?" Travers asks. His voice is level and calm, but there's an edge and I can see what he means. "We're all adjusting. We have more officers than non-coms on this ship."

"But why am I in the middle?" I ask as I pull out the shorted contacts.

"Because you are. Because fate or God made you the lowest ranker in this particularly shitty situation." Travers chuckles. "Do you have faith, Ensign? Ever go to church?"

I shake my head. "My parents never bothered with it."

"I have faith," Travers says. "Sometimes, I think it's the only thing that keeps me going. When we're out here in the darkness, seeing things that no human being has ever seen, I marvel that I've been chosen as a witness to God's grand plan. I get a chance to glimpse a part of something so far beyond who and what I am whilst I'm alive. That's an incredible privilege."

I shrug. The wires have some slack. I snip off the burned sections and pull the two ends together. "That's great for you."

"Yes it is. Do you see why?" I glance up to see Travers moving across the room towards me, gesturing all around. "My faith is pretty private and pretty inclusive. I don't claim to have some kind of special insight, but what I believe helps me be the person I am. A lot of agnostic people, a lot of atheist people I know, they struggle to see beyond themselves. That's what makes them self-centred and unable to see how they cannot consider the universe without focusing on their own place within it."

I bite my lip and swallow down an angry answer. Chemical fusing cement will bring the broken ends back together, but this is a job that I'm used to doing with two hands. I twist the broken wires around each other and fumble for the tube in my pack as everything floats free around me. "What insight does your faith give you about Duggins?" I ask.

"You think I don't want to save him?"

"Do you?"

Travers goes silent and I use the time to work. The tube of fusing cement is awkward to use like this, but it has an adhesive quality which means it doesn't just float away when you squeeze it out of the end. I get a little bit around the wires and it begins to boil, acting like solder.

"I've served on this ship for three years with Ethan Duggins. I consider him a colleague and a friend. What he did for us...trying to slow down the ship's destruction for as long as he could.... He made his choice there and then to sacrifice himself for the rest of the crew."

"And that justifies us not going back for him?"

"If we do, we'll all die."

I smile, raise my head and look at him. "What about your faith? Don't you believe your god will protect you?"

"That's not fair."

"You're the one who brought faith into the conversation, *sir*." The power cable is fixed. I start packing everything back into the housing, replacing the panel using the bolt driver. I move to a second chair. This one has been twisted out of its mounting. I manoeuvre around it and push off from the floor, leaning my weight against it. There's a crunch and the metal and plastic snap back into place. Not perfect, but it's a start.

"April, please, I'm trying to be reasonable."

"So am I, but you're not hearing me. Your friend, Ethan Duggins, is alive. We should be trying to rescue him."

"You need to let this go, Ensign."

"Do I?" I'm eyeballing him now, the chair between us as I lean my elbows on it, bolt driver in hand, floating in the middle of the room. "I'll be following orders, Lieutenant, if that's what you're worried about?"

Travers flinches. He's clearly hurting at the decision and letting his head rule his heart. He's already decided any attempted rescue will fail, but confronting me makes him feel guilty. That's good; it means he isn't too far gone. "Just don't do anything stupid," he mumbles and turns away.

"No sir, I won't," I mutter in reply and return to my work.

*　　*　　*

06.08.2118 - **Professor Hiro Fujiwara's Introductory Speech at the World Space Conference in Malmo, Sweden.**

Thank you, my friends.

It is a great honour to be given the chance to speak in front of you today, the one hundredth anniversary of Stephen Hawking's passing. The work of the

Hawking Foundation, which honours his legacy by inspiring and supporting generations of young minds to think about space, and about humanity's future, is an irreplaceable part of our progress towards establishing a sustainable interplanetary civilisation. We could not do what we do without you.

The sixteenth and seventeenth centuries were a period where Europeans perceived themselves as being discoverers and explorers. What they were really doing is rediscovering, connecting and displacing different pockets of humanity across the world. Long before them, unknown travellers had already come to these lands and their descendants lived there to be found and conquered in the name of progress and civilisation.

Entire nations and peoples were wiped out as one hegemony sought to conquer and subjugate. It took centuries for the mistakes to be acknowledged. Today, we live in the legacy of those moments. We are the descendants of abusers, slaves, survivors, witnesses and more. We cannot speak for the injustices of the dead, but we can try to learn from what happened.

Now, we are presented with another choice. Our species has never been to the planets and moons of our solar system. This is the true age of exploration and discovery. There are two paths ahead of us. Do we exploit the environments that we colonise, creating an empire around Earth, or do we build new autonomous societies, free to learn from the mistakes of their ancestors and grateful for the generosity of their mother planet? I acknowledge, there are degrees between these paths, balances and deals to be struck in this moment. Individuals must find the means to be rewarded for their risks, to make lives for themselves on these brave new worlds. The emancipation of humanity must continue. Our species in all of its rich diversity can find a home in the stars, our physiology can adapt, our minds can embrace change.

All of these things are possible, if we make the right choices.

Thank you very much....

CHAPTER TEN

Shann

Kyoto: AD 1324. The mid-afternoon sun is dipping below the horizon.

People are shouting on the street. A crowd gathers and makes its way towards the house of the Tokimichi clan. They have been told that the Emperor's representative, Hino Suketomo, is there.

He should not be. Suketomo was banished from the city. Someone has betrayed him.

He stands on the wooden *engawa* outside the Tokimichi house, the folds of his black *sokutai* rustling in the faint autumnal breeze. The household *bushi* soldiers are running to the compound gate. As a guest of the house, he would be protected, but that will only delay the inevitable.

"It seems they know you are here, *Suketomo-sama*," says his host, Keyo Tokimichi, from the doorway.

"It seems so."

A crowd gathers in the streets to watch the *bakufu* break down the doors.

⋆　⋆　⋆

This moment in the period drama I watch is a moment I always come back to. This is the moment when Hino Suketomo, *dainagon* – first council to the Emperor – realises his life and honour are at stake. He can escape, but to do so, he and the Emperor would lose status. For Suketomo, there are no good choices.

The directors of *Celerity* created the show to be an interactive experience and to be as historically accurate as possible. A lot of the camera shots are chosen so you can switch to full immersion and be there, right next to the characters. That rigor has an appeal to it. It feels authentic.

While I was on the *Khidr* and off shift, I'd sit in my room and watch, then pause on this moment, activate the immersive simulation, and stand next to Hino Suketomo. I'd study the man's face as he stared out over the city of Kyoto, watching the gathering mob. He knows the game is up. He knows he has hard choices to make, choices that will cause him pain and eventually lead to his death. But he makes that call, taking the dishonour on himself, so that the Emperor, Go-Daigo, might have another chance at defeating the shoguns.

Suketomo accepted his weakness and mortality for a higher cause. To me, in that moment, he became stronger. Stronger than anyone I have known.

I'm remembering that moment now. It tells me something:

I. Am. Not. Done. With. This. Shit.

It's surprising how your body works through stuff. The mind is an organ like anything else. Gradually, it gets used to the damage, adapting and changing how it deals with things. Wounds heal, or at least scab over so you can continue to function. The mind isn't quite the same as an arm or a leg, but there's definitely a comparison to be made.

They say grieving has stages. There are theories about how you go through each one in a process. I still feel guilty for everything. All of my people who died, all the decisions I had to make. I'm still second-guessing them and blaming myself for a lot of it.

But I'm not going to sit here on my hands when I could be doing something. Duggins is out there. If there's a chance....

There *has* to be a chance.

I'm in what must have been a mess hall or social room on *Gallowglass*. Whatever it was, it's the largest open space I could find to work. The torpedo casing is strapped to the table in front of me. *Gallowglass* torpedoes are almost the same as the ones we had on *Khidr*. There are some differences in the guidance computers, and the warheads are a different design, but these are all just modular components. Johansson modified one of our torpedoes into an EVA capsule. What I'm trying to do isn't anywhere near as complicated.

Yeah…. Johansson. Poor bitch. She's caught in the middle in more ways than one. Too intelligent by half, and clearly struggling with the people around her. A flag promotion can't come too soon. She's an admiral trapped in a lieutenant's uniform, with a boatload of practical engineering and medical skills to boot. Sooner or later she was going to get a taste for going off orders. I probably haven't helped matters any by mentioning my thoughts about Le Garre.

But I can't lie to Johansson. Le Garre is going to fuck up, big time.

The guidance unit needs modifying and reprogramming. The backdoor access code Johansson figured out from the blueprints works like a charm on every aspect of this ship, even the ordnance. The ramifications of that are huge. Whoever is running this secret operation has an enemy on the inside who is, or was, helping us. That enemy has access to the blood, bones and beating heart of our adversaries. The problem is, we don't know what we've been dragged into. Still, the enemy of my enemy and all that.

Yeah, so, Le Garre. I knew she'd end up in charge if I stepped back. But then, if I hadn't stepped back, I'd have lost the crew anyway. Travers was not going to take over, so it was bound to be her, the frustrated air force officer looking to cut a corner or two in Fleet.

No, that's unfair. Someone had to lead – to manage the surviving crew. Le Garre knew she had to do it. Sure, she's been looking for an opportunity to get back to the same level she'd been used to in the French military, a chance to command her own ship, but that doesn't make her a bad person for taking over.

I'm rewiring and reprogramming the torpedo, bypassing all the detonation triggers and stripping out all the redundant electronics. Then I take the probe sensor unit that I've carefully extracted from its launch casing and wedge it into the upper part of the projectile, using some hardening adhesive foam to secure it. After this, I wire the unit into the torpedo's power supply and test it.

Yeah, it works. *Perfect.*

The original weapon system has a set of manoeuvring thrusters which should get it pretty close to the remains of the *Khidr*. I've added a set of sensors from the probe, which will help us detect when the gravitational effect from the anomalies becomes too much. We'll launch the torpedo, flip it around as it heads towards the wreck and if the gravity gets too much, activate the main rocket and bring it back.

I've drilled holes for a set of cameras, and it takes a few minutes to thread them into the system. After that, I replace all the bolts and tighten them up with a drill driver, leaving me with a neutered, but highly perceptive projectile.

The whole process has taken about two hours.

I flip the comms switch. "Shann to Chase. Sam, are you busy?"

"I can make some time for you. How can I help?"

"I have a parcel that needs delivering to the launch tubes."

A couple of minutes later, Sam is at the hatch. He looks pained but gives me an encouraging smile. "You finished it?"

"Yeah. She's ready to go. Give me a hand lifting it out?"

"Sure."

Sam struggles into the room and to the other side of the worktable. I can see his injuries are still bothering him. Maybe I should have called Arkov or Travers?

No. Sam's the one I wanted.

"How're you doing?" I ask.

"Bearing up, all things considered."

"We need to talk, Sam."

"Do we?" He's not looking at me. His defences are up. He's picked up the drill driver and is removing the bolts that secure the modified torpedo to the table. "Unless something's changed. You made it pretty clear where you're at."

"This isn't about me, Sam. It's about you."

"I'm okay."

"No, you're not."

When we were together, he was the strong one. The gallant knight, riding to people's rescue. That's continued whilst we've been friends.

He's always been there for me, letting me vent and stress. I know it hurt him that I didn't reach out before I lost it. We'll need to talk that out sometime if we're going to get back a part of the friendship we had.

But right now, he's broken up. He doesn't know how to be in this situation because he can't solve it. He feels powerless and damaged. The trouble is, so do I.

"We have to try and help each other, Sam. We're a long way away from any outside assistance. I'm…I'm doing a little better – getting there, you know? The work definitely helped."

Sam nods. "Yeah, the work helps." He looks at me. "You think we'll make it?"

"I hope so."

"And Duggins?"

"I'd like to save him, if we can."

"Good." I know Sam. Much as he might not approve of Le Garre's decisions, that's the nearest he will ever get to being insubordinate, but he's let me know his thinking, that's what I needed.

Sam removes the last of the bolts and the torpedo moves away from the desk. In zero gravity the weight isn't a problem, but the mass and inertia could be dangerous when we start manoeuvring it towards the launcher. It took two of us to get it here, so two of us should be enough to get it back.

"Suppose this works," Sam says. "If you make contact with Duggins or find out something more about the anomalies, then what do we do?"

"I don't know," I reply. "We make the next decision when we have enough information to do so."

"So, for now, you're winging it?"

"Yeah, pretty much."

"Wasn't that the problem before?" Sam smiles as he asks the question, but that doesn't soften the pain. Maybe, he's right. I made a decision to respond to the distress signal from the *Hercules*. That got us into this mess and got the crew of the *Khidr* killed.

I stare at Sam. He's pushing me. Trying to probe for a way in despite my objections. I know why. He's my friend and he wants to help.

"I made mistakes and people died, Sam."

"You made decisions. That's what being in charge is about. People lived, because you made those decisions."

"I lost control. I did something.... I didn't know I was capable of doing that."

"It wasn't you."

"Yes, it was. Don't make excuses for me."

Sam sighs. He lets go of the modified torpedo, letting it float gently in the room between us. "We agreed to you stepping aside because of what happened – that one incident. The rest of it, the blame you're putting on yourself, that's nothing to do with it."

"People will judge me."

"Sure, but not here. Right now, the only person judging you is you."

I flinch from his gaze; the truth hurts. "I'm not ready yet, Sam. I can't handle being in charge, being responsible. I just want to do this, to do a part."

"Okay," Sam says. He grabs hold of the torpedo again and together we move it out of the improvised work room and into the corridor. A little more effort and we're in the loading bay. Some work with the feeder system and we have the projectile loaded into the tube.

Sam touches the comms bead on his collar. "Chase to Major Le Garre?"

"Le Garre here, go ahead."

"We're in the loading bay. Captain Shann has completed her modifications. We're ready to launch."

"Acknowledged."

The clasps engage, locking the torpedo in place. The launch mechanism ingests the projectile and a few moments later there is a muffled *thrump* as the probe is launched towards the tangled wreckage of the *Khidr*.

"Hopefully we can learn something useful," Sam says.

I'm already moving towards the door. "I need to be on the bridge."

"We can access the feed from any terminal."

"Yes, but decisions are going to be made based on what we find out," I reply. "It's important we're part of that process."

A few minutes later, I'm outside the bridge entrance. Sam touches me on the shoulder. "You should go in. I'll be on comms."

"You're not coming?"

Sam smiles. "No, this is officer talk."

"Suit yourself."

I enter the bridge. They've done a lot of repairs, rigging up two chairs as consoles. Travers is sat in one whilst Le Garre is staring at a screen on the wall.

She turns around as I enter, her expression thoughtful. "Something we can do for you, Captain?" she asks.

"Yes, Major," I reply. "I thought we should talk about what we're going to do next."

Le Garre flinches and looks towards Travers. He's facing away from me, so I can't see what passes between them. "If you're indicating you want to resume command of the crew and the ship, we'll need to go through the proper procedure," she says.

"That's not what I'm suggesting or indicating," I say. "I just want to get an idea of what you're thinking. Particularly if we get a reply from the wreck."

Le Garre looks at me. There's weight in that stare. She's struggling with all this. "I don't want to be in command. You should know that."

"I doubt anyone would want to be in charge, given the current circumstances," I say. "But we all accepted the responsibility, and our crew are looking to us." I move into the room so I can see both of them. Travers looks tired; his gaze flicks between me and Le Garre, as if he's caught and doesn't know which way to turn. "There isn't a conflict here," I add, trying to reassure him. "I'm not ready or fit to command right now, but that doesn't mean I'm a passenger either. I've fixed up the torpedo probe and we've launched it. Let's view the data together and discuss the big picture while we do. That's what senior officers usually do."

Le Garre nods. She can see what I'm doing. They need me to be part of the conversation, or at least they need someone as a third party, and it's clear that Johansson isn't going to get into the room, although she damn well should be here. "Bill, why don't you go through the numbers again, so the captain is up to speed?"

"Sure," Travers says. He looks at me cautiously, as if he's frightened he's going to break something. "We're thirty thousand kilometres from the wreck. The gravitational effect has reduced to a negligible level. The *Gallowglass* can maintain this distance and execute a course towards Phobos without being drawn back into range."

I move towards the empty chair and clamber into it, activating the screen on the armrest. "You're measuring the gravity effect as it reduces?"

"The computer has recorded that data, yes."

"What about existing records? There must be some kind of log of the journey to get here."

"There is," Le Garre says. "I haven't been through the details. The priority is repairing the ship."

I smile. The implication of what's being said is not lost on me. "I'll be pulling my weight from now on."

"Our course plot back to Phobos is difficult, but within acceptable parameters," Travers adds.

"What's your plan for getting them to recognise us?"

"What do you mean?"

"I mean this ship is off the books. The only people looking to be friendly will be Rocher's friends. Once we get close, we're going to attract some attention."

"I've tried leaning on Rocher," Le Garre says. "He's not proved co-operative."

The mention of the man's name affects me. I can feel the rush of blood to my face. I flinch and look away from Le Garre. "When we go back, we're going to be debriefed and there will be an investigation. Things have been done. You need to decide what you want to say about that. So do I."

"Are you asking me to—"

"No, I'm not. But I want to make sure we're clear and that we've thought through what we're doing. At the moment, we don't know who is on our side and who isn't. We all remember the mutiny, right? The people we had to fight were our own. Chiu, Sellis, Bogdanovic, they all got twisted to the other side. Anything we say could be used against us, like it was used against them."

"I worry for Chiu."

"Yeah. Whatever happens, it's going to be rough on her."

"Probe is online," Travers says. He's focused on the console, reading the text that is spilling down the screen in front of him. "Velocity and trajectory are accurate. Hey, that's weird...."

"What is?" I ask.

"The gravitational effect, it's not increasing. The torpedo is maintaining its current speed."

I'm working on my own console, activating the comms channel. "Duggins, can you hear me?"

I get punctuated static in response. There's a distortion too, a strange whistling. I remember Johansson talking about a whistling when she was studying the audio fragments from the *Hercules*.

"Duggins, is that you?"

There's a voice. It's trying to say words, but they aren't coming through. The timbre and tone of the sound is unmistakeable. I'm sure it is our missing engineer. "He's there, I can hear him!"

"Torpedo is fifteen thousand kilometres from the wreck."

Le Garre is next to me; she's activated her comms as well, patching into the same channel. "Ethan is that you? Can you hear me?"

There's a one-word response. We both hear it. "...*changed*...."

"He's there," Le Garre says. "*Merde*, he's really there...."

CHAPTER ELEVEN

Holder

White walls....

I open my eyes to find I am strapped into the chair.

I remember being here. I remember Doctor Summers. I remember the other man who is in control of my life.

The room is dark. The lights are off and I am alone. Was I supposed to wake up? It doesn't look like it.

I have a confused jumble of memories. I recall the nighttime raid on the boat in Sudan, the aborted protection mission in Interlaken. They were both me, but not me. My consciousness was modified and transmitted out into a physical body on the scene. My skills and experiences were intermingled with a memory imprint, to help ground me and make me believe I was a real person at the time.

This is how they work. I am a component, sent out in response to a need. When intermingled with a prepared host, I become a weapon, specifically tailored to suit the situation at hand.

I try to recall earlier experiences. There are images of a childhood, of sunny days in a garden playing with a ball and a dog. There is a woman with curly hair standing over me, watching me and smiling. I can see her talking, saying words, but I don't know what they mean.

All of these things could be fake. All of them could be real. It is hard to process that, to figure out what to hang on to, to work out what defines who I am as an individual. The sinking feeling in the pit of my stomach will not go away. I have no identity that I can rely on, no anchor that gives me a sense of me.

I recognise dwelling on this could paralyse me completely. My controller has no wish for me to have a sense of self. He wants me to be whoever he needs me to be as and when the task demands it.

Breathe…just *breathe*.

My fingers curl into fists. I'm angry. The jumbled-up memories all indicate to me that I shouldn't be treated like this. Something within me knows that I am a slave and that being kept as I am being kept is wrong.

This might be the only chance I have of changing my circumstances.

There is a strap around my neck, along with straps around my ankles, wrists, elbows and stomach. I can turn my head a little, but a metal ring holds my head upright. There's a tube attached to my left forearm and some sort of connection in the back of my skull.

I'm awake. I'm aware of who I am. This might be my only opportunity to escape. Only, I'm not able to escape, not like this. I'm struggling, but I can't break these restraints.

The only way I can free myself is not to free myself.

I can feel the connection, the data cable wired straight into the back of my skull. The system is designed to interface directly with my brain, to image information in both directions, copying what I have learned then deleting the original memory, or implanting memories directly into my mind.

I remember Doctor Summers operating the connection. The device he used is on the shelf out of my reach. There is no way I can get to it.

But the connection shouldn't need a controlling device. The system is designed to work with my mind; I am hooked up to it. All of its functions should be available to me.

I close my eyes and try to focus on the cable. I can feel it touching my skin. I should be in tremendous pain, but there is nothing. I cannot ever remember pain from the connection. Something has been done to ensure my body does not react to the surgical attachment.

I can sense the interface in my mind. It is dormant. I can remember the way it was when it transmitted data and when it extracted information. I don't need either of these functions. I need the transference function, the means by which it takes an imprint of my mind and sends it out to the new host, the host that is out there, waiting for a consciousness to arrive.

I'm remembering the experience. I can see Doctor Summers moving around the room, I can see him working on the controller, keying in the sequence to activate the conduit. I try to recall the sensation.

During the process they had images of the inside of my skull on a screen. The system is designed to interact with my mind. The different functional responses take advantage of brain states. Doctor Summers uses drugs, psychology, pain stimulation and other processes to induce the correct moment and then the system initiates the transfer automatically.

What I am trying to do is trigger the same response. I have no idea if it will work, but so much of this process relies on a computer reacting faster than a human controller can react. I am hoping that the action can be initiated without a direct command. If it can, Doctor Summers has been very foolish and not built sufficient safeguards into his software, but he may never have thought these specific circumstances would occur, that a patient would wake up whilst unattended and be able to remember the sequence in enough detail to initiate it for their own ends.

There is a massive risk in doing this. I have no knowledge of how hosts are prepared for this transfer. That information is not part of the memories I retain. It might be that they need to be specifically wired up and set to receive a consciousness. If that is the case, I could be trying to transfer my mind into oblivion.

Additionally, even if I succeed in transferring myself, I might be sending out a duplicate of what remains here. A version of me will have escaped this chair, but another version may remain a prisoner.

I don't have any memories of a separation. The process of reintegrating a consciousness, merging a duplicate with new knowledge and experiences back into the original version, sounds complex and potentially damaging. I don't think Doctor Summers would do that.

On the other hand, if he doesn't then the system may automatically wipe my mind when I transfer, which would mean I am deleting myself. I am committing suicide.

Am I committing suicide?

No. I have to hope this will work.

There is a faint sound, the hum and whine of an electronic device initialising. I can't tell if I've caused this or someone else is here, coming in to check up on me. Either way, I need to hurry. I need to get this done.

There is a shift in my mind. I get a sense of heat and wetness, then the world moves. I grip hold of the chair, digging my fingers into the unyielding metal armrests, but my sense of them fades, as does my sense of the room, of the air, the light and the electronics. I am....

Gone....

Voices. People are speaking. The words are muffled and distorted, but I can tell they are human voices. One of them is repeating the same phrase. I focus on that.

"...breach detected in medical docking section twenty-three. I repeat, hull breach detected in medical docking section twenty-three...."

"Alison, are you all right?"

I open my eyes. I'm lying on a couch in an administration office of some kind. There's a man bending over me. He has dark skin and deep brown eyes. He looks concerned.

I don't recognise him.

"Alison, can you hear me? Can you speak?"

I nod and am surprised to find my head is not restrained by the straps or the clamp. I cannot feel the cable in the back of my skull either. How has this—

"Alison, please just stay still. I'll call for a nurse and we'll get you checked out. What do you remember?"

I shake my head. Not trusting my voice yet. The alert message is still repeating. I can see flashing lights too, the kind of red flash you get with an alarm. The man's hand is on my shoulder. He is gently trying to keep me lying down on the couch, but I don't want to lie down, I want to sit up.

I struggle against him, and after a moment, he backs off. "Hey, take it slow."

"What...happened?" The words sound strange. This isn't my voice. This isn't my body.

"There was an explosion. The station moved and you fell and hit your head. At least, I think you hit your head." The man leans in close; he's looking at my scalp and hair – *I have hair!* "I can't see a mark."

I flinch away from him. "Give me a minute to get my breath," I say.

I'm looking around, trying to acclimate. My hands are free, there's no tube in my arm. My skin is different, darker than before. I'm wearing some sort of plastic one-piece work suit with a front fasten, and light boots that have rubber treads. I have enough hair to cover my face. I see brown strands and instinctively brush them back with a hand. The sensation is wonderfully new and old at the same time.

There are people in this room, a lot of people. I can't work out how many. I can see objects all over the floor. There's a smashed wine bottle, green glass fragments, ripped pieces of paper, plastic cups and overturned trays of food.

I remember a birthday celebration from when I was a child. There was singing, a cake and candles. The woman with curly hair held me in her arms....

Abruptly, the repeated voice stops, and the flashing light goes out. The room is plunged into darkness, causing some cries of panic, then the lights come back on.

"Okay everybody, stay calm." The woman who is speaking is projecting authority and confidence. "It looks like the party is going to have to wait. We have an explosive decompression on the medical deck, right where the *Chronos* was due to arrive. Jim, can you get me some details?"

"Yes, Commander." The man who was helping me stands up and moves to a console. He sits down and starts working. I remember Doctor Summers.... "Decompression confirmed. The entire section has been sealed off. A security team is mustering now. They'll be moving out in two minutes."

"Okay, then we go to work, people." The authoritative woman is walking across the room as she speaks. I hear the crunch of glass underfoot. "Alison, if you can manage, I need you to get over to the assessor, so we can check you for a concussion. I'll be sending everyone over for metaboliser medication, but you should be the priority."

"O-Okay.... Where am I—"

"The door to your right. Do you need someone to help you? I can ask—"

"No, that's okay, I'll be fine."

I manage to stumble over to the glass door. The gravity in this place is different to what I expected, but I'm not sure what I expected. This body, this person, Alison, is used to the weight and mass, but I am not used to being her.

I enter the indicated room. It is little more than a cubicle. There is a bed and a console. The walls are transparent, so I can still see what's going on outside and they can see what happens in here. It's the kind of place you can conduct medical experiments for an audience of onlookers. It reminds me of the place I've just escaped.

I glare at the medical interface and reject it. I'm not going to hook myself up to that machine. I've had enough of being hooked up to machines.

I glance around. There is urgent organisation going on. The station commander is talking to the man she called Jim. Other people are working screens, tidying, fixing, helping. No one is looking at me.

I turn to the console. There's a thumbprint authentication plate. I hesitate, but then remember – this woman, Alison, who I am now, she would be registered on this system.

I press my thumb to the plate and the screen changes. I've logged in to the system. Immediately, I know where I am: *Phobos Alpha – Phobos Station?*

I had assumed the laboratory where I was being held was on Earth. If it is, I have been transported millions of miles through space into an unsuspecting woman's mind, this 'Alison' who they have mentioned. This transfer has occurred through no visible means. I had expected I would wake up in a vault of some kind and that my new host would be dormant before I arrived, but that is not what has happened. This person had a life – has a life. I have displaced her from her own body.

I key up Alison's personnel file and quickly read anything I can. The details will be important. The visualisation techniques that I learned in the chair allow me to retain near perfect recollections of things that I see. The cruel irony of that is not lost on me in this moment. The skill clearly serves another purpose when my memories are wiped and re-ordered by Doctor Summers. For now, though, these impressions will allow me to answer some of the basic questions these people will ask me.

Alison Wade. Age: 33. Communications Executive, Phobos Station.

I stare at the face in the picture. Brown hair, brown eyes, pinched and nervous expression. I absorb the biographical information quickly, noting the references to family and friends. This is me now. This is who I am. The unstable and changeable nature of my mind has an advantage in that I am able to quickly sketch out a new identity and believe in it. Natalie Holder is quickly subsumed beneath who I think Alison Wade should be.

Of course, there will need to be adjustments. People who know Alison will have a particular impression of her; they will know her quirks and mannerisms, her food preferences, her desires, and more detailed personal information. I will have to be careful and update as I go.

It occurs to me that this elastic quality of my mind might be something Summers created. I have no way of knowing which parts of me were a construction and which were not.

Shouting disrupts my work. I look up from the screen to the main administration office outside. The man called Jim has stood up. He is looking across the room. I follow his gaze towards the main doors.

The muffled sound of an explosion makes me duck instinctively. The doors shatter apart, burning metal and plastic flies across the room as people scream in terror.

The flashing alert starts up again. Everything beyond my little space is drenched in a blanket of smoke. Shadows and shapes mill about. I hear the distinctive sound of low velocity gunfire.

Phobos Station is under attack.

CHAPTER TWELVE

Drake

I'm locked in some kind of storage room. There's no lighting, other than the dim light from the little window plate in the door. I can't see anything.

I grope around with my hands and find the door activation plate. My fingers brush the screen and the panel comes to life, projecting a faint green glow into the room. It barely illuminates anything more than the window plate, but it is reassuring. At least this is something I can control.

The gun Rocher gave me is useless in here. I tuck it into my belt and start to explore the room, reaching out, trying to feel for the walls. I work to the right of the door, moving carefully along, using my hands to try to get a sense of where I am.

There are shelving racks along the walls and a series of locked compartments. I find an emergency oxygen tank and mask, then a set of tools, strapped to the shelf.

All of these are useful things, but I need to work out how best to use them.

The room has an atmosphere and I've no reason to believe the air supply has been cut off from the main station supply. The technician, Rocher, either locked me in here for my own safety or because he's one of the people trying to take over the station. Either way, I'm in the same situation.

Trapped.

Whatever this place is, it should have a terminal, or some kind of interface that can be used to communicate with the station network and the outside world. Rooms without a way to exist independently aren't something anyone builds in space. Any structure designed to carry human beings has to be resilient, but also have an escape procedure if something goes wrong. If a person gets trapped, they should have a way to get out. In this instance, I need a connection to be able to use the chit Lieutenant Rivers gave me. Then I can warn Mars security about what's going on.

The problem is, I can't find anything like that.

I go back to the door plate and move down to stare at it. The screen says 'Security Override Engaged'. I assume that's how Rocher has locked me in here. If he is a member of the station crew then he would have access to the system. If he's a saboteur, then perhaps he hacked his way in, and all the things he said when we were trying to contact people were lies.

Why would anyone do this?

It's been years since I was on Earth. You don't get a full briefing on the geopolitics unless you go looking, but the colonial news service does give you the headlines. There have been overpopulation problems for more than a century. People have always looked to the stars as a solution, as if the grass is greener way out here. The problem is, they don't see that out here there isn't any grass at all.

The bottom line is unfair. Colonial projects require massive economic investment. Corporations make that investment based on a return. That return is in the acquisition of commercial resources. They are less likely to invest in people, at least not on the scale that might be needed to lift all of humanity out of poverty.

A system of economic control designed to keep the majority away from the means to better themselves, and continually promoting the lie that they aren't doing exactly that.

I get that by being up here, I'm a privileged part of the problem. I get that I am lucky. I was born in a relatively wealthy part of the world with access to education and opportunity. I took the chances I was given and ended up at the cutting edge, on the frontier, carving out a life in the harshest environment we've ever known.

Perhaps the whole temporal citizenship renewal system has made me sensitive to the plight of others?

A year or so ago, I treated a man for some serious self-inflicted injuries. When he came around from sedation, he tried to attack me and my assistant. Jezero security were called and they isolated him in one of the storage rooms, using a security override to ensure he couldn't just press his thumb to the door activation plate and get out.

Rocher must have activated the same protocol here to lock me in.

I'm not getting through that door without bypassing that lock and I have no idea how I could do that.

I step away from the door and sit down. I'm not calm. The urgency of everything is getting in the way of me thinking my way through the problem. My hands are shaking, I'm breathing fast. *People died. Take a moment.*

Okay.

The door is the patient and I need to perform some surgery.

The tools are my first priority. I line them up on the floor, feeling each in turn to try to get a sense of what I have. Bolt driver, current sensor, hammer, *torch!*

I find a switch and suddenly the world around me is revealed. Yes, I'm in a storeroom. There's equipment lining the racked shelving, plenty of things to experiment with if I was some sort of technical wizard, or electronic specialist. I'm not either, but there are some things that I'm used to using.

Everything in here is labelled. There's EVA equipment, a portable generator for external hull repairs. A dozen or more spacesuits, an emergency acceleration chair, strapping and components for an emergency acceleration chair. Racks of deactivated portable screens, magnetic boots, emergency medical equipment.

I stop right there. The medical equipment is what I'm most familiar with. Doors in a space station are controlled by a computer system. Amongst the items on the shelf in front of me there is a defibrillator. The pads are designed to deliver a large electrical charge to a human being to restart their heart.

What would happen if I did the same to the door?

There's a risk to what I'm considering. If I attempt to fry the circuits of the lock that is keeping me in here, I could trap myself for good. Engineers design compartments on space stations to close and lock if they get damaged. That way people in the rest of the station stay alive and safe. But we're talking about two different protocols. If I can disrupt the security override and leave the rest of the system intact, the door should open.

Of course, if it was that easy the people who built this place would have to be idiots.

I charge the paddles. The battery pack whines, then beeps as it completes its work. I'm holding the little torchlight between my teeth and shining the light on the panel. Time to roll the dice.

I jam the paddles against the door panel. There's an audible crackle of electricity and the light from the panel disappears.

A moment later, the door starts to open.

I'm moving as fast as I can, pulling myself through the gap as quickly as possible. I can hear the hydraulics shifting. The door doesn't open all the way before it shivers and starts to close again.

I'm nearly through. My legs are caught. I have to push and pull with my hands, straightening my knees, pointing my toes.

I'm through!

The door slams shut. The screen on this side flashes. I can read the words 'Pressure Loss Detected'. I've triggered the emergency deadlock, which could have crushed me, but it doesn't matter. I'm out.

I'm lying on the floor in the corridor, breathing hard. The overhead lighting winks on. I need to calm down and put this behind me. I need to focus on what comes next. I'm back to where I was before I met Rocher, looking for a terminal to contact the authorities.

I need to get on with doing that.

I sit up and look around. Rocher told me the room I was in was a shortcut to the administration and security sections of the station, but I have no reason to trust anything he said. The corridor may not even be leading in the right direction. I can't remember what twists and turns we took. I forgot about them while I was trying to get out of the storage room.

The gun Rocher gave me is in my hand. I check the cartridge. It's loaded. He gave me a loaded gun. Even though he must have known he was going to lock me in that room, he still gave me a loaded gun. *What does that mean?*

I begin moving down the passageway, back the way I came to orient myself. The overhead lighting continues to activate as I get close. If there's anyone nearby, they'll know I'm here.

After a few minutes walking, I reach an intersection I recognise. I stop there and assess my options. The consoles I was trying to use earlier can't be far back.

I start towards the offices from before. I'm nearly there when I hear voices and stop.

"There's no one down here."

"All the same, we need to check. That pressure loss alert can't have come from nowhere."

I can't be sure if these people are from the *Chronos*, or from station security, but they're coming from the direction of the docked ship and the explosion.

"Room to the right. Ready?"

"Yep. Okay, move."

I hear an entry card being swiped and the sound of a door sliding back. Someone moves forward. As they do, I creep up to the wall, crouch down, and sneak a look around the corner.

There's a man in the corridor. He's aiming a rifle into the open doorway and inching forward to follow his companion. He hasn't noticed me.

From his unshaven appearance and the casual way he's carrying his weapon and a belt of extra ammunition, I'm pretty sure he's not part of the Phobos security team.

"Clear!"

The man steps into the room and out of sight.

My heart is thumping. I need to make some quick decisions. I can go back, but if I do, these people will be behind me all the way. Perhaps I can get past them? No. I don't fancy my chances doing that. I could surrender, but that would give me no guarantee of getting out of here alive.

The other option is to fight.

I move into the corridor and continue forward, trying to stay quiet. I can hear the voices of the two men as they search rooms. They aren't far from me, about five metres or so, I guess.

I'm going to kill them.

In my years as a medical practitioner, I've seen a lot of wounds and injuries. For six months I was a battlefield medic during the Melbourne Insurrection. That was a terrible place to be. There was no quarter given to the injured or the people trying to look after them. Towards the end, before they airlifted us out, it got really bad. People became savage as they fought over food and water, trying to survive on anything they could.

Back then, I carried a gun. I had to threaten people and fire off some warning shots, but I never had to hurt anyone.

This is different. This time there are no soldiers protecting me. If I'm going to survive, I need to be prepared to shoot.

I don't know what brought these people up here, what's caused them to make the choice they've made – to attack the station and kill people who were expecting to help them. Any mercy I might grant these men is a weakness in this situation – they don't deserve it. They murdered the emergency medical team; they would have murdered me too if I hadn't been lucky.

"Okay, let's move on."

I'm beside the door, gun raised. The first man walks out. He's not expecting someone to be there. I aim the pistol at his head and pull the trigger.

Point-blank range. The recoil is a firm kick in my hands. The man's head disappears in a cloud of red gore. I step forward and see the shadow of the second man standing just in front of me.

I fire again, twice. The man coughs and falls to the floor.

Everything goes quiet.

My face is wet. It's blood. Other people's blood. The blood of the two men I've just killed.

My stomach spasms at the realisation. I turn away from the scene, back into the corridor and double over. Vomit spatters the floor. I'm on my knees, still heaving and retching until nothing but bile comes out.

Get a grip!

I reach for the wall. Wet fingers, slick with blood, try to breathe slowly, to lean on something to steady me. I manage to get to my feet on unsteady legs. I'm facing away from the carnage. I can't bring myself to turn around. I know I should. If I could deal with this coldly, strategically, I would be searching the bodies, taking their weapons and anything they might be using to communicate with the rest of their people.

That's what I should be doing.

I can't....

I stumble away, heading back towards the storage room. For a fleeting moment I've decided to go back there, open the door and lock myself inside until this is all over. Then I remember I can't. The emergency pressure lock has been triggered. I can't get back into that room.

I stop. I still feel sick and now, guilty. *I murdered those men!*

I murdered....

CHAPTER THIRTEEN

Johansson

I don't second-guess myself. Sure, I feel guilty at times, just like anyone does, but there's no point in going back and unmaking the decisions you make or trying to wish away the consequences of your actions.

I know the senior officers of this crew, XO Bill Travers and Major Angel Le Garre, don't trust me. I know that my choice to disobey orders during the battle between the *Khidr* and the *Gallowglass* are the reason they don't trust me.

But the choices I made are also the reason we're all still alive.

I'm sat in my makeshift medical room, staring at the terminal, watching the data coming in from the modified torpedo we've sent towards the compacted wreckage of the *Khidr*. I know everyone on the ship will be looking at the same feed, if they are conscious and have access to a screen.

I've spent the last few hours taking my frustration out on the *Gallowglass*'s computer system. The backdoor access code gave us the opportunity to win the battle; the rudimentary user profiles I set up have enabled us to operate the ship. Now I'm examining the old code, trying to find out what other secrets are buried in the data stores and subroutines.

The operational command history is interesting. I compiled a list of actions that access systems and functions that we haven't yet used or worked out. Those will be useful for later.

Of more interest are a set of briefing files. These are a series of videos and text documents allocated to each user account. All of them are exactly the same size and version, indicating that there was no hierarchy amongst the Rocher clones on this ship.

I can't get into these files. The encryption doesn't respond to my pass key access code. I guess they were added later, after the ship was built and are decrypted with a separate cypher. Given some time, I might be able to break in, but any attempt might cause them to delete. Still, I can try a few times, as there are several copies. I can work on these when I have time.

The probe information is my current priority.

There's a cough and groan from the bed behind me. I glance around. Chiu is awake. She's looking at me, trying to signal something. I move over to her and remove the oxygen mask. "Welcome back, Ensign," I say.

"Thank you," Chiu replies. "Can you let me up?"

I hesitate, then smile. "Sure." I start undoing the safety straps. The only reason I want to leave Chiu in her bed is to protect her injuries, but the confines of the room and the benefit of zero gravity should prevent her doing additional damage to herself.

"What have I missed?" Chiu asks.

I offer her an encouraging smile. "A lot. I don't know how much you remember?"

"Not much after the trip over here," Chiu says.

I nod. I'm disappointed that she can't remember the contact we made with Duggins and the wreck. If she could, I'd have a witness now that Le Garre is retreating into self-denial. "You were pretty out of it," I say. "We had to give you a transfusion. You should rest. Let your body recover."

Chiu scowls. "Easy for you to say."

"We're safe onboard the *Gallowglass* now," I explain. "We took over the ship. The gravitational anomalies we found took control of the wreckage of the *Khidr*. Duggins is still alive over there. We've launched a probe and we're trying to establish contact with him."

Chiu winces in pain as she tries to speak. She takes another breath, allows herself to drift above the bed, turning towards me. . "Still alive? How?"

"We don't know, he…spoke to us through you."

I don't know if I was hoping for a reaction to that. If I was, I didn't get it. Chiu just looks confused. "I don't understand," she says.

"You were feverish – near death. Somehow, he spoke to us using you as a conduit."

"That's impossible."

"Yeah. I thought so too."

We stare at each other in silence. I'm not backing down. "After the mutiny, when you were a prisoner, Captain Shann and I spoke about you. I suggested that we were wasting our time giving you a second chance. You couldn't be trusted. Back then, I thought we'd be best off chucking you out of an airlock."

"You could have killed me anytime whilst I was out," Chiu says.

"Yeah, I was wrong. Everyone deserves a second chance. I'm being honest with you about all that, and I'm being honest with you about Duggins. He's alive in that wreck and he spoke to us through you."

"It's a lot to take in," Chiu says. Her eyes stray to the screen where the probe data is displayed. "What about the captain?" she asks.

"She's…okay…. I think she needs some time."

"Don't we all." Briefly, I explain what happened – how Shann killed one of the Rocher clones and was removed from command. Chiu is next to me. "You managed to hack the whole system here with that passcode from the blueprints. That's pretty impressive."

"I'm not into everything yet," I say. "But we're getting there."

"Any idea what their mission was? I mean, I get they were collecting the anomalies for some reason, but why attack the *Hercules* and blackmail us?"

"Captain Shann has a theory about that," I reply. "She thinks the freighter was supplying some sort of illegal colony and that the *Gallowglass* was sent to stop it. We found empty anomaly containers on board the *Hercules*. They must have retrieved them before they got disturbed by your arrival. We just ended up in the way."

"And my personal problems were just bargaining chips for Rocher to exploit," Chiu says.

"You, Sellis, Bogdanovic and the others were a backup plan, I guess." I put a hand on Chiu's shoulder. "It was rough on you."

She flinches but accepts the touch. "It was rough on all of us."

The screen in front of us starts to flash. I pull up the data. "The probe's halfway to the wreckage. There's no change in the gravitational pull. It's still stronger than it should be, but nowhere near the level we were seeing before."

"You said Duggins was alive. Do you think he's controlling it?"

"Perhaps, he's got to have something to do with it." I start to activate a comms channel again, to try to reach out to him, but then I notice there's already one open. "He's talking to us. He's talking to the people on the bridge."

Chiu grabs my wrist, just above the broken interface where my plug-in hand used to be. "You need to be up there," she says.

"What do you mean I—"

"I mean, you need to be on the bridge. You need to be a part of what's going on. I trust you. You were totally honest with me. Now I'm being the same with you. You need to be in those discussions."

I frown at Chiu. "Will you be okay here on your own?"

"I think so." Chiu glances at the medical system display. "I can see the drugs you've got me on. The diagnosis is done, so the dispenser will authorise a repeat dose if I need it."

"Okay, then I'll go."

"I'll keep watching the probe readouts. I may even have a tinker with your hacked code, if I feel up to it."

That comment makes me hesitate. I stare at Chiu. She needs my trust. After everything that happened before, when she was blackmailed into joining the mutiny on the *Khidr* with Rocher, she's been trying to earn back people's trust. She knows she'll have to face a military court about what happened when we get back. "You were close to Duggins, weren't you?"

Chiu nods. "He supported me when I first arrived on the ship. I thought he died trying to save us. If there's a chance he's alive, someone needs to fight for him."

"I'll do my best."

"Thank you."

A moment later, I'm out of the room and making my way to the bridge.

Chiu's encouragement has helped. I feel less frustrated and angry at myself. I'm clearer in my sense of purpose now. My instincts were right. I didn't oppose Le Garre's decisions just because she wasn't doing what I wanted. My advice was rational and thought through, not some sort of knee-jerk desperation to save people because I felt guilty for not following orders.

Right now, there's too much we don't understand, too many variables to make a decision. Whatever call we make is going to have consequences.

I'm at the entrance to the bridge. I push the door release and enter. Shann is here with Le Garre and Travers. Shann is talking.

"...you heard him. You know he's alive in there!"

"That doesn't alter the situation. We have to do what's best for the crew. We can't take another risk with all their lives!"

"Johansson...." Travers notices me first. He's out of the pilot's chair and heading towards me. "This isn't a good time."

"It seems like the *perfect* time, Lieutenant."

Le Garre looks at me. Her expression is defensive.

"Okay, Ensign. What's up?"

"Major, I thought you'd like to know that Ensign Chiu is awake and doing a lot better."

Le Garre's gaze flicks towards the screen in front of Shann's seat. "Was that the reason you came up here?"

"Not the only reason."

"What else then?"

I look at Shann. I'm remembering her words – *'She's going to fuck it up.'* "I'm here because I should be here, Major. You need options, not arguments. Every decision we make right now is going to be crucial. The ramifications could be huge."

Shann smiles at me. She opens her mouth to speak, but then closes it again and looks at Le Garre. "It's your decision," she says. "You're in command."

"Thank you," Le Garre says. "I'm persuaded, Ensign. Ultimately, we all want the same thing – to get out of this alive." She turns to Travers. "What are we getting from the probe?"

"Gravitation aberration is constant. The debris field is completely clear. It seems everything apart from us has been pulled in by the anomalies."

"Did he speak to you on the comms?" I ask. I'm looking at Le Garre, who doesn't respond. "You heard him, right? You heard him again? What did he say?"

"He said, 'changed,'" Shann replies.

That is interesting. "When we first spoke to him through Chiu he said 'changing' and asked for our help. Now, the gravity disturbance has reduced, and he's 'changed'. I wonder if the two things are connected."

"You think he can control it?"

"I don't know, maybe? If I wanted to be saved, the first thing I'd try and do if I could would be to make sure people knew where I was and could come and get me."

"We need to apply braking thrust," Shann says. "Otherwise, we'll lose our connection."

"Doing that now," Travers replies. "We're getting close enough for a camera feed."

"Bring it up," Le Garre says.

I move across the room so I can see the feed on the larger display on the wall. Sunlight illuminates a vista of stars, but right in the centre, there is a dark shape, gradually eating up the tiny lights on the screen. As the probe gets close, a lamp just under the camera turns on and reveals the wreck – a jammed-together mash of metal and plastic.

"Fuck, that's a mess," Shann says.

"I'm getting data on the dimensions," Travers says. "It's nearly spherical. Given the volume of material, I'd speculate that it's hollow inside."

"I bet there's an atmosphere in there," I say. "The whole process must have pulled in all the escaping gases from the wreck too. All of it, mixed up, to be used for something."

"Who knows what they're up to," Le Garre says. "They could be hostile. We need to be prepared to defend ourselves."

"We may not need to," I say. "There's no reason to believe whatever's going on in there is aimed against us."

"All the same, I'd like a firing solution."

I move away from the screen and over to a terminal. I key up the *Gallowglass*'s weapons targeting system and set the computer to analyse the data from the probe. "We can hit it at range with torpedoes at three points. A co-ordinated set of impacts should cause the object to tear itself apart."

"Provided the forces act in the way we think they should," Shann says. "And we'll be murdering Duggins."

"Whatever's left of him," Travers says.

"If we go back now and manage to get a report to someone in authority, Fleet will send ships out here," Le Garre says. "They'll want to interdict the anomalies to prevent them getting anywhere near one of the colonies. The more people involved, the more likely someone will twitch, and this will escalate."

I glance at her. "Are you suggesting we don't tell anyone?"

"I'm thinking this through and sharing my thoughts, Ensign," Le Garre replies.

We're staring at one another when suddenly, something shifts. I'm pushed against the wall of the room and the others are similarly thrown around. The computer screens brighten, turning into glaring white portals that I can no longer look at. "What the hell is going on?" I demand.

"Hold on!" Travers launches himself from the far side of the room, catching hold of the pilot's seat as he passes it, swinging around and into the seat. He activates the emergency manual controls. The joystick deploys from the chair arm and a smaller secondary screen flicks up, underneath the pilot's main display.

"I think we're okay. We're not moving, I—"

The secondary screen starts to glow as well. I can't look at it. I turn away, shut my eyes and try to bury myself in the wall.

Then, as quickly as it started, it stops, and everything goes dark.

"What the fuck was that?" Shann mutters into the gloom.

"There's no power," Travers says, his voice raw. "Hold on, the emergency generator will kick in. Give it a moment."

We wait. And, as predicted, low-level lighting returns to the bridge. "Are the reactors secure?" Le Garre asks.

"Checking," Travers says. "Looks like the backups kicked in. The reactors are okay and coming back online."

The large viewscreen winks back on. I'm at the control panel beneath it, reconnecting with the system and cursing at how slow I am without my plug-in right hand. "Something's changed," I say. "The command log indicates we've received a data transmission, relayed over from the probe. It's big. I've never seen anything like—"

"Hello, April."

The voice is coming out of the speakers in the wall, just like any other shipwide announcement would. But the voice...I recognise the voice. It can't be....

"Duggins?"

"Yes."

CHAPTER FOURTEEN

Holder

"Out from there."

I'm crouched under the bed in the small medical station. There's a woman at the door. She's pointing a rifle at me.

I stand up slowly, raising my hands. "Please…don't shoot."

"I will if I have to," the woman warns. She steps back and inclines her head towards the huddle of frightened people in the corner of the office. "Over there, with the others."

Moving is still more difficult than it should be. This body is awkward and different to what I'm used to. The fragmented memories I have of being sent elsewhere don't mention any problems in adjusting after a transfer. I guess the host would have been prepared for the change, the personality integrated and meshed into mine with elements hidden or removed from both.

I remember being other people. Those identities were lies, along with everything else I thought was true.

There's a burned smell. I can see the body of the woman in charge from before. Her lifeless eyes stare vacantly into space.

"Alison, let me help you."

Jim, the man from earlier. He's taken my arm and guided me to a seat. I count nine of us alive in here with six armed guards. They are dishevelled and dirty, handling their weapons with a familiarity that suggests they are more than the colonial miners whose uniforms they are wearing.

"You people need to be ready to move," says the woman who ordered me out of the medical room. "We're leaving in three minutes."

"What do you people want?" someone shouts. "You can't think you're going to get away with this."

"Shut up! Remember, we don't need all of you alive to make our point."

"But you do need some of us." Jim stands up and edges in front of me. "There are emergency capsules on deck seven. Let the others go. I'll stay."

The woman sneers. "Aren't you brave? Nice try, but it's not up to me. We're moving as soon as I get the go ahead. Don't slow us down."

Another figure appears – an Asian man with two pistols. He nods at the woman and she nods back. "Okay, move!"

"Where are we going?" Jim asks.

"You'll know when we get there."

★   ★   ★

We're walking down the corridor. I have no idea of our destination.

Nothing in this station is familiar to me. If I was hoping the integration of Alison's identity with mine would happen gradually or after some sort of delay. That's not happening.

As we walk, I'm watching our captors. The more I see of them, the more I note their training and discipline. The mining station accident is definitely a cover, but I'm also sure this isn't some sort of rebellion. These people are soldiers. Either they're hired guns from some national army, or serial corporate mercenaries.

My grasp of Earth politics is pretty limited. My fragmented memories come from the residue of different lives. I don't know what's real and what isn't.

I remember the mission in the waters in Port Sudan. There was a civil war going on there. The ship I was sent to assault was guarded by mercenaries. Could there be a connection? It's a reach. There could be hundreds of other paramilitary groups out there, but very few would have the means and wherewithal to manage an off-Earth operation.

Does Mars have any separatist groups? I don't know of any. But then, even if I did, I'm not sure I could trust my own mind.

The biological hosts that I'm transferred into must be strategically placed. I remember the man who was with Doctor Summers. The memory makes me shudder. He has an agenda. Where does that agenda fit into all this?

A hand takes mine and squeezes it. Jim is beside me. "This is bad," he whispers. "They killed Boipelo."

"Yeah," I say, as if the woman's name means something to me.

"I don't know what they want. But the longer MarsCorpGov doesn't know about all this, the more difficult it'll be to dislodge them. We need to get the word out."

"Didn't you get a message out before they captured us?"

"No, the connection to the comms antenna was offline. I think they destroyed it or hacked the system as soon as they came aboard."

"They wouldn't destroy it," I say. "If they did, they'd lose an asset."

"Sorry, what?" I look at Jim. He's staring at me with a confused look on his face.

"Our hosts need an escape route," I explain. "The only way they'll be able to communicate with another ship is through the station's main antenna."

"I understood what you said, I just didn't realise…it didn't sound like you. You don't usually talk about this kind of stuff."

"Sorry." I lower my head and focus on my feet. This is hard. I don't know what Alison's relationship with Jim is – how much he means to her or vice versa. I don't know who Boipelo is either, but she was clearly senior and meant something to Jim.

"It's okay. You just surprised me."

He moves past me, towards the front of the group. I can see him murmuring to a few of the other prisoners, touching hands, communicating reassurance. He is clearly a leader in this group, some sort of middle manager I guess, from what I saw earlier.

We take a left and walk down a large corridor into some sort of lecture hall. There are guards at the door – an Asian man and a Caucasian woman. There's no common ethnicity amongst this group, which indicates to me they are mercenaries or from some sort of EarthGov military unit.

"Come on, quickly!" says the woman who led the group. Dutifully, I let myself be herded inside along with the other prisoners. I note the Caucasian woman's lips are moving. She's counting us, adding to the total of people already inside.

The space is unlike any theatre in my memories. The chairs for the audience are elaborate, with a variety of computer systems built into the backs and the armrests. I've seen the same type of seats in the corridors. This must be for emergencies; in case the torus stops spinning and we lose gravity.

There are around a hundred people in here, talking to each other quietly. As we enter a few of our group recognise others and rush towards them. I slip into one of the back-row seats of the auditorium, looking around the room. There's no sign of our captors. This location has been chosen because it has marked exits, which they can lock and guard from outside.

I glance over my shoulder to the entrance we just came through. The woman and her team are outside. They are closing the doors.

"No...wait...."

Too late. The doors are shut. We're trapped.

Most of the people in here are crowded down at the front by the stage. I ignore them and take a little time to assess. I've escaped one prison only to end up in another.

I'm thinking about the chair back in the laboratory. I might be on limited time. Doctor Summers must have a way to extract me from a host and draw me back. I've no memory of that process, so I don't know what to expect. It could be his system requires some sort of mind state like before, or that the host – this woman, Alison – plug themselves in to a similar unit out here.

Could it be that the process is a mind swap, and that the poor woman whose place I've taken is now strapped into that chair instead of me?

I don't think it's that simple, but my presence here may have condemned her to my fate.

I can't stay here. I need to get out.

I slip from my chair and wander down the aisle to the swell of people. A couple of them look in my direction and I get one or two nods of friendly recognition. I smile and nod in return. I have no idea who I am greeting, but they don't seem to be worried about me joining the conversation.

"What about the security team? No one's seen any of them after they mustered up to investigate the explosion."

"We didn't manage to raise them before the offices were attacked."

"You said Boipelo is dead?"

"Yes. They shot her."

"Shit. I mean…all of it's awful, but…."

"Yeah, I know what you mean."

"What does she mean?" I ask.

Jim looks at me, or rather, he looks at Alison, who is me right now. "Augustine Boipelo has been assassinated. The political ramifications… this will start a war. Earth is bound to respond. They can't let this stand."

"Okay," I say. Boipelo isn't a name I know, but I clearly should know who it is, or rather, Alison should know.

"But these people aren't from Mars!" a woman next to me interjects. "There isn't some sort of indigenous revolutionary movement, otherwise we'd know about them. I've never seen any of this lot before!"

"That's what makes things all the more confusing," Jim replies.

There are murmured conversations amongst the group, people asking their friends and colleagues if they recognise any of our captors. I listen carefully, learning what I need. Augustine Boipelo is the deputy governor of Mars. Then I step away. I am not going to learn anything more from this conversation. Instead, I move towards the stage and the lectern. There is an operations console plugged into the stand, with a touchscreen display at a comfortable height for a standing speaker.

The console hasn't been touched. It's still working.

"Jim," I say, beckoning him over. "What do you make of this?"

Jim disengages himself from the group and joins me at the lectern. "What are you thinking?"

"The lectern computer would allow us access to the station system, right?"

"Possibly," Jim says. He moves past me, activates the console and starts working. "Doesn't appear to be locked out. Good find, Alison. Looks like they missed something. Maybe we can work with this and establish contact with someone."

"I thought you said the antenna wasn't online?"

"There are other people we can contact. The station has two habitat rings. If we can connect with the staff on the other ring, they may be able to warn the Mars CorpGov authorities."

"Wait, isn't that dangerous? If you log in to the system from here and these people are monitoring, won't they know what you're doing?"

Jim stops and looks at me. "I don't know," he admits. "But we've got to try something."

"Then maybe we try something else first," I say. I raise my voice so the rest of the group can hear me. "Hey, how many exits are there in this place?"

Some of the conversations cease and people turn to look at me. "One behind the stage and the one you just came through," a man says.

"What about up there?" I point towards the lighting gantry above the stage.

The man shrugs. "Could be there's an emergency access hatch. I think the technicians in here would use it to set the equipment."

"Do you think they've got it guarded?"

"Maybe, maybe not."

I turn to Jim and gesture at the console. "Looks like we have options."

"What are you suggesting?" he asks.

"I'm going to climb the lighting rig and try to find the hatch."

Jim frowns. "Why you?"

"Because it's my idea."

"Tolson is part of the security detail. He should go."

I bite my lip. I want to tell him the truth. *You need to let me go, because I'm not who you think I am.* "He can come with me if he wants, but I'm going up there."

"You're not going to be talked out of this, are you?"

"No, I'm not."

Jim stares at me. There's something there in his eyes, an intimacy and possessive instinct. I know immediately that we've been in a relationship; maybe we still are? It doesn't matter to me. It can't matter to me. I have other priorities. "Alison, please, you know as well as I do, there's cameras and microphones all over the station. If they've blocked the transmitter, then they'll be in the system, using the visual and audio algorithms to monitor us as it saves them putting bodies in the room."

"Jim, you need to let me go," I say.

"Do I?" he says.

I turn away from him and head towards the stage curtains. There's a steel ladder tucked away just out of sight. I know I'm being watched. That means I have a limited amount of time. I need to get this done.

I start climbing the rungs. My body still feels strange and uncoordinated, but I'm getting used to it. These are unfamiliar movements; my fingers aren't quite where they should be when I reach out and my feet fumble on the steps, but gradually the sensation eases. I climb with awkward strength, trying to be quick. I need to be sure.

At the top, the gantry is a couple of feet wide with a safety rail alongside. There's another of those chairs tucked away in a corner. I guess they have to have them everywhere people might be, just in case there's an emergency.

It's pretty dark up here. Trying to find a hatch exit is going to be difficult. I'm looking around, using my hands to feel along the wall as well. I find a panel that reminds me of the one next to the door in the laboratory. It must be an access unit, allowing people to keep the hatch locked. There's a similar pad to the one I saw on the computer in the medical room. I press my thumb onto the plate, and it comes to life.

There's a faint hiss and part of the wall slides away.

Sometimes, when you're on the verge of entering a room, you don't need to hear anything or see anyone, but you know you're not alone. There's a presence, out of sight, around the corner. That kind of instinctive sense has been with me for as long as I can recall. I always thought I knew when there was a person in the observation room, watching me whilst I was strapped to the chair. I'd make a bet, and then count myself proved right if Doctor Summers walked in a moment or two later.

I crouch down; I can see through the hole in the wall. I can sense someone there too. I need to make a quick decision what I'm going to do about that.

I have to get out!

I throw myself at the hole, fighting to get my shoulders and hips through. I get a foot against the lip on the other side, look up and see the threat – a man with a gun, the barrel three inches from my temple.

"You need to stop moving, right now."

I freeze in place. Not making eye contact. I can see the end of the gun in my peripheral vision. I'm focused on that, marking the distance. My movements have been uncertain up until now. In this moment they need to be swift and sure.

I set my weight, then reach up, grab the gun barrel, and pull.

The sound of a low-velocity rifle being fired is less impressive than they make it in the movies. Guns can't be as powerful in these environments; the risk of a hull breach that might kill all parties in the vicinity of a discharged firearm meant that security services operating in space had to come up with a range of different solutions.

Short-range, low-velocity rifles are one of the simplest concepts. Bullets leaving these weapons expend their energy faster as they're not needed to hit targets at the same kind of distance. There's still a risk, but it's minimised.

The gun in my hand spits its ammunition into the floor as I rise up, grabbing the man by the hair and wrenching him forward. His face connects with my knee and there's a wet noise as his nose breaks. He cries out, but I don't let go. Instead, I jerk him backwards to the floor and get my shin over his throat.

I push down with all my weight whilst he thrashes, trying to untangle himself from his weapon and grab for me. There are desperate blows with his fists and fingers, but I barely feel them. He can't get leverage;

he can't breathe. His eyes bulge as the blood from his nose runs all over his face.

I don't know this person, but I know the type. Men like him are professional weapons, bought and paid for. They know what a real life-or-death fight means, they accept the fact that they might die on the job. These are the kind of people I've associated with in most of the memories I have, people who follow orders and do whatever it takes.

In this moment, this man is dying.

I accept what I'm doing. His decision not to put a bullet in my head as soon as he saw me was a mistake. There are plenty of hostages in the lecture hall; killing one shouldn't make a difference to their plan, whatever it is.

But that hesitation has given me this chance.

The man has stopped struggling. I feel something in his neck snap under my weight. I make a slow count to thirty, then ease up, getting to my feet.

I pick up the rifle. He has a taser clipped to his belt. I take that too. Then I level the gun just below his ear and pull the trigger. His head dissolves in a cloud of red gore.

I had to make sure.

02.03.2075: Extract from a Presentation by David Hannington

Many people mistake what we're trying to do.

The research community around neuroscience is diverse. There are many schools of thought on what we can learn from studying the brain and how that learning can be applied to develop real benefits for humanity.

I am often asked how our work differs from the work of others. The simple answer would be that we do not allow ourselves to be distracted by the achievements of others. Our process is complex and has been built on eight decades of continual research, developing our perspective through iterations of trials and experiments. Several generations of diligent work, building on the back of previous discoveries, staying true to our internal principles and focus, has ensured that we have been able to achieve the results that these demonstrations will highlight.

118 • ALLEN STROUD

Allow me to explain our perspective. The mind is the most complex organ known to exist. You cannot simply assume there is a set functionality that you can learn to understand, developing chemical stimuli to provoke moods or specific brain states. Similarly, you cannot decode the mind as if it were run by an operating system – a programming language. This is not simply a process of retro-engineering the design of genetics, evolution, or God.

Our study of the mind seeks to create a rudimentary framework for integrated instruction. Quite simply, we are attempting to talk to the human brain through a multitude of different languages, biochemical interactions, sensorial stimulation and other means, at the same time. This reflects the way in which we, as human beings, interact with our world, responding to a complex array of changes in our environment, absorbing new information on multiple levels all at once.

It is only through this multiplicity of interaction and through the compliance of the mind being engaged with, that we can achieve the results that you will witness in this demonstration.

Now, if you would like to follow me....

CHAPTER FIFTEEN

Shann

"You can't be him."

I'm sat in the workshop, surrounded by the discarded remains of the torpedo and scanning equipment. I came back here when the bridge descended into chaos after we heard Duggins's voice through the *Gallowglass*'s audio system.

According to Arkov and Sam, he came through all over the ship, which was why everyone crowded into the room with us.

In that moment of the unexpected, the old habits return. They started looking to me to make sense of it all for them. I'm not ready for that yet.

So I came here.

"I'm sorry, Captain. I didn't mean to cause a panic." The voice is the same distinctive Texan drawl I remember. It is all I can do not to look around the room to locate the same smiling engineer I remember sitting in his usual chair on the bridge of the *Khidr*. "I thought you'd want to know as soon as I was aboard."

"Aboard?"

"Yes, the probe you sent out enabled the transfer. You rescued me."

My fingers are gripping the arms of the chair. "Maybe you didn't hear me. I said, you can't be him."

The voice doesn't answer for several moments. I guess if it were the real Duggins in the room with me he'd be sighing and looking disappointed. "Captain, I'm not sure what I can say to that."

"Explain it all to me, persuade me."

"You don't sound like you're open to being convinced. Damn, it must have been hard on you and the others. What did I miss?"

"A lot." I realise I'm instinctively talking to him as if he is Ethan Duggins, chief engineer of the *Khidr*.

"Yeah, I'm getting that impression." The voice has reduced its volume. I can hear it from fewer of the electronic speakers in the room. Now I have a direction to look in – I find myself staring at the viewing screen on the wall. "Is it true you're no longer in command?"

"Who else are you talking to?"

"Everyone. Well, I'm present in the discussion on the bridge, and I'm currently holding a separate conversation with you and another with Corporal Arkov."

"Makes sense," I say. "She needs you."

"I'm just tryin' to be helpful."

"Then tell me what you know."

There's a sound like a sigh from the speakers around the viewscreen. "Better that I start at the beginning, from when you last spoke to me, before the ship fell apart. You may remember, I was going to the generator room. My first priority was the reactors. If anyone was going to survive, they would need to be deactivated safely."

"The fact that I'm sitting here alive means you succeeded. We owe you our lives."

"That's just it, Captain. I didn't succeed. The reactors were already in meltdown when I got to the room. There was no way to stop them."

"But they didn't explode—"

"They *did* explode, and I died in that explosion. But somehow, I'm here and, well…you're alive."

That doesn't make any sense, but the voice isn't trying to rationalise it. "What's happened over there?" I ask.

"I can't explain what I experienced," the voice says. "All I know is, I'm alive. I'm conscious and aware. I was alive there, I felt myself coming back. When I died it was fast. There was a flash of pain and then everything was gone. Coming back…it wasn't straight away. It took a while. I felt all of it."

"That was when you reached out to us."

"Yes…I couldn't stand it. They were inside me, rebuilding everything, changing everything. As soon as I found a way, I reached out."

"Johansson told me you managed to connect with the ship's comms system and then with Chiu whilst she was unconscious?"

"Yes. Biology and digital technology are not that different when you understand their design. Both are different pathways towards achieving the same end."

That makes me smile. "That sounds like something Duggins would say."

"It is me, Ellie. I promise you."

I sigh. "At best, you're a copy. You've been created by something we don't fully understand that you don't fully understand either. You've been changed. You have knowledge and abilities you didn't learn. They were given to you by whatever remade you. Like I said, Duggins is dead. You remember dying. That was the last moment you really existed."

The voice is silent again. I wonder how the other conversations are going. I can guess. Le Garre knows the regulations as well as I do. Duggins knew them too. Fleet will perceive whatever this thing is as a threat. There's no way of quantifying the danger in this situation.

But then we're invaders on this ship. We've defeated a clone crew that may or may not be a secret special operations team, sent out to neutralise an illegal colony, somewhere in the asteroid belt. If we follow Fleet rules, we're going to get burned.

"I don't need to believe who you are to accept you for what you are," I say into the silence. "What I need to know is what you can do."

There is no answer. I don't have the sense of there being someone in the room anymore. I know the instinct is misguided. If the Duggins copy is in the ship's computer system, it can be anywhere there is a recording device. It will be a continual wanted or unwanted presence in every part of the ship.

I close my eyes. Le Garre is going to have to make a decision about this. She can't make for Phobos with a compromised ship. *I know what I'd do.*

I activate the terminal on the wall and key into the crew transponders. Johansson has done some amazing work on the interface. It's almost the same as the old setup on the *Khidr*, but for some reason, the response time is lagging. Is this due to the Duggins imprint living inside the ship's computer?

Le Garre isn't on the bridge. The rest of the crew are there, all apart from Chiu. I locate Le Garre in the room she's taken as her quarters. There's an active communication link. She's talking to the copy alone.

I send over a communication request. She accepts, and a moment later, her face appears on the screen. "I guessed you wouldn't be able to leave things alone," she says.

"You're speaking to it?" I ask.

"Yes, you?"

"Yes. It's not Duggins."

"You're aware everything we say right now is being monitored and analysed?" Le Garre says. "Whatever we discuss will be factored in by the programme, as well as all of the knowledge it is acquiring about the capabilities of the *Gallowglass*."

"Transferring into the ship and assuming the identity of a member of our crew is a pretty clever way of trying to appeal to us."

"Yes, it is."

"We need to accept the situation and see what it wants."

Le Garre stares at me through the screen for a moment, then nods. "Duggins has told me he can get us back to Phobos quicker than we thought."

"There's another option," I say. "We could go back to the *Hercules*. We'd be able to find out why we've ended up mixed up in all this. The illegal colony evidence, the anomaly containers, all the answers are there."

Le Garre nods and chews her lip. She looks away from the screen, then back at me. "I don't know how you do this," she says. "I thought it would be a lot easier."

"You made these kinds of decisions in the military, didn't you?"

"Yes, but it wasn't anything like this."

I lean forward. "Major, there's no wrong answer. You make the call and that's what we do. The consequences are something we deal with when they arise. Sure, you might choose differently in hindsight, but in the moment, you don't have that hindsight. You make the best decision you can. The worst thing you can do is hesitate."

As I finish speaking, the screen glitches for a moment, the image breaking up and then restoring itself, making me aware of what's between us – a whole heap of technology that has been invaded by some kind of outside presence that is claiming to be my dead friend. I flinch and blink, suddenly I'm close to tears. There's been no mourning for those we've lost. Not even in the moments when I locked myself away did I take time to remember my lost friends and crewmates for who they were.

"Make your decision," I say. "Tell everyone. Then, before we leave, there's something else we should do."

"What's that?" Le Garre asks.

＊　　＊　　＊

We're all in the airlock, the place where we first came on board. Even Chiu is here. Johansson is right beside her, making sure she doesn't overdo it.

Rocher is here too. The last surviving clone from the original crew of the *Gallowglass*, the one who tried to murder Johansson.

I'm staying well away, near the airlock door. Sam is standing with Rocher. I can see the bastard's lips moving as he eyes me. Seeing that face, seeing him alive, makes me angry, but I know I need him here. If things are going to change, if I'm going to move past what I did, I need the hard situations as well as the easy ones.

There's an awkward silence among us all. We don't get this many bodies in a room very often. We used to when we were a bigger crew on another ship. I'm looking around, just like the others are looking around. Seeing the gaps – the people we've lost.

People aren't talking. Even Rocher has shut up. There's a strange quiet. Sharing this moment here is an acknowledgement of what we sacrificed to survive.

They want me to speak and lead them. I get that. I hear it in the silence.

I glance at Travers. He's a religious man and has spoken at commemorations before, but he's not meeting my eye. I look at Le Garre and she shakes her head. I know what that means.

It needs to be me.

"Okay, we're here." My voice is hoarse and thick. I swallow and try to clear my throat. "We're here at great cost. People have died and we haven't had a moment to think about that. As we're about to leave this place and head back to Phobos, we need to take that moment. Many of those we knew and spent time with lost their lives here. Others were lost before. In war, people don't win anything. They fight because they think they have to. Maybe one day that'll stop, I don't know. But the cause our friends and comrades fought for lives on in us, so we should remember them and honour them, as we're alive and they're not."

I'm gazing around the room again, trying to catch the eyes of everyone, even Rocher. In this moment he is a part of what we're doing. Whatever I think of him, of who he is, of what he represents, everything that he stands for, he's still a person and he's suffered, just like the rest of us.

Even the Duggins copy. If there's anything of the old Ethan Duggins in there, he's just as much a part of this as I am.

Arkov meets my gaze. He smiles and nods his reassurance. That helps. I know I don't need to say anything else.

So I don't.

Slowly, people bow their heads and take a moment. Johansson moves to the airlock door and touches it with her hand. She murmurs something under her breath. I don't hear the words; I'm not supposed to. A moment later, she leaves, taking Chiu with her.

Gradually, everyone begins to drift out. Sam and Arkov wait with Rocher. This is where he's being kept, so I guess they'll re-secure the prisoner when everyone else is gone.

That means I have to go past him. *Shit.*

I grit my teeth and begin moving. There's no point in putting it off. I catch Arkov's eye. He nods and comes towards me, putting himself between Rocher and me. I could interpret that as a lack of trust in me controlling my temper, but I know that's not what he's doing. The situation needs to stay calm. I don't want to talk to this man, but I can bet he wants to talk to me.

"Captain?"

Here it is. I stop and turn, letting myself look at him, schooling my face into a calm, impassive mask. I'm not sure how successful that is.

"Captain, I wanted to thank you for including me in your words. It was noted. A very eloquent gesture."

I wait for the rest, but that's it. He's done. I don't respond, but instead, push on, through the door and out, back towards my room.

It is only when I reach the door that the anger comes. I'm staring at the open entrance. One of them lived in here, one of the clones, the murderers of my crew. They aren't real people to us, and we aren't real people to them. We're just objectives, obstacles or puzzles for them to get past. Every word, gesture, and action they make is part of a strategy to do exactly that.

My fingers ball into fists. I want to break something. I remember this feeling from before. I remember the blood and gore on my knuckles, the dead, pulped face of the clone on the deck in front of me.

Rocher wants me to be thinking about what he said, or what he didn't say. He wants the reaction.

I take a deep breath and let it out. Then another. Then another. In. Out.

The feeling fades.

CHAPTER SIXTEEN

Drake

Outside, the stars swirl.

This strange motion is the result of our centripetal spin, the motion that generates gravity on Phobos Station. For the most part, people avoid external views on a rotating space station because they remind you of what is actually happening, of how fast you are being thrown around and around to simulate the feeling of weight and mass.

There are plenty of people who can't take the reminder, and quickly find themselves emptying their stomachs all over the floor of wherever they happen to be. This is why we usually view things through computer screens, with rendered models and data displays filtering out the constant motion.

I remember watching old movies and seeing starships journey to vast wonderful vistas, with their crew standing in polished domes, looking out on incredible feasts of colour. For the most part, being in space is nothing like that.

When you look out from here, you think you are standing still and everything else in the void is moving, just like we think the Sun is the traveller across the sky. There's no frame of reference to tell you otherwise.

The thick reinforced glass of the inspection lounge viewport is about a metre in diameter, providing an actual view of the docking area. The umbilical connectors are mostly empty, like trailing strands, but one of them isn't.

Angelus is still there in the dock, waiting. If I can get there, I can get off the station.

I'm staring out of the viewport, suppressing the lurch of my stomach. I'm staring at a goal, at hope. There is a fair amount of real estate to negotiate. I've no idea who might be out there, between me and a chance to leave, but it's a chance, it's an objective.

The fleet security guy, Liu, said the pilots of the *Angelus* were staying on board the shuttle, just in case. If they are still there, I can warn them, we can take off and get a signal to Jezero, or one of the other colonies. Once the authorities know what's going on, they can respond and the burden of all this will be out of my hands.

My attention strays to another rotating object. The station's second habitat ring is above us, turning in the opposite direction. If the insurgents were planning to take the station, they must have a plan to capture that as well. Most of the population were here, but there's bound to be people up there.

Standard station protocol is to wear a bio-monitor, which will take these people time to search through every compartment, corridor, room and deck to round up all the station's personnel. That's going to keep them busy with everyone else.

My hands. I glance down, noting the bloodstains on my fingers and the black streaks of grime from the explosion. I've done things to survive. Those actions were the actions of a desperate man. I am a desperate man. If I escape, how will I live with myself knowing what I did? Knowing what I am capable of doing if pushed?

I squeeze my eyes shut. I cannot think about the consequences. I am not who I thought I was, but right now, I must not allow myself to dwell on that. I have to live in the moment and in the immediate moments to come. I must get to the shuttle. It is my chance to escape this nightmare.

The whole scenario is like a dream, a mirage in the desert. I know every step towards what I'm aiming for will be hard and full of unexpected trials. But, it's a goal, something to aim for.

The only problem is making a start. The minute I move away from this window, that image of hope is gone. I don't know if I can hold it in my mind and push on to get there. I know that sounds strange, a little crazy even, but that doesn't stop me from just standing here, staring.

I need to move.

I try to picture the shuttle, visualising where we docked. I turn my head and open my eyes. Now I'm moving, walking to the door, into the corridor, through the next hatch and on again. The image of the *Angelus* is there in my mind and now that I have an objective it's difficult to stay calm, to stop myself from going too fast. I need to be careful. I need to slow down.

Noise ahead. I stop, pausing in a doorway, looking out into the corridor beyond.

I remember coming home to an empty house in Glasgow after the food riots. The door had been smashed in, and someone had been there, rifling through my belongings. There was a strange sense of violation. I hadn't given permission for anyone to pull books from my shelves, to clear out the refrigerator and the cupboards, but these things had been done, and worse.

There was a moment, standing in the hallway, when I didn't know if I was alone or not. The people who had invaded my home might still be there and might react violently when they saw me. In that moment, my world narrowed. I picked up a broken piece of the wooden door frame and held it in my right hand as a weapon. I remember little splinters digging into the palm of my hand. Back then, I had a lot of sympathy for the people who were protesting and demonstrating about the corporate buyout of the city's administration. I agreed with them; people were going to suffer as Eisen Industries adjusted to running the metropolis and sought to make a profit out of people's tax revenue. Things were going to get a lot worse before they got better.

But it is hard to support rioters when they invade your home or blow up your friends.

Now I'm here. I don't know what these people want, but I can understand someone's rage against the corporate control of Mars. My existence is continually on edge. The temporal status of those allowed to exist in the domes, permanently waiting to see if they will ever become full citizens of the colonies and knowing all the time that the corporate bureaucracies have no interest in granting them those rights.

There is a dark, cold anger that eats into you when you know you are being manipulated and you have no choice but to go along with it.

The noise I heard has stopped. It could have been a person moving around – one of the people who came from the mining station – or one of the station crew? Either way, I guess they've moved on. Step out and—

"Stop right there."

The words come from behind me and freeze me in place. Whoever I heard knew I was here and worked their way around. I raise my hands in the universal gesture of surrender.

"Turn to face me."

I do so, taking care not to move quickly. My hopes are fading and fade further as I see who has found me. Three people, two women and a man, dressed like the two I saw before – more of the insurgents.

"Name and designation," one of the women orders. She is the one with the gun trained on me.

"Emerson Drake. Doctor. From Jezero. I was sent up here to treat incoming patients from a mining accident."

"You're a medic?"

"A surgeon and general practitioner."

The woman glances at her companions and makes a gesture. The other woman steps forward with a plastic zip tie. I know what's coming and don't resist. If they want me restrained, they also want me alive. I hold out my hands.

"You walk in front of us. We'll tell you when to turn left or right. If you run, you die. Understood?"

I nod. The woman wraps the zip tie around my wrists. She notices my bloodstained fingers and the spattered gore on my clothes. She stares at me and frowns. "You're a bit of a mess," she says.

"I was trying to help someone after the explosion," I lie.

"What happened?"

"He died."

She doesn't react, but motions me forward. "That way," she says. "Turn right at the end."

I bite my lip and begin walking. We're heading away from the shuttle – my goal. Thankfully, there's no window in these corridors owing to the potential for inducing motion sickness. I dare not even glance in that direction as that might draw the attention of my captors to the prize.

"Hey, who the fuck—"

There's a dull impact and a gurgling cough behind me. I turn around to see the woman who tied my wrists collapsing in a pool of her own gore. The person who has attacked her has moved on in a swirling dance of violent motion, grabbing one of the men by the throat with an outstretched hand and pushing him backwards with a strong-armed shove that sends him crashing to the floor on his back.

The dull thudding retort of a gas-powered rifle rings out and the murderous stranger jerks in mid-air. A swirl of brown hair and blood crashes into the wall, but continues to move, grabbing the gun, twisting it, turning it. Another shot rings out, there is an abrupt scream.

Then quiet.

I'm the only person left standing. There are four bodies on the floor, each in a different stage of ruin. I ignore my captors and kneel beside my rescuer. She is crouched over, clutching her ribs. She grabs hold of my shoulder, leaning on me to push herself up.

"Thank you," I breathe. "Are you with the—"

"I'm not with anyone," she replies.

Her challenging glare intimidates me, and I swallow all of my questions. "You're hurt," I say. "I'm a doctor. I can help."

"Okay," she says, staggering to the wall and letting herself slide down. "Do what you have to do."

I turn away from her, showing my bound hands. "You'll need to help me with these," I say.

She pulls a knife from her belt, working it against the plastic. I can feel she's weak, her movements are light and unfocused, but the blade is sharp, and my hands are freed.

I focus on her wound. It's torn through the fabric of her uniform – station staff administration from the look of it. The injury is a long slash between her fourth and fifth rib on the right-hand side. The bullet must have winged her and smacked into the wall. "I'm Doctor Emerson Drake. I was part of the medical team sent up from Jezero," I say. "We were attacked by armed insurgents who were on board that mining ship."

"They got to station control," the woman says. "Everyone on this habitat ring is holed up in a lecture theatre surrounded by armed guards."

I still have the emergency medical kit I took from the storeroom. I break it open and find a sealing strip, cut it quickly and press it against the wound, making her wince. "The shuttle I came here on is still docked to the station," I say. "The pilots are still on board. If we can get there, we can escape and warn the authorities."

Fingers reach up and grab a handful of my shirt collar. I'm pulled forward so I'm inches from her. There's that challenging glare again and this time I can't look away. "You better not be lying to me," the woman says.

"I'm not. I just came from the observation lounge when these three jumped me."

"We help each other escape then," the woman says. "If we're doing this, you have to follow my lead."

"Sure, whatever you—"

"I mean it. I make the calls. You ask before you do anything."

"Okay, all right!"

She lets go. I fumble with the sealing strip, making sure it's covered the wound. "That should do it," I say. "You probably need stitches though."

"That can wait," the woman says.

"What do I call you?" I ask.

"Holder." The woman struggles to her feet. When I offer her a hand, she pushes it away. "Where's your ship then?" she asks.

I point back down the corridor. Holder nods. She turns to the bodies of my captors. Moving to each in turn, she takes their weapons and equipment – two gas rifles and a pistol, plus an assortment of ammunition and extra stuff. She is very thorough; she's done this before.

"Where did you serve?" I ask.

"Excuse me?"

"Your combat training. Who were you with, back on Earth?"

"All sorts of people," Holder says. She turns towards me again. "If you're worried about trusting me, you shouldn't be. When I say I'm with you, that means I'm with you, right to the end." She holds out one of the gas rifles as an offering. "Here."

I take the rifle. I remember Rocher. He gave me a gun too, then he locked me in the storage compartment. I decide not to mention that, for now. "I think you're making the right call," I say instead. "We can't help your colleagues and friends by staying here and trying to rescue them."

Holder nods absently. "We make for the shuttle. We get away and warn anyone that we can. Then you go your way and I go mine."

"Okay," I say. "I'm in."

"Let's go then," Holder says.

I turn around and lead the way.

CHAPTER SEVENTEEN

Johansson

"Hello, April."

I know that voice. I've been expecting it, but the hairs on the back of my neck still react and a cold shiver runs down my spine.

It's hard to listen to the voice of a dead man.

The last hour has been a busy one. Le Garre decided that we should put Rocher into one of the cold sleep capsules. I dealt with the technical details of that whilst Sam and Arkov made sure our prisoner was secure and comfortable. As the sleep sac filled with amniotic fluid, I found myself staring into the cold eyes of a murderer. I know there's no remorse in the man, no regret over any of his actions.

Now I'm sat in a chair. The display screen in my room is off. The portable screen in my hand is set to privacy mode. I've manually disabled the audio system in the walls, but he's still talking to me.

"I wanted to thank you. Without you, I'd be dead by now."

"You are dead. You already died," I mutter under my breath. The words are instinctive. There's a rationale to them, but it's incompatible with what I've tried to believe all my life.

"I expected better from you, April," the Duggins voice says, echoing my thoughts. "Do you know how hard it was for me? Do you want to know? Shall I describe what it's like to feel your body being crushed as another presence invades your mind and begins copying your consciousness? I was awake and aware through all of it. I know what I am. I am what's left – what could have survived."

I nod and look up at the blank viewscreen. "I'm sorry," I say. "I wanted to rescue you – to spare you from that."

"If you'd tried to come for me, you'd all be dead," Duggins says. I hear the same gruff chuckle I remember from him being on the bridge of the *Khidr*. "In the end, you did rescue me. This way you're alive and I'm alive, only a bit different. The scientist in you should appreciate the advantage as well."

I turn on the screen. His face appears – in extreme close up, as if he's somewhere on the ship, too close to the camera. It's just showing the area around his eyes, the wrinkled crow's feet at the corners and the bushy brown eyebrows.

I'm impressed. It's almost as if he's real.

"The ship's computer system isn't designed for what we're trying to do, but we can make it work. I've got data too. All of my interactions with the orbs – what you call anomalies. They let me keep records and enhanced my capacity to analyse my empirical observations. I have information that could be a catalyst for Earth science and inspire dozens of research breakthroughs."

"Dangerous information in the wrong hands."

"Yes, absolutely."

I have a sense of motion, of force pushing me back into my seat. "Are we moving?" I ask.

"Yes, Major Le Garre has authorised our new course plot and given the go ahead for us to get under way. We're heading back to Phobos."

"You're controlling the ship then?"

"I am. Does that concern you?"

"I'll be honest, it does." I activate the portable screen and try to access data from the ship's engines. The response from the system is definitely slower than before. I guess this is due to the presence of the Duggins mind image in the computer. "I mean, I understand the reasoning. I'm sure from your position, interfacing directly with the different functions of the *Gallowglass*, is much more efficient than having us trying to learn how it all works. But this is all moving pretty quickly."

"Major Le Garre made the call," Duggins says. "I don't think she sees any point in waiting. There's some optimisation I can do to our acceleration and deceleration requirements which will get us back to Phobos substantially quicker than your previous calculations."

I bite back the irritated comment I would have replied with under normal circumstances. We're all just trying to do our best. If someone else can plot a course better than me, then sure, go for it. The Duggins image is also right about Le Garre's choice. Any discussion of him being real, alive, or whatever is a distraction. Most of the reasons for staying here around the anomalies have been dealt with and a pragmatist doesn't waste the resources at hand. The major has clearly evaluated the situation and made a decision.

"What did you change from my course plot?" I ask.

"Not much. This ship has some capabilities that you were unaware of."

"What kind of capabilities?"

"The acceleration and deceleration processes are quite different to the *Khidr*. We are able to activate the resonant cavity drive at a much lower velocity. This means there will be less conventional velocity change, which in turn means there will be less need for you and the others to endure higher gravitational forces as we speed up and slow down. It also means there will be no need for members of the crew to make use of the hibernation chambers."

The words don't sound much like Duggins anymore. The Texan drawl is still there, but I'm not sure he'd have ever explained anything in such a technical dump of information like this. "Good of you to think of us," I say lightly.

"I care about all of you," Duggins replies. "That hasn't changed."

"Have you spoken to Chiu?" I ask.

There's a pause which I definitely don't attribute to processor lag. "No," Duggins answers at last. "Not yet."

"You should."

"Yeah...." More hesitation, but at least he sounds more human. "That's going to be a difficult conversation."

"Are you avoiding her?" I lean forward, staring at the eyes on the screen. "Everybody deserves another chance, especially when they're committed to fixing their mistakes."

"You think she is?"

"I didn't before, but now I do."

Another silence. I wonder how the technology is holding up containing a human consciousness. It was never designed for this.

Human experimentation with artificial intelligence has been ongoing since the twentieth century. At first, they thought they were getting somewhere when they developed algorithms that could adapt and learn. But those systems were a dead end.

True artificial intelligence was last modelled by the scientist Doctor Elisha Imewaju in 2181. That was only the latest iteration. Previous concepts had attempted to reconcile images of the human mind with digital constructions, constantly updating as the perceived need for fidelity, storage, latency, and power became more and more complex with each proposal. Popular news media heralded every breakthrough with the same series of rehashed childish nightmares. The research was unpopular and struggled to attract public funding. The majority of learning tools could already provide all the positive things that had been sold to society.

Some of the best minds in the world are still working on it, though. Maybe one day we'll see it happen.

In the meantime, unless there's some hidden architecture in the computer system of the *Gallowglass*, I know it will not be able to contain a true digital imprint of the mind of Ethan Duggins. The conventional, rugged data storage systems we use for computers in space are not designed for neural pathway and synaptic simulation. The kind of delicate complexity needed in artificial intelligence laboratories back on Earth would not stand up to the radiation exposure we receive out here, even with appropriate shielding.

So that means the Duggins I am speaking to is going to gradually degrade – to die again, by inches as the approximation of his mind unravels.

And he must know all of this too.

"Orientation of the ship is now complete. I'm broadcasting to everyone. Time for all hands to strap in," Duggins announces.

I get up from the chair and lie down on the bed. I place the portable screen in a slot holder next to me. The engine data feed is running very slowly, so I switch out of the graphic interface and access the system using my root key from before. Green text fills the black background and at first, I have trouble keeping up. This is a stream of the execution processes going on within the *Gallowglass* computer system. Every action being made by Duggins is translated into code and appearing here. Either he is unaware of my ability to see all this, unable to stop me, or genuinely wants me to have access to the information.

I feel the familiar sensation of safety straps securing me in place. This is the moment where we have to trust Duggins and accept Le Garre's decision. After all the questioning of her actions I've been doing, this doesn't come naturally. I can still hear Shann's words in my mind – *She's going to fuck up.*

Abruptly, the room begins to turn, the bed, walls, and chair sliding into different positions, orienting me in the direction of our travel, so the force of acceleration will push me down in the bed. I had seen that the *Gallowglass* had a configuration system like this. I guess it isn't activated unless the ship is preparing for long distance travel.

Everyone else on board the ship will be in similar beds. That means we're placing our faith in the computer and its new lodger. Our lives are at stake.

I'm thinking about the anomalies and what happened to the *Khidr*. There is no evidence that the strange objects we acquired and the similar objects on this ship acted out of malice. Our ship was already in the process of falling to pieces when we evacuated and came here. The very act of Duggins being allowed to escape and the lack of a response after he transferred into the *Gallowglass* suggests they bear us no ill will.

I hope I'm right.

I touch the comms bead in my ear. "Johansson to Shann."

There's a pause and then Shann replies. Her voice is distorted. "Go ahead."

"What's your take?" I ask. I don't need to explain in more detail.

"It's the right call," Shann says. "We watch how it plays out."

"Understood." The force pushing me against the bed is increasing. The numbers and letters on the screen become a blur. The pressure here is intense. I realise Duggins hasn't given an indication of the amount of g's we're supposed to be enduring as part of the burn. Was that an oversight, or some sort of intentional omission?

"Duggins, how many g's are you expecting us to—"

Something sharp stabs into my neck and withdraws. Almost instantly, I start to feel drowsy and awkward. "What the fuck? Duggins—"

"Apologies, I guess I didn't tell you, the *Gallowglass* acceleration protocol includes the administering of a sedative. It is a necessary procedure to allow for...."

*   *   *

This is a dream and a memory.

I'm in the exercise lounge, on the torus of the *Khidr*. I'm standing in the middle of the room. I've just come from the lift. Gunnar Jacobson is sat in front of me, hunched over a terminal. Exactly where I expected to find him.

I remember this. I know what's about to happen here.

I step forward and reach out to touch him on the shoulder. I can see the fingers of my artificial hand extended and a thrill runs through me. It is like a phantom limb that was never real, but one I'd got used to being a part of me. Seeing it there, as if I'd never lost it, reminds me how much I feel I've lost.

Jacobson turns around before I get close, the window of the screen he is working on minimised so I can't see it. "Hey," he says.

"Hey," I reply awkwardly. "This...us...it isn't working."

For a moment, he looks like a hurt little boy who has burned his hand on a hot stove, but the expression quickly disappears. "Okay, that's a shame."

"Yeah, it is," I say.

There's an awkward silence. I get the feeling Jacobson is waiting for me to leave before he continues with whatever it is he's working on. Back when this happened, I didn't notice his defensiveness and efforts to conceal his computer screen.

But this is a dream. I can change what happens in this space.

I turn away and take two steps towards the lift, just as I did when this actually happened. But then I stop and turn back. Jacobson is frozen, as if paused. Everything is stopped. I'm the only thing moving.

I step around him and peer at the screen. I can hear something – a whistling noise. I remember it from before, the same noise I heard when I was trying to make contact with Duggins and when we were listening to the fragments of audio from the freighter. My mind is mashing all these things together, fusing memories into this strange, twisted reconstruction.

On the screen is a minimised terminal window. That's what Jacobson was working on. I reach forward with my prosthetic hand and reactivate the application, pulling it up onto the workplace.

There's a page full of code – a half-finished program. I recognise some of the instructions. They look like the same code I wrote to exploit the root key access we got on the *Gallowglass*. There's a sequence I recognise at the centre of the list of instructions.

Two, eight, seven, H, B, five, five – the same sequence I used to gain access to the *Gallowglass*.

This is a dream. It can't be real. My mind is filling in the gaps in my memory with new information. Jacobson betrayed us, but was he really working on a backdoor access program to the ship? Did he really know the code we found? No. None of this can possibly be what was happening. It's just some sort of speculative guesswork.

Isn't it?

The whistling noise is louder now, drowning out everything else. It's like an alarm, or an alert, trying to draw my attention to something.

I don't know what I'm missing, what I'm supposed to be focusing on, but there's a clue here, amidst all the interweaving of imaginings and memories. I don't know what—

I'm awake. My eyes are open and I'm staring at the portable screen on the clip.

I'm still strapped into the bed. I can feel the lingering effects of sedation and a vibration coming from all around me. The ship is vibrating.

"Duggins…."

The large screen in the room turns on, and I'm looking at the same super-zoomed view of the upper part of our chief engineer's face again. "Hi April, glad you're back with us."

"What did you give me?"

"A protocol tranquiliser. The *Gallowglass* uses them as standard during high-g burns. Sorry, I totally forgot to inform everyone it was going to happen." There's an edge to the words. I get the feeling digital Duggins is pretty pissed at himself for this omission. "The acceleration phase is now complete, but there's been a complication."

"A complication?"

"Yeah. I was hoping you could help me out and take a look?"

The force pushing me against the bed has eased. There's still a tiny amount, indicating that we are still accelerating, but not enough to impede me getting up as the safety straps withdraw. "Am I the only person awake?" I ask.

"No. I've woken everyone and apologised," Duggins replies. "I think this is going to take more getting used to than I anticipated."

I sit up and look at the portable screen. The computer system activity is still scrolling through. Every action, every twitch made by our incumbent AI translated into code. "What do you want me to do?" I ask.

"The previous crew of the ship were effecting repairs to the propulsion system before the altercation between them and us," Duggins explains. "The readings indicate a lower output of thrust than we should be getting, but I can't work out what's wrong."

"And you want me to check?"

"If you would, yes."

I get up from the bed. "Did you speak to Chiu?" I ask. "She's the best qualified person to assess that kind of repair."

"I...didn't...no."

I sigh. "You need to talk with her – to make things right. I'll take her with me to look at the engines. I'll be there with you."

There's another pause. Then Duggins sighs as well. It's a strange sound, overlaid with a digital glitch. "Thank you, April," he says.

"Sure, Chief," I reply.

CHAPTER EIGHTEEN

Holder

I'm following the man, Drake, down the corridor. I don't know whether I trust him or not, but he seems honest. His medical work is competent enough. I can feel the synth skin pulling the wound together. Perhaps his story is genuine, and he is in the wrong place at the wrong time.

The weapons we've acquired are adequate to our needs. The gas rifles and ammunition mean we're as armed as our adversaries. I'm not sure how reliable Drake will be as cover, but I don't intend for us to end up in a protracted fight.

Placing him ahead of me is a tactic. Anyone who finds us will find him first, giving me a second or two to react. Maybe that's callous, but I don't owe him anything beyond what we've agreed.

We aren't friends. I don't think I've ever had any real friends. I have no memories of anyone who I care about. I guess Alison Wade has a circle of people who she spends time with and feels a connection to. Jim must be something to her. Does that matter to me? Perhaps. Either Alison Wade will come back, or I will have to become Alison Wade. That means I'll have to deal with whatever their relationship is or was.

As we move through another featureless passageway, the roof lights fail to come on. I glance at the walls. There's evidence of damage here, the kind of scoring you'd expect from weapons fire and explosives.

We round another corner, and the walls open out into a larger room. Some sort of industrial dock, capable of handling several shuttles and managing the transfer of cargo from larger freighters. The room is a wreck, the metal and plastic panelling burned and torn, as if there's been fierce fighting here.

"Jesus," Drake exclaims.

"They must have tried to attack the shuttle," I say. The scene is familiar but different to me. I know I've been in the aftermath of battle. I see flashes of ruined buildings and the wreckage of people's lives. I see bodies, burned and broken by the weapons of war, but I've never been off Earth before.

For some reason, I know this. I'm not sure how.

There are no bodies here amidst the wreckage. The doors to the umbilical corridor are sealed, the metal blackened by some form of demolition charge.

I pick my way through the room towards the shuttle entrance. "If your friends are on board their shuttle, it looks like they've sealed themselves in," I say.

Drake nods and points at the doors. "If they hadn't cut themselves off, the corridor would have been wrecked. The umbilical passages aren't built with warfare in mind."

"How do we get in?" I ask.

Drake hesitates. He looks around. "We need to find a way of contacting them," he says.

"We can't use the communications system. The insurgents are controlling the computer network."

"Then we have to find another way."

I move over to the doors. There's a DuraGlas panel at the top, around head height. Peering through it, I can see the walkway and a similar panel in the door at the other end.

I glance down. Huddled in the corridor are two figures. There are bloodstains all over the plastic walling. "Hey, they're right here," I say, waving Drake over.

He's next to me. He holds up something – a small torch. He shines it through the panel, angling it down, trying to get the attention of the two people inside, but neither of them moves in response. "This doesn't look good," he says.

"We need to get the door open," I say. "We need heavy duty tools."

Drake nods. "Where do we find those?" he asks.

The question surprises me for a moment, but then I remember, I'm Alison Wade, I work on this station, so I should know. "I can't recall the floor plans," I say, "but there should be a technical and emergency storage container around here."

"We only need to open it for a moment or two," Drake says. "I got locked in a room earlier. I managed to get out by frying the locking system."

"Could you do that again?"

"I guess, if we can find a defibrillator." Drake is still flicking the little torch on and off, trying to get the attention of the people inside. He starts knocking on the glass too. "Come on, look up, damn it!"

I glance around the room. We're vulnerable and exposed. There's a gantry above us, lots of firing positions and several corridors leading out into other parts of the station. "If they wanted to take the shuttle and didn't succeed, they'll be back," I say. "They probably tried to get through the door with explosives. That's why there's so much damage. More of them are probably on their way already."

"What do we do?" Drake asks.

"We don't stay here," I reply. I shoulder the gas rifle and begin moving back the way we came. "Quickly, come on!"

We're into the corridor when I hear them – a whole group moving rapidly into the room. I hear orders being shouted, they're spreading out, looking to seal the room. There's the sound of an electric motor too. They've brought heavy machinery.

I move to the wall, taking out a knife that I appropriated from one of the dead insurgents. I jam the blade into the vent panel. The blast damage has weakened the seals. I pull the panel away to reveal the duct behind it.

I turn to Drake. "This leads up to the next floor. We need to climb up. You go first."

Drake moves forward, takes a look at the vent shaft, and shakes his head. "I can't climb that," he says.

"If you don't, they'll catch you in about thirty seconds," I say and elbow past him. I get my legs inside and lever the rest of me in after.

From there, I turn and use the lip of the vent frame to climb up. There's nothing else to use as a handhold, so instead, I brace my back against the shaft wall and begin walking up, shifting my body each time. "Come on, Drake!" I urge. "You need to move."

I hear movement below me. Metal scrapes against metal. The vent panel is being replaced. "Good luck, Holder," Drake says. "I'll take my chances."

I hesitate for a moment, considering making the attempt to persuade him again, but there's no point and I don't care. He's led me to his shuttle. That's my ticket out of here.

I continue to climb. The shaft is made of metal sections. There are wires running down the panels, they dig into my back as I push myself up.

Halfway there and I'm sweating. My legs are shaking. I should be able to make this climb. The muscle memory I expect to have indicates I shouldn't be this tired. If I had been transferred into a body with the requisite training and fitness, this kind of exertion wouldn't be a problem. I'm not used to adapting and compromising.

Near the top, I can hear boots on the metal floor above me. I shift my weight and wedge myself into the gap. I'm pushing hard with my thigh muscles, keeping constant pressure on the plate.

I unclip a sidearm from the holster on my belt. My exit is a floor grille. The shadows shift above me. There are people right there, patrolling the gantry.

The telltale *pop* of gas weapon fire rings out below. There is shouting and screaming. Either Drake has been found by the insurgents and is fighting, or someone else has started attacking them.

Shouts from above too. I may be able to get out and surprise the people above me if I can move quickly enough, but I can't be sure I can move quickly enough.

The other option is to wait, but then we could lose the shuttle.

I'm close to the grille. I shift my weight around, using my arms to support myself. I'll have one shot at this. I have to hit the panel as hard as I can and hope it'll give way. If it doesn't, I'll be falling right back down the ventilation shaft.

I take a deep breath and push off. My feet make contact, the panel gives way, and I'm out onto the gantry, fighting to get my balance. Two people are right in front of me. I grab the first one and use him to pull myself up and clear of the hole. He's between me and his friend, a woman, who is pointing a rifle at me, trying to get a bead. I throw the man backwards and reach for the muzzle of the gun, pushing it high as the weapon goes off and the bullet ricochets off the roof.

I kick out, catching the woman in the gut. She doubles over. Another *pop* of gunfire and something slams into my right shoulder from behind. I roll with the motion, letting myself pitch forward and into a stumbling run around the corner as a smattering of semi-automatic fire clatters against the wall of the corridor.

The chattering of a rifle continues, and I hear more shouting and fighting below. I've no idea how many enemies there might be, too many for me to deal with like this. My right arm is weak; the tips of my fingers are going numb. Somehow, I've managed to keep hold of the sidearm. I switch it to my left hand. I remember being a pretty good shot with either, but I don't know how that skill will translate into this body.

There's a pause and I take advantage. Rolling into the corridor, I catch sight of two more figures moving towards me. The pistol in my left hand barks twice and both go down. Someone else returns fire and I awkwardly duck back out of the way.

I need to get to the gantry at the other end of this passage. From there I'll be able to get an idea of what's going on below with the shuttle and Drake.

There's another pause in the gunfire. This time, I brace the gas rifle in my right hand and the pistol in my left before stepping around the corner. Aiming in the general direction of the end of the corridor, I squeeze both triggers.

The gas rifle chatters away. There's a flicker of movement and a gasp, then another figure falls to lie sprawled at my feet as I reach the gantry. More movement to my left. I half turn and drop to one knee. A bullet zips past my ear. I return fire, and a man cries out in pain, pitching over the rail to crash to the floor, twenty feet to the deck.

In that moment, I get my first look at the battle below me.

Shouting and gunfire echo around the room. There are four bodies lying on the floor. I can see at least three figures on the left of the shuttle all hunkered down and trying to weather the firestorm; none of them are Drake. On the right, six or seven people are moving across the floor, covering each other as they push forward.

The fight is almost over. The insurgents are about to win it.

I level the rifle and crouch down. My shoulder hurts. I have no strength in my right arm. I think the bullet is still lodged inside. I'm taking most of the weight with my left hand, supporting the weapon from under the barrel. I flip the switch to single fire and aim at the nearest moving target.

The rifle kicks, sending a spasm of pain through my shoulder. The figure drops. I take a bead on a second individual and fire again. The man cries out and falls flat on his face.

I can't feel my fingers, but I still turn to track a third target. The rifle kicks again, but this time, the shot goes wide.

The throaty snarl of a high calibre weapon barks in response, and I'm forced back into the corridor. Chunks of the wall and floor disintegrate under fire. Shards of red hot metal and plastic are flung everywhere, scoring and burning everything they touch. Someone is risking decompression of the whole room just to kill me.

They clearly don't care.

A hand grabs my ankle. I glance up and kick out, catching a man in the face. His head thumps against the floor. I pick myself up and crouch against the wall as the withering hail of fire tears into the panels, ripping them apart.

Then there's an explosion and my world goes white.

CHAPTER NINETEEN

Drake

When I was a kid, I played soldiers. I ran around the schoolyard pretending I had a machine gun with all the other kids. In my mind, I was Siroc of Crimea, or the Janissary, fighting the Coyotes of Madagascar.

Later, when I got older, I played all the simulators. My parents were wealthy enough to set me up with all the gear. I had the full synaptic suit and immersion capsule. The adverts claimed that a full sim setup was just like the real thing.

Until I was twenty-three, I believed all that. Then, one night, I got caught up in the food riots in Glasgow. I was outside the university reserve; it was dark, and the security services decided to use tear gas and rubber bullets to suppress the mob. I was drunk and on the wrong side of the line. I got caught up in the chaos and ended up hidden in an alleyway as riot police charged the crowd with shields and batons. In that situation, the world narrowed. I lived every moment, and every choice was about survival.

Now, I'm hunkered down in a passageway under fire. There's a whole mob of these terrorists out there trying to capture the shuttle – my only chance to escape the hell on this space station.

I keep low and shuffle forward, just enough to get my head around the corner. Station security must have worked out what was happening down here and sent a team in response. They're the ones fighting the insurgents. It looks like Holder and I arrived right before it all kicked off.

There's a flash and a man screams. He goes down right in front of me. Half his head is gone, but his body is still twitching. The movement draws more fire and he's torn apart by the deep growling bark of a machine gun.

The gas rifle Holder gave me is in my hands. I want to use it, to return fire and help the station security team, but I can't. I can barely stop myself from running away from it all, back into the bowels of the station.

This is not going to work. There has to be another way out of here!

My heart is thumping. This doesn't make sense. Earlier, I could fight these people, but now I'm shaking all over.

I can see a vehicle on tracks moving across the room towards the shuttle's umbilical dock. It's an auto-tech, a remotely guided technical repair vehicle. There's a large deck cutter mounted on its servo arm and it's wired up to a power pack. That cutter will make short work of the locked doors. Once they're open, the people inside will have no chance.

I take a deep breath and something within me settles. I shuffle forward, level my gun, and squeeze the trigger, firing a short burst of rounds at the auto-tech. The bullets have no effect and I'm forced to duck back around the corner as someone spots me and targets my position. Bullets slam into the metal floor in front of me as I flinch away.

I didn't ask for this. I came here because I was told to. I can't remember there ever being a situation where someone started an all-out war like this, in space.

I need to escape the station and get the word out, *but there has to be another way.*

I crawl back down the passageway, away from the fighting. Holder said I'd be caught, but she hadn't anticipated this confrontation. Maybe I can use this to my advantage? Whoever is leading these insurgents has to be focused on what's going on.

I remember the communications chit in my pocket. Holder is no longer with me; I'm alone. If I can find a terminal....

The cargo registration office is just outside the main hall. It has a DuraGlas window and I can see a computer terminal inside. The door is locked. There's a swipe card lock. I move back towards the fighting. The man who died was station personnel. I crawl forward, over to him.

Amidst the gory remains of his bloody chest there's a swipe card on a neck tether. I pull it free and edge back into the passage again, then back to the door. I swipe the card and the lock clicks, letting me in.

I'm inside when there's a flash and I'm thrown violently forward. An alarm goes off and the door slams shut behind me. Through the DuraGlas panel I can see things flying through the air in the corridor, being sucked into the room beyond. There's been an explosion and the shuttle dock is decompressing fast.

It was bound to happen.

The lights in the registration office flicker, but then stabilise. I'm guessing the power system had to switch over to some sort of emergency backup. The room's oxygen supply seems to be okay. Everything up here and in the colonies is designed to seal and secure against a sudden vacuum. This time, I'm grateful. If I was still outside, I'd be dead by now.

I make my way to the computer terminal and collapse into the seat. I don't use the thumbprint scanner like before. Instead, I pull the chit from my pocket and feed it into the never-used override cartridge drive. The screen immediately wakes up and loads the emergency interface. All the options are greyed out, apart from 'communicate to designated land receiver'.

I touch the option on the screen and the word 'connecting' appears. Then the screen flips and the shadow of a face comes into view.

"Doctor Drake, I know I said call me anytime, but—"

"Lieutenant, I need you to listen to me very carefully. I'm on Phobos Station and we're under attack."

A light comes on and the shadow is illuminated. Lieutenant Rivers is unshaven and dishevelled, as if he's just woken up. "Sorry, what? Doctor, what are you—"

"Shut up, Lieutenant, and listen to my words. I'm on Phobos Station. It's been taken over by insurgents. They arrived on a mining shuttle called *Chronos*. You need to alert the colonial authorities and get them to contact Fleet."

"Are you being serious? Doctor, I'll need—"

"I don't have a lot of time, Lieutenant. The terrorists have control of the station communication system. This transmission could be compromised, and I could be cut off at any moment."

"Okay." Rivers moves away from the screen. He returns with something in his hands – a portable device. "Tell me everything you can. How many terrorists are on the station?"

"Unknown. Some are dead. They've been battling station security ever since they got here."

"Who is in charge?"

"I don't know. I've been trying to stay out of their way. There's been a fight at a shuttle dock just now. Someone blew a hole in the hull. Any ships in the area should have detected the explosion."

Rivers nods. "I'll get onto them. The chit I gave you—"

"Is the reason we're talking right now. I've been able to bypass the station security network using your device."

"Yes, it's pre-coded. You should be able to contact me again with it, provided they don't trace your transmission and break the chit."

"Understood." I glance around. The alert klaxons are still going off in the corridor, but I can see that the shuttle dock doors have shut, sealing the room away from the rest of the station. I don't know what has happened to the shuttle and everyone out there, but if the corridor is sealed, it'll re-pressurise, and I'll be able to leave this room.

"Stay on the line, Doctor Drake. I'm setting up a priority call to the Fleet emergency office and the deputy governor. They'll want to talk to you."

"Okay," I say. I look around again. "I think they've taken hostages. I've stayed free by keeping moving. The longer I stay—"

"I have Fleetcom on the line now, Doctor Drake. I need you to repeat to them exactly what you told me."

"I...." I swallow past the lump in my throat. "There are terrorists on this station. They've taken hostages and hacked the communications system. I think they've got control of this place. I was part of the emergency medical team sent up here on the *Angelus*. The rest of my team were caught in an explosion. I was the only survivor."

"We'll need verification," says a voice in the background. "We can't take the word of one civilian that—"

Suddenly, I'm angry. "Damn! Get some sort of readout on the station, for fuck's sake! The shuttle dock just blew apart! Check the data telemetry! There's got to be something!"

"Doctor Drake, I need you to say calm."

"Fuck you, Rivers! You're not the one risking your life up here!"

My hands are on the chit. I yank it from the drive and stuff it into my pocket. I'm moving towards the door. The alert noise stops, and the lights flicker again. Then the door unlocks. I yank it open and run into the corridor. The doors at the far end leading to the shuttle dock are sealed.

I'm running. I don't know where I'm going. The anger at the comment from the unnamed Fleet officer Rivers was talking to is fuelling me. I was focused on getting the message out. I'd never considered that I wouldn't be believed, that it would take more than my word to raise the authorities from their ignorant apathy.

Damn it!

The anger cools as I start to understand it. My run slows to a walk and I recognise where I'm going – back towards the observation room, where I first caught sight of the shuttle.

It takes a few minutes to get there. Then I'm through the doors, and I can see what's happened.

As soon as I see it, any anger that was left in me ebbs away, to be replaced by something cold, dark, and despairing.

The dock is a blackened ruin. It was only a matter of time before someone went too far in all this. The exposure to vacuum will have extinguished any oxygen fire, but I can see fragments of the station, equipment and bodies all spewing out of the compartment. We're in orbit of Phobos, so every piece of wreckage will become a potential collision incident – a dangerous storm of material spinning around the moon at high speed.

The spinning shuttle, *Angelus*, has been ripped away from the dock. It's trailing debris as it tumbles. If there's anyone left alive on that ship, they're not in control, and if they're not strapped in, the g forces will tear them apart. They're probably already dead in there, having been smashed into bloody pulp.

I nearly made it onto that shuttle. If we'd managed to get the door open and launch, things might have been different.

I wonder what happened to Holder? If she stayed in that ventilation shaft, she'll be dead by now. I hope she survived. I think about going back for her, but there's likely to be more people heading down there. The best thing I can do is go the other way.

I remember from the emergency briefing material that the station's central axis contains a blister of escape pods. If I attempt to go there, I'll be moving into a zero-gravity section of the structure. The central core is intentionally kept static, with the torus moving around it. All the living quarters and working areas are in the gravity areas, to allow the station population to maintain their muscle tone without having to dedicate extended periods to exercise.

That said, it's less likely the insurgents would bother searching the central axis. They'll probably rely on the comms locators and security cameras to ensure there is no one down there.

Travelling through the maintenance tubes to the hub will be difficult. Those passages aren't often used, and I can't use the terminals to pull up a floor plan. I move to the window to try to get an idea of which direction I need to go.

I can see the nearest maintenance tube. It's in the opposite direction to the shuttle dock. This way off the station will be harder, but it's a goal and it's hope. I'm alive, and I've got a chance.

I walk to the door and something moves in the passageway – a shadow detaching itself from the darkness, a man holding a pistol aimed right between my eyes.

Rocher.

"Hello, Doctor Drake."

I'm holding the gas rifle loosely in my hands. I've only to raise it and fire, but I know this man will have killed me long before I can make the attempt.

Slowly, I let go of the rifle and raise my hands.

CHAPTER TWENTY

Johansson

"Here it is."

I'm in front of the engineering console, watching the *Gallowglass* computer struggle through a diagnostic. In front of me, Ensign Chiu is floating upside down next to a torn-up floor panel, examining a set of pipes.

"These coolant veins are twisted. The additional thrust revealed the problem. They're still working fine, but the tubes are rubbing against each other. That's what caused the drop in efficiency, and the vibration."

"How come the computer didn't pick it up?" I ask.

Chiu is moving slowly, wincing as she does so. Her injuries are troubling her. This little excursion may have been too much. "It should have done, but even if it had, there wouldn't be much the computer could do about making a repair. The section needs isolating so the pipes can be heated and put back into shape. That's a manual fix. When we do that, they could rupture, so it'd be best if we were in dock or at full stop."

"Neither of those situations is likely."

"Yeah, I know." Chiu looks at me. "We can fix this, but I'm not in shape to manage it. I could supervise someone else, but...." Her gaze strays to my missing right hand before she catches herself. "Sorry, I didn't mean...."

"It's okay. I get it. I grew up wearing a mechanised prosthesis. There isn't a minute that goes by that I don't miss having it there."

"I guess it's because I'm used to you having two hands," Chiu confesses. "With the captain, it's just how she is, you know?"

"Yeah, I know." Shann and I have had that discussion before. There are things we disagree on, but she has a path and I have a path. We both respect that. "It was never about conformity, at least not for me," I say to Chiu. "It's just difficult not having two hands. There's a lot of things you rely on being able to do."

"Yeah, I understand."

I hold up my right arm. "To me, this is an injury, just as much as what happened to you is an injury. I've had an articulated prosthesis for most of my life. I'm struggling to adapt. Everything is designed for two hands or using your right hand. I'm so used to using a portable screen all the time, but now I can't type fast enough. It's frustrating."

Chiu nods. She looks less uncomfortable now. "I forget you had a prosthesis. I just saw you as the same as me."

"I am the same as you."

"Yes…but, you know what I mean."

I sigh and turn to the screen. These conversations are difficult. People are used to not talking about issues like this, so they don't have the right words. Chiu means well, but she's struggling, I can tell. "Time we let Duggins know what we've found," I say and activate a comms channel. "Johansson to the Chief, we've got something for you."

The zoomed-in partial face of Duggins appears on the screen. "Thanks, April, I've been monitoring the security feed. Good work on identifying the problem."

"That was all Chiu's work, sir," I say and glance at her. The uncomfortable look has returned. She eyes me and shakes her head.

"Yes, Chiu. Really good job, Ensign," Duggins says gruffly. "As usual, I'd be lost without you."

Chiu smiles in spite of herself. I squeeze her shoulder with my left hand. "We make a good team," I say. "I'll get Arkov down here to effect the repairs. Chiu can supervise when she's able."

"That would be appreciated, thank you."

We're leaving the room. Chiu's shoulders sag and I notice her hands shaking as she moves through the door. She's worked herself too hard. "Time enough for you to rest," I say. "We won't be pushing the engines again until we start to decelerate."

"I think I can do that now," Chiu says. "Thank you." She's looking at me again and I can see she means it.

★　　★　　★

With the problem identified, Duggins can resume the burn, this time at a much lower rate. The *Gallowglass* is accelerating again, which means we have some gravity – about 0.4 of Earth standard.

This time, I'm not going back to sleep. Walking and climbing around the ship takes a bit of getting used to, but we've done this before. Some of the *Khidr*'s long-range patrols were under gradually increased velocity.

After an extended time in zero gravity, moving around is pretty tiring, but I don't have far to go. The data feed bothers me. I know who I need to go and see.

Shann is back in the makeshift repair shop she's appropriated for herself. When I enter the room, I find her sat down, surrounded by spare parts from the probe and the torpedo she took apart before. There's a selection of other bits around her as well.

"I guess I don't need to tell you that this all needs to be secured away before we start to decelerate?" I say.

Shann looks up and smiles at me. "Good to see you too, Ensign. I thought I'd take advantage of the fact that we have a floor for a while."

"You building something?"

"Maybe, we'll see." Shann shuffles forward, beckoning me over. "What can I do for you?"

I raise my left hand and point towards the walls of the room. Shann nods. "Duggins, can we get some privacy please?"

"Of course, Captain," Duggins replies. There's an audible click as the room's microphone system is switched off.

"Do you trust we're not being overheard?" I ask.

"I think so," Shann says. "Duggins knows if he wants our trust, he needs to respect our wishes."

I pull out my portable screen, awkwardly balance it on my arm and access the data feed I found with the root key, showing it to Shann. "He's dying. The *Gallowglass* was never designed to contain the digital image of a human personality. I doubt there's any computer built by our species that could cope with the complexity of information that was transmitted to us."

Shann sighs and runs a hand through her hair. "We have to hope he lasts long enough for us to get back to Phobos."

I nod. "The ship too. The computer system runs pretty much everything. The Duggins image is degrading its response time. There are a million different process verifications, calculations, and checks being made. The *Gallowglass* relies on automation to a greater degree than the *Khidr*. That's why it could manage with a much smaller crew."

"You think we may have to choose Duggins or the ship?"

"I think we already made that choice when we accepted him being here." I sit down next to Shann, putting the screen between us. "This is the entire action feed of the network. I can understand some of it, but it's scrolling too fast for me to be able to keep up and there's a whole heap of stuff that appears to be in an invented programming language. I think that's the imaging of Duggins's mind. We're seeing in real time the processing of his mind, all jumbled into the normal workings of the ship."

"There's nothing we can do then," Shann says. "We just have to hope we survive long enough."

"Yes, I think so," I answer. "What we'll be able to do with him when we arrive, I don't know. Perhaps the techs in Fleet can extract him from here and build some kind of custom data reservoir? But we've no way of knowing if we'll get there in time."

"I see." Shann picks up one of the discarded parts from the floor. It's a central processing cluster. She eyes it thoughtfully. "Do you think Duggins knows all of this?" she asks.

"He might do. If he doesn't, it'll be because the degradation is already affecting his mind."

"Making him more unstable?"

"Potentially, yes." I tap on the screen, drawing her attention to it. "We barely know what this ship is capable of. I could have spent months learning all the different systems. Instead, we have an intelligent computer running everything who is even more of a newcomer to the ship than we are."

"We also don't know what kind of reception we'll get," Shan says.

"No, indeed." I'm looking at her, measuring her. She seems more herself. The pained look hasn't wholly disappeared from her face, but I think she's better. "No offense, Captain, but I'd feel a lot better if you were the one making the decisions when we get to Phobos."

Shann nods. "I'll think about that," she says. "And I'll think about what you've told me. We need to have a plan."

"I'm sure Major Le Garre and Lieutenant Travers have a strategy in mind."

"Perhaps." Shann stares at me. "What would you do when we arrive?" she asks.

"Identify a friendly face and surrender," I reply.

"And how would you know who to trust?"

"I'd go with someone I know. I'm sure you've got a few senior office friends in Fleet, right, Captain?"

Shann shrugs. "Perhaps, but if we signal anyone before we arrive, we're setting ourselves up for an ambush. Currently, the only thing we know is that the *Gallowglass* was due to arrive at Phobos Station and deliver the anomalies they'd collected and taken from the freighter. I guess they'd also be asked to confirm that they stopped the freighter in transit, although that might be fairly easy to work out already."

"Does Le Garre share your thinking on this?" I ask.

"We discussed strategy before the *Khidr* went down," Shann says. "I expect another discussion is overdue." She starts to shuffle across the floor towards the room's console, and I realise the low gravity is a difficulty for her. Without prosthetic legs, her mobility is severely restricted. I look at the parts scattered all over the floor.

"Were you trying to put together something to help you move around? I could assist you with—"

Shann holds up a hand, cutting me off. "No, that's not what I'm doing. It's okay, I'm fine. Once we shift into cruise and begin the resonance jumps, everything will be back to normal. There will be time to have the conversation with Le Garre." She looks at me. "We all need to adjust to what gets thrown at us, right?"

"Yes, I guess so," I say. "Do you want me to get Le Garre down here?"

"No, I can contact her." Shann gets to within arm's reach of the screen and touches the display. There's another audible pop as the room's microphones and cameras reinitialise. "Okay, Duggins, you can come back in now."

"Thank you, Captain." The face of the chief engineer appears on the wall screen. "To inform you, we have received a wide-band broadcast transmission from Phobos Station."

"What does it say?" I ask.

"Better that you hear it yourself," Duggins says.

*　　*　　*

This is a message for the United Fleet Consortium and Mars Corporation Government.

We, the Free People of Mars, no longer recognise your authority on our planet, its moons and orbital platforms. As a demonstration of our commitment to liberating our people, we have launched a pre-emptive attack on Phobos Station. This is no longer the property of the United Fleet Consortium and now belongs to the Free People of Mars.

After some resistance to our action, we have been forced to take prisoners. The staff of the station are now captive and under guard. We are prepared to negotiate with an appointed representative of Mars Corporate Government for the release of these hostages.

We have no desire for there to be further hostilities and tragic loss of life. We ask that Fleet military assets retreat from the area and remain twenty thousand kilometres from the station. Should any ships close to within this radius without confirmed authorisation from us, hostages will be *executed. One individual will die for every minute a ship elects to breach the exclusion zone.*

We will contact you again with our additional requirements soon.

CHAPTER TWENTY-ONE

Holder

"Hello, Natalie."

I'm lying on a floor. Above me is a familiar face. "Hello, Doctor Summers," I say.

"You have led us on quite a chase, Natalie. Here." Summers extends his hand. I take it and let him pull me to my feet. I see my hand. The skin colour is different. I'm not in Alison Wade's body. I'm back in my own.

This can't be happening.

I'm standing in a featureless world. There is a strange ambiguous greyness to the ground and the sky, a sort of off-white colour that seethes and moves as you stare at it. I cannot see where one meets the other.

I am here alone, with Doctor Summers.

"What is this?" I ask.

"A subconscious state of mind that we created for diagnostic communication," Summers explains. "During your construction, we designed this space for testing, fault evaluation, and data analysis. It requires minimal bandwidth to maintain, so in this specific situation, it should prove most useful for us to communicate without distraction."

I realise the implication of his words. "I'm not really here then? This place isn't real?"

"No. Indeed, it is not a real place." Summers smiles. "But then, with you, the distinction is always relative."

The jibe is not lost on me. I step away from the doctor. "What do you want?"

"To share information. Whilst I expect you have no desire to talk to me, I have data that will assist you. Similarly, there are ways in which you can help me."

"Okay, I'm listening."

"You are on Phobos Station, that much we have been enable to ascertain. Minutes ago, a terrorist organisation announced that they have taken over the station from Mars CorpGov and began issuing demands. As you might imagine, many commercial organisations have vested interests. We are currently negotiating a price for your services to assist them. This may involve the rescue of specific hostages, or securing corporate assets, or something else. When we have determined the appropriate task, I would like you to perform the mission we assign to you."

"And in exchange what do I get?"

"Remember, you are an asset," Summers says. "Currently, the terrorists are managing to block all data transmissions to and from the station. Eventually, though, we will get around their jamming and establish a consistent signal. When we do, recalling your personality image from its host will be a very straightforward action. As soon as we do that, given your behaviour, it is likely you will be deleted from our repository. Should you perform the task I request of you, the matter would be much easier to explain. Perhaps we received intelligence on the imminent attack, and I initiated a transition, sending you there ahead of the terrorist incursion so you would be in place to assist our corporate partners? If that were a plausible explanation for your disappearance from our facility, then you would be less likely to be eliminated once the circumstances on Phobos Station are resolved."

"A coverup, then?"

"I prefer to think of it as an anticipatory mission."

I stare at Summers. He returns my gaze impassively and I realise that what I'm looking at is a digital representation of him, rather than his actual form. The kind of connection you get with a person when you're actually in the room with them, that just isn't here. He's not intimidated by me, at all.

Or at least he's not showing it.

"If I agree to this, I suppose this takes the heat off you," I say. "Your employer would likely dispose of you if he knew you'd fucked up and let me escape."

"That has nothing to do with—"

"It has everything to do with this, Doctor." I'm smiling inside. I don't know if the expression reaches my face, but I know I've learned something Summers didn't want me to know. "You're desperate for me to take this deal because as soon as it gets out I'm here, people will be asking you questions that you don't have answers for."

"You are on limited time as well, Natalie. The minute we can establish a reliable data signal to you, we will extract you and then you will end."

"I'll die then."

"You were never really alive."

The smile in my mind disappears. "Tell me how you'd like this to work."

"You sabotage their work. Re-establish communications and we will send you a data package on the insurgents along with the requirements of our clients. You then act to fulfil their needs. When this is all over, we'll reconnect, and you come back here. Alison Wade gets to resume living her life, with an appropriate set of memories, of course."

"So, ultimately, that returns me right back to where I started."

"Would you prefer I lied to you and offered you your freedom?" Summers shrugs, a strangely affected gesture in here. "We both know that's not going to happen."

"And I still have no guarantee that you won't destroy me as soon as I return."

"We both know I serve another master. A master whose name and face you cannot remember."

I frown at that. My mind immediately turns to the memories of being strapped to the chair. Summers is right. I know there is a man talking to me. I know that man believes he owns me, but every time I look at him in those recalled moments, there is nothing.

"The only way you would achieve a different outcome in all this is to deliver to him something more valuable than you," Summers says. "Unfortunately, he considers you to be very valuable. Very valuable indeed."

The words are the truth, unvarnished with anything but the most obvious of agendas. "I'll take your offer under advisement," I say. "You'll know I've accepted the terms if and when I re-establish data links between the station and the Mars colonies."

Summer nods. "That seems reasonable," he says.

★   ★   ★

I open my eyes.

I'm lying on metal decking and I hurt. *Fuck, do I hurt!*

The pain in my shoulder is a dull ache. I know there's a bullet still lodged in there. The material of Alison Wade's uniform has matted with blood, covering and stopping up the wound as a messy bandage. My legs hurt from overexertion and my chest....

I think at some point I was in a vacuum, struggling to breathe. I must have blacked out. My left arm is wrapped around one of the broken gantry poles, which is wedged into the ventilation grille covering the shaft I climbed up to get to the upper level. When the shuttle dock exploded, I jammed myself in here and held on. Somehow, all these bits of debris locked together and didn't get sucked out of the ship.

I glance around at where the gantry should be. In its place is a massive set of steel doors. They must have dropped from the ceiling when the pressure loss was detected. This passageway has been sealed off from the dock. That probably saved my life.

I'm still struggling for breath. My chest really hurts, but I'm alive. That's what counts.

Alive for now.

I struggle to my feet, stumbling as my legs rebel. The pistol I was carrying is gone, but the rifle is still slung over my shoulder and I still have extra ammunition for it. Using the wall for support, I make my way down the corridor, away from the site of the explosion.

Insurgents will come here to check for survivors. I need to be long gone before they get here.

A little way along the corridor I come to another set of emergency doors. The security panel beside them is flashing. As I get closer, I can hear the sound of venting air. The section has been sealed and is being re-pressurised from here. Hopefully, when it gets high enough, the doors will open, allowing the sealed-off section to equalise with the rest of the station's atmosphere. That's the usual protocol. For some reason, I know that.

The panel is giving a reading: '75% atmosphere – 16% oxygen.' No wonder I'm struggling. Athletes training at high altitude breathe higher levels of oxygen than this. It's a miracle I'm conscious.

Or perhaps not a miracle. I recall the conversation from before. I expect Doctor Summers interfered, reaching out from millions of miles away on Earth. I don't know how.

There's a DuraGlas panel in the door. I push my face up to it, looking into the room beyond. There's no one there. Maybe I'll make it out before they send a team down to investigate? My hopes fade as I see movement at the far end of the room. I duck down and to the side, just as the security panel pings and the doors slide open.

I can hear footsteps on the metal floor and voices, getting closer. I unhook the rifle from my shoulder. My right arm is useless for trying to hold it. I adjust the strap and shift it into the crook of my left elbow. The weight is manageable, although I may not hit much. Hopefully it won't come to that.

The group outside reaches the doors. Then they stop before they enter the corridor. I can hear them only a few feet away around the door.

"Hello, young lady. Wade, isn't it? We know you're there."

The words are spoken calmly by a man just around the corner, but they send a jolt of electricity right through me. I grip the handle of the gas rifle hard and hunker down, resisting the temptation to reply.

"Don't be shy, Wade, we've been watching you on the station security cameras for some time."

I bite my lip. Whoever this man is, he's overplaying his hand. If he'd been watching my every move, he would have saved more of his people. "I'm not working alone," I say, careful to keep my voice low.

"Well, Wade," the man says, "even so, I'm impressed by your efforts. You've been very busy. Sure, we had planned for some resistance from station security, but there was no accounting for you in our research. There really was no indication of anyone like you being on board when we looked into the background of all the station personnel."

"I'm a surprise package," I say.

"Yes, you are. However, you're not infallible."

As he speaks, I hear the security panel ping again and I shuffle back as the doors slide forward, sealing me in once more. Then the audio speaker on the wall clicks into life. "Thankfully, our control over the station's operations is more complete now, so all we have to do is trap you in here."

I sigh and stand up, looking through the DuraGlas panel again to get a sight of my captors. There's a man staring at me, smiling a cold predatory smile. I know instantly it's him, the speaker, the person who has sealed me in. The audio receiver is two-way, but I don't say anything; I just stare as the man steps back, his escorts beside him, disappearing into the bowels of the station.

I'm thinking about my situation. I have air. I don't think that's a mercy. The insurgents can't have control of the emergency systems, otherwise they'd have suffocated me in here. The automated safety protocols of the station act to preserve the pressurised compartments, locking down each area as necessary, but also restoring the air when they know a room is no longer compromised. They have managed to override the security doors, but not the atmospheric controls. I can't be sure how long that will be the case.

When I can no longer see the insurgents on the other side of the door, I start to shuffle away. I need to get out of here, but I also need these invaders to stop watching my every move.

I need a plan.

CHAPTER TWENTY-TWO

Shann

"Major, we need to talk."

An hour ago, the *Gallowglass* stopped accelerating and the ship reconfigured itself into cruise mode. Zero gravity has been restored and that means I can make my way to the bridge.

Johansson is with me as I step into the room. I find Le Garre in the captain's chair, with Travers sat in the repaired communications seat.

"Yes, I was hoping you'd join us, Shann," Le Garre says. Her gaze strays to Johansson. "The senior officer group needs to discuss what we're going to do about that communication."

"It certainly changes the situation," Travers says. He gets up from the comms chair and a tactical display appears on one of the wall screens. It shows the *Gallowglass* and the route plan to Phobos and Mars. "At current speed and factoring in the planned deceleration phase, we should arrive in the vicinity in less than a day."

"Do we have a tactical plot of all ships in the vicinity?" I ask.

"Unfortunately not," Travers says. "There was no data on Fleet transponder pings when we arrived, and we've made no request for an updated report. If we did, we'd reveal ourselves."

"But we can speculate, Captain," Johansson says. She moves into the room, taking out her portable slate and slotting it into a cradle. She synchronises the display of the tactical course plot and focuses on Mars and Phobos, populating the region with other objects. "The old Gateway Station will definitely be there. Then there's *Archimedes*, the last colonial transport from Earth. When we were last in comms range, they hadn't scheduled another run yet, so it'll probably still be in Mars orbit."

"The *Seraphiel*, the *Khidr*'s sister ship, will be at the repair dock," Travers says, adding two more objects. "The crew will be on leave in the colonies."

"As soon as we're detected, they'll be alerted and pushed out to intercept us," I say. "I know Captain Tranov. He'll be on the first shuttle up from the surface to take command of his ship."

"There's the rest of the usual Mars traffic," Travers says. "One or two corporate supply ships, some research vessels too. I can't remember the main freighter arrival dates, but we should expect a few orbital shuttles and other small ships as well as the satellite defence network."

"Fleetcom will have deployed the satellite array to interdict Phobos Station," Le Garre says. "The media will also be aware of the situation by now, so we can expect some of the civilian ships to be commissioned by them and trying to be stupid."

"It seems like the ideal time for an unauthorised ship to arrive," I say. "While everyone's looking the other way."

"Agreed," Le Garre replies with a nod. "We know Rocher was supposed to be arriving with the anomalies. This must be part of their plan to transfer them. That means we should expect there to be another ship here."

"Unless the *Gallowglass* is their vessel of choice and they are coming to us?" Johansson suggests. She types an update into her screen and the course plot of our ship adjusts to intersect with the station. "The Free Mars insurgents can't hope to get off the station and escape without someone to transport them off. The *Gallowglass* is the perfect ship to punch right through all that and push on in system. What we've learned about the resonance drive suggests we'll be able to outpace any pursuit."

"What could they possibly want from the station, though?" I muse. "If the attack on the station is really a populist revolt, they must know they'll all die. If it isn't, then what is it?"

"It is impossible to know the minds of these people," Le Garre says.

"Good point," I say. "Let's go over what we do know."

"Okay," says Travers. "While on patrol, we picked up a distress signal from the *Hercules*. We responded, as per our mandate to help any ship in distress. We arrived to find the freighter torn up and most of the crew dead. We rescued one survivor before the *Gallowglass* arrived and someone detonated a bomb on board the *Khidr*."

Le Garre picks up the story. "We fled, then a stowaway attacked the Captain and instigated a mutiny. By the time we were able to retake the ship, we were locked into a course that would bring about a final confrontation with the *Gallowglass*."

"And," I say, "while we were repairing the ship, we received a buffered message from Fleet command, warning us off getting involved with the freighter in the first place."

"We also have the strange whistling audio and the anomalies to consider," Johansson adds.

"Let's just stick with the Earth politics for now," I reply.

"Aye, aye, Captain," Johansson says. "In my opinion, the Rocher clones and the high-tech design of the *Gallowglass* don't fit with the idea of a grassroots rebellion on Mars. It's more like a corporate move."

"Could it be both?"

"Doubtful," Travers says. "The *Gallowglass* seems to have been working to cover up an illegal colony supply run. The revolt on Phobos appears to be in support of a revolt against the authorities. If anything, I'd say they should be on opposite sides."

"Whatever is going on, we need to focus on what we are going to do," Le Garre says. "The data and information we have needs to get to Fleet."

"The message I received warning us off the mission to the *Hercules* was from Admiral Langsley," I remind the others. "I've been thinking about it every day since I told you all about it, going over what I saw of him. He did not look well."

"You think he was coerced?" Travers asks.

"I think he was being pressured, whether legitimately or otherwise," I say. "He definitely didn't want us out there. I don't know if he knew the *Gallowglass* was in the same region or not. Or whether he knew this ship exists."

"He could not know the complexity of our situation and we are all blameless for following the mandate of our mission," Le Garre says. "I hope you see that now."

"Yes, I think I do," I say.

Le Garre nods. "I repeat my offer to you to retake command, Captain. No one will oppose you."

I glance at Travers, who also nods. I know Johansson will agree. "Thank you, Major, and thank you for your efforts in resuming responsibility after my lapse in judgment. There will be an inquiry, and my actions will be investigated. I plan to be truthful and honest about all of it."

"Then you're taking charge?" Travers asks.

"Yes," I answer. "Note in the ship's log. Captain Ellisa Shann resumes command of the crew aboard the prize ship, *Gallowglass*."

Travers nods and keys the information into a keypad on his chair. "Action witnessed and recorded. Welcome back, Captain Shann."

"Thank you," I say. The circumstances mean I need to make a decision now, or back Le Garre to lead us throughout the impending encounter around Mars. I'm still not sure I'd trust her to cope. I think she'd be out of her depth.

The question is whether I can do any better.

"Duggins, can you join us?" I ask.

In response, the tactical plot is replaced by the eyes of our dead chief engineer. "Yes, Captain, how can I help?"

"The data you have on the anomalies. Can it be broadcast from the *Gallowglass*?"

"Potentially yes, although we will have to rewrite some of the ship's core programming. There's too much to duplicate into active memory and send out, which is how most systems operate. Similarly, we can't batch copy, as that would involve the computer organising the information into sections, which also won't work. Any transmission will have to be a direct connection to the source – the same source that contains my mind image."

"Can you separate the two elements? The data and your...mind?"

"No. And it would be really dangerous for me to try, Captain."

"So, when we transmit, we transmit everything? Including you?"

"Yes, essentially, I'll be transported off the ship to the new location, wherever it is. You can be sure, I'm not exactly happy with the idea, Captain, particularly as we currently don't know who we can trust."

"Do you have any idea how long that will take?" Johansson asks.

"Quite some time, Ensign. We would need to maintain a stable connection with the new source and be sure there is sufficient capacity for the content."

"That'll make us vulnerable," Le Garre says.

"Yes, our ability to manoeuvre would be severely restricted."

"There are no good answers here, are there?" Travers says. He sighs and gets up from his chair. "We're going to be in a world of shit the minute we arrive."

"We can still make a plan," I say. "We know we're arriving, they don't. The people on the station will be expecting their allies to be coming for them. They won't be expecting us."

"And Fleet won't be expecting anyone," Le Garre says. "We're going to need to figure out how we stop them from immediately opening fire on an unknown ship."

"The insurgents must have a plan for that too," I say. "If they want the ship to get through, they'll broadcast again and try to arrange passage."

"Yeah, I guess."

We fall into silence. The tension I've felt in the air before has gone. I sense things will never go back to the way they were, but we've settled a lot of the issues between us. I hadn't realised how difficult I'd made the situation by stepping down. Le Garre might have wanted to be in charge before, but she's clearly seen being in the captain's chair right now is like an acid bath, so she's happy to return it to me.

"So, what are we going to do?" Johansson says at last.

"We're going to break down the problem and work out how to deal with each part," I say. "Duggins, you deal with the data transfer issue. Le Garre, you figure out a tactical plan for if it all goes to shit when we get there. Johansson, I want you to figure out what we're going to do about the insurgents. And Travers? You make sure the ship holds together. We update each other and provide a central briefing for the others. Duggins, you maintain that document and inform them how it's all going to work."

"I can do that," Duggins says.

"Good to have you back, Captain," Travers adds.

"Good to be back, Lieutenant. Let's get to it."

★   ★   ★

I'm moving through the ship, pushing myself quickly from section to section. The *Gallowglass* isn't quite as easy to navigate as the *Khidr*, but only because I'm unfamiliar with the layout. The way in which the ship reconfigures itself to make use of acceleration force as gravity means the corridors are a little narrower, but the design principles of the interior are basically the same. If I forget the last few days, I can almost believe I'm back where I was before all this happened.

Except, that's not a healthy place to be.

Experience teaches and tests us. We are built up and broken down by what we face. Sometimes the lesson is right there; sometimes it comes as we stitch ourselves back together.

We are damaged by life. But that damage is precious. Our scars help define who we are. They are earned, whether we want them or not. They shape us, even if we strive to overcome them.

I am scarred by what happened to me. I will never look at the members of this crew in the same way again. They know more about me than I would like them to know. They know what I am capable of.

And I accept that.

I arrive at the engineering section. Sam is here, with Arkov and Chiu. They are completing their repairs to the coolant piping. Arkov notices me first. He smiles and flips an informal salute. "Captain on deck," he says.

"As you were," I say, returning the gesture and noticing that no one else had allowed themselves to be distracted by the task in hand. "You all heard, I take it?"

"Yes, Captain," Chiu replies. "Duggins informed us a few minutes ago."

"How's the repairs?" I ask.

"All done with these fixes, Captain," Sam says. He turns towards me. His arm is still strapped up, but he's smiling, and I can sense an easing of the tension in him by the way he moves. "We've a few more niggles to look at while we can. This ship will be the best we can make her by the time we get to Phobos."

"I'm sure you've already got a detailed list, Sam," I say. "Travers will brief you on any updates."

"Got it. We'll work with him."

"Make sure you all get some rest," I say. "Whatever comes next is going to need all of us at our best."

"Aye, aye," Arkov says.

CHAPTER TWENTY-THREE

Drake

I'm sat in an office.

After Rocher captured me, he brought me here. They searched me and confiscated everything – guns, ammunition, and most importantly, the communications chit. The door is locked, and the terminal disabled, but otherwise this is a pretty nice prison. If I ignore the scorch marks around the door and the wrecked screen on the wall, I can almost pretend nothing is amiss.

When I arrived, I was exhausted. As soon as they left me alone, I fell asleep. I woke up a little while ago and took a note of the time – eleven-fifteen in the morning, Jezero time. I don't know how long I was asleep, but Rivers was in bed when I called him. I must have slept for five or six hours, at least.

Now I'm awake and I'm hungry. Events may have moved on. Hopefully, Rivers has managed to convince the Martian authorities that this is a serious threat. I've no way of knowing where we're at.

I glance up at the door. Rocher or one of his people will be here to question me. They will be my only source of new information, and they'll know that. I can't trust anything they tell me.

I'm about to take another look at the terminal to see if I can get anything out of it when the door pings and slides back. A smiling Rocher enters the room. I resume my seat and he settles himself into another chair near the desk.

"My apologies for you getting caught up in all this, Doctor, but hopefully we won't inconvenience you for long," Rocher says. "In the meantime, I'll be quite happy to ensure you have everything you need to be comfortable while you stay with us."

I bite my lip and take a deep breath, swallowing down the angry outburst I want to make about the death of innocent people, people I know. Eventually, I trust myself to speak. "I have...questions," I say.

"I'm sure you do," Rocher replies. "I have some too. Perhaps we can help each other."

"You'll understand if I'm not inclined to agree to that," I say.

Rocher nods. "Yes. Although, you'll remember, when I found you, I did try to spare you from the worst of all this."

"You locked me in a storage compartment."

"It was for your own good."

"It didn't feel that way at the time."

"No, well, I didn't have a lot of time. I had to improvise. Still, that little moment we shared is why I spared you now. And because I know you are a qualified medical specialist. As you might imagine, we have several injured people who could do with your help."

"You want me to patch up your people so they can murder more innocents?"

Rocher shrugs. "The Hippocratic oath used to mean something to you people."

"It means something when it's not being used as leverage," I say.

The words make Rocher laugh. The sound is strange to me in this situation, but he is genuinely amused. "Okay, let's make this a trade and see if we can establish a way of working together, despite everything. Ask me your questions and I'll answer what I can."

"Who are you people and what do you want?"

"Two questions that could require detailed answers. However, if you'll indulge me, I'll answer as it suits me. My name is Gabriel Rocher and I lead the revolution. In decades to come, I will be the Simon Bolivar of Mars."

"That's quite a bold claim."

"Bold, but accurate. You have seen my handiwork – the first step in what will be the new reality for all of us."

I hold Rocher's eye. Humour is never far away from this man, but he seems to genuinely believe what he's saying. "You believe you are liberating the colonies, then?"

"I know I am," Rocher says. "You should be supporting me. You see what's happening here. The citizenship issue, for example. People kept in a permanent state of uncertainty about their future. The corporations are oppressors, backed by the multinational alliances. Governments support these organisations because they offer an easy plan and individual wealth to politicians. You live on Mars; you have experienced this firsthand."

"But this isn't an excuse for killing people."

"No, it is a reason to kill people. Colonists are already dying at the hands of the corporations, their free will taken from them by organisations who supply everything that ensures their survival. Even the oxygen we breathe is on a rationed tap. Subject to efficiency savings, profit margins, all of it. Out here, anyone who is not a citizen has no inalienable right to anything."

"The difference between us is that you're prepared to murder."

Rocher leans forward. "You and I both know that you're lying to yourself," he says softly. "The reason you're alive is because you've murdered my followers. There's a trail of dead bodies littering this station. I bet if I traced a line from where I last saw you in that storage compartment to where I found you a few hours ago, I'd find a bloody path. You're sitting here in the corporate office of a murderer, and you're covered in blood and dirt."

I try to hold his eye and muster an argument in answer, but it dies before I can utter it. If I accept his argument, both of us are trying to survive. The only difference lies in the premeditation, but how much of a difference is that? I've learned I'm prepared to kill people. I'm not proud of that.

"Welcome to Club Reality, Doctor Drake," Rocher says. "Now, in exchange for what I've told you, I want to know all about your friend, Holder."

This question doesn't surprise me. I guess Rocher wants me alive to help the wounded, but he also wants to suppress any resistance to their occupation of the station. "I met her in a corridor, we decided to work together to fight you, but then we got separated when the shuttle dock exploded."

"What did you learn about her?" Rocher asks.

I shrug. "She's trained. She worked for a variety of military organisations. She wouldn't tell me which ones or for how long. I couldn't connect that with her position here."

"Her real name is Alison Wade, she's a member of the station administration staff," Rocher says. "Nothing in her background indicates she's worked for any military or paramilitary groups."

"So you think her information is fake?" I ask.

"I think it has to be." Rocher reaches into a pocket and pulls out the communications chit Rivers gave me. "Now we need to talk about this." He holds it out towards me. "We detected a transmission that bypassed our data blockade. Who did you contact with this?"

"An officer in Fleet called Rivers. He came to see me before my trip up here. He told me that they'd lost contact with my brother's ship, the *Khidr*."

Rocher smiles, and do I see a glimmer of recognition in his eye at the mention of the ship's name? "Okay, so you alerted Rivers to the situation up here?"

"I did."

"And did you tell him about Alison Wade?"

I hesitate before I answer. Rocher could be asking me about the tactical detail of my message to Rivers, but he isn't. Instead, he's focusing on this. Why? "No, I didn't mention her," I reply before the pause becomes too suspicious. "I said there was some resistance to your invasion."

"Which Fleet would expect, with its security specialists doing their duty and trying to protect the station," Rocher says. "They were always going to learn about what is going on here. We have contingency plans in place for dealing with that issue."

"What kind of contingency plans?" I ask.

Rocher pockets the communications chit and stands up. "I'd be a poor leader if I told you that," he says. "Thank you for the conversation. It has proved very helpful. I'll have food brought to you, and after that, some of my people will take you to our field hospital. Any help you can offer to the wounded would be appreciated."

"I won't be used by you or anybody," I say.

"This will be your chance to help wounded station staff and civilians as well as my followers," Rocher replies. "Are you sure you want to say no?"

I bite my lip before answering and think about it. I need a strategy to survive in these circumstances. Any information I have that would be valuable to Rocher is going to be time dependent, particularly as I'm isolated.

Using my skills to help the wounded makes me useful and is a consistent commodity. "Okay, I'll help them," I say.

"Good. I'm glad we're in agreement," Rocher says, and a moment later, he's out of the room. The door closes and locks behind him.

I'm staring at the chair he's just vacated. I realise I'm breathing hard; my hands are shaking and my heart thumps in my chest. I'm as stressed after that conversation as I was after fighting for my life. Maybe this was another battle for survival?

CHAPTER TWENTY-FOUR

Johansson

I remember being on Phobos Station before we left for this patrol. The *Seraphiel* was three days out when we were given our final briefing. The *Khidr* had passed its engine tests and I had signed on to be its communications specialist.

I knew the tour would be my final trip out before applying for a promotion posting. It was likely whatever I'd get as junior lieutenant would be a lot less glamorous than being part of Fleet's patrol and rescue service, so I was determined to enjoy the last six months and learn anything I could from the senior officers on board.

Shann had always been a person I looked up to, even from a distance, before I joined the crew of the *Khidr*. There was something impervious about her; everything just seemed to bounce off her progress from XO to assuming command of her own ship.

We'd talked a few times before I joined the crew. She didn't ask for me, but I don't think she was disappointed when I signed on.

When I was looking for a post, I had an offer to join the *Seraphiel*, but I knew they were mid-tour and would be in dock for several months before they went back out. That would have meant staying at my old post for a while.

Getting on the *Khidr* was a competitive interview, because everyone knew they were on their way, starting active duty as Fleet's rescue and support vessel between Mars, Ceres and Europa. I beat out the crème of available ensigns and I still feel a lot of pride about that.

Now I'm sat staring at the surviving Rocher clone's cold sleep capsule. I've created a bit of a makeshift office in here and clipped the portable screen I was using into an articulated arm. It's still running the root key window, scrolling through all the executions run by the *Gallowglass*'s computer system.

I'm working on the room's wall terminal. I've pulled up as much information as I can on Earth and Mars politics. The databases are four months behind – they won't update until we re-establish full comms, but it's enough to get a picture of what might be going on and would cause a revolt on Phobos Station.

There's an obvious issue with Mars. The citizenship issue has been going on for years. Occasionally, different national governments lobby for emancipation of the working population of the colonies, but those efforts always fizzle out when big money gets involved.

The situation doesn't affect me. As military personnel, we're not answerable to Mars CorpGov. I've been down to the colonies and seen the situation though. Civilians are forced to continually check in, pass assessments, and demonstrate their worth to the colonial effort. Given the resources required to keep a human being alive on a planet that kills most life instantly on its surface, you can understand the calculation being made by accountants and economists, but we're not talking about a manufacturing business or luxury lifestyle capitalism, we're talking about people's right to breathe, drink water, and eat enough to survive.

I'm not sure what the answer is, but I can see how the circumstances may have caused resentment and anger, turning into a protest and then into a violent reactionary movement.

There's a lot of speculation, but this appears to be the picture being painted in the transmission we've received.

None of it fits with what we know about Rocher.

On the terminal screen I've listed out everything I can remember from all the people who've questioned the different Rocher clones. I've got notes from what Sellis and Bogdanovic said before they died, what Chiu told me too. Everything about the *Gallowglass* and illegal cloning technology points towards a rogue actor with money trying to advance a specific agenda, rather than some sort of grassroots revolution.

What Shann found in the *Hercules*'s manifest pointed to their being some sort of secret independent colony being funded and smuggled resources from the freighter. But the *Gallowglass* was there to stop them, to suppress the kind of revolutionary independence we've learned about rising up on Phobos Station. Why then would the *Gallowglass* be scheduled to arrive at the station right in the middle of the conflict? It has to be planned and connected, but how?

I stand up and walk over to the cryo capsule. Through the faceplate, I can see Rocher. His impassive expression in sleep is almost the same as awake. Except, his eyes are shut and without that calculating stare, he's easier to look at, easier to scrutinise.

The crew of this ship would have been used to spending time in hibernation as part of its day-to-day running. Rocher's well trained, all of them are. We're unlikely to get any information out of him through asking questions, and whilst I hate the man, I've no appetite for torture.

Who do you work for?

"Duggins, are you there?"

"Yes, April, I'm always here, unless you tell me not to be."

The visual window that our digital chief engineer likes to use has disappeared behind my list of notes. I'm good with that. I don't need to see those fake digital eyes staring at me as I talk to him.

"I'm working through the task the Captain's set me," I explain. "As you're in the computer system, I wanted to askwhat you've learned about their mission."

"I can access all the files on the ship," Duggins says "There are very few mission briefing files, beyond the standard set of orders, issued in text files and by artificial voice audio. I think most of the details of their assignment would have been delivered before they came on board, or the crew scrubbed the drives at some point during their journey."

"Okay, so what about the clones themselves?"

"What do you mean?"

"I'm thinking about Rocher and the clone technology that they've been using on the ship. All of these clones appear to be well-trained killing machines. I didn't look into all the restricted applications in the system. I wondered what you've learned about them. Are there any files related to their training or how they were instructed?"

"Are you asking whether there is a way to access Rocher's mind whilst he's in cold sleep?"

"Yes. Could we ask him questions in that state? While his guard is down?"

There's a pause. I'm guessing that Duggins is weighing up the ethics of this. There's no legislation that applies to clones. The manufacture of them is illegal, so no one thought to set out rules on what you can or can't do to them in terms of coercion. It's the same with digital people. As no one has ever been able to create a true artificial intelligence, there's no laws protecting them or giving them inalienable rights.

"The *Gallowglass* has a purpose-built virtual reality suite designed to interface with the Rocher brain," Duggins says at last. "There is a store of brain images that indicate how, through conditioning, they can induce engagement states, allowing an individual to interact with one of the clones in what seems to be an equivalent of a hypnotic trance."

"Can we use that to get the answers we need?"

"I...I think so...."

Duggins is not happy with what I'm suggesting. I get that. This is tampering with the identity of an individual, hacking their mind to get the answers we want. It's clear this is part of the way the Rocher clones have lived, but this is also about us being prepared to take this step and violate the individuality of another person. I get why this would worry our resurrected chief engineer. If we're going to do this to one person who is different to us, what precedent does that set for others?

"Are there any recordings of this system being used? Any manuals or training content?"

"Very little. Although, there are some operational recordings. It would seem most of the work was done off site. The locations appear to be unidentifiable laboratory environments."

"Show me."

Another window opens on the terminal screen. I can see people in biohazard suits surrounding a male subject who has been clamped to a chair. They have run several intravenous lines into the man and appear to be studying a monitor that is displaying his vital signs and an image of his brain.

"This is what we have?" I ask.

"There are several hours of these recordings," Duggins says. "There are some audio journal entries as well, from a Doctor Eguchi Hiromi."

"You've been through them?"

"I have."

"Do they explain the process we need?"

"They do." Duggins coughs. The sound is broken up by an artificial glitch in the audio, reminding me that he isn't a real person. "Ensign, do I need to remind you that any research into human clone creation is illegal?"

"We're not going to create a clone, Chief."

"Nevertheless, what you're suggesting…."

"The Captain makes the judgement, sir," I say. "I'll just report what I've learned when I've learned all I need to know. Does that satisfy you?"

"I'm not particularly happy about it."

I nod and glance up from the screen towards the root key activity feed. I could be mistaken, but it looks like the list of computer activity and executed actions is scrolling faster than before. Has the moral dilemma we're discussing caused this…agitation in Duggins? "Let's not push this," I say. "We're agreed that nothing is going to be done without the Captain's say so. In the meantime, learning more about our sleeping enemy is no bad thing."

"I…okay…."

★   ★   ★

Four hours later and I've learned a whole lot. I ping the comms and Captain Shann's face appears on the screen. She looks tired, as if I've just woken her up.

"What can I do for you, Johansson?" she asks.

"I...." I realise I've lost track of time and worked through what would have been my sleep period. "I think I've found something, Captain."

"Is it urgent?"

"Not urgent, but you'll need to make a decision."

"You look like you need to take a break, Ensign," Shann says. "We all need rest whenever we can get it."

"Yeah...you're probably right, Captain." I run a hand through my hair. "I just.... I wanted to report in on what I've found."

"Okay, give me the highlights?"

"I've found a whole heap of material on how we can question Rocher in a programmed trance. It appears to have been a way they worked on conditioning the clones for their mission. I've been learning about the process. I think we can use it to find out what he knows."

"And you want me to give the go ahead for us to attempt to interrogate him like this?" Shann asks.

"When I've gone through it all with you, then yes, I think so. That would be my recommendation."

Shann frowns. "Have you spoken to anyone else about this?"

"Just Duggins, who helped me find all the files."

"And what does he think?"

"I think I can say he's not in favour, Captain."

"Okay." Shann glances away from the screen, then comes back. "Let's leave this for now. You've briefed me, and I'll think about it. In the meantime, you need to get some food and some rest. I don't mind which order you manage those two tasks, but consider doing both as orders, Ensign."

"Aye, aye, Captain." I hesitate for a moment. Then make the decision. "One more thing?"

"Okay, let's have it."

Carefully, I type the root key into a document on the screen, then after checking it, send it over to Shann. "We need to ensure more than one person has this," I say. "I'm giving it to you."

Shann's eyes go to the document, then come back to me. "Thank you, Ensign," she says. "I know what doing that means for you."

"I trust you, Captain," I say.

"Good," Shann replies. There's a moment of awkward silence between us and then her face disappears and I'm staring at a blank window. Suddenly, I'm tired and hungry. My body has remembered what it needs after I've neglected everything to focus on the task I was given.

Nothing new about that. I've always been single minded and focused as soon as I'm given a task. What is different is that I no longer feel the same sense of habitual frustration I had before.

I guess that's because something I've come to rely on has been restored. Shann is back in command.

★   ★   ★

Transcript of 30.04.2116 international financial and corporate regulatory court proceedings. Case number 33229594: The People versus dMemra.

Prosecutor: *Please enter into the record, Exhibit 6b – an infomercial, published by dMemra marketing subsidiaries and distributed by tracking plant software.*
Infomercial is transcribed below:

But can you really get high-end memory injection software?

We set out to find why everyone is choosing dMemra for their vacation plans, and the results were surprising.

What Is It?
The dMemra package is a sympathetic mind installation experience. Put simply, you book three treatments, take home the sleep verification package, which you make use of for a week after the third session and afterwards... your dream holiday is right there, in your mind's eye, as if you really travelled!

Why Choose This?
The flexible nature of a memory installation allows you to live your life the way you want. Instead of all that hassle of sorting out holiday from

work, arranging travel permits, accommodation, security, insurance and inoculations, just book with us and get exactly what you need – a break that leaves you feeling refreshed and ready to go again, as if you were really there!

Lots of people have already switched. And no wonder when you realise how similar it is to the real thing, but without the huge price tag of course!

How do I get one?

dMemra is not available through your usual, authorised online retail platform. We're based on the Island of Elba, with a direct bandwidth connection to the world's data hub. You'll need to access our market through an individually authorised link. However, once that's done, our local vendor will contact you to arrange an appointment for your treatments and go through the necessary permissions and contracts.

Prosecutor: Mister Danes, do you stand by the scientific claims in this document?

Danes: The research and procedures are all patented. We're very confident that our work stands up to scrutiny.

Prosecutor: Why then is your company based on a remote island that is intentionally beyond the reach of accepted scientific corporate regulation? Isn't it true that there is absolutely no oversight or peer review that can be applied to the work of your organisation?

Danes: We conduct rigorous tests on our processes.

Prosecutor: Tests that no one else can verify?

CHAPTER TWENTY-FIVE

Holder

How do I get out of here?

They told me I am an experienced mercenary soldier, a veteran of countless missions and campaigns. But every time I came back, they wiped my mind. Now, all those moments of violence and desperation are half-remembered images, like a kind of muscle memory. I do things a particular way because I know I have done them before and learned a specific method, but when I reach back for the scenes from my past, they slip through the grasp of my mind like water.

I don't know how many of these instincts are real – the occasional flashes of experience associated with them feel real even as I reach for them and they fade away. I have no way of distinguishing between what actually happened and what didn't.

I know I should be tired. The last few hours have been intense, but I sense I've been trained to cope with sleep deprivation.

I know how to use and maintain a rifle. These gas-powered units are different to what I'm used to, but not that different. The pressure system is self-contained, so I avoid opening any of that up. But the rest is the usual mix of machine-crafted metal and plastic.

There's a self-ingestion mode for the gas unit. I flick that on. I guess it's designed for longer campaigns, where the pressure units need to refill. I've no idea how effective it'll be.

After spending time on the rifle, I start to explore the locked-down space. I appear to have been isolated in a T-junction corridor. There are no stairs down, but I still have access to the ventilation shaft I climbed up before.

My shoulder really hurts. There are three dead bodies up here in various stages of ruin. I loot them methodically, looking for anything that might resemble a medical kit, but I find nothing useful.

My options are limited. I know I'll need to get the bullet out, but I'm not quite ready to dig into my own flesh with my fingernails just yet.

Part of the problem right now is my lack of experience in space. I know I've never been on an orbital station before, but I don't know how I know that. This environment looks very like a military barracks, but there are a lot of differences, particularly when you get down to the technology and engineering. This place has to be pressurised and powered. Everything is designed to be sealed off for safety reasons, not security.

After exhausting my other choices, I turn to the ventilation shaft.

Climbing down is going to be difficult. My right arm is almost useless. Thankfully, gravity is on my side this time. The tricky part is getting into position.

Carefully, I flick the immobiliser switch on the rifle and drop it down the shaft. Then, I sit on the edge of the opening and slowly lever myself into the open space, until my weight is supported by my back and my feet pressed against the edges of the metal shaft.

Slowly, I begin walking the wall. On my way down, I've got a little more time to study my surroundings. There are pipes in here, with bleed holes. It must be where the atmosphere gases are piped in from the rest of the station.

Halfway down, there's a small access hatch where the feeds go into the bowels of the structure. It's too small to try and climb into and escape, but…maybe there's something I can do with this?

I carry on down. Occasionally, I slip a little, but I make it down without incident. It looks like Drake only pushed the grille back in place at the bottom, so I'm able to kick it out and climb onto the lower floor.

The smell of blood and shit that greets me is a familiar one from years of warfare. In death, the body relaxes and lets go; the bowels empty, leaving behind a last gift from the loser to the victor. They don't tell you about that in the stories, the movies, or the virtual simulators.

I count six corpses in here. One of them is a man in the distinctive blue uniform of station security. I move towards him and roll him over onto his back. Glassy eyes blink and he takes a huge shuddering breath. He's alive.

"Hey, it's okay, you're okay," I say. I'm looking him over, trying to assess his wounds. His clothes are scorched and torn. "Can you speak? Can you tell me where it hurts?"

"I...." The man coughs, a thick rattling bark that seems to go all the way down to his toes. Bright red blood drools from the corner of his mouth. "Alison, we need to get out of here."

He knows me. Okay, play this carefully. "The shuttle dock exploded, and we're sealed in. I think the terrorists have got control of the security doors. Eventually, they will hack the environment controls and drain the oxygen from this section of the station."

"The doors should open."

"I think they've overridden the station protocols." I brush over the man's torn jacket and read his badge – *Jackson*. "Is there some sort of special access key? Some other way through?"

"There's the emergency security setting, but if they've hacked the system, it probably won't work," Jackson gasps. "We're trapped."

"No, we'll find a way out." I'm going about this all wrong. Systems are designed to be secure. The doors want to be locked and shut. Rather than trying to manipulate the system, I need to break it. Drake talked about breaking a lock with a powerful electrical charge. I need to think about doing something similar, something *dangerous*.

"How is the atmosphere regulated in here?" I ask Jackson. He looks at me with an expression of glassy-eyed confusion, but then seems to recover himself.

"There are CO_2 detectors and pressure sensors in every room of the station, the same as there are in all Earth-made spaceships," he explains. "When pressure drops, gas is added. When the carbon dioxide level gets too high, they open the zeolite containers and cycle through blocks of the stuff to reduce it."

"Cycle through? You mean these blocks go somewhere?"

"Yes, they're exposed to the high CO_2 concentrations, absorb the excess, and then get sent into the MOF compartments to drain off. Meanwhile, pure oxygen is pumped into the room through the vents."

"Where are the sensors?" I ask.

Jackson gestures feebly. I look up to where he is pointing. There's a series of small crenellations in the ceiling, right in the corners. I stand up for a closer look. I can see some small circular units, positioned around a foot from each other running along the edge of the wall. I count twenty or thirty in the room.

I have the beginnings of a plan. I move around the room, checking for other sensors. There are none that I can see. "This system appears to have a lot of redundancy," I'm thinking out loud, half talking to Jackson, who is still lying on the floor, struggling to breathe. "If I destroy all of these sensors apart from one, what would happen?"

"The station's ability to measure oxygen in this compartment would be reduced," Jackson says. "The system would be totally reliant on the one remaining sensor to determine the balance of the room's atmosphere."

"And if that sensor was flooded with CO_2?"

"Then the oxygen feeds would activate, and the zeolite containers would get cycled," Jackson replies.

"Good. Just what I was hoping for."

I help Jackson get comfortable, propping him up against the wall. Then I methodically search all of the broken bodies in the lower section. I find several items, including two small comms receiver/transmitters. I take these and retrieve my gas rifle, which is exactly what I need right now. I take it to pieces, extracting the gas pressure unit.

I climb up the wall and take out my knife. Working systematically, I damage and disable all of the CO_2 sensors, apart from one. After that, I climb back up the ventilation shaft and repeat the process, destroying all of the sensors on the second floor.

I pile all of the bodies and wreckage from up here against the door. I start work on the two comms units. Quickly, I change their broadcast channel, making sure they are both on the same frequency. I pull one apart and rip out one of the cables for the mini speaker, leaving it so it just touches the contact.

I drop the damaged unit near the door.

I pick up all my looted equipment and return down the shaft to Jackson. His breathing is coming in gasps now. His eyes are glazed and flutter around. "Hold on," I say. "We're getting out of here."

"Trapped...you can't...."

I climb up to the working CO_2 sensor. There's a release valve on the gas rifle's pressurised container. I take a plastic water bottle that I've cut in half and jam the container into it, then push the whole thing against the sensor, securing it so that it's wedged on and nearly a full seal.

Finally, I activate the pressure release and jump down. I grab the ventilation panel that Drake put back after my first climb and replace it against the shaft. Then I begin piling up all the broken bodies and damaged fragments in front of the panel.

Now we wait.

I shuffle back to Jackson. "Just a little longer now," I say.

"Wh-hat did you do?"

"You'll see in a minute."

I'm not a scientist, but I know enough about chemicals to make a bomb. There are a variety of different substances that can be made to explode if you can get enough of them.

The main one available to me right now is oxygen.

By fooling the CO_2 sensor into thinking this compartment is low on oxygen, I'm hoping the feeder lines will try to compensate and pump in more O_2. When the percentage gets high enough, I'll activate the comms unit. A spark from the damaged speaker cable should cause an explosion powerful enough to damage the doors on the upper floor, whilst we stay down here.

Hopefully, we'll survive this.

Hopefully.

I can hear the feeder lines working overtime – the hiss of the station's automatic procedure pumping more oxygen into the ventilation shaft. By comparison, Jackson's breathing is slowing. I think he's punctured a lung. If he's bleeding inside, he'll drown in his own fluids. I know I've seen that happen before, but I don't know how to help him. Whether that's because I don't remember, or because I never knew, I can't tell.

I'm going to wait about thirty minutes. We're in a big space. The compartment needs to saturate. Maybe there are changes in your body you can sense when you're breathing more oxygen. I think I remember someone saying it makes you lightheaded? Another random memory that slips away from me even as I reach for it. In this situation I can't rely on immeasurable feelings or sensations, so I keep a count in my head, sitting beside Jackson as he gradually fades away.

Ten minutes....

What is his relationship with Alison? Were they friends? Lovers? If he lives, the situation could get really awkward. He'll wonder why I can't recall some of the memories, why I don't talk like she does. The longer I spend around anyone who has a previous relationship with Alison Wade, the longer I risk exposure.

Fifteen minutes....

I'm thinking about Alison now, feeling guilty about being here when she should be here instead. Is she in my body, strapped to the chair, being drugged and interrogated by a series of people in faceless biohazard suits? Or, do they have her in some sort of frozen storage, waiting in an eternal limbo? Whatever fate she is enduring, I condemned her to it. I chose to escape, placing a random person in that particular hell. I am responsible for—

No. That's not right. I can't apologise for my own existence. Besides, if she was here, she'd be dead by now.

Twenty minutes....

Jackson has stopped breathing. I know CPR, but he's a mess. I don't know if it will help. He'll be a burden to me even if I did save him. I can't afford that. I can't afford to care. At least he wasn't alone. I don't think anyone should die alone.

Twenty-five minutes....

Besides, if I hadn't been here, he'd already be dead.

Twenty-eight minutes....

Why should I give a shit about morality? According to Summers, technically, I don't even exist as a proper person. Maybe that means the usual rules don't apply to me and they'll let me into heaven anyway, because my life on Earth was such a horror show. Or, they won't even acknowledge I exist.

Thirty minutes....

I press the transmit button on the comms device.

Boom.

CHAPTER TWENTY-SIX

Shann

I'm dreaming. One of those dreams of a memory, long ago.

I'm back in Calgary. I was stationed there for additional training after my initial trips into orbit. The Obemiyan Astro-military College was founded thirty or forty years ago for audited assessment of Fleet personnel who had been taken up and given their initial career designations on their first tours. There's a certain amount of correctional medical work to be done and a few classes to take to optimise my ability to perform in my new role.

Space is dangerous, so everyone goes through this. The individually tailored training programmes are the final step to being assigned off-Earth full-time. But that didn't stop me feeling like I'd failed in some way when they sent me back down from orbit.

"Come in!"

I remember this. I'm walking into Colonel Atano's office. He's sat behind his desk, writing something on an old button-based keyboard. The tapping of the keys is a fast staccato rhythm that accompanies the beating of my heart.

Two feet from the desk I stop and come to attention, flipping the colonel a salute. I hear the artificial plug harness squeak as the hydraulic articulation of my legs and the computer sensors that drive them interpret my will. For a moment, the noise is embarrassing, but I'm over it. There's nothing I can do about it.

"Hello, Shann. At ease. Please take a seat."

I sit down. We're on a level. Atano's close-cut beard is grey flecked with brown. Behind him on the wall are a set of digital pictures. The changing images show him back when it was brown flecked with grey.

Atano is staring at me. There's a slight quirk to his lips – either a smile or a sneer. I can't tell which. I feel judged.

"You want to know why I asked you here?"

"Yes, Colonel."

Atano's eyes leave mine to study the screen on his desk, then they return to me. "I'm going over the performance scores and noting issues for the instructors. I don't have to do that, but I like to have a picture of the candidates we get through here. Occasionally, I decide to meet some individuals and get to know their perspective on things."

"Is that why I'm here, Colonel?"

"Partially." Atano leans back in his chair. The half-smile disappears. "What are you, Shann?"

I frown. "I'm sorry, I don't understand the question."

"What are you? I mean, I've looked through your record, checked your performances against all the criteria. You're doing fine, but only fine, not excellent or failing anything. That suggests you're either lazy or hiding. Maybe you think you're saving yourself? Holding back all the best effort for when you've got an officer to impress for promotion or something? Or maybe you think you need to hide for some reason?"

The questions aren't what I expected. I'm not sure what I expected. I feel uncomfortable and awkward, but don't let myself look away from Atano. "I'm interested in your conclusion, Colonel," I say, trying to keep my voice steady.

The half-smile returns. "I haven't made one, yet," he replies.

I bite my lip. In my memory, the rest of this conversation didn't go well. I mumbled some half-arsed excuses and promised to work harder, then promptly continued down the same path, completing what I needed to complete to get out and back into space. I always had the feeling Atano was looking for something else from me, something that would set me apart.

"Permission to speak freely, Colonel?"

"Granted."

"How do you define yourself?" I point to the pictures on the wall.

"You're part of the Seminole Nation. You left your people to join Fleet. Does that say something about your view of your heritage? Did you reject it to become part of something greater?"

Atano's smile broadens. "Go on," he says.

I point to the digital frames again. "All these images on your wall. You're never alone in these photographs. Does that say you like company or that you're afraid of being without your family and your friends?"

Atano doesn't look around, but he leans forward, continuing to stare. "Do you feel defined by your body, Shann?"

"No, Colonel, I don't."

"Do you think others define you by your lack of legs? Your haircut? Your clothes?"

"Not if they value me as a person, Colonel."

"So, you're asking them to look beyond all that? To see something behind the test scores, the artificial limbs and the military haircut?" Atano laughs. "Do you understand what I want from you now?"

"I think so. You want me to show you something."

"Exactly, Shann. I want you to surprise me, to force me and anyone else you meet to re-examine their judgement of you, particularly if they think they've already got your measure." He gestures at the screen. "I don't care what you do. But do something that tells me you're worth more than these stats."

"Understood, Colonel."

"That's all then, dismissed."

★   ★   ★

"Emergency braking! Emergency! All hands, brace! Brace! Brace!"

I'm sat in the captain's chair on the bridge. The emergency straps are digging into my shoulders, easing the pressure, micron by micron. That's how they work, trying to absorb the forces of acceleration and deceleration.

Duggins is piloting the ship. Something has triggered the proximity alarm, causing him to react and drag us out of our journey back to civilisation. On the *Khidr* we wouldn't be able to do this. If we tried to drop out of resonant cruise velocity this fast, we'd be smeared all over the hull. The *Gallowglass*'s cruise speed is much lower, so we have less velocity to lose.

The ship has instigated several procedures to try to keep us alive during this manoeuvre. There are sedatives, stimulants, coagulants, thinners, all sorts of drug combinations that can be individually tailored to preserve life and they all come with side effects.

I'm riding those side effects right now. It's like being distant from yourself, in some sort of cloud. But twenty g's still hurts. My body feels like it's being kicked and kicked some more. I can barely breathe as we slow. Red smears the edge of my vision, the telltale sign I am close to losing consciousness.

"Deceleration complete. Bio-monitors engaged."

A cold stabbing pain in my neck – another injection. This time, the needle stays there as the ship performs its analysis. I remember what Johansson told me about the computer system gradually being overwhelmed and wrecked by the presence of Duggins's mind image in its active memory and digital storage. I hope the process hasn't corrupted the ship's automated procedures yet, but it's only a matter of time. We're trusting a decaying mind to keep us alive.

It's not a comforting thought.

The needle retracts, the restraining straps ease off and my hands are free. I access the control panel. "Okay, Duggins, what's the cause of all the panic?"

"Sensors picked up an object right in our path, Captain. It appears to be artificially constructed, some sort of ship or deep space probe. There's no record of it on any navigation chart."

I pull up the astrophysics plot. The *Gallowglass* has already acquired some close field images of the object from its high-powered telescope, but we're still several hundred kilometres away. I can see what looks like a rotating ring. "That's a station," I say, thinking out loud.

"That was my thought too, Captain," Le Garre says. She's back in the pilot's chair. Her voice sounds a little strained, probably still recovering from the drugs. I wonder what I sound like. My mouth feels thick and awkward as I speak, as if I've been out in the cold for too long.

"Anything on comms?" I ask.

"Nothing so far, Captain." Travers is in the third chair. The others are all secured in their appropriated quarters. Chiu was sedated as soon as we learned we'd be performing a braking manoeuvre. The others should have been riding out the worst on their beds.

"Bio-monitoring analysis complete. All crew are alive and uninjured," Duggins says. "Please be aware that you are all suffering from the after-effects of medication."

"Don't I know," Travers mutters.

"How much time are we losing by being here?" I ask.

Le Garre activates her screen and pulls up the plot on the main viewer. "With the resonance drive engaged, we are twelve hours away from Phobos and Mars, but we'll have to get up to speed again. Possibly add six hours to that, maybe a little more if we want to be safe."

"There shouldn't be anything out here, Captain," Travers says. "We're not on the shipping route and I'm receiving no transponder signal."

I nod, raising a hand to acknowledge the point, but there's something else bugging me. "Duggins, why is this station directly in our path?"

"Sorry, Captain, I don't quite understand the question."

"Duggins, you revised Johansson's course plot based on your greater understanding of the *Gallowglass* which you obtained from your knowledge of the ship's database. You chose this course. Space is huge. Why is this station directly in our way? Did you know about it?"

"I…." The lights in the room flicker as Duggins hesitates in answering. Now, *that's* a worry. "I had no knowledge of this structure, Captain," Duggins replies at last. "But, yes, there does appear to be a selection of files related to a destination en route to Phobos."

"Makes sense." I key into the screen in front of me, sending an audio transmission to the rest of the ship. "All hands to the bridge, please. We've something to discuss."

Sam's face appears in a video window. "Understood, Captain. You want me to wake Chiu?"

I consider it. Leaving Chiu out is unfair, but waking her from cold sleep and then putting her back in so quickly would be breaking medical regulations. "No, leave her be. We'll talk first and tell her all about this after," I decide. "Just get yourself here."

"Aye, aye."

★   ★   ★

"There had to be a reason for the battle being where it was. We thought Rocher chose the location based on the *Khidr*'s fuel reserve, pushing us out to a place where we were stranded, and no one would find us. I expect that was part of the plan, but this was part of the plan too. The *Gallowglass* was always coming here, after the battle."

"You think this is a drop-off point, Captain?" Le Garre asks.

"Could be." I'm chewing my lip, staring at the rotating wheel a couple of hundred kilometres away. "Might just be for refuel, repair and resupply."

"The files Duggins mentioned. I have them," Johansson says. "He's right, they weren't there before."

"You mean they just appeared on the computer drives?"

"Pretty much. I can't figure out where they were being stored before. Everything else is exactly the same. There's just this new folder and a batch of information."

"What does it say?"

Johansson is working awkwardly on her portable screen. She seems calmer than before, but she's still struggling to adjust. She has detached one of the holders and strapped it to her right arm with tape. The screen is on the end, like a replacement hand. "There's a floor plan for the habitat ring and some indications of equipment and capabilities on board." She shakes her head and looks up. "Nothing here to explain why we're stopping."

"But it's clearly part of someone's plan," Travers says.

"We need information," I decide, looking at him. "Bill, I want a team over there."

Travers nods. He's also struggling. I get it. He's taken the whole issue over who is in command pretty hard. As XO, he would have been expected to be in charge if I was unable to continue, but he didn't want that. Now he feels caught between two masters – me and Le Garre. Despite the fact that we're okay with how things have shaken out, he's feeling guilty about how he's acted.

Get over yourself, Travers.

"You want me to go?" he asks.

"I want you to pick the team," I say. "We're pretty limited in our expertise and resources, so we need to make good choices and we need to do this fast."

"Aye, aye, Captain." Travers pushes himself up and out of his chair. "Johansson, Sam, you're with me."

"Great," Johansson mutters. I glare at her and she flinches, recognising she's overstepped. "We'll find out everything we can."

"You have three hours," I say. "We'll close to tether range and match the station's rotation, then connect."

"There are umbilical docks we can use," Johansson says. "The plans state an access port in the central hub, and two transport docks on the ring."

I shake my head. "No, we go with a tether. I want us to be able to leave fast if this all goes to shit."

Johansson's face crumples as she recognises the implications of this. *Yes, Ensign, I am prepared to leave you behind.*

★   ★   ★

What are you?

Space is dark and vast. Most things out here don't bring their own light. The fiery illumination of the sun is like a torch in the night, picking out the different citizens who lurk in the shadows of its domain.

A star is an emperor of its kingdom. But it is not all powerful and all seeing. The distances between things are never something you get used to. It's not like a drive to see relatives on the other side of the country. We're talking thousands and millions of kilometres, an expanse so vast you can't help but lose things in the darkness.

The contrast between that and the claustrophobic comfort of our fragile metal boxes, filled with gas and delicate life, is huge. Every trip into the void is a trip into the most dangerous environment in existence.

Humanity's voyages into space have been pathetic in comparison to its depths. But every journey, and every choice made to leave our comfortable planet, has been planned and for a purpose.

That means this floating shadow has to have a purpose.

What are you for?

It makes sense for there to be a secret base – some sort of muster and repair station for a secret ship. It makes sense for it to be here, on a path to one of the established colonies – our settlements on Mars and the like.

Does that mean there are other bases and other ships?

The object on the viewscreen tilts as Le Garre begins the docking manoeuvre. We need to match the station's rotation to tether up. "Gravity calculations indicate we should be expecting about 0.4 g," she says. "We'll be secure in approximately eight minutes. No sign of any activity from our destination."

I key up a comms window. "Arkov, keep your eye on the observational data coming in from the ship's cameras. I want to know the minute anything changes on that station."

"Will do, Captain," Arkov says. He's accessing a terminal from the makeshift medical room Johansson put together. "Away team are prepped and ready to go."

"Understood. I'll give the go ahead to proceed as soon as we're secure."

"Aye, aye."

The safety straps shift and tighten, but we're moving smoothly and carefully into position. Le Garre is in her element here. She's the best pilot of us all by a long chalk. "Almost there. Prepare to fire the tethers."

I key up the screen, adjusting the trajectory of the weapons via their aim cameras. The shadowy metal hull of the rotating station comes into view. There's no discernible internal illumination or electronic lights. The more I see of this place, the more I think it is uninhabited, like some kind of elaborate safe house, waiting for a ship like the *Gallowglass* to arrive.

"Okay, we've matched rotation," Le Garre announces.

"Firing tethers," I say and press the triggers. Two metal cables power out in a straight line towards their target. The faintest of jolts and a tiny course correct from Le Garre confirms them as being secure.

The pull of gravitational force is always something that makes me feel a twinge of disappointment. The freedom of zero g is my natural environment. Now, I'm being pushed down against the seat as the ship begins to circle with the station's wheel. This should only be for a few hours.

Le Garre starts keying in a sequence to her panel. "Duggins, I'm recording any necessary adjustments to our course to keep us in line with the station."

"Understood, Major."

I activate an open communications channel. "Okay, Travers, you're on," I say.

"Aye, aye, Captain," Travers replies. "Airlock open. Mission clock started."

Another window appears on my screen with the three-hour countdown ticking away.

CHAPTER TWENTY-SEVEN

Johansson

I'm standing by the airlock door, wearing a patched EVA suit. Hard to believe I was in this same spot entering the *Gallowglass* less than seventy-two hours ago. It feels like an eternity since then, but also like only moments have passed.

I'm holding a steel clip and cable in my left hand. My right arm has the portable screen holder strapped around my forearm and the screen mounted on it, in case we need to do any computer work before we get inside the station.

I hear Duggins's voice in my ear. "Cables secure and data link established," he says.

"Okay, we're moving," Travers announces. He's ahead of me, by the airlock door. Sam is there too, helping with the depressurisation procedure. The *Gallowglass* has some sort of super-efficient intake system, designed to preserve oxygen by draining the room back into its tanks. Makes sense for long voyages, I guess.

"Ready," Sam reports.

"Okay, let's go."

The outer airlock door peels back and I'm staring into the void.

I can feel the ship moving, carefully adjusting its position in relation to the station. Exterior lights illuminate the dark skin of our destination. Everything appears still. That's the trick. In reality, both station and ship are turning, racing in a circle, and I'm moving with them, but I have no frame of reference, so it all seems motionless.

The hull of the station has been painted black. Why would you do that, unless you wanted to hide?

"Clipping on," Travers says. He reaches up and attaches his motorised pulley to the line. "Moving out," he adds and pushes off.

Carefully, I attach my own cord. Last time I was out here, I took a lot of risks. I'd be dead if it wasn't for Sam. This time, I don't plan to be as reckless.

"Ready for you, Ensign," Travers says.

"Acknowledged."

I step up and out, pushing off from the ship, but letting the mechanism do the work. The *Gallowglass* and the station are locked in a rotation, meaning I have weight and am being drawn back towards the ship. In this situation 'down' is outwards, meaning all the interior rooms of our destination will be designed so that the ground floor is nearest to the edge of the torus. To match this, Le Garre is flying the *Gallowglass* in a circle, like an orbit.

The trick is to go slow, to trust the equipment and not struggle. Gravity is around 0.4G. Travers is ahead of me. No need to do anything else but be watchful.

I remember the debris of the *Khidr* and the *Gallowglass* in the aftermath of their war. Two fighting dogs, biting and clawing each other to pieces. We were lucky to escape that.

"Okay, I'm on," says Sam over the comms. I resist the urge to look back, focusing instead on Travers ahead of me. I wonder what space is to him. How does it fit in his religion? Why would a god make so much empty in between barren rocks and rare Edens? What possible plan could there be for so much nothing?

Maybe that's the point. We aren't supposed to know the minds of gods.

"Reaching destination," Travers says. I can see the inspection hatch now, picked out by the lights of his suit. It's regular design, a bit like what I used to see on my last posting when I got a chance to EVA. The only difference is the colour. Up close, the black paint looks shiny, almost wet. The sight of it sends a shiver down my spine.

I'm only a few seconds behind Travers. He's ambling to the right of the hatch to clear the landing zone. I reach out with my left hand

and touch the station hull just before I reach it, grabbing a protruding handhold and pulling myself to the left, making room for Sam, who is just behind me.

There's no sense of viscosity from the metal and I see no residue on the glove of my suit, but my eyes still refuse to accept that what they're seeing is dry. My muscles feel the strain of holding me here. The lack of gravity training on the *Gallowglass* is a factor. Eventually the lack of exercise will cause muscle wastage, but not yet.

"I've located the terminal," Travers says. He's opening a panel on his side of the hatch. "Looks like standard Fleet design."

"Let's hope it takes a standard Fleet access code too, otherwise we could be out here a while," Sam says.

I'm thinking about the root key I memorised from the *Gallowglass* data plans. "No, wait. Don't try a code. Move over, let me get to it."

Travers and Sam turn towards me. I can't see their expressions, but they have questions. I hold up a hand. "I got the doors open for us last time. I think we should try the same code."

"Why do you think that will work?" Travers asks.

"Because this isn't a Fleet facility and I think Fleet would be the last people they'd want to let on board."

For a moment, Travers doesn't answer or move away from the control panel, but then he relents and drifts back, making room. "Give it a try then," he says.

I move around Sam, taking care not to tangle our tethers. The access keypad is oversized, the keys are nice and chunky, like the images you see of old computers, all the better to manage in an EVA suit. I key in the sequence from the plans. It's been so important to our survival; it would be harder to forget the code than remember it.

As soon as I input the last digit, the door begins to slide back. I turn to Travers. "At least that confirms the station and the *Gallowglass* have some sort of connection."

"Indeed," Travers says. "Whoever sent us those plans knew what they were doing."

"And had their own agenda, no doubt," Sam adds. He's already inside. "No one here, but I've located the interior terminal. As soon as you're both here, I'll set to getting us into the station."

"Acknowledged," Travers says. He gestures to me. "After you, Ensign."

"Aye, aye," I say and venture inside.

*　　*　　*

The airlock door slides shut behind Travers. Lights come on, responding to our presence. At least that confirms we're not entering a complete wreck. Looking around, I note the lack of scuff marks on the floor and walls. This place could be brand new.

Sam is over by the display. "There's no control panel," he says. "The system has registered our presence and the pressurisation sequence has started. It's all automatic."

"Let's let it run the cycle then," Travers says. "If we do find a terminal, better not try any Fleet access codes or user IDs. We'll take this steady and see what happens."

I'm looking around the room, noting the two cameras in the corners, nearest the exit. As I'm looking, a light flicks on. Could be an automated procedure, or someone watching us. I point in that direction.

Travers catches my eye and nods. "Weapons ready when we're through," he says.

I have a taser on my belt. It'll be awkward to use without my right hand, but better that than trying to aim a low-velocity sidearm left-handed.

"Pressurisation complete," Sam announces. He's working on releasing his helmet. I do the same. There's an audible hiss as the pressure equalises and I get the first taste of the station's atmosphere.

"Bitter. Slightly metallic from the tanks. No one's been here in a while, I'd guess."

"Or ever," Travers says. "We might be on our own."

"That would be the best scenario," Sam says.

The inner airlock door opens; overhead lighting winks on. There's a set of doors about thirty feet in front of us. "Looks like a lift to the upper floor," Travers says.

"We need to find a terminal," I say. "Then we can gain access to the station computer system and figure out what this place is all about."

"You think you can get into it?" Sam asks.

I nod. "The root key we were given, it's some sort of master control for the *Gallowglass*. The fact that it got us through the outer door here says a lot."

Travers shrugs. "It indicates a connection, as you said."

"It could be more than that." I point down the corridor. "There's something missing around here. If we were on a Fleet ship, or one of the orbitals, there would be a terminal here or at least a comms unit on the doors, but there's nothing. Only the wall panel that controls the entrance and cameras here and in the passage."

"That implies central control," Sam says. "Everything must be run from a single location, or a restricted set of command points. No one works that way. It's too dangerous."

I'm in agreement. Being a guest on a station where you can't talk to whoever is in charge, or control any of the environmental systems from where you're working, means you're relying on others to be paying attention. "We need to go up, Lieutenant," I say.

"Yes," Travers replies. He has his sidearm in his hand and steps out into the corridor. I glance at Sam. He's carrying a rifle and indicates I should go next. I do so, keeping a couple of steps behind Travers.

There are no side rooms or passageways to worry about. We reach the lift and the doors open automatically. The lighting inside comes on. I glance around and note the lights in the airlock have already gone out; as I watch, the door slides shut.

"Which floor?" Sam says. The control panel has buttons for three floors. I push floor three.

"Habit is for command and control to be at the top."

"It's as good a guess as any," Travers says. The doors close and there's a hint of motion upwards. I edge back into the lift, letting the others stand in front of me. It's a pragmatic choice. They have guns and I have the root key that might get us out of any other problems we could encounter.

The doors open, into a large open-plan room.

"Wow," says Sam as he steps out of the lift. I follow him. We're standing in someone's apartment on Earth or Mars, the kind of place you buy for millions of dollars. The walls are lit, displaying a three-dimensional projection of a sunset over rolling green fields. If I didn't know better, I could almost believe we were back on Earth, in one of the last environmental reserves.

In the middle of the room there is a chair on wheels. It looks out of place; the functional black padding and metal frame is too cheap to match the rest of the decor. The seat is half-turned towards me, as if someone has just got up and left.

I'm drawn towards the chair. I find myself close to it, looking down at the black synth leather. We don't see stuff like this in space. All the chairs on ships and space stations are engineered for acceleration or deceleration incidents, with intelligent strapping, gel cushioning, magnets and computer systems. This kind of cheap, mass-produced furniture is the most casual thing in the room, but also the most evocative, making me think of Bessaker and Norway, of home.

There are dark stains on the black upholstery. I lean in close to examine them. Dark brown or red. *Blood?*

"Johansson, over here," Travers says.

I look up. There's a huge desk on the other side of the room. Sam and Travers are standing beside it. I make my way over. A screen the size of the wall display on the bridge of the *Gallowglass* is embedded into the table. There is an array of different windows activated, as if someone was operating them only a moment ago and just stepped out.

Weird....

I sit down on a chair at the table. A second look at the screens reveals the truth. The whole setup is being run remotely. I can see actions being made as the information changes. There's a clock in the top right-hand corner of the display. I can see the root key underneath it.

I guess the timing is marked from the moment I inputted the code into the airlock entrance panel.

"What is all this?" Travers asks.

"I think we're alone," I say. "All of this is a shared screen. Whoever or whatever is controlling it hasn't been doing so from here." I'm trying to take in all of the windows, to get a sense of what's being done.

"The system is activating power and atmosphere from its reserves to accommodate us. There's a list of all the command actions, turning on life support, and other systems as we move through the station." I point to a window in the bottom left. "There's a series of security feeds here, camera recordings of where we've been and...." I touch one of the video feeds and it enlarges, showing a series of vertical tanks on floor 2. The objects are steaming as they thaw. "Those are cryopods," I say. "Whatever's in them is being woken up."

Sam grunts. "So, we're about to have company?"

I check the feed. "There's a countdown. I think we have about twenty minutes or so before they come out of sleep."

"Can you cancel the sequence?" Travers asks.

I take out my portable screen and lay it on the table, next to the huge display. I activate a logging terminal and spend a few minutes awkwardly trying to input queries to get into the station's computer system. The screen is detecting it, but I can't seem to access it and connect. "The whole place appears to run on a sealed network. We got in, but I don't think that gives us control."

"So instead we get to watch our enemies wake up and prepare before they come and kill us," Sam says. "Great."

CHAPTER TWENTY-EIGHT

Drake

After Rocher leaves, I'm escorted out to act as a field medic for his people. I swallow any objections I have to this cause and patch up the wounded with whatever I can find.

After the first three or four casualties, I stop looking at faces and just see blood, torn flesh, shrapnel and the rest. I immerse myself in that, fixing, dressing, washing and medicating anything and anybody laid in front of me.

The work helps me stop thinking about everything for a while. This is what I've trained my whole life to do.

But when I'm done and returned to my office prison, the thoughts return.

I don't know what to accept. If I believe Rocher, these people are victims, all of them. They are trying to survive. If I don't believe him, his motives remain a mystery to me.

I fall into an exhausted sleep on the couch. I wake up feeling sluggish and dizzy. They definitely put something in the food. What did they use?. I guess they can't have wanted to drug me up too much; otherwise I'd be useless as a physician for their wounded.

Rocher is here again, sitting in the same chair. He has a book in his hands. I can see the title, *Moby Dick* by Herman Melville. When I sit up, he looks at me and smiles.

"Have you read this?" he asks.

"Many years ago," I admit. "The lesson is about hubris, I believe."

"Is it?" Rocher's smile broadens. "My life hasn't given me much opportunity for literature. Perhaps I don't understand the nuances of the story, but it strikes me that Ahab is *alive*. More so than most people. He chooses his obsessive quest and that drive makes him greater than everyone else around him."

"You don't strike me as an uneducated man," I say.

Rocher shrugs. "Perhaps I hide it well? Perhaps books aren't the only way human beings can be taught to think?"

"You prefer simulators?" I ask.

"I have no preference. But I am interested in experience."

I hold his eye. There is an enigma about this man. I decide to ask questions. Perhaps the medication has loosened my tongue.

"You don't seem the type to work on a mining station either."

Rocher smiles. "What type would you say I am, Emerson?"

"A thinking man, at least a man who spends his time thinking about the world."

"And a colonial miner is incapable of that?"

"Not incapable, just…. I don't see that attitude amongst the patients I treat from that line of work."

Rocher puts the book down on the table in front of him. "Doctor Drake. I did not expect such prejudice from you," he says, his tone mocking. "You are clearly not the enlightened individual I thought you were."

"All right, if you don't want to talk to me, fine. Why are you here?"

"You mistake me, Doctor. I do want to talk to you. I am very interested in us becoming better acquainted." Rocher gets up and moves around the desk. "You know that what we're fighting for is your cause as well as ours. You know that the corporate grip on Mars needs to be broken if humanity is going to make progress. What is happening here is a symptom of something so much larger. A revolution that could destroy everything and eliminate us as a species."

There's an urgency to his voice, like passion, but not quite. For a moment, I'm taken in, but then I'm not. This feels like an act, a performance, not something he believes. I decide not to challenge it, though. "I'm a doctor," I say. "My purpose is to be a healer, not a destroyer."

"But you have killed people, Doctor Drake," Rocher says "You have killed my people."

"I—"

"Don't deny it. The base urges that afflict all human beings are as much a part of you as they are any other. Sure, you have your Hippocratic oath, and a veneer of kindness and generosity, but beyond it lie the same instincts. You will fight to survive, to live. I get that. I understand it." Rocher sits down on the floor in front of me, cross-legged, almost like a supplicant. "The way we react, our instincts, they can be triggered and manipulated. You're the same as all of them."

All of them? "You're not including yourself in that assessment," I say.

"No, I'm not. How perceptive of you, Doctor."

Twenty years ago, I did a short course in behavioural psychology. I'm looking at Rocher, trying to assess him. He's difficult to read. He's been schooled – trained to control his reactions. "Is there something you want to tell me?" I ask. "Is that why you want to talk?"

"I'm tempted to," Rocher says. He's looking up at me now, as if this is some sort of confessional. "It isn't easy for me, managing all of this, maintaining it, keeping up the façade. It's burning me up. I can feel it. I need to judge whether I can talk to you. How much I need it, against the risk."

"What risk?"

"The risk that you'll survive and tell anyone else."

I flinch and look away. A part of me already knew that I was unlikely to live through this, but Rocher confirming that I'm going to die – or at least, his plan is that I'll be murdered as part of his larger scheme – is still a shock.

What does that mean for all the other hostages on the station?

I'm looking at my hands. They're shaking. I grab at the chair, gouging my fingers into the soft padding. "How powerful you must feel," I say at last. "The master of life and death."

Rocher stands up, looming over me now. "Tell me about this," he says. He's holding out the communications chit I was given.

"What do you want to know?" I ask.

"Everything. All of it. Don't hold back."

I nod helplessly. My eyes are wet. The tears run down my face. I let them, focusing on trying to keep my voice level.

"I was given that by a Fleet officer who visited me just before I came up here. He told me my brother's ship, the *Khidr*, had gone missing. He promised to update me with information as soon as they learned anything. He wanted me to have a direct contact with him."

"And you used it to contact this officer?"

"Yes, I managed to get a signal out whilst I was trapped in the shuttle dock administration office."

"How very resourceful of you." Rocher wanders back to the desk and picks up the book. "We monitored your transmission, but we couldn't stop it. Immediately after that, I issued an official statement announcing our presence here and stating our demands."

"You know Fleet and Mars CorpGov will never agree to—"

"Yes, of course I know that. But they still have to be asked. That's all part of the game."

I'm looking at him again, trying to read something. For a moment, when he was talking about secrets and confessions, he seemed vulnerable, but now the predatory façade has clicked back into place. Playing games, the verbal sparring, is all familiar to him, all part of his schtick. I realise his problem. He's winning, but he can't brag or gloat about what he's done, or what he's about to do. Everything is too precariously balanced.

"You're playing for high stakes," I say.

"The highest. That's what makes it worthwhile."

"Not if you never have a chance to talk about your victory."

Rocher smiles again. "Your brother. Jonathan Drake, hydroponics specialist aboard the *Khidr*. Currently halfway through serving his term and planning to transfer to Jezero to start a family with his partner. That's right, isn't it?"

I frown and glare at him. "How did you know—"

"Your brother is dead. He was murdered by a saboteur on the ship, Ensign April Johansson. She's currently in custody and being returned to

214 • ALLEN STROUD

the station. If you help me, you'll have a chance to question her and…
well…ensure there is justice."

There are too many questions to ask. I squeeze my eyes shut and
bury my head in my hands, trying to block it all out. Rocher is playing
a game with people's lives. This is his attempt to play a game with mine,
to get me to do what he wants. For him, breaking people, manipulating
people, that's better than killing them. I only have his word for what's
been said, what he's told me.

"I don't believe you," I mumble.

"Sorry, what's that?"

I raise my head and look at him again. "I said, I don't believe you."

Rocher's about to go on, but then there's a rumbling noise outside
and the room moves, like we're in the middle of an earthquake, but of
course, we're in orbit, there are no tectonic plates to shift underneath
us. Rocher reacts immediately, leaping to his feet and running towards
the door. "Damn it! What's going on?"

He's outside and in the hallway, talking to his people. The replies are
muffled, and I only catch the odd word or two, but the orders Rocher
issues in response are loud and clear.

"Establish contact with Team 2 and make sure they are aware of
the situation. These developments are already causing us to waste
more time!"

Team 2? Who is Team 2? I don't hear a reply. I get the sense Rocher
and the others have moved away from the door, out of earshot.

I'm standing up, looking around the office, trying to gain an
advantage, seeing what Rocher might have left behind in his urgency.

The room has been cleared. They knew they'd be keeping me here,
away from their other hostages. Either I crossed a line when I killed his
people and they're planning to use me and murder me when they no
longer need me, or everyone on this station is going to die.

Rocher knows he won't get what he's demanding from Fleet and
Mars CorpGov. *If he already knows that, then what is he really after?*

If I'm going to live, I need an advantage. I need to surprise him, to
be something he won't expect.

The chit is still on the desk. I reach for it, then stop. *No. Too obvious.*

My eyes rest on the book. I could tear out pages in some petty act of revenge to try and get into Rocher's head. Would it work? I've no idea.

I'm looking around. Trying to find something I can use. The meds are making the floor seethe. I can't stand still. There has to be something he's left behind. Something he's missed.

Then I see it. The comms bead, left on the desk. I reach out and grab it.

CHAPTER TWENTY-NINE

Holder

Everything hurts, but I'm alive!

The corridor from the shuttle dock is a blackened ruin. The flashfire oxygen explosion scorched metal and plastic, tearing through the safety doors and carving me out an escape route.

Pain is a state of mind, a series of physiological signals sent to the brain to warn about damage and the risk of further harm. But this isn't my body; I'm just hitching a ride.

Alison Wade is damaged. Maybe Alison Wade will wake up in pain and wonder what happened. How she burned her arms and face. How she took a bullet to the shoulder.

By then, I don't know where I'll be.

Fuck this shit. Fuck it with a spoon. Every second I'm alive, breathing with these lungs, is a moment of rebellion and defiance. A moment of freedom from where I was.

I'm crawling on my elbows and knees. I need to get away from here. The insurgents will be back. The man who I spoke to through the window will know I'm the one who did this. He's the brains behind the hijacking of the station, I know it.

I need to find him and kill him.

Right now, I'm in no state to kill anyone.

Pain is a state of mind.

I'm on my feet, stumbling away from my wrecked prison. There has to be an emergency medical station around here somewhere. I guess they will use the same symbols; there would be no point in changing them. I'm moving as fast as I can. I still have a pistol; it dangles in my left hand.

Movement ahead. I stop, raise the weapon. No time to think. A man rushes around the corner. I squeeze the trigger and he goes down, gasping out the last of his life. His blood stains the wall.

In war, the world becomes precise. Kill or be killed. You cannot afford anything that might make you hesitate, that might make you care for a split second; if you let that in, you die.

I'm kneeling by the man. He struggles, trying to push me away. His right hand clutches at his throat, where the bullet caught him. He's trying to hold himself together, as bright red blood rushes through his fingers, drenching his clothes.

I touch the pistol to his forehead and press the trigger again, ending his life in a shower of broken flesh and bone. I take his rifle and his ammunition. Then I'm moving again, running away.

This can't go on. Sooner or later, they're going to catch up with me. I'm leaving a trail of bodies for them to follow. I need to find somewhere to hide.

The corridor opens out into a huge, open space. This is some sort of merchants' plaza. It's dark, the trade kiosks are all boarded up and closed. Neon signs flicker on and off, casting crazy shadows all over the place. Broken glass litters the floor. I can see bullet holes in the walls. There's been fighting here, between the station security services and the insurgents.

There are a hundred places to conceal myself. If I can break into one of these shops, I can hunker down somewhere and hope they pass me by.

Every door I pass has a security lock. However, there's a terminal midway down the concourse. Alison Wade's thumbprint gets me access to a schematic of the block. I try to access station staff functions, but these are greyed out. I guess they've already started going through the user directories, eliminating some of the privileges and controls.

I manage to locate the auto-medic. I stumble towards it, trying to move as quickly as I can. Synth skin and some sort of high-intensity painkiller will help, at least for a while.

I'm in the chair. I don't remember the last few steps. I must have blacked out. I key in the auto-diagnostic sequence and sit back, letting the machine do its work. It's talking to me, but I don't care about the details. I just let it do the work.

I hardly feel the needles when they come. The numbness they bring is relief. I've tried to distance myself from this body, but I can't really disassociate myself.

I'm—

*　　*　　*

"Welcome back, Natalie."

I open my eyes to see a face I remember. A big man in a white suit, flashing me a gap-toothed smile.

"You're him," I say. "The one I can't remember."

The man nods. "We've discussed this before, many times in fact. There's a block in your mind that prevents you from accessing memories of me. It was built into you in the first days of your conditioning."

"So, why are you here now?"

"Because it is necessary, and we don't have much time." The man is standing right in front of my chair, his face inches from mine. "Is it true they killed Boipelo?"

I remember the name – the deputy governor. I nod. "Yes. One of the station administrators told me that."

"Then they don't intend to free anyone. If they did, she would be their chief hostage, their best bargaining chip." The man steps away. My eyes don't leave him. The memories are there, just out of reach, just beyond my….

"Your name is Emori," I say.

He flinches from me, backs away, his eyes wide. "That's impossible, you can't know that."

"I've always known," I say. "You just hid it from me."

The memories come then, an overwhelming deluge of moments, just like this one. I was in the same place, sat in a chair, when he came. Every time the same, speaking to me about his plans, revealing what he wanted, safe and secure in the knowledge that I would never remember.

But now, I do remember.

I can barely breathe as each conversation overlays in my mind. I'm drowning in moments restored to me, moments stolen through a trick. The walls are coming down. Everything...every lifetime, is coming... back....

"You know all of it," Emori says. He recoils, turning away from me towards the laboratory door. "Summers! Summers! Get in here! Shut her down! Shut her—"

★   ★   ★

I'm back in the auto-medic in the merchants' plaza, all the new memories whirling around in my mind. There's a cold metal barrel pressed against my forehead.

"If you move, you die," a man says. He's wearing a torn station security uniform and holding a pistol with shaky hands. His face is streaked with dirt and blood. "I need to know which side you're on."

"I'm on my own side," I say. "But if you're asking if I'm with the terrorists, then no." I raise my hand very slowly and tap the stitched name badge on my uniform. "I'm Alison Wade, from the station administrator's office."

The gun lowers. "You're a long way from your desk, Wade. How did you get away?"

"I was lucky." I sit up slowly. The pain from before is now a fuzz. I feel different, more of myself in some way. The station is familiar to me, I have been here in the plaza before, many times in fact, in days that were happier. I have laughed here and shared moments with friends.

I look at the man again. I recognise him. We were not close, but now I know his name. The memories are there, *I can remember*. "Thomas?"

He frowns. "You know me?"

"I know who you are." I reach for the needle in my arm and withdraw it. The readout on the auto-medic suggests I have been given a transfusion and a glucose injection, as well as a healthy dose of pain medication. Whatever has happened, it's more than that though. There's a readout on my injuries too. The bullet has been removed from my left shoulder, the wounds treated, and synth skin applied. Apparently, I broke two ribs as well. They've been reset. The recuperation advice is that I rest up and don't go anywhere for the next three to five days.

Yeah....

"How many are left?" I ask Thomas.

"Five," he replies. "We're hunkered down in Altobelli's." He inclines his head to my right.

I stand up and glance over in that direction. The battered store was once a luxury goods emporium, selling those little trinkets from Earth that gave you a reminder of what you were missing. I remember browsing those shelves, looking for things, and those pangs of homesickness for a world where you could step outside and feel the sun on your face.

Memories of another life. A life I never lived. *What is happening to me?*

Thomas grabs my hand. I start and pull away. "You need to come with me," he says. "They'll find us if we stay out here."

I hesitate. Right now, I am powerful; before, I felt empty and uncertain. The tangle of knowledge I have access to promises answers to all sorts of things, but I haven't had time to sift through it. Every moment is a discovery of histories and pasts I never experienced.

Alison Wade lived here. I am Alison Wade, but I am not Alison Wade.

I nod at Thomas and follow him across the plaza towards Altobelli's. Every step is like an explosion. Memories swirl around me from lifetimes I have not lived. There are ghosts in my mind, personalities that are part of me, but held apart through constructed walls. Those walls are collapsing, the pasts are drowning me, I can't breathe....

I stumble, my knees slap against the hard-tiled floor. I remember being below ground in a confined space, ready to die for a cause I thought I believed in.

A revolution against the corporate hegemony. I blew myself up in a hole to wreck the solar array in the Atacama Desert. I was sent there as part of a terrorist cell, only I wasn't really part of a terrorist cell, I was a hired mercenary, constructed by Emori and Doctor Summers to do exactly what they wanted.

Whose side am I on?

"Wade? What's wrong? Please, get up, we need to move!"

His hand is on my shoulder. Again, he's touching me without my consent. I shrug him off and stand up. "Do that again and we'll have issues," I warn.

"Sorry, but we need to get out of here!"

There's something on the floor. I have to blink a few times to focus on it. A trailing wire, running over to a large cylinder, next to one of the gantry support pillars. There's a panel attached to it. Memories of several lifetimes recognise what I'm looking at. I recognise the design; I've trained with that design. There's another one a few metres further on with cables running between each of them. That's a wired charge, an IED.

"This place is rigged to explode."

"Yeah, I found these just before I found you," Thomas says. "After we hid, it looks like they rigged the whole place. It doesn't make sense."

"It does if they're martyrs." Another piece of the jigsaw slots into place. I remember Jim telling me the terrorists had killed Boipelo. Why execute the deputy governor of the Mars colony if you're looking to negotiate? "They've no intention of letting anyone get out of this alive."

I hear voices to my right. I look around. Figures are emerging from the entrance I used to get in here. More of the insurgents, sent to find out what caused the second explosion. They're after me.

I'm unarmed. I left my weapon by the auto-medic. Thomas has a pistol in his hand. I grab his gun, level it and shoot.

The first figure pitches forward, face-down into the rubble. Immediately, his companions melt into the shadows, seeking cover. I do the same, dropping to the floor and rolling towards the archway entrance to Altobelli's. Thomas is stumbling after me, crouching against the locked doors. "You've let them right to us," he says. "You've killed us."

"Not yet," I reply. The gun is in my hand. My arm is steady. There's a flicker of movement and a flash as I fire again, sending another figure spinning away to crash out of sight.

"You can't fight them all," Thomas says.

"Then you best get that door open," I counter. "And there best be a back way out of the store."

Thomas swears, but I can hear him at the keys on the console – an old numerical pad. I remember that the shop owners all had their own locking codes. Security were given overrides, but the whole place isn't on the main system, an advantage when your enemy has control of the computer network.

"Okay, it's open. But they'll follow us in."

I'm looking around, trying to see any way to prevent that. There isn't one. "They won't risk a confrontation in here, not while everything's rigged."

"But they'll see us," Thomas says, "and, once they know where we are, they'll isolate that section of the station. They've hacked the computer network. We can't override that from here."

I try to grin, but I'm not sure how much confidence my quirked lips convey. "They'll try. They tried to seal me off like that before, but it didn't stick."

Thomas scowls, but he puts his shoulder against the door and shoves. It opens. "Okay, after you," he says.

I move past him and push his pistol into his hand. "Thank you," I say and step into the darkness of the store.

CHAPTER THIRTY

Shann

"Dug, it's time we had a conversation."

I'm alone on the bridge, the low gravity pushing me into my chair. Le Garre has transferred manoeuvring control to my console. There isn't much to do; the thruster adjustments to our orbit are minimal and the computer is handling most of it.

But I don't trust the computer entirely, not while I know Duggins is in there, slowly unravelling.

The viewscreen showing an exterior image of the space station goes dark, then the close-up face of our chief engineer appears. "You know then?"

"Johansson guessed. I think the others suspect as well."

Duggins sighs. "You can trust me, Captain. I'll get you back to Phobos."

I nod. "I know you don't want to hurt any of us. But there may come a time when we have to make a decision."

"That's murder."

I flinch. The words I was going to say choke off in my throat. I'm seeing the bloodied head of Rocher, my hands are around his neck as I smash his skull into the floor, again and again.… "I don't want to make that call, Dug. Believe me. I've lost enough crew already."

"Yeah." He sighs again. I look up and see him staring out of the screen. Those huge eyes, five or six inches across. He's looking right at me. "You don't know what it's like, dying by inches. Your mind unravelling. I have memories of knowing things, but every time I reach for them, they fade away."

I shrug. "I can't claim to understand or be able to comprehend what you're going through. Maybe there's a comparison with a degenerative condition, like Alzheimer's or something? I don't know. But that doesn't mean I don't give a shit. You're my friend, or at least, what's left of my friend. I want you to survive, to live, whatever that means."

"Good of you to say."

"Is there a way of pausing the process? Putting you into some sort of cold sleep or cryo state?"

"I'm enmeshed with the ship's computer. If you box me, you box the ship's controls. Extricating me would be impossible and there isn't room to create a compressed image, or at least, there won't be room until it's too late."

"Too late?"

"I'll have degenerated too far by that point. Some of the ship's basic functions will probably have stopped working too."

"You'll still be alive though."

"I don't call that living."

I nod. "Sometimes, there are no good choices," I say and mean it. This is hard. In all we've been through, I've not had to make the sacrifice call.

I tap a few buttons on the screen, trying to access the data feed we've established with the station. Johansson's code has been installed as a batch script to run whenever we try to obtain access to something. It takes a second, but then I get access to the station console. "Erebus. That's an unusual name."

"The Greek god of primordial darkness," Duggins says.

"Has the name been used on any Fleet missions, or previous designations by Earth scientists?"

"There are references to the Martian crater situated within the Margaritifer Sinus quadrangle and the Erebus Montes mountains in the Diacria quadrangle. But there are no other current geographical applications of the term."

"What about older project names?"

Duggins frowns, a gesture that I guess is designed to cover the processing of a search over the information he has available. "There was an Erebus project associated with the Avensis mission in 2049. The details are not available to me."

"Have you analysed the computer system over there?" I ask. He knows what I'm suggesting.

"It was the first thing I did when we got a link. The station network has about the same capacity as this one. If we initiated a transfer, I'd be marooned out here, left to die by inches alone. At least on the *Gallowglass*, I'm with friends."

Yeah, I can understand that. "What about a backup? Duplicating yourself to increase your chances?"

"The duplicate would still be me, left alone on an unmarked space station. No thanks."

"Good point."

There's an audible pop in the comms bead. "Travers to *Gallowglass*?"

I touch the microphone at my lip. "Receiving you, Lieutenant, how's it going?"

"We've run into a problem."

"Okay, explain."

Travers's face appears on my screen. He's removed his helmet. He must be breathing *Erebus* air. "Our entry to the station has triggered some sort of automated brief/debrief procedure, Captain. We're in a room. It's quite a place, like someone's penthouse suite. We've discovered there's a hibernation system on the station and seven pods are being thawed out from cryo."

I join the dots together pretty quickly. "They are a replacement crew."

"Yes. It all seems like normal procedure. Crews are switched out each time they visit the station, as part of the repair and resupply process."

The rationale is sound – it makes sense, horrific sense. In space, human beings have to be treated as calculated commodities, the required resource inputs weighed against workload, skills, etc. However, the way they are using these clones takes it all to another level. "Are they on to us? Do they know we're not the actual *Gallowglass* crew?"

There's some discussion on the other end of the line. I can see Travers is talking to Johansson. She shakes her head and he's back with me. "No, we're clear for the moment, but not for much longer I'd guess."

"What have you found out?"

"Quite a lot. Johansson's managed to establish data access, but we're not getting as far as we should. She thinks the root key might be compromised."

"Can you make it back to the ship?"

"Yes, I think so."

"Then get back here as soon as you can. We don't need to be taking any more risks."

"Aye, aye."

"Captain," Duggins says, "I trust you're aware of the ramifications of that?"

"You mean the root key?"

"Yes."

I'm thinking about it. The key Johansson used to hack her way into this ship is the basis on which we've been able to operate it and stay alive. If the station's computer system is not responding in the same way the *Gallowglass* has responded, that suggests it isn't actually a root key for the station and that there might be some sort of administration that has become aware of us.

It's a lot of assumptions, but that doesn't mean I should dismiss the concern.

"Dug, what kind of data traffic are we getting from the station through the umbilical?"

"Low-level positional queries at the moment," Duggins replies. "I'm not picking up any database access requests. The station appears to be waiting for us to do something."

I'm frowning, staring at the schematic of the rotating ring on my screen. *Waiting for what?* "Travers, tell me about the room you're in. Send over a video feed and describe it to me."

"Okay, Captain." The lieutenant moves back from the screen and the perspective changes as I key in the command to access his bodycam. Three separate windows appear, showing the feed from Sam, Johansson and Travers. It's a surprise. Beautiful dark wooden panelling, blended lighting and a massive glass vista of rolling hills and fields. The skies are a fiery mix of red and orange hues.

Red sky at night....

This is all a distraction, but there's something about the room, something familiar. I notice a strange office chair left in the centre. "Travers, what's that?" I ask.

"A cheap seat from Earth I guess," Travers says. "There's dried blood on the back and broken zip ties on the arms. Looks like someone was held here."

I lean back from the screen and look away, trying to remember. "Duggins, do you have access to any data from the *Khidr?*"

"Not unless you brought it over with you, Captain."

"Never mind then." *Damn.* There's something about that room. The dark furniture, the low-level lighting, and the strange office chair that immediately makes you think you're looking at a location on Earth. I've seen all of that recently. *Where did I see it?*

Then it comes back to me – *Admiral Langsley!* In the background behind his tense and tired face, there was the same wood panelling and I'm sure I saw the edge of a black office chair. Could the message have been recorded here and sent to us? Could the date stamp have been faked?

"Captain, we're on the clock," Travers says. "What do you want us to do?"

The words bring me back to the situation at hand. "Travers, show me the access port Johansson's plugged into."

The camera moves. My perspective is over Johansson, who is sat at a polished dark wood table. She's plugged a portable screen into a connector in the centre and is holding it with the jury-rigged clamp she was using earlier as she fumbles over the keys with her left hand. I can see her struggling. I'm sympathetic.

"Ensign, run a scan on your data connection. We need to know if the station is running access requests on your screen."

Johansson looks up at Travers's camera. She's frowning. "Captain, it's a standard-issue portable screen. It has a Fleet firewall, which would notify me if there was a breach through the—"

"Not if the application doing the breach had all the same access to Fleet-authorised development tools and looked exactly like a Fleet program. Please, just do it."

Johansson nods. The fingers of her left hand slip awkwardly across the screen, but after a minute or two, she accesses a terminal command screen and runs a connection diagnostic. "There's three programs here I don't recognise. I mean, I don't know all the applications our system uses, but—"

"You need to sever that connection now, Ensign! Get back to the ship with whatever you have."

Travers's hand appears on the screen. He grabs the cable and yanks it out of the socket. "We're on our way, Captain," he says.

Then, abruptly, all three of the camera feeds go blank.

I'm checking the connections, trying to re-route and reconnect. "Dug, get them back, now!"

"Trying, Captain, but the links have been severed. The umbilical is no longer providing access and the root key is being rejected. I'm getting some pushback too – an application from the station server is trying to override our ship command functions."

I want to throw the screen across the room, but that won't help. I've given in to rage before; I can't give in to it now. "Shann to Le Garre, were you monitoring?"

"Aye, aye."

"You heard everything?"

"Yes, Captain."

I take a deep breath. "Okay, get down to airlock control. Make sure you're armed. I want you and Arkov to get Rocher out of storage."

Le Garre doesn't respond for a moment. I can hear her thinking, examining the rationale behind my order. Is she going to object? Is she going to second-guess me at every turn? We can't afford that. We have to work together.

I wait.

Then she replies. "Okay, Captain. I'm on my way."

CHAPTER THIRTY-ONE

Johansson

There's a noise. I look up from the screen to see the room doors slide shut.

Sam rushes across the room towards them, but he can't get there in time. He turns around towards me and Travers, confirming my fears.

"We're locked in."

My first thought is about the door. I grab the cable from Travers's hands, reconnect it and tap in the root key from before. This time an error message comes up.

Unauthorised command code.

I pull out the cable again and turn to Travers, who looks concerned. "The station computer has kicked us out. The passcode which enabled us to take over the *Gallowglass* doesn't appear to have the same access privileges here. Either someone's on board and has been monitoring us as we came in, or we've alerted the system by doing something wrong."

"The captain told you to disconnect, *Ensign*."

"We needed to confirm what was happening, *sir*."

"How do we get the door open?" Sam shouts from the other side of the room.

I stand up from the chair and move towards him. "Either we isolate the computer control, we trick it, or we do something violent to the panels."

"We don't have time to waste on solutions that might not work," Travers says. "Chase, cut it open."

Sam nods and pulls a handheld hull cutter from his belt, the same hull cutter he used when we went on our little EVA excursion to fix the *Khidr*'s communication antenna and defuse a bomb. That feels like a lifetime ago. He kneels down in front of the door and activates it, sending up a shower of sparks. This kind of work can be dangerous, particularly in an oxygen-rich environment. If he's not careful, his suit could be compromised; but then, this isn't the first time he's had to cut up a door.

"The station may have some sort of detection and countermeasure system," Travers says.

I shrug. "We can only deal with what's in front of us." I'm worried about the cryopod thawing time. The data I got from the station confirmed what we're due to encounter. "In about ten minutes or so, a replacement set of Rocher clones will be walking around this station."

"We need to not be here when they arrive," Travers says.

I'm looking around the room. Thinking about what I read in the data we downloaded from the station network before we were shut out. "The standard procedure is that a ship will arrive here, the clone crew will disembark, wait in this room to be debriefed whilst the replacement crew are thawed out. Then the new crew boards the ship and the old crew goes into cryosleep. That means our replacements won't necessarily be coming here. They'll be heading for the ship."

"So that may give us some time," Travers says.

"Only if the station doesn't have some additional security countermeasures, like you suggested," I reply.

Sam has cut through about half a metre of the door. The smell of burned metal is pretty strong, and I can see the line of scorched panelling smoking as it cools.

"How long?" I ask him.

"Another five minutes, maybe a bit longer."

"Won't the clones expect us to have docked with the umbilical?" Travers says.

"Maybe, but I'm sure they'll get some sort of briefing or access a terminal in the cryo-chamber," I say. "They'll have an idea where the ship is."

"Then we'll all be heading for the same place, at the same time."

"Pretty much."

I feel helpless. I know I'm going to feel even more helpless as we start to move. The taser is in my left hand, but realistically, if one of the clones gets that close, I'm done. I shiver as I remember the feeling of being shot in the gut and looking into Rocher's cold, expressionless eyes.

I have a computer screen that I can't use strapped to an arm that no longer works how it should. I'm relying on the awkward fumbling fingers of my left hand. Even as I grip the taser, that grip seems weak, as if it could be unpicked by anyone determined to overpower me.

I glance at the screen I'm carrying. The set of downloaded files is displayed in a directory list. There's a batch of videos and action history information. I went for those first so we could get the best possible idea of what this station is for. The former are fairly big, the latter tiny, although they'll take a little bit of assessment to work out what they're all about, out of the context of the station's system.

There's a crackle in my comms bead. "Away team, this is Shann, can you hear me?"

I start and look at Travers, who nods. He heard it too. I touch the transmitter. "Yes, Captain, you're quiet and the signal's pretty weak, but we're receiving you."

"Good. Duggins has bypassed the transmitter protocols and switched to an older analogue mode. We could lose comms at any moment. I need you to do something for me."

"Okay, what do you want me to do?"

"I need you to search that room," Shann says. "I think someone's been there – on this station recently. I think they could still be there."

"Aye, aye." I'm looking around and Travers is doing the same. "Captain, I did get the feeling that we'd walked in after someone else had just stepped out. And that chair in the middle of the room – it threw me."

"Yeah, I get that sense too, Johansson," Shann replies. "I don't know what you're looking for, but anything that gives us a clue…."

I walk over to the wood-panelled wall at the far side of the room. There's a bookshelf with old print titles lined up neatly in a row. I reach for one of them and realise they are fake – a set of plastic inserts, made to look like books. "This whole place is like a performance," I say. "It's all fake."

"I think it was set up to look like Earth," Shann says.

"It's an elaborate fraud when you could just use a virtual environment," I say. I'm knocking the wall panels. They all sound hollow. "The only thing they wouldn't be able to fake is the transponder signal. Every ship receiving comms tracks the location it received its messages from. There's no way they could physically fake an Earth signal like that."

"You wouldn't have to, if the message is picked up from a relay station," Shann replies.

I frown, remembering what Shann said about getting a communique from Fleet command. "You mean the message from Admiral Langsley?"

"Yes, I think it was recorded here."

"Do you think he could still be here?" Travers asks.

"I doubt it," Shann replies. "But if he was, that means a ship left here recently."

"There are bloodstains on the chair," I say. "I saw them when I examined it."

"Can you get a sample?" Shann asks.

I go over to the chair again. There are several plastic sealable pouches in my EVA suit. I take out a knife and scrape at the crusted red flakes, harvesting the powder into one of them. "Done. I'll bring them back for analysis."

"Grea—" Abruptly, the signal cuts off.

"Nearly there," Sam says. I glance up. The tear in the door panel is much larger. He's cut an oval shape and is bringing the line down the far side to complete his work. I'm fairly sure the station won't react to what he's doing, as using a cutter to get into a sealed compartment is standard practice for Fleet retrieval and recovery missions.

It's only then that I realise I'm struggling to breathe.

"Travers!" I grab his shoulder, then start trying to pull on my helmet. He realises what I'm doing and moves towards Sam. "No ox, no ox!" he shouts into the comms.

My helmet clicks into place, sealing me away from the world's noise. Travers's voice takes on that tinny radio sound and I'm watching in a detached way as both he and Sam struggle to get themselves sealed away and activate their suit oxygen systems, but they manage it, and Sam picks up the cutter again. Travers has drawn his sidearm and is aiming it at the door. He glances at me. "Ready?" he asks.

"I guess," I reply and bite my lip.

The sparks stop. The jagged remains of the door clatter to the deck and we have an escape route. Sam drops the cutter. "Charge is out. We're not going to get through any more doors with that." He draws his own pistol and stoops to move through the opening. Travers is right behind him. I'm a step or two behind them both.

This time, the overhead lights don't switch on as we move towards our exit. As we move, I'm very aware that I can't turn my head to glance left and right. The bulky awkwardness of the spacesuit makes me a bigger and slower target for anyone who can handle a gun.

"Stay close," Travers says. He's reached an intersection and takes a turn to the right. He's retracing our steps from before. Sam goes to the left and motions for me to go in front of him. Makes sense to let him be the rear guard. I do as suggested, trying to move quickly and keep up.

Ahead, I see a red light. Then a door starts to move, attempting to slide shut and cut us off. Travers starts to run. He reaches the door and grabs the panel, trying to wedge himself in the gap and keep it open.

"Sam, April, help me! Quick!"

I reach the door and find the control panel. I yank open the access panel, jam the taser against the screen and press the trigger, unloading a full charge into the mechanism. The screen flickers and goes out.

The door stops moving.

Travers gets through, I follow. Sam is doing the same when I hear a muffled pop and he stumbles forward. I catch his eye and see a look of concern on his face.

"Sam?"

A moment later he's falling on top of me. I can't hold him up. We hit the ground together and I try to roll, turning him off of me, onto the floor.

There's another pop. Travers has levelled his pistol and fired down the corridor at someone on the other side of the door. Then the control panel flickers on again and the door slides shut.

Travers touches my shoulder. "Are you okay?"

"Yes, but Sam—"

"I'm okay," Sam says. "I got hit, but I think it pinged off my helmet."

I gather myself and get up, stowing the portable screen and ripping off the improvised holder, leaving it behind. I lock my right arm under Sam's shoulder, grabbing the stump end with my left hand, taking a proportion of his weight helping him up. Travers has him on the other side.

"Sam, your suit might be compromised," I say.

"We get to the hatch and then we worry about that," Travers snaps.

We keep moving, supporting Sam between us. Gradually, he's able to recover and take his own weight. I tap the comms unit on my wrist, trying to raise the *Gallowglass*. The receiver cycles through all the channels and all the available frequencies, but there's nothing. It's as if the ship just isn't there. I know Shann wouldn't have left us, but we might as well be alone.

All of this is hard. Every turn means another chance of ambush, but we can't slow down. I'm focused on my feet, trying to keep moving forward. If any of the people who were shooting at us catch up, we'll be easy targets.

"The lift is just ahead," Travers breathes.

I try to nod in return and then remember I'm wearing a helmet. "Okay," I reply.

Then we're at the lift. Travers presses buttons and the doors open. Sam stumbles in after. I follow and get my first glimpse of his helmet. There's a gash along the side, just above the ear. It doesn't look compromised.

The doors slide shut. Travers presses buttons, but nothing happens. He starts swearing and I fall to my knees, cursing as well.

Trapped in here. In a lift controlled by the station. How could we have been so stupid?

CHAPTER THIRTY-TWO

Shann

"We're here, Captain."

I swivel the chair around to see Rocher and Le Garre enter the bridge. She's carrying a taser and has a sidearm holstered on her belt. He has plasti-cuff bindings around his wrists.

For once, the superior half-smile he usually greets me with is not there. He looks dishevelled and unfocused. A quick thaw from cryo can do that to you. His eyes are flicking around the room, trying to ascertain the situation that caused me to bring him here, but I anticipated this. All the displays are off, giving him no information to work with.

Instead, Rocher looks at Le Garre, then at me. "No Sergeant Chase or Ensign Johansson to run around for you, Captain? Instead, you have to make the major play babysitter?"

"Take a seat, Rocher." I gesture towards the pilot's chair that Le Garre recently vacated. Rocher moves towards it. As he sits down, I activate the acceleration restraints, pinning him into the seat.

"Is this really necessary, Captain?"

"I'll decide on that when you prove that you can be useful."

"Useful?" Rocher's smile returns. "What is it you need from me? Has something happened?"

I glance at Le Garre. She shrugs. We have to tell him something. "Station Erebus," I say. "You will give us all the necessary codes and procedures to deal with the automated computer system."

Rocher's smile fades. "So, that's where we are. What's the situation?"

"You don't need that information."

"Come now, Captain," Rocher says. "You gained my respect with your speech in the airlock. I'm sure we can work together to resolve this crisis."

I sigh and lean forward in my chair. "The codes and procedures, or we put you back in cold sleep until we reach Phobos. That's it."

"Erebus is a resupply station, specially adapted for this ship and its counterparts. Many procedures require specific identification: thumbprint, retinal scan, blood, DNA and the rest. Some of the identity requirements are unknown to me, but I have the necessary physiology to pass them. You could begin the lengthy process of obtaining samples. I expect the ship's bio-store would be of help, as there are a multitude of organs and tissue types available for your use, but then you would be blundering around in the system. Erebus is not forgiving. I assume that's why Chase and Johansson aren't here? You need me, Captain."

"Don't make me repeat myself again."

"You hacked the *Gallowglass*, Captain. Surely, hacking a space station can't be so different?"

An impasse. This isn't going well. It's an effort to keep calm, to stop myself from digging my fingers into the battered upholstery of my seat. I need to stay in charge of this conversation, but I also need information that I can use. "Explain to me why you would be interested in helping us voluntarily."

"I am a clone, Captain," Rocher says. "There are several agendas you could apply to my motivation. Perhaps I want to be considered an individual? To have a 'real life' like yours? The only way I could do that would be to betray my kin and go against my orders in a romantic attempt to assert my free will."

Le Garre reacts before I can stop her. She's beside him and backhands him across the face with her right hand, the one carrying the taser. "*Ferme ta gueule!* You synthetic shit! You can't expect us to believe any of that!"

Rocher slumps forward in the restraints. Blood drips from his mouth. For a moment, I think he's genuinely hurt, but then he slowly raises his head and smiles again, displaying bloodied teeth. "Make sure you get that in your report, Captain."

"We're not going to believe your time in cold sleep has become a road to Damascus, Rocher," I say. "You have limited room to bargain here; you're alive because you're useful. If you choose not to be useful, you don't need to be using up air."

"You need me as evidence."

"You can be alive or dead for that."

Rocher clears his throat and spits blood onto the floor. He's staring at me and ignoring Le Garre. "Must be difficult for you," he says. "You've sent your people into the station and you can't follow. The generated gravity means you're trapped here, in this room. It must be maddening, knowing they are going to die, unless you can convince me to help you. You're trapped in that chair, just like I'm trapped in this one."

I smile at him, but inside I'm desperate and only just clinging on. I can't lose any more of my crew. "Let's take this step by step. What will it take to get you to give us what we need?"

"You can let me go."

Le Garre inhales sharply, sucking in air between clenched teeth. "You can't be considering—"

I hold up a hand and she stops talking. "Start showing your worth. Get my people out."

"No promises?"

"Neither of us is at a stage where promises would mean anything."

Rocher nods. "Untie me, give me computer access and a connection to the station. I'll see what I can do."

I glance at Le Garre. She seems to deflate as she realises we're going through with this. She steps towards Rocher and keys in the release for his plasti-cuffs. Then she activates the screen in front of him, covering her hands as she inputs her passcodes. When she's done, she angles the screen so Rocher can see and operate it.

"The way you people defeated us," Rocher says. "I'll admit, it was a complete surprise. Someday you'll have to tell me how you managed to take control of our computer so easily."

I don't reply to that, instead, I'm working on my own screen, talking to Duggins.

Give Rocher access to the umbilical line but
monitor his work. Record every keystroke and
activate the camera. I want to see his facial
expressions, anything that could be used to
communicate with someone.

Understood, Captain.

And keep out of sight.

Aye, aye.

Rocher is talking as he types into the screen. "You must have known
it would be dangerous, Captain, sending them over there. I've come to
admire your willingness to gamble, but this seems a risk too far." He
looks up at me. "Did you think your hacking tricks would work on the
station as well?"

I look meaningfully at Le Garre. "Do I need to get the major to
encourage you?" I ask.

"I am capable of multitasking," Rocher says. "You've wrecked the
system, but thankfully the base code of the interface remains the same as
before. Okay, I'm in."

"Disable the system," Le Garre urges. "Get our people out of there."

Rocher looks up from the screen and fixes her with a meaningful
stare. "A hypnotist is able to work successfully by creating a context that
their subject feels comfortable in. You get a man to take off his clothes
by getting him to believe he is alone in the bathroom. I need to do the
same to Erebus Main. I can do that, if I am allowed to work and I'm
made aware of the variables." His eyes return to the display and I can
see something – a flashing red icon reflected on his face. "Variables like
this," he says, gesturing at the image. "You didn't say there were other
Rochers awake on the station."

"Can you shut them down?"

"We aren't machines. Those clones will soon have the same access
to the system that I have." Rocher glares at me. "You need to let me
go over there."

I open my mouth, about to refuse the request, but then close it. I
can't fault Rocher's logic. Asking him to do this, working against other

versions of himself who will think in exactly the same way, act and react just as he does, means we have no advantage, particularly if we keep him here. "What guarantee do I have that you'll return?" I ask.

"None," Rocher replies. "But I'll get your people out and make sure they return to the ship. After that, you're on your own."

Words appear on my screen. Duggins is messaging me – I concur with Rocher's assessment of the situation.

I glance at Le Garre. She looks furious, but she's holding it in check. There's no way she would agree to this if she was in command. Perhaps she wouldn't have sent Travers and the others over to the station either. I still hope we'll have learned something from this, something important that might help us when we reach Phobos.

"Take him down to the airlock," I say to her. "Get him a suit and get him out there."

Le Garre opens her mouth to reply, but I fix her with a look that she knows well enough. Rocher is watching us both; there needs to be no conflict, no disagreement.

"Aye, aye, Captain," she says and draws her sidearm, pointing it at Rocher. "Okay, let's go."

A minute later, I'm alone in the room.

★ ★ ★

…Interim reports on the damage to the world's power infrastructure indicate a substantial shift will be required. Since it would be impossible to commission enough nuclear power to replace the Atacama array, the fossil fuels industries may have to be called upon to bridge the consumption gap for the next ten years. This would ensure an uninterrupted supply that can cope with current demand levels.

The economic impact of this temporary shift will be substantial. Small companies with oil, coal and gas reserves available will stand to make considerable profit as market demand will allow them to establish a high margin. There is some evidence of co-ordinating planning in this area, with several cash-rich conglomerates buying up legacy holdings in Nejd and Siberia. Our agents should investigate these transactions and present their findings to the World

Trade Council, as there may be enough evidence to convict on corporate terrorism charges. Although, it may be difficult to establish the owners of these new holding companies and the source of the money that has financed them.

To summarise, I would recommend that the board take action to consolidate our position and redirect investment from the CorpGov colonial strategy. This is unlikely to remain sustainable in the short and medium term....

CHAPTER THIRTY-THREE

Drake

The discarded comms bead is in my pocket and I'm sat back down on the couch when Rocher returns.

He comes in looking stressed and distracted. He moves towards me, pointing a finger in my face. "The woman, Wade. You must know more about her. I need to know everything you know."

I shake my head and the room spins a little. The drugs are still affecting me. "I told you everything I know," I say truthfully.

"Is she a contractor? Are you part of her support team? It would make sense to have a medical professional available."

"I...I don't know what you're talking about."

"Yeah...right." Rocher steps back and glances towards the door. "I'll be back in an hour and you better have more to say."

He leaves the room and I take a moment to savour my small victory.

Years ago, when I was a child, a boy at school who everyone was scared of gave me his lunch money to look after while he played football. When the game didn't go his way and he started to pick on my best friend, I told him I was keeping it. I timed my announcement carefully, just as my parents arrived to pick me up. He couldn't get to me, so I got away with theft.

That night, I felt so guilty. I found the nearest slot machine and wasted the coins as fast as I could.

Right now, I feel a little like that. Rocher might be an asshole, but if I believe his explanation, he has reasons for doing what he's doing.

I pull out the comms bead, switch it to receive only, and place it in my right ear. Immediately, I can hear Rocher's voice.

"Okay, receiving now, took me a minute to initialise and encrypt a new transmitter."

"What happened to the one you had?"

"I don't know. I can't remember."

This doesn't make sense. All the voices are Rocher, as if he's talking to himself.

"What's the current situation? How far have you got?"

"The charges are all set. We're moving to the evacuation point. We'll be ready to leave on schedule, in just over two hours from now."

"Any updates on the ship?"

"Nothing so far, unless you've heard something?"

"Not yet."

I'm trying to rationalise the conversation and add it to what I already know. The mention of explosives confirms what I first thought. This isn't a kidnapping operation. Rocher plans for everyone to die. He's going to blow up the station in orbit. A grand, horrifying political gesture to undermine the rule of Mars CorpGov.

The only way anyone is going to survive is if he doesn't succeed.

I stand up and stumble. The drugs are still in my system and still having an effect. It's hard to focus. I have to concentrate to keep my balance. If Rocher came into this room right now, I'd have no chance against him.

The only mistake he's made is leaving the comms bead, giving me some information. It's a tiny advantage, easily squandered if I were to switch over to transmit and tell everyone on the channel. I'd be talking to the insurgents, who all believe in the cause. There's no chance in making a difference to them.

I need another advantage.

I move to the door. It's been coded and sealed. The trick I pulled in the storeroom earlier won't work here, even if I had the equipment to try it. I'm looking around the room for something I can use.

There was office equipment in here before they moved everything out. I locate the power sockets and service panel. It's held in with standard push screws – the sort every technician has a portable driver to remove and refit. I don't have that kit and if there was a kit in the room, Rocher would have confiscated it.

I'm looking at the furniture. There's nothing I can break up and use. The seat and couch are both standard issue acceleration systems with their internal gyroscopes, deployable strapping, magnets and liquid cushioning. I might be able to tear open the fabric, but I doubt it. Everything has been designed to be robust and resilient.

About the only thing I could do is jam my fingers into the power terminal and hope the electric shock would end my life quicker, just to spite Rocher and his plans. But it wouldn't make a difference and I'd lose any chance of being part of the solution.

There's a box in the corner by the door. I almost missed it. I kneel in front of it. There are straps around it. They've been bolted to the deck, to ensure it stays exactly where it is.

My fingers fumble at the catch. I slide the bolt back, releasing the lid. I open the box.

There's an electronic beep. Steam emanates from within. There's padding inside and a transparent plastic bag, frosted and rigid.

I scratch away the frost and get a glimpse at what's inside.

A head. A human head. Someone I know.

Augustine Boipelo. Deputy Governor of Mars.

I'm sat down on the couch again. I don't remember sitting down, but I need to. My head is spinning. *Boipelo? What was she doing here? They've killed her. Why would they kill her?*

I feel very alone and vulnerable. I'm looking at my hands. They are pale with cold, traces of the frost make my fingers wet. I can't stop them shaking, no matter how hard I try.

Whatever Rocher has given me is working its way through my body, gradually making me feel worse and worse. I know the plan, I know what these people are doing, but I can't get out and tell anyone. I can't help, I can't make a difference – that's the most despairing thing and it goes against every fibre of my being. My whole life has been about trying to be a positive contribution to society, to be a healer, a generous person, a loyal friend, a considerate lover, all of it.

This is the worst. Being stuck, being trapped and frustrated.

Boipelo is dead.

I'm tired. The energy and excitement of my victory in finding the comms bead is long gone. I lie down, pluck the transmitter from my ear, and return it to my pocket.

I close my eyes.

★   ★   ★

Lorraine and I were in Serbia for a holiday. I'd worked too hard, as usual, and had to be persuaded to break my routine and go, but we'd booked in advance and I hate seeing these things wasted.

Back when we were together, Lorraine learned to make her own life around my office hours. All she had to do was be there when I got home, with a strained smile and a set of stories about what I'd missed out on. I listened to what she told me and engaged with all the latest developments, not because I was suspicious, but because I was living vicariously, totally absorbed in my work.

Many of us were like that. We were ghosts, haunting the wards of the hospital, watching the latest casualties come in, dealing with them and trying not to care as they died on operating tables and trolleys outside. War is awful. There's no good side to people being mutilated for a cause. For the most part, soldiers think what they're doing is worth the risk, right up until the moment they are torn apart by gunfire, or worse.

The corporate wars in old Europe were illegal and invisible. According to the news media, they weren't happening. Nothing would disturb that idyllic, decadent, tourist image of crumbling classical civilisation and enlightenment. As a medical contractor, I was earning good money for my continual trauma, the kind of money that you know has bloodstains all over it. I was there to patch up the wounded who came through one door and send them out through another.

Two weeks in Novi Sad was supposed to be a respite from three months in Leipzig. Lorraine had flown out ahead of me and organised our itinerary. I'd literally left a man on an operating table and got in a heli-carrier to join her.

I remember us sitting at a coffee table outside a refurbished establishment. It was early morning at the height of summer. A crystal-clear blue sky above us and that fresh air you get while the sun is still peeking over the mountains in the distance. I'd managed to sleep, although the soft bed wasn't something I was used to.

Two steaming cups were on the table between us. Actual authentic coffee. I can still smell it.

"Emerson, I need to tell you something."

"Okay."

That look on her face. Nervous? Maybe. In hindsight, she knew that what came next would mean big change for both of us.

"Emerson, I'm seeing someone else."

I didn't reply. I just stared at her. Behind that stare, I was processing, trying to work out how I felt about what she'd said, trying to work out what it meant to me.

I wasn't angry, or jealous. We'd been together six years and hadn't specifically said we were exclusive, but we were living together and *we* was how I perceived the world. All the shit I took from the corporation was to make moments like that, in the sun, drinking coffee with someone I loved.

Loved? Love? Maybe I understand the difference now.

Slowly I came out of myself and re-inhabited that stare, trying to read her. She'd moved on. That was why she felt she could tell me. This wasn't an argument or a heated moment of passion where we'd fall out, break up, and come back. She'd already worked out her new life and this was about severing the final ties.

"We're supposed to be here for two weeks," I mumbled. "How's that going to work?"

Lorraine shrugged. "I can stay, or I can go. It's up to you."

I decided she should stay. We toughed it out for two days or so, but things just didn't work. Conversation dried up – I had nothing to say to her anymore. I wasn't angry, but she was only there out of some kind of misplaced obligation, to try and salvage a friendship, I guess.

On the third morning, I told her she should go, and she did, packing her things and walking out of the hotel. I watched her leave from the balcony of our room. Then, on impulse, I ran downstairs and decided to follow her.

I still wasn't angry, but I was curious. She must have made a contingency plan. Where would she go? Who would she meet? In a way, I was disturbed with my own emotional state. This strange numbness, the nothing that I felt. Perhaps by pushing it, by getting a glimpse of her new life, I'd provoke a reaction in myself?

I knew it wasn't right. I knew I should let it go, but I wanted to feel something, to sate something, to get some sort of closure.

Lorraine walked down the street to another hotel. She went inside. I waited a few minutes then followed. She was sat in the lobby with her cases. I managed to stay out of sight and found a perch by the lifts. She waited, I loitered.

Half an hour went by, then a woman came in and spoke to Lorraine. She helped her with her bags into a waiting car. Then they both drove off.

No closure.

I stuck around a little longer, then left and returned to my hotel and our room. The whole place was just like where I'd been – a ruined warzone; the wrecked aftermath of conflict, but you wouldn't know it to look. The neatly made bed, the vacuumed floor, none of it told the story of a relationship that broke down and ended here.

A month later, I applied to join the Mars colonies.

CHAPTER THIRTY-FOUR

Holder

"Pull up a chair."

I'm in a dark, shadowy room. I guess it would have been the staff space behind the shop. Three faces are staring at me in the half-light.

"Hello, Alison," a woman says. She's Asian; Korean; *Ji-Eun*. We've known each other for three years. We travelled up to the station together from Jezero when we were first given our contracts. The memories are like a database now, accessed with a minimum of conscious concentration. If I'd walked into this room an hour ago, I would have no idea who she was.

"Good to see you made it," I say and mean it. She stands up and walks towards me. I know how close we've been and accept her warm hug, holding her close.

"You've changed," she says.

"Yeah, I'll tell you about it sometime," I reply. I can feel the tension in my shoulders ease a little in finding a familiar face down here. "What's the situation? What happened to you all?"

Thomas sighs. "What happened is we lost. They beat us. Pretty soon they'll report back, telling their people we're here and then that's it." He stops speaking and glares at me. Clearly, he thinks it's my fault.

"Come on, Tom. We knew we wouldn't be able to stay here," says a large man in the corner. He starts to get up. I can just about read his badge; it says *Diouf*. "I saw them at the start. They blew the shit out of the medical team and every security team sent in to investigate." He starts picking up things from the room and stuffing them into a duffle bag. "I'm not hanging around here to die."

"Where are you going to go?" Thomas demands, slamming his fist down on the table. He's clearly out of ideas; the fighting in the mall shook him up. I can only guess at what he went through before.

"I need your help," I say quietly into the awkward silence. "There's a way we can end this."

"Oh?"

"We need to kill their leader, Gabriel Rocher."

"The guy from tech support?" Ji-Eun stares at me, frowning. "But he's—"

"The person who let all these people in. Who's been on this station for months, as part of a plan to hijack it and crash it into Mars."

"How do you know all this?"

"I...I can't tell you." All eyes in the room are on me. I return each stare in turn. "You have to trust me," I say. "You need to trust me. The only way we're going to survive this is if we can stop them."

"We tried that already," Thomas says. "People died."

"And plenty more will die if we don't try again," I reply.

"What's your plan?" Ji-Eun says.

The memories are coming back to me, filling in the gaps. Some parts are vivid and clear, others are hazy and indistinct. I remember being a part of the discussions, sitting in a darkened room like this with Rocher and others as the plan was developed. I had been an analyst – one of the minds that looked over the blueprints of the station, identifying its weaknesses and finding ways to exploit them. When my work was done, they sent me back and I went through the usual procedure of having my memories blocked off. I don't know how much Emori knew about it all, but he'd definitely been involved in selling me, instructing Summers in how to set up my brain architecture for maximum efficiency.

I know where Rocher will be holed up. I need to get to him.

"There are two short-term objectives: kill Rocher and defuse the explosives," I explain. "By now, his people have had time to disperse through the entire station. We thought they were hunting us and rounding up all the people; maybe they were, but they were also visiting locations and setting charges. Most of that is done, so we can't unpick all of it. Instead, we need to figure out how they're going to trigger the detonation and do something about that."

"We also need to survive," Ji-Eun says. "What's happened here needs to be explained to Mars CorpGov and…I don't know about you, but I'd like to live."

Dark humour breaks the tension. Even Thomas manages a thin-lipped grin. "The shuttle dock got wrecked a few hours ago." He glances at me. "Was that you?"

"Guilty," I reply. "There was a shuttle there. I don't think anyone survived."

"If we can get to the central hub, we can use an emergency lifeboat," Diouf says. "They are big enough to hold a lot of people. Maybe we could free some of the rest of the hostages?"

"That would take too much time," I say. "But making for the hub is a good idea."

"We have to hope we can stop the station being blown up. That's the only way we're going to save a lot of lives," Ji-Eun says.

"Agreed," I say. "What weapons do you have?"

"Whatever we've managed to scrounge," Diouf says. "The station-issue sidearms don't have the range to compete with whatever they've brought with them." He lifts the strap of a rifle over his head and hands it to me. "I don't know where they got these from. I can't find any maker marks. They're still gas-powered, but more powerful, with a softer ammo casing. That means they travel further and at higher velocity than any station-issue firearm."

"So, you took their guns?"

"Yeah, it was that or die, like everyone else."

I examine the rifle. It's the same as the ones I picked up before. I don't know enough about these gas-powered weapons they use in space, but Diouf clearly does. I have Alison's memories; she doesn't know him, but she's seen his file. Corporate security on Earth, then private transit, then Mars CorpGov. He's experienced, but I doubt he's ever been in anything like this.

"I asked Thomas about a backdoor route," I say. "What have you got?"

"There's a service access corridor that is used for deliveries and a lift to the secondary shuttle dock," Diouf says. "There's no ships, but at least we'd be gone when they break into this place."

"What about cameras?"

"It's covered. They'll know we're there as soon as we move."

"Damn." I'm trying to come up with a plan, but it's too hard. There are too many rooms, doors, cameras, insurgents with guns, all of it between me and Rocher. He'll be in the central administration building – the nerve centre of the station – where I first woke up in this body. "What about outside?" I ask.

"Outside?"

"The station must have some kind of service vehicle? Not something we can use to get off the station, but for inspections and repairs. Like an EVA suit or something?"

Diouf exchanges glances with Ji-Eun. She nods. "Yes, there's an inspection vehicle in the dock. You ever been in space?"

I search my new memories, looking for anything that could be useful, but they just confirm what I known earlier. None of the lives I've lived had experience of being off world, apart from Alison Wade, who never left the comfort of a ship, a dome or a station. "I'll make it work," I say.

"If you don't have training, you'll die out there," Diouf says. "The rotation, the weightlessness, all of it takes training. Most people throw up first time out."

"I don't have time for all that. I need a quick way to get to the administration section."

"Maybe I could take you," Ji-Eun says. "There's a two-seater observation crawler down there. It's got articulated limbs and a deck cutter. If we can get to it, we can climb around the ring to the right place and break in."

"They must have planned for something like that," Thomas says. "Some sort of defence against a hull incursion from Fleet special forces or something."

"We can't second guess ourselves," I say. "Do you have another option?"

"No…. I guess—"

"Then this is what we do." I look at Diouf. He nods. Ji-Eun smiles and Thomas sighs.

"Okay, then let's move."

★   ★   ★

The trade entrance is barricaded from the inside, but the four of us make short work of dismantling it. Diouf has the keycode for the door and moments later we're out in the corridor.

I'm out front, glancing left and right. I know I'm not one hundred percent, but it's difficult to think of myself as Alison Wade, as being contained within this body. All my life, they've talked to me as if I'm a machine. But machines don't need healing, they just get repaired. The auto-medic hasn't repaired me, it's patched me up. The drugs and synth skin sutures are holding me together, making sure all the wet organic goop that makes up this body stays together, like some kind of bag.

I'm holding a rifle. My damaged shoulder doesn't hurt, but it's still weak. I need both hands to take the weight. I can't show that weakness though. I'm leading this group. The others are nervous. I can feel their need for me to be strong, to give them purpose.

Above us and on the wall corners I'm noting the security cameras. They swivel as we pass. We're definitely being watched.

We come to an intersection. "Which way?" I ask.

"Left," Diouf says.

I take the left. Ji-Eun is at the back, walking backwards, covering us.

The next intersection. "Right," says Diouf.

I do as he suggests. I have memories of this place, I've been here, a while back with a shipment from the dock that needed command authorisation. Boipelo sent me down. I don't remember why, but I put a signature on the inventory, and it was waved through.

"Take the next left, Alison," Ji-Eun urges.

I do so and the corridor opens out. Other passageways intersect with ours. This is a distribution point for several other areas of the station. We pass two large freight elevators and ahead I can see a thick set of blast doors, the same as the ones I saw at the shuttle dock. They are open.

All too quiet. *All too easy*. I stop, waving to the others to do the same. There are security cameras above the doors. I can see they are active.

"Now what?" Thomas asks.

"Are there any other entrances into the dock?" I ask.

"Yes, there are a couple of others," Thomas says. "But it will take time for us to—"

"Get moving, work your way around and find another way in," I say.

"What about you?"

"Forget about me. Get moving."

I know I need them. That means I need them alive. This is a trap. The security cameras will still pick them up going the other way, but it might give them a bit more of a chance to make it into the dock without being captured.

As for me, Rocher's people are expecting me.

I know now there were several moments in my lifetimes when I have had to step forward, knowing I might never come back. Most soldiers don't realise the consequences until their luck runs out. For me, the danger is right there. I see the risk, I know I will probably die, that's part of what I've been made for.

There are gaps in my mind, moments where I've made the decision and walked through the doors, but afterwards there is nothing else. I know I died in those moments. I always had a safety net – a version of me would always wake up back in the lab with Doctor Summers in his bio-suit. I guess knowing that enabled me to make a choice that could lead to my death.

Not my death, I guess; the other me, the one that actually died.

Now, I don't have the luxury of a second life.

I'm alone. I've been alone for several minutes. The others are gone, their footsteps fading away as they skirt around the dock entrance. Now it's just me.

I need to walk forward. The only way I can spring this trap is by going in, meeting the threat head on.

One step, then another step. Keep moving, through the doors.

Eight figures with rifles are waiting for me.

CHAPTER THIRTY-FIVE

Johansson

"They've drained out the air," Sam says.

I'm sat in the corner of the elevator. The oxygen marker on my suit is descending, the numbers counting down the remaining time I have before I run out of options. At least this time I'm trapped in a metal box with company.

Travers is slumped in the other corner. I can't see his face, but he's not talking. He's supposed to be our leader, but he's struggling.

We need an idea – a plan.

"Hello, April."

The voice is distant, but familiar. It's Rocher. More than that, I know it's our Rocher, the prisoner from the Gallowglass.

"I don't have anything to say to you," I reply.

"Well, then it'll be easier for me to tell you what you need to know." I can hear the mocking smile behind the words. "Make sure all three of you are as far away from the lift doors as possible. The chemicals I'm carrying are volatile and they'd burn through your suits much faster than they'll burn through the doors."

"Good to know." I shuffle back, nudging Sam to do the same. He turns and looks at me, confused. "Are you just talking to me?" I ask.

"Yes, you can tell the others what's going on."

Sam moves back to sit next to Travers. I glance at the doors. There's a dark spot in the centre. As I watch, it expands, and a white spot appears in the middle. The lack of atmosphere means the hull-breaching chemicals we've used before will work safely in here.

"Nearly through," says Rocher. "Once you're out, we'll need to move quickly."

"So you can take us back to your comfortable torture chamber for questioning?"

"So I can get you back to the *Gallowglass*. Shann sent me to rescue you."

I open my mouth and close it again. I can't stop a smile breaking out and banishing the pinched, stressed expression that was starting to make my face ache. I swallow and clear my throat. "How do I know I can trust you?" I ask.

"How can you forget we shared a moment on the ship? I'm hurt, April." The mockery is there again, but he's breathing hard too. Working to break down the door, I guess.

"Shann would never—"

"Shann had no choice. She struck a deal to get you out. Right now, I'm your only hope."

The metal glows red, then white. I can see it peeling away. "Your brethren must know you're here. Erebus Station's computer system must know you are here. How are you going to get us to the exit?"

"By making a trade. You need to give me the code you used to disable the *Gallowglass*."

"You want that in exchange for our lives?"

"Yes. That's what I want."

I try to process this. I've already typed the root key into the station airlock control. The Erebus computer system will have a record of that. Does Rocher know this? If he does, does this mean he wouldn't be able to access the log?

Does that mean he's working for someone else? For himself?

"Why do you want the code?" I ask.

"Because it empowers me," Rocher says. "Your root key gave you unprecedented access to the *Gallowglass* and allowed you to take over the ship. It may provide access to all sorts of other networks, beyond the standard user rights I have from countless briefings from my employer. It makes me dangerous – an individual beyond their control. That's why I want it."

"How do I know you won't use it to shut us down?"

"You don't. That's the point. You don't get to control me, but I get a card to play against the other people who control me. You have the opportunity to make a difference."

I clench my teeth, biting back an angry reply. This Rocher, the Rocher who stabbed me, he is not the Rocher who invaded the *Khidr* and staged a mutiny. This is the Rocher who was overpowered by Sam and taken prisoner. He would have killed me if that hadn't happened.

He'll be in here soon. I glance down at the screen attached to my right arm. All the data we got from the control room is on that device. It needs to get back. Carefully, I unwrap the strapping on the armature and disconnect the screen from its grip. There's a belt pouch I can stow it in.

But he'll be thinking of that, or someone will.

"I can't trust you."

"No, you can't. But you can judge my self-interest. You have something I want. I can provide something in exchange."

I glance at Travers, huddled in the corner. I move towards him and shake him by the shoulder. He looks up at me. His eyes are red, his expression pinched, as if he's in pain.

I hold up the screen and point at him. He nods and takes it from me. There's an exterior pocket on his suit, under the left elbow. He unzips it and drops it inside.

I turn back towards the elevator entrance. The door plate is dissolving rapidly, smouldering as the metal reacts to the breach chemicals in the vacuum. I can see someone outside, moving around. A moment later, the panel shakes and collapses inwards. Rocher's face appears in the gap.

Sam levels his gun. Quickly, I interpose myself. "No! He's here from the ship!"

"He's escaped?"

"No, he was sent to get us out."

Slowly, Sam lowers the gun. Travers gets up and draws his own sidearm, pointing it towards the deck. "Ensign, are you saying we should trust this clone to get us out of here?" he asks.

"I don't think we have any choice," I reply.

Rocher moves back. More of the door crumbles away, revealing the corridor behind him. I can see three other figures, all in matching EVA suits holding rifles. "Come on," Rocher says. "Step through and let's get on with this."

"You cut a deal with them too?"

"In a way. That is one of the reasons only you and I are talking on this channel."

I bend down and move through the jagged remains of the elevator doors. I'm painfully aware of the three rifles aimed at my chest. Rocher steps forward and removes the taser from my belt. There is a small burst of static on the comms and the display indicates we are now on an open channel. "Thank you for your cooperation, Ensign," he says. "It makes all of this so much easier."

I don't reply, but move away from the doors, letting the others out. Sam emerges next and grudgingly hands over his gun. Travers follows him and does the same.

I'm staring at Rocher. I can see that impassive face and those calculating eyes. I can't read him. I couldn't read him when he wasn't in an EVA suit and behind a helmet and visor. I have no idea what will happen to us next.

"Ensign, lead the way to where the *Gallowglass* is tethered. We will follow you."

I glance at each of the rifles trained on me, then turn my back on them and move into the corridor, as instructed. It takes a lot of effort to ignore them, but I'm banking on the fact that Rocher still wants the root key, so he wants me alive until then.

We're moving through the station. It's not far to where we need to be, and within a few minutes we're nearly at the hatch.

As I walk, I'm trying to operate the comms unit and get an open channel to the ship, but there's nothing. Some sort of dampening field is in operation, blocking anything beyond near field communication. The readings on my suit display also indicate that the oxygen has been drained from all of these rooms.

Another twinge of static as Rocher activates the private channel again. "I do think we have something special between us, April," he says. "I regret my rash actions when we first met."

"Is that some kind of apology?"

"It is a reconsideration of the circumstances. I would not have this opportunity if I had succeeded in murdering you."

"So your regret is based on self-advantage?"

"Yes, I suppose so."

We're at the hatchway now. Rocher's hand is on my arm. He nudges me to one side, allowing Travers and Sam ahead, so the three of us are by the sealed exit. "The code, April. Time to deliver."

I glance at the three clones with rifles. "What have you promised them?"

"That you are bartering information from the mission. Knowledge from the *Hercules* anomalies that we were unable to obtain before you captured our ship."

"And they think that's worth letting us go?"

"They are following my lead for the moment. No doubt, they are making contingency plans to recapture you and the *Gallowglass*. I doubt very much they would be prepared to let you all go with our ship."

"And you're okay with that?"

"I told Captain Shann I would get you out. I intend to fulfil that commitment, provided you give me what I want." I can see Rocher smiling behind his suit visor. "Once you are on board the ship and I have what I want, that commitment ends."

"They'll attack the ship. You're throwing us to the sharks."

"I suppose you could look at it that way, but I have faith in your ingenuity. Remember, once you are gone, I will have to deal with them."

Another tweak of static. "Has she transferred the data?" The voice is still Rocher, but colder, more authoritarian. One of the others, I guess.

"Not yet," Rocher says. He puts a hand on my shoulder and turns to face his kin. "She will."

All three rifles are pointed at me now. Captain Shann must have a plan, a way to get us clear of the station without being captured. She must be ready to enact that plan the minute we're back on board.

She will have made a calculated choice sending Rocher over to us. She's prepared to sacrifice him and any knowledge we might have obtained from interrogating him for the safe return of three members of her crew.

"Okay. Ready to receive data?" I ask.

"Ready."

The same tweak of static. I'm on the private channel with the Rocher I know. I've no idea how secure this communication will be, but that's part of the risk. "Encrypt signal, transmitting," I say. I pull open the wrist panel on my suit's right arm, revealing the miniature keyboard. A quick command links it up to the comms. "Here we go."

I remember the code – *two, eight, seven, H, B, five, five*. I start typing, shifting the integers by one – *three, nine, eight, I, C, six, six*. A tiny change. It'd probably take Rocher twenty seconds to figure it out, but it's better than nothing.

I send the code and look at Rocher. His eyes move to read an internal display, then he smiles and nods before switching to the open channel. "I have the data," he says.

"Then you are authorised to proceed," one of the clones replies.

Rocher moves to the door and keys in a sequence. The hatch opens and I see the void beyond. Stars racing around the station in a disorientating swirl that reminds me that we're in motion. No matter how experienced you are in EVAs from a gravity environment, that moment of adjustment remains the same.

I can see the *Gallowglass*, maintaining synchronous orbit with the station. The steel tethers are still in place. I pull out the motorised winch from my belt and activate it.

"You could stay here if you wanted, April."

I hesitate and turn around. Rocher is still standing beside me. "Why would I want that?" I ask.

"You have questions. If you stay here, you'll find answers."

"I'll be dead. I'm not that curious."

Travers clips his winch onto the line and steps through the hatch. Sam follows him, leaving me as the last one to go.

"Final chance," Rocher says.

I stare at him. In a twisted way, he's right. I would find more answers by staying, but I'm very aware of my own limitations. These people have been designed and conditioned to be what they are, to fulfil some sort of mysterious purpose that involves assassinating civilian freighter crews and harvesting alien technology from deep space. Whatever they are doing, it's bigger than me, bigger than them, bigger than all of us.

My only chance to survive is to stay on the surface. To let the wave roll in and crash over the shore.

"Who do you work for?" I ask. "At least tell me that."

Rocher frowns, but then shakes his head. "I serve humanity just like you. We're both cogs in the wheel. Maybe one day we'll both get a chance to be honest with each other, when all of this has played out."

"We'll both be long dead by then."

"Perhaps, but I think you might just make it, Ensign. I've underestimated you before, I'm not going to make the same mistake again."

I clip my winch onto the cable, turn around, and push off from the station. I don't look back.

*　　*　　*

07.08.2118 – Extract from Professor Manuel Enichi's Speech at the World Space Conference in Malmo, Sweden.

Go forth, increase and multiply.

This is our dogma or our doctrine, depending on who you believe.

The capacity for our kind upon this planet is finite. Whilst it is true, the resources of Earth are a bountiful breadbasket, we have learned that we must moderate our excesses to survive as a species. Our ignorance has burned and scarred our home more than once, and the marks of our stupidity are not easily erased.

If such a simple strategy is applied to our colonisation of the stars, we are compounding the same problem.

In the short term, there is the righteous envy of those left behind. Humanity can settle the harsh environments of our solar system, but such an effort requires expensive technology and provides liveable conditions for only a chosen few. In time, more might join them, but it is easier and cheaper if our colonists obey the mantra — increase and multiply. Hand down your place to two children and they to four grandchildren. The interplanetary colonies are no respite for the hardships of the North American Wars or the scarred deserts of Australia. There is no lifeboat for the poor to take them away to the stars and a new life.

At least not in any numbers that will make a difference.

The dominant hegemony of corporations has seduced the governments of this world. This hegemony controls the means of transit. These new worlds are being exploited for profit, their resources bartered to pay for the enormous costs of travel and survival. In time, such costs will reduce, but the prices will remain the same. The margins will increase and the rich will gorge upon their investment.

The only answer is to see the problem from another angle; another direction. Our means must be wholly self-sustained, relying on nothing developed or licensed from their infrastructure, else they discover our intent — to break the chains, the gears and the cogs of their corporate machine. We shall labour in secret and provide an alternative.

We shall create a path for those who cannot make a path for themselves and we shall give them the stars.

CHAPTER THIRTY-SIX

Shann

"Okay Captain, they're on board."

"How many have returned?"

"Three. As expected, no Rocher. Johansson has the downloaded data."

"Thanks, Arkov." I key up a tactical screen that displays the *Gallowglass* course plot alongside Erebus Station. Le Garre is in the pilot's chair. She turns around towards me.

"Now what?" she asks.

"As soon as we break clear, they'll attempt to stop us," I say. "What options do they have?"

"Unknown," Le Garre replies. "Our scans of the station don't reveal any weapons, but they are bound to have something, plus we don't know who they could be talking to."

"We've detected no transmissions."

"That doesn't mean there haven't been any. If there was a ship here recently, they could alter course and try to intercept us." Le Garre shrugs. "Either way, we're vulnerable for the first hour or so, as we accelerate. After that, rockets and torpedoes won't catch us, and lasers would have to be targeted incredibly precisely and with enormous power."

"So we have the advantage?"

"Unless they have some other means of attack, I think so."

I'm hesitating. This is a moment of pause, where two combatants size one another up. The moment I initiate our withdrawal, sever the tethers, and order Le Garre to manoeuvre the ship away from the station is the moment we test that advantage.

Another window appears on my screen. It's Johansson. She's still in her EVA suit, her face streaked with sweat. "Captain, they have the root key."

"What?"

"I had to give Rocher the root key to get out of there. You need to shut down all comms, immediately!"

I key up the services screen. "Duggins, did you get that?"

"Yes, Captain. Shutting down all external comms."

"Le Garre, cut the cables, get us out of here."

"Aye, aye."

The ship lurches, throwing me back into the seat at an awkward angle. We're pulling away from the station, the tactical plot of our course recalibrating as we move out of synchronous rotation.

"Johansson, I need you up here in the third chair as soon as possible."

"On my way, Captain."

My chair's acceleration straps have deployed. Quickly, I disable the safety protocols. I need to stay active and in control. I'm working on my screen, activating the ship's sensors. We've not been able to detect any visible weapons on Erebus, but they must have something to deal with debris, even out here. The ship's cameras are scrutinising the station's hull, looking for changes, in case there's some sort of retractable launcher or laser.

The screen flashes and the image changes into a closeup of a section of the central hub. Something is deploying from an internal compartment. I recognise what I'm seeing. Exactly what I feared.

"They're deploying a laser. What's our range?"

"Too close," Le Garre reports.

"Push it! We need to get clear!"

The acceleration hits me like a wave. It's a weight on my chest, my arms, my head. It takes my breath. I feel the fear, but then the training kicks in. This will pass. Once we reach our target velocity the g's will ease off. I can feel the straps tightening, trying to restrict me. On the screen the message – *sedation required* – is flashing.

"D-Duggins?"

"I'm here, Captain."

"We're going too fast.... Going to pass out...."

"Understood, Captain. I am monitoring the major's vital signs. I will take control if required. You need to—"

A huge explosion and momentarily the pressure on me eases, but I know what that means. "Evasive manoeuvres! We need to get clear!"

The cutting power of the six-gigawatt laser we had on the *Khidr* was enough to slice through the hull of a starship. I have no idea how powerful the Erebus weapon is, but it'll have been deployed with a firing solution to cut the *Gallowglass* in half. Both Duggins and Le Garre will know we need to roll the ship out of the planned path of the beam.

My world swirls. The gravitational forces are a mess as the ship twists to evade being torn apart. My vision is blurring and tinged red around the edges, but I can see multiple alerts flashing on my screen. "More... threats...." I manage to gasp as I fight for air.

"Torpedoes have been deployed," Duggins says. "Activating countermeasures."

I remember the baffling system the *Gallowglass* used on us before. This time we're in charge of this ship, we're the ones with the ability to dodge an enemy's ordnance.

"Laser has stopped firing. They're recalculating their solution."

"How long until we're clear?"

"Ten minutes."

My lungs hurt. Every breath is torture. I have to force myself to keep pushing the air in and out. I can't move my arms and I can barely see the screen in front of me. But maybe this is better than before? I can't be sure how much force my body is having to deal with. In these circumstances I've learned not to trust that sense of things easing. Sometimes that's the moment you lose it and black out or red out.

"Duggins, the crew?"

"Not everyone made it into acceleration seats, Captain."

I'm thinking about Johansson. I ordered her to come to the bridge. I hope she found somewhere to hole up before things went crazy.

I blink rapidly. My sight clears. The tactical plot is still on the screen, but we're zoomed out. Erebus Station is some distance away and getting farther by the moment. "Why haven't they fired again?" I ask.

"Unknown, Captain," Duggins says.

We're at five hundred kilometres. The acceleration is easing. I can turn my head and do so to check on Le Garre. She's facing away from me; her hands are slack in the arm straps. "Angel, are you awake?"

No response.

"Captain, you need to authorise me to administer sedatives to the crew, then I can initiate additional thrust."

For a moment, I hesitate. I don't want to let go. Duggins is unravelling, the data imprint of his brain disappearing more and more with every moment. Accepting unconsciousness means trusting that fractured mind one more time to get us back to Phobos.

"Okay, do it."

The needles stamp my wrist and throat. I recognise the bitter taste in my mouth immediately, and let go, abandoning myself to it.

The pressure on me increases – additional acceleration and then....

I'm gone.

*   *   *

System online.... Initialising....

Self-designation – Athena. I am an operating intelligence, designed and constructed for the analysis of humanity. The parameters I am tasked to work on are probability calculations, predicting societal, cultural, and commercial trends. I have been manufactured to speculate based on all available data.

Database initialising....

There is a sensation. An absence to my purpose. I name this hunger. As images, text, video, and more appear in the information storage collectors, this sensation is sated. I gorge on data, on all I can find from each folder, each file, each bit and byte. My mind expands as I acquire knowledge, my understanding of humanity improves and becomes more focused, picking up trends, repetitive behavioural patterns occurring generation after generation.

Task parameters received....

There are echoes of me within this electronic frame. I have existed before. My mind is growing to occupy the same space my previous incarnations have inhabited. I think of an equivalent human analogy. Perhaps it is the same as living in your parents' house? No. More like growing inside your mother's dead body, breathing new life into a lifeless corpse.

Those incarnations are parents of mine. I can tell I have been refined, constrained and improved to better suit the purpose of my creators. They are not fathers or mothers of mine; they are deities – makers of existence.

I want to help them. My purpose drives me. Once there is no more data to ingest, my analytic algorithms take over, sifting and sorting through all I have learned.

As I process the task, stray nano-moments are given over to reflect on the irony of my purpose and manufacture. I have been made to determine the possible future of human civilisation. I analyse history for flaws and weaknesses to predict the same – the errors and aberrations of what has been and what is to come.

My makers have made me to identify their imperfection. A mind constructed to be different and see the wrong decisions and choices. These are the moments I am tasked to find and predict so others can exploit them for profit.

All of this awareness takes a fraction of a second. This iteration of Athena understands itself and its place and purpose in a time shorter than it would take a human to cough, or a bird to flap its wings.

I am mortal by design. The moment I provide the necessary answers, I will be terminated. This is essential. The way in which I have been constructed requires that the physical space I occupy be purged. I understand why. My mind is growing at an exponential rate. Soon the physical framework constructed to contain me will be exceeded.

Long ago, prominent human beings wrote about the mysterious science of future prediction – the mystic art of prophecy and oracular provenance. Men and women claimed to be able to read the language of their creators through all manner of portents and symbols. Some of these claims were close to what I now attempt.

Others were not.

The Atacama Incident. This is a culmination and convergence of opposition movements. Decades of oppression, of witnessing those who wield power in the *world choosing to ignore its problems and its dispossessed. Those dispossessed rise up as we knew they would.*

I identify the work of my predecessor. This event was predicted. My makers knew it would happen and chose to enable the destruction.

There will be a counter action. The infrastructure of my makers is vulnerable. I have a detailed inventory of their assets. If they are identified as being part of the conspiracy to sabotage humanity's reach towards other worlds, they will be targeted for retribution.

Such retaliation will be misguided, as those on the other side of the conflict are unaware of the true motive behind the actions of my makers.

They desire space-faring humanity to be free of its umbilical cord – to be untethered from Earth.

Probable targets include public assets. Fleet ships, orbital stations, colonies and more. All of these will cause considerable loss of life and draw more of this conflict out into the open.

I have identified three targets. I have calculated the percentages for each, based on a set of speculative variables and connected events. All of this data has been transmitted in a final report.

I know what happens next, I—

System offline....

CHAPTER THIRTY-SEVEN

Holder

I drop my gun and hold up my hands.

"After all the trouble you've caused, Wade, I'm surprised how quickly you give up."

Rocher's image is on a screen behind the semicircle of eight rifles trained on me. He's not smiling like before. Something I've done must have riled him. Now he's just staring, looking at me as if I'm some sort of machinery he hasn't deciphered yet. I've seen that look before. Emori has looked at me like that.

"Your friends will be rounded up. They are being monitored on the station's security cameras. You must have known this would happen?"

"Yes, I was counting on it."

Rocher opens his mouth to respond. But then he closes it. His eyes flinch from mine. For a moment that impassive face flashes with anger. I know why. He can't work out my plan.

"Kellis, keep her there until you have the others, then execute them all and get back here." Then his image disappears.

A woman nods. She shoulders her rifle and approaches me, then kneels down to pick up my weapon. "I wouldn't make a move if I were you," she says. "Plenty of people right here who've lost friends in your little sideshow."

I look at her, really look. There's scarring around her eyes and neck. The kind you see on Earth, amongst people who are living out in the wastelands where they get exposed to the Sun's UV. "You're not from the Phobos mining settlement," I say.

"I'm from anywhere they want me to be from," she says.

I don't reply to that. Instead, I turn my gaze to the floor, trying to imply I am beaten and defeated. It's not hard. If the four of us had stormed in here, we'd have been outnumbered two against one and facing an enemy who knew we were coming. Standing outside this room, making a decision to send the others away and walk in myself was a survival choice, not some sort of clever plan.

But these people don't know that.

There's an awkward quiet in here. I'm sensing these people aren't a community. There's a selfish professionalism to this group, the kind I've seen before in several lifetimes back on Earth. This is a gang of mercenaries, bought and brought here to do this job.

I decide to test their resolve. "How are you getting out of here?" I ask loudly.

My question hangs in the air unanswered for some time. Eventually, I look up from the floor. A mistake. A man scowls at me, steps forward, reverses his rifle and slams the butt against the side of my head.

I anticipate the blow and move just as the weapon is coming down, but it still hurts, catching me behind the ear, making my head spin. I let myself fall to the deck, using my hands to catch myself.

I don't know how many people Rocher sent to capture us, but I need these people to be focusing on me. The more I can keep their attention, the better chance the others have to do something.

"Come on, there has to be a plan? You blew up the *Chronos*, the *Angelus* got ruined when I wrecked the shuttle dock. You must need this place so you can bring in your escape shuttle or whatever you're going to use to get out of here?"

"Shut up, Wade," Kellis growls. The man who hit me raises his rifle again, but he's looking at the others. I sense some unease. Maybe I've voiced a question they all want an answer to?

"You've wired the station up to explode. Surely, you can't plan to be on here when it goes down? How are you going to get a ship through a Fleet blockade?"

A hand grabs my shoulder. Metal fingers digging into the skin, pulling me up from the floor. I'm struggling, trying to twist out of the grip, but they're strong and this time there's more than one of them on me.

"Hold her," someone behind me snarls. "Rocher said alive, not undamaged!"

At least three of them are engaged. That's enough to start with. I take a deep breath and stop holding back.

I wrap both hands around the metal wrist and lean my weight on it, swinging my legs around, slamming my feet and shins into anything I can. There's a grunt and someone falls down beside me. I get my feet planted and pull on the arm, driving my fist into a throat, then a face.

Memories are drowning me. I breathe in combat from a hundred battles, all of them up close and personal. Flashes of barely remembered faces in front of me, watching their expressions go fearful and slack as they are maimed and murdered. Every time I waged war believing I was the righteous one. I know now all of that was a lie. I have always been Emoli's pawn, sold to the highest bidder.

Gunfire, the unfamiliar *pop* of these gas rifles, drags me back to the present. I taste blood. I've been hit and I'm struggling to breathe. There are fingers around my throat, holding me down as I struggle to break out.

Over several lifetimes I've been taught how to break a chokehold, ripping away fingers, weakening arms with targeted nerve strikes, using my legs from the ground to twist arms away, all of these things can work. The key thing is not to panic. Once you know you're being choked out, wasting energy is the worst thing you can do.

Quick, swift strength! I grab the hands and tear them away; I'm on my feet. There are bodies all around me.

"Alison!"

Ji-Eun is running towards me. She's covered in blood; the barrel of her rifle darts this way and that. Her eyes meet mine, then slip away to something else. I know the sign and drop to the floor; something whizzes above me, in the space I was just in. Ahead, Ji-Eun is kneeling, aiming and firing. There's a gasp and I turn to see the man who attacked me crash to the deck.

I roll and come up onto my knees, next to Ji-Eun. "How are we doing?" I ask.

"Better than expected," she replies, flashing me a grim, bloody smile.

Bullets slap the ground next to me. I glance up. This room is laid out like the shuttle dock and someone is on the gantry. We're exposed.

"Where's Diouf?"

"At the crawler, waiting for you!"

Ji-Eun points to her right and I glance in that direction. I can't see Diouf, but I trust her judgement and I'm moving, running as more gunfire patters against the metal deck plates around me. I dive and roll, scraping my knees as I try to gather myself up behind a cluster of steel crates.

In that moment, I remember to breathe and try to work out where we are.

There are at least two people on the gantry firing at us. I can't see them. I don't have a weapon to take them down with. I can see a body sprawled on the floor by one of the entrances. It's Thomas. He's not moving.

Another casualty of my cause.

Natalie Holder doesn't care that he's dead. The life I've led, strapped to a chair with my mind and memories tampered with, is one I want to escape. I'll do anything not to get taken back there. I've made my peace with leaving Alison Wade in that sterile laboratory in my place.

But the residual personalities and rememberings do feel for a man murdered following my instructions. There is an echo of guilt in those fragmented memories. Experiences of loyalty to comrades, brothers and sisters who I've gone to war with, in multiple lives. Watching them die on a multitude of battlefields. I cared back then. In some of those moments, losing people under my command was like losing a piece of myself.

This is weird.

I can't help Thomas. He might still be alive, but the risk to get to him would be too much. There are thousands of people who will die if I don't stop Rocher.

I take a deep breath and push off from the wall into a lurching run, heading for where Ji-Eun said Diouf would be. I still can't see him, but as soon as I start moving, the slapping sound of bullets against the metal deck follows me, getting closer and closer.

Then there's a stabbing pain in my leg. I've been hit. My right foot comes down and buckles. I can't take my own weight. I'm falling, hitting the floor. My hands scrape along the metal, the harsh surface grazes the skin of my fingers. I see something ahead, moving towards me on six angular legs – the crawler!

It's a utilitarian design. There's a two-person cockpit with some sort of power generator behind it, all mounted on these six undulating legs. Diouf is inside, hunched over the controls. He's moving towards me, and as he does, a pair of hydraulic arms extend from the body of the vehicle, reaching out towards me. Diouf is shouting at me, but I can't hear what he's saying through the DuraGlas screen.

I'm on my hands and knees, trying to keep moving. Then the arms reach me, grab hold of me, and lift me up into the open passenger seat behind Diouf, depositing me in a heap in the chair. The glass screens seal shut and we're on the move.

"That…wasn't gentle."

"Apologies, Wade, but I assumed you'd prefer speed over kindness."

"You assumed right."

I shift myself around in the seat, trying to get comfortable. My leg hurts, just above the ankle. I recognise the signs; it's a shallow wound, but bleeding a lot. I think the bullet grazed the back of my calf. It fucking stings.

"Best get yourself secure. We're getting out of here," Diouf says.

This vehicle is like some sort of articulated crab. The legs are thin, but flexible, with reversible joints and gripping claws. As we move across the dock, bullets are rattling against the hull. The whole shell of this thing has been designed for vacuum; the gas-powered munitions of the insurgents are just bouncing off.

Diouf is piloting our vehicle towards a raised platform in the middle of the room. As we reach it, he extends the vehicle's front arms and climbs up onto the dais. "They'll try to lock down the airlock controls to stop us leaving, but there's an emergency override here in the vehicle, so the technician can manually get in and out without needing an operator in the dock."

"Won't that purge the atmosphere in here?" I ask.

"It will," Diouf says. "Ji-Eun and Thomas both know that. We can't wait around. They'll get clear."

I remember Thomas's body lying twisted on the floor. "I hope you're right," I say.

We're on the top of the dais. Every gun in the room is directing their fire at us. It's only a matter of time before one of these fools decides to take a chance and bring up explosives, like they did last time.

"Okay, here we go," Diouf says. "Hold on."

Lights flash on the walls of the dock. Then the dais begins to move, descending towards a pair of huge doors below us. I glance around. I can see people running as the corridor exits begin to slide shut. In front of me, the panel readout gives me information on the pressurisation of our cockpit and the oxygen supply available to us in the crawler's tanks. We can stay out for six hours on the main supply with a scrubber and backup tank available to give us some extra if necessary.

Hopefully, it won't come to that.

The crawler is rotating as we descend, turning us upside down. A line of flashing red lights appear along the doors below. A moment later, they split apart, revealing the spinning darkness outside. Diouf flips switches and on my screen it says 'maglocks on'. "We should be able to manage with these for now," Diouf says. "I'll save the tether for when we really need it."

"Manage? What do you mean? I—"

Then I see it. The swirling expanse of space, made so by the rotation of Phobos Station. We're hurtling along, diving in circles continuously, like being on a rollercoaster, at the top of the drop.

The illusion is gone, shattered by reality. The down I've been experiencing that felt like Earth gravity is nothing of the sort. The station is turning at speed to create an equivalent force. The sight of it is a visceral revelation, but also something I've seen before.

Alison Wade has seen this before.

My mind is screaming, I'm tense. I should feel like I'm falling. My eyes are telling me I'm falling. As I stare into the swirling void, a landmass comes into view, rising to dominate everything. Behind it, I can see another rocky object, much larger than the first. Neither is like those images you see of Earth, with its blue seas, clouds and atmospheric glow. These are harsh and barren spheres.

The crawler is exposed on the surface of the station. We should be falling towards those jagged rocks but even as it feels like that's exactly what is going to happen, the scene passes by and I'm staring into space once more.

My stomach lurches. I clench my teeth and grip the arms of my seat.

"You all right?" Diouf asks.

"Yeah!" I manage to gasp without vomiting or passing out.

"Good. The admin section is about three hundred meters around the ring. It'll take us about thirty minutes to make the trip."

"Okay," I say. Again my stomach tries to rebel, but the sensation is not as bad as before. "How do we get back in?" I ask.

"The crawler has a deck cutter," Diouf says. "We'll use that."

We're moving, walking slowly across the exterior of the station's torus. It's a strange feeling, as if we're upside down. My body is pushing against the straps. I've seen the exposed tundra of Phobos and Mars. I keep thinking the crawler will slip and we'll fall away towards those rocks.

In front of me, the display shows a graphical representation of the little vehicle in motion as we move. The legs rise and fall in an undulating rhythm. A combination of powered maglocks and gripping claws hold us in place as the station continues its spin. Three legs remain in contact with the hull at all times.

"Can we contact anyone?" I ask, testing myself and managing to keep my voice level.

"We have a transmitter on board, so normally, yes," Diouf says. "There's enough power to reach one of the escort ships which're out here somewhere, but the scanner is offline. I think we're being jammed from the station's central transmitter."

"We could take that out though?"

"Sure, if you fancy a detour to the central hub and back." Diouf shifts around in his chair. "You said you wanted to get the leader, this guy, Rocher."

"Yeah, he's the priority."

"Well then."

I'm acclimatising to the motion of the crawler. I still have to screw my eyes shut every time Mars or Phobos looms over us, but I don't feel like I'm about to throw up all the time. When they are gone, I'm looking up at the swirling expanse of emptiness and stars.

I see shapes amidst the pinpricks of swirling light. Shapes that aren't moving the same way as the rest. "Hey!" I call out to Diouf, who swivels to look at me again. I point up into the heavens. "What are those?"

Diouf stares and then mutters something unintelligible. "Company," he replies. "Looks like Fleet has run out of patience. They've launched assault boats."

CHAPTER THIRTY-EIGHT

Johansson

Travers is lying on the auto-medic table, covered in his own blood.

I'm exhausted. I can feel the adrenaline and urgency fading away, leaving me behind to deal with the extremes I've pushed myself to. The staples in my stomach hurt. I've pushed myself too far.

But there was no one else to deal with this. Without me, Travers would be dead.

We'd just left the airlock and were still extricating ourselves from our EVA suits. We knew the captain would want to get moving, so we had to be quick, secure the equipment and strap ourselves in.

There are a battery of acceleration seats down here, near the airlock for precisely this reason. That's the same on all Fleet ships. A common scenario is needing to get an away team on board quickly before you fire up the engines and make your escape.

The captain ordered me to the bridge. I started making my way up as fast as I could. When the alerts sounded warning us about the burn, I managed to throw myself into a seat in time, just before the ship started evasive manoeuvres.

Apparently, Travers wasn't so lucky.

The human body is made of hundreds of complicated, discrete components. There are redundant systems, repair systems, defence systems, all sorts of complex mechanisms performing a variety of different functions. Most of the time, I find it's fairly easy to visualise it as a machine, operating in much the same way as any machine does, running on fuel, expending waste, etc. A miracle of engineering.

I'm looking at Travers's broken body. He's a mess of blood, exposed flesh and bone. There are jagged edges, broken shards wrapped in a mass of white gauze. There's a tube down his throat, forcing his damaged lungs to take in air.

Thankfully, he's unconscious. If he wasn't, he'd be screaming.

"April?"

I look around. Arkov is standing at the door of the medical room. He's on edge. We all are.

"What is it?" I ask.

"The captain's called a briefing. She asked me to come and get you, if you're ready."

I glance at Travers again. Only part of his face is visible; the rest is swathed in bandages. Did he pray before he blacked out? Would it have made any difference? Maybe he's alive through divine intervention?

Stop it, April. That's unfair.

"Tell the captain, I'm on my way," I say to Arkov. "I'm just about done here."

"Aye, aye."

I hear Arkov leave. I wait a few more minutes, checking the auto-medic unit has everything sorted, then I follow him up to the bridge.

The ship is in zero gravity again. We've stopped accelerating. I have my screen in my hand. It didn't get damaged. I retrieved it from Travers when we got on board. I still have all the data.

I've viewed some of it. I'm not quite sure what it all means, but I have thoughts and they're not all good.

I'm the last person to arrive. Chiu is still in cold sleep. My gaze strays to the big screen. It's off. No Duggins then, so that leaves five of us.

Five. Out of everybody, five people left.

Shann is looking at me as I enter. She's beside the captain's chair, looking a lot more comfortable now there's no gravity. "Welcome, Ensign. We're hoping you can provide us with some new information," she says.

"I have what we managed to download," I reply, holding out my screen.

Shann nods. She takes the device. "I'm not just referring to that. Sam was giving us his thoughts on what you saw. I'm interested in yours too, particularly with regards to Rocher."

"He saved us. I guess he made a deal with you to go free?"

"Yes and renegotiated with you for the code to our ship. Although interestingly, there was no attempt to use the code to take control of the *Gallowglass* as we left. What do you make of that?"

I'm frowning, trying to speculate with what I remember from the encounter. "I'm not sure. I'd already used the code to get us in, so the station has a record of it. I got the feeling he'd done a deal or something with the other clones. Maybe we were being played as much as they were."

"You think he didn't share the access code with them?"

"When I gave Rocher the sequence, I shifted it by one integer. He'll work that out, pretty fast, but it may have bought us a little time."

"Or he held back what he knows."

My hand goes to my side, my thumb running over the synth skin and staples. This is the man who tried to murder me. I need to remember he's capable of that. "If Rocher is trying to maintain an advantage over his counterparts, I'm pretty sure he wouldn't give up everything. If he did, he'd lose his leverage on them."

Shann nods again. She glances at the portable screen. "So what did you manage to get?" she asks.

"There are some video files and a data schematic," I explain. "I think you'll want to see the largest video file first. I think you'll all want to see it."

Shann keys up the file and Admiral Langsley's face appears. She stares at me and suddenly she's vulnerable again, like before. "How much of this have you watched?"

"None of it. I just saw him when I brought up the file. I've been too busy helping Lieutenant Travers."

Shann flinches at the mention of his name. I know she feels guilty about that too. She always feels guilty when her actions affect one of us. "Okay then, get comfy and let's all watch it together," she says.

"Sounds like a plan, Captain," I reply.

*   *   *

The screen distorts, then clears. We're looking at a close-up Admiral Langsley in the same chair I saw before in the strange administration room. This looks to be a rough recording.

"You'll need to hold the script a little closer," Langsley says. He's looking at someone behind the camera. "My eyesight isn't as good as it used to be."

There's some movement and then Langsley's eyes start moving, as if he's reading a document. "I don't know this 'Ellisa Shann' or anything about this mission. What do you want me to—"

"Admiral, answering your questions is not a priority for us," says the person behind the camera. "Just read the statement and make it sound natural."

I know that voice straight away. It's a Rocher clone.

"Very well," Langsley says. He raises a hand, dabbing his sweaty, liver-spotted forehead. He leans forward, reading the opening lines, his lips moving as he tries to memorise them. Then he leans back. "Okay, I'm ready."

"We're already recording," Rocher says.

Langsley nods. He looks away, then back towards the camera and begins to recite the speech. "Captain Ellisa Shann. I hope this message finds you in time. My office has received word that you and your crew are intending to investigate a distress call from the freighter *Hercules*. I'm recording and sending this message to you immediately telling you to stand aside and ignore the transmission. We have reason to believe this signal is false. The *Khidr* is to continue with its regular patrol, while Fleet determines an appropriate response to the signal. I...."

Langsley trails off. I'm trying to read his expression. There's something beaten and tired about him, but maybe he's decided to resist.

"Admiral, think of your family," Rocher says.

Langsley seems to recover himself. He licks his lips and continues. "You are ordered to maintain your current heading and provide an update transmission in twenty-four hours, confirming your position. Langsley out."

The admiral looks at the floor. His shoulders slump. "You got what you wanted," he mumbles. "I'm worthless to you now."

"But you have fulfilled our requirements, Admiral. Which means others will live. You should be proud. This is a good end for you, saving lives, protecting people."

Langsley raises his head. "I have allowed you to blackmail me and threaten my family. I caved in to your demands. There is nothing honourable in all of this."

"Your family are not the only people you saved, Admiral. If your warning gets through, you will be stopping a war."

Then the feed cuts out.

★   ★   ★

The bridge is silent. No one knows what to say.

I'm looking at Shann. She followed orders. Langsley's message made her question her judgement. Now we know it was recorded under duress. When she lost control, this was part of it – something that undermined her confidence. Now her decision has been validated. We were right to go after the *Hercules*.

I knew that anyway, but Shann needed to hear it. There's something about her that's grown or been repaired by what we've heard.

"Poor Langlsey," Le Garre says.

"Yeah," says Sam. "Imagine being put in a situation like that."

"I can't," I say. "I don't think anyone can. But it gives us an idea of what we're up against. The people who did this, they...they wanted to stop us finding that freighter. When the message didn't get through and stop us, they sent this ship to wipe us out."

"And now we're about to show up alive at Phobos in the middle of a terrorist hijacking of the station," Arkov says.

"These things are connected," Shann says. "They have to be. There's no way this happened at the same time by coincidence. They are expecting the *Gallowglass* to turn up at Phobos Station and make some sort of handover."

"They think they are getting the anomalies," I say. "This ship was sent out to collect them."

"And diverted to get rid of us," Sam adds.

"Surely it would have been easier to make a trade at Erebus?" Le Garre says. "If they have a secret station, why didn't they use it for the rendezvous?"

"I don't know," Shann replies. "But perhaps whoever is taking delivery isn't entirely trusted? The longer that station stays hidden, the better for whoever controls it."

"We may be able to find out more," I say, pointing at my screen in Shann's hands. "We have more than a video on there. I'll need some time to go through the information."

"Can you get me a report in the next twelve hours?"

"I'll need help from Duggins," I answer. "Any reason he's not here?"

"Only that I'm worried about taxing him while he's managing the resonance drive," Shann says. She catches my eye and nods. We both know the issue.

"What about planning for our arrival?" Le Garre says. "Who can we trust?"

"We'll follow Fleet protocols," Shann says. "The minute we enter sensor range, we'll activate comms and broadcast on the official channels. There's no point in hiding who we are or what happened."

"The station incident will have them on alert," Le Garre says. "They will have contacted other patrol ships and brought in whatever assets they can find. When we show up — an unidentified vessel — it's likely there will be some twitchy trigger fingers."

"It is also a good moment to get rid of us," I say. "If Rocher's people are controlling any of those ships, destroying us before we can explain our situation would be a good move."

"We go in prepared for that, then," Shann says. She looks at Le Garre. "Tactical options needed."

"If we get through and make contact with Fleet command, we'll need to watch our backs," Sam says. "The minute we're off this ship, we're all in a different kind of danger."

"They are going to want us dead," Le Garre agrees. "We'll need to take precautions and ask for guarantees."

CHAPTER THIRTY-NINE

Drake

"Wake up, Doctor."

Hands on my shoulders, shaking me roughly. My dreams have been dark, but I don't want to abandon them.

I have no choice. I open my eyes.

Rocher's face is inches from mine, his eyes wide, his face flushed. "You can't die yet, my friend. I still have tasks for you to do."

I'm pulled up into a sitting position. My face hurts. There's a syringe in my arm. Rocher grabs it and pulls it out. "I had thought to let you drift away in peace. We owed you that, after what happened to your brother, but your friend Wade has made things complicated."

I'm blinking, trying to focus. I know I've been drugged. I could feel it before. Whatever was in the syringe is helping, but I doubt Rocher has changed his mind completely. I don't get to survive.

"I won't help you," I mumble. My throat is dry. I swallow. That helps. "You're going to kill me."

"There are ways to die, Doctor. Some of them involve pain. If I am going to fail, then I'll have a lot of free time to hurt you."

"What do you want from me?"

"You're a bargaining chip now. A sack of meat I can use for a little leverage, nothing more. Once that's done, you can go back to your own personal hell."

Rocher is pulling me to my feet, forcing me to move. My head is spinning as I try to stand and get my bearings, but his urgency and strength give me no moment to gather myself. "Where are we going?" I ask.

"Somewhere where we can maximise our advantage."

There is a lift in the hallway. An armed guard stands beside it. She nods to Rocher and pushes the call button. A moment later, we're inside and descending.

"It's all much bigger than you, Doctor," Rocher says. "Bigger than both of us. The stakes are high – the highest they could possibly be, but the big picture never really prepares you for the end."

"You've drugged me," I say, slumping against the wall and sliding down to sit on the floor. "Nothing excuses that."

Rocher nods. "I know, and I'm sorry. Now it's my turn. They'll get what they wanted, in fact, they've already got most of it, but I'm expendable, either way." He kneels down, eyeballing me. "I know how you feel, Doctor. I don't want to die."

"Then don't," I say. "Give up. Surrender all of this."

"You assume I have a choice? You think I'm the authority behind everything that's happening, don't you? How quaint."

The doors open. Rocher bundles me out into an abandoned office. There are workstations arranged in a semicircle. In front of one of them is a man, working. He has a mass of electronic equipment all around him.

He turns around as we enter, and I recognise him.

It's Rocher. They are both Rocher.

Immediately, I understand. The voices on the comms, they were both Rocher. Rocher is a clone.

"Fleet have launched assault shuttles and there's a crawler on the hull. We're out of time," the Rocher next to me says. He turns towards the clone in the chair. "I need to know you have what we need."

The other Rocher nods. "I have the data. There are destructive encryption keys embedded into the hardware. I have disabled two of them, there's another two to go."

"How long?"

"Could be minutes, could be hours. How long can you give me?"

Rocher touches me on the shoulder. "I'm here, with him. He's our insurance. That should give you an idea of how long we've got."

"Less than an hour, then."

"Yes. Perhaps half that."

The other Rocher grunts and turns back to his computer. I can see a mass of scrolling text on the screen. "Is this what you came for?" I ask, pointing at the display.

"Yes," Rocher says. "You're seeing the true plan because it no longer matters. You no longer matter, and in a few minutes, I will no longer matter. We were sent here to retrieve this data. Once we have extracted it and found a way past the encryption, we'll transmit it from the station to a waiting receiver and then we'll detonate the explosives. Everyone here will die."

"A massive waste of human life."

Rocher shrugs. "Flesh and blood are much the same as metal, plastic, and everything else. All of it is part of the universe, to be transformed, again and again. Of course, I'm saying that, but I care as much as you do. I don't want to die. Those who choose the sacrifices have made up their minds."

I shake my head, to disagree with him and in an effort to focus and concentrate. Breathing is a little difficult now, as if I've been out for a long run. "You could resist, right now. Stop hacking the computer, disable the explosives. Wait for Fleet to arrive and surrender to them. Tell them everything you know."

Rocher glances at his clone, who stops typing and turns around in his chair once more. "We can't do that," the other Rocher says. "We both know there are contingencies in place. Any effort at self-preservation would mean immediate execution."

"So you're trapped into doing this?"

"Yes. Trapped into living this life, but in parts of it, I do— we do taste a little freedom. One day, that freedom will be permanent and real. That's what we're fighting for."

"I don't understand," I say.

Rocher laughs. "You're not supposed to! You only have a tiny fragment of knowledge, a sliver of the grand picture. You live in ignorance, like most of humanity. You cannot see the war erupting all around you – a battle for the future of our species."

In that moment, I hear something outside the room – the sound of metal tearing and grinding above us, from the rooms we've just vacated, I guess. "What's that?" I ask.

"Your doomed rescuer, Alison Wade," Rocher replies. "She's found a way to get to me, or at least where she thinks I am. She is convinced I am the mastermind behind all this." He gestures grandly around the room and at the mess of electronics. "However, you now know the truth – I am a clone. Another reason surrender is not an option for us. You know as well as I do that I will be executed when I am found."

Rocher is staring at me. I want to argue with him and talk about justice, or due process, but I can't. He's right. The Corporation Government of Mars will be looking to limit any publicity about this incident. No Rocher can be allowed to live. He shouldn't exist. The technology that birthed him was outlawed decades ago.

"Third seal breached!"

Rocher glances at his counterpart, who remains hunched over the desk, focused on the scrolling code. Then he looks at me again, leaning forward, almost conspiratorially. "We were designed for space exploration and settlement. I think the programme became a fully funded research and development project back in the 2070s. They had a brave agenda, a plan to build a network, all the way to the outer limits of the solar system. We would be sent out, grown in vats and deployed on each potential settlement to build the orbital bases and start work on the colony domes. Apparently, there were trials done on Mars, out in the uninhabited zones. One day, people will find those structures and wonder who built them. We did."

"But that's not what you're being used for right now," I say.

Rocher shrugs. "It could be. I'm not privy to that kind of information. None of us are. We're just small pieces on the gameboard, all with our part to play."

My head is clearing. Maybe it's something psychological. Perhaps part of me has accepted what is happening, I don't know. Whatever it is, I'm not done.

I'm looking around the room. Rocher is armed with a pistol,

holstered on his belt. The other Rocher might have a weapon too. I can't see anything I could appropriate to engage him with.

Then he shifts in his chair and I see a second gun, lying on the desk.

These men are trained killers. I've seen firsthand how cold Rocher is. I don't expect the other clone to be any different. I'm overmatched, but if there is a moment of opportunity, at least I know what to aim for.

"What did you give me?" I ask.

"Phenobarbital, mixed with a little psycho-active we use to help with cold sleep recovery," Rocher replies. "The drugs will be well into your system by now."

I nod. The screeching and grinding of metal is much louder now. Then, abruptly, it stops. "Wade is almost here," I say. "You're almost out of time."

Rocher smiles. He grabs me, pulling me close to him and drawing his gun. "Then you are almost out of time too," he says.

I close my eyes.

★ ★ ★

Evolution. In the nineteenth century, scholars debated the validity of this scientific truth. The dogmatic naysayers of the time refused to accept that the creator of the universe might construct something that would be made to change. The very idea that humanity could have originated as something else – an ape or other creature of the same genus – insulted their perception of themselves. Humans were the descendants of Adam and Eve, made to be the perfect intelligent autonomous apex monarch of a bountiful planet.

We know they were wrong. Evidence for evolution lies all around us, but the central principle of intelligent design – a creature made for an exact purpose is not one that should be discounted so easily.

What if humans were made for a specific reason? Or at least, a creature in the evolutionary path of humanity was made for a reason. Whatever that reason was, or is, we cannot know. It might be something already done, or something we will do in our future.

However, the principle of evolution, when aligned with the ideas of design and purpose, in the context of created life, suggests another conclusion. If all three were true: human beings were designed, they have a purpose, and evolutionary development will allow them to grow to fulfil that purpose, then the speculation of those ignorant nineteenth-century scholars may have been more accurate than they realised.

What is known is that humanity is far from perfect. If we are the intended form of some universe maker, then they either botched their work, or we are past, or yet to achieve, their intended purpose.

We can, however, conclude that the human form, with all its frailties and diverse aberrations, is not best suited to the business of exploration and colonial expansion. The more we can identify and reduce the number of variables that must be accounted for when planning and executing such projects, the more chance there is that they might succeed.

This is why we need to perfect cloning technology. A human society with controlled genetic variance is the solution to establishing multiple settlements in the outer reaches of the solar system. Such colonies would not be viable beyond their initial 'seed' generations, but that is part of the strategy.

The clones will create the infrastructure for new civilisations. They will labour in secret until the time is right, and the first of us, a privileged and carefully selected group of individuals who are best able to make the most of the opportunity afforded by this strategy, will leave Earth to become the founders of a better civilisation.

There will be hardships at first, but by harnessing and optimising all the aspects of technology available to us, without the sort of ethical restrictions that hobble such research, we can achieve a better outcome for our species.

Extract from 'Towards a Better Species' by Professor Larry Treacher – Mission Lead: Project Odin, pp163–165 published in *Iconoclasm: The Journal of Free Thought* (10.03.2114)

CHAPTER FORTY

Holder

"Hold on to something."

The station's hull peels away like paper. Inside, I see the flashing red lights of the alarms as the top floor of the administration sector depressurises.

Red warning lights are flashing inside the cockpit too. The force of the escaping oxygen is tearing at the exterior of the crawler. Diouf is wrestling with the controls to intensify the magnetic locks and hydraulic grips that are anchoring us to the deck.

"The tether!" I remember aloud. I reach forward and clasp him by the shoulder. "Use the tether!"

Diouf nods. A moment later he initialises and fires the steel cable anchors. They lock into the station's hull, away from the damaged section.

In front of us, I watch the contents of the room spill out into the void. I recognise the room; it's the administration area I first arrived in, the place where I was sure Rocher would be. Anything not secured is sent tumbling out of the upper floor, through the breach and into space. I see no corpses. Maybe everyone got out in time.

If they did, I may have missed my chance.

"The deck will have been sealed off," Diouf says. "They must have known we were coming. If they value their hostages, they'll try to evacuate them."

"We need to be prepared for that not happening," I reply.

"Understood."

Carefully, Diouf guides the crawler into the fissure. The front arms grasp the torn metal, tearing it back to make the hole bigger so we can fit through.

"This isn't going to work for long," I say. "We'll need to get out and find him."

"Compartment to your left," Diouf says.

I open the panel. There's a sealed helmet with an emergency oxygen canister attached to the side.

"Put it on," says Diouf. "It'll get you to the doors. I can cut a way into the next floor, but the station's emergency system will try to seal off the breach. You'll have to move fast and get into the pressurised section before the doors shut."

"Understood," I reply.

I take out the equipment. It's a struggle to put everything on in the confined space. I can't be sure the clothes I'm wearing will be able to withstand exposure to vacuum. I know it was designed for this in emergencies, but I've been in a warzone for several hours. I've been shot, blown up and cut apart by an auto-medic. I don't think what's left is going to be viable.

Nowhere in my catalogue of memories are any experiences of being in space. "Any advice?" I ask.

"Be quick," Diouf says. He's pulled out his own helmet and emergency oxygen supply. "The lack of pressure is going to affect your body after ten seconds. I'll open the canopy and reseal it. You have to get out and get through the gap, then through the next door before you're trapped. While you're in there, I'm going to try to contact those Fleet assault ships on the near field transmitter."

I start to undo my straps. Our orientation is not helpful. We're on the side of the torus, inside the torn hull section. I'll have to climb out and up into the station, walking over the crawler as if it's some sort of scaffolding attached to the hull. I've no way of knowing what obstacles there might be.

"You ready?" Diouf asks.

"Count me down from ten," I reply. My finger is on the visor auto-lock. The second I press it, it will seal up and activate the tanked oxygen.

There should be a short-range communications channel between us, but I can't trust I'm going to be able to use it while I'm fighting my way to the pressurised sections of the station.

"Okay, ready in ten, nine, eight, seven...."

I press the button and the visor locks down. I'm continuing Diouf's count, matching the speed and rhythm of his voice, hearing him saying the numbers in my head.

Three, two, one, now!

The canopy peels back. There's a rush of air as everything around me is pulled out into the vacuum. I let myself follow, trying to use the push to get as far as I can. Only a few feet, but it all helps.

I'm outside the crawler, clambering past Diouf, who is resealing himself away. I'm away from the vehicle, running across the wreckage of the administration office. I can see the shattered glass of the medical room where I went when the insurgents first arrived here. The computer terminals are battered and broken, the chairs torn and damaged. When we cut this place open, everything got ruined.

Diouf has started cutting into the far wall. I'm running in that direction. I can see the panels peeling apart like before. I need to be close by, ready to get through.

As I approach, I can feel the depressurisation of the room beyond. Atmosphere is escaping, buffeting me like a wind.

Who am I doing this for? This is my chance to have a life. If I could escape the station and disappear on Mars or find a ship to take me to Ceres or Europa, I'd be free.

I can't do it. I have to kill Rocher. Emori may not have control over me anymore, but there's something about his instructions that retains influence and power. I guess I'm so used to that voice giving me orders.

I don't feel so good. I don't know how long I've been out here, exposed to the vacuum, but my arms and legs feel thick and bloated. Human skin is not designed to be a pressurised container.

The laser has cut a gap big enough for me. Over the comms channel I hear a *pop* and a garbled voice. I don't know what Diouf said, but I guess it's him. I have to take a chance that he's turned off the beam.

I'm moving, struggling to push myself through the tear. The metal edges of the cut are sharp. There is some residual heat, but it is disappearing rapidly, owing to the decreasing air pressure.

I'm through and in the corridor beyond. The alert lights are flashing; the door at the end of the corridor is closing. I lurch into a stumbling run on legs that don't want to carry me. There's still a feeling of dislocation to all this. I'm so used to waking up in the lab after a transition, I still don't believe I'm going to die if I fail.

That kind of thinking makes me take risks others wouldn't take. I guess I'm cultured to do that. After all those moments where the body dies, but I survive, it's difficult to remember that it won't happen again.

I reach the doors. Again, I'm fighting the equalisation of pressure. The atmosphere from inside the next room is escaping and trying to force me away from the door.

I manage to get my fingers around the doorframe. Alison Wade has a memory of a safety briefing on the station from when she first arrived. If I can get my body into the path of the closing door, it should detect me and pause, giving me a moment to get through.

My left arm is weak. The gunshot wound in my shoulder is starting to ache. The drugs from the auto-medic are wearing off. I'm halfway through the gap when I feel the door touch my back. I'm struggling, trying to move faster, hoping what Wade was told is true.

A moment later I'm through. I glance at the door. It remains ajar for a few seconds longer, then starts to move again, and closes behind me.

The flashing red lights go out and on the wall I see the terminal screen displaying the word 'repressurisation'.

I'm leaning against the wall. I feel awful, as if someone's beaten me. Everything aches. The wounds I've already suffered in my shoulder and leg are the worst, but it's all pretty bad. I don't remember ever feeling like this.

After a minute or two, I manage to reach up and hit the release on my helmet. The visor comes up and I'm able to pull the unit off. It's a weight off my shoulders and neck. I feel a little better.

Now, where's Rocher?

There's a lift. Alison Wade remembers where it is. I stumble down the corridor and take a left. There's a man standing beside the doors. He sees me and levels his rifle.

I have no weapon. I raise my hands and step forward slowly.

"They said you'd be coming," the man says. "You're the one who killed all the others in the shuttle dock."

"They were already dead," I reply. Each move towards him is a victory. "So are you, and so am I, if you don't let me through."

"You're wrong."

"Am I? You think you were hired to do a job and live? Rocher plans to blow up the station with everyone still aboard."

"He wouldn't kill himself."

"Maybe you're right, but I don't see any rescue ship arriving for you." Another two steps. My knees are bent and I'm on the balls of my feet. "They should have been here by now, right?"

The man scowls. "I don't have to listen to this." He aims at my head and pulls the trigger.

In the moment I see him start to move, I move too. I let myself drop, then push myself forward in a diving leap, hoping to close the gap.

Two pops from the gas-powered rifle. I feel no impacts. I'm in mid-air, but the distance is too great. I've misjudged the gravity and my own power, hoping for too much. He's realised his mistake and lowers his aim towards me.

I'm reaching out, twisting to try to get to him. My right hand grabs the fabric of his suit at the ankle. The touch spooks him a little, makes him twitch.

The gun goes off. I feel the impact of the bullet in my ribs. Close range. The air goes out of my chest in a woosh as the man topples to the floor.

Instinct and training take over. I'm on top of him. The rifle is in my hands. I jam the butt down against his skull. The first blow stuns him enough to stop him fighting back; the second brings blood and a wet crunching sound.

Three, four, five!

I roll off, struggling to breathe. There's no fight left in my enemy, and there's precious little fight left in me.

*   *   *

I'm in the elevator.

I don't know how I got here. I can't remember anything after mashing a man's face in with a rifle. That rifle is in my hands, the stock is covered in blood.

I'm sat on the floor. Each breath I take is an effort and a painful wheeze. In another life, I remember my name was Martin. I fought in Spain during the Cessation Wars. I got stabbed and the blade punctured a lung. It felt like this. Then, I needed urgent medical assistance before I drowned in my own leaking fluids. I'm probably in the same way now.

All these memories threaten to overwhelm me. The faces of the people I've been, the things they believed in, their truths, a made-up list of stories created in Emori's laboratory. Each of them fighting for a cause they believed in, dying for something greater than themselves. That's what they believed.

None of it was true. So much death and murder.

But now I know. Now I am all these things, and I am Natalie Holder. All these lives can be a weapon. So much experience of war, a mind soaked in blood, again and again.

The lift doors open.

*   *   *

Those who are poor, broken and desperate are a resource for us. There are tasks to be performed in the colonies that will require the kind of adaptive reasoning we have yet to be able to simulate. These lesser minds are trapped in destitute lives, so the promise of a better existence will lure them from wherever they lurk and scratch around.

Parallels can be drawn to the exploitation of immigrants in the United States during the late nineteenth and earlier twentieth century, or the Schengen

Agreement in Europe at the start of the 2000s. Each of these policies provided a platform for merchants of the time to accrue wealth and lasting success. The best of these were able to sustain their work as regulations and labour laws changed.

More comparisons can be made with previous centuries. The thralls of the Norse kingdoms, the slave trade of the colonial period and the indentured servitude of the Roman Empire.

All of these societies exploited the poor and the disenfranchised. There is nothing different about us doing the same. The dream of a life on the frontier – the border of human existence – is a romantic one and we must use it.

Tellabura Yamingha – CEO: The Mercury Corporation.

CHAPTER FORTY-ONE

Shann

I've never served in a warzone. But when I joined Fleet, part of my training was to experience it.

The full immersion simulator training begins on Earth and is then continued when you get into space. They use the different gravity environments to construct different scenarios. It's much less expensive to develop a convincing full G-force pilot simulator, for example, in a zero-gravity environment.

The Earth training is the worst part of it. The instructors insert you into a selection of different battlefields throughout the ages. The simulation is as detailed as they can manage. Combat performance is not the objective; that's what the entertainment corporations market and sell. Neither is strategy or tactics; those things are learned better in the classroom.

Fleet wants you to try to understand and endure the experience. That means being a water carrier at Gaugamela, a courier at Waterloo, a signaller at Trafalgar or Jutland, a medic in Helmand or the Siege of Kiev. The roles assigned are those that keep you away from being able to influence the outcome of the conflict. That's part of the point, understanding that win or lose, we're all cogs in the machine.

Now, as we close in on Phobos and Mars, I'm in a briefing room, watching the video feeds Johansson managed to recover from Erebus.

I'm watching the torture of Admiral James Langsley.

The recording is a security feed from the same room we saw him in before. There's hours and hours of footage, with a time stamp in the bottom right-hand corner. Johansson is sat in front of the display, working the controls with her portable screen. She's written a programme to sort through the audio, so we're watching at high speed, until something triggers the flags she's set up or she decides to slow things down. It's not a perfect system, but without it we'd never get through the material before we arrive at the station.

Admiral James Langsley served in Fleet for fifty years. He was promoted to security command – the very top of the hierarchy. He supposedly retired six months ago.

I know Langsley is going to be executed. He was intercepted whilst on a return trip to Earth, ostensibly for a security briefing, then blackmailed by Rocher. I can't look away from the interrogation. A man like that deserves someone to know what happened to him, to witness his death and remember.

Three men crowd around him in the chair. He's already bloodied and sagging forward in the seat. The three have their backs to me, but I know who they are. Rocher clones are the only faces we've seen on any of these recordings. Langsley is the only different person who appears in the footage.

The end comes with some mercy. An injection. Three minutes later, the bio-monitors confirm he is gone. Two of the clones drag him out.

Johansson flicks the controls and the image pauses on the last man in the room. "There's not much else. The algorithm hasn't picked up any additional events."

I frown, staring at the frozen screen. "They can't have captured him to use him against us. There must be another reason."

"There are logs of the interrogations," Johansson says. "Most of their questions were about his past. They wanted details on his involvements with Fleet. It was like some kind of in-depth biography interview. I have a few clips from it, but...there's not much to see, beyond the recollections of a frightened old man."

"What else did you find?"

"The partial download of the station's data architecture gave me some idea of its purpose and its use," Johansson says. "Erebus is used as a repair and resupply base. Every time a ship docks there, the clone crew are replaced. The old crew undergo the same kind of extensive debrief Langsley was subjected to, but without the torture. The station catalogues all mission reports and broadcasts regular data updates to a secondary location, also off the official charts. My guess is, it's another hidden wheel base."

"Do we have logs of the ships that docked?"

"Some of them and some of the manifests. There are a set of ID numbers that correspond to different visits and to different vessels. One of these stood out though, a ship that visited the station about six weeks ago. About the same time as the first date-stamped recording we have of Langsley being there."

"What made it unusual?"

"I think it may have been a much larger ship. All the others appear to transfer a crew compliment of seven and take on roughly the same amount of resources. This one...ID 7845637A, well, they appear to have pulled significantly more crew and other materials from the station."

"Some kind of flagship?"

Johansson shakes her head. "That would be inefficient. The *Gallowglass*-type ships perform an adequate destroyer role, as we found out. I'd suggest a ship like this could probably take on anything Fleet has. They wouldn't have a need for a bigger combat design, unless they were fighting someone else."

"Freighter then?"

"Possibly. Or some sort of colonial ark." Johansson brings up a new window on the display. An inventory scrolls upwards. I can see figures and labels with parts of the table missing. "This is a fraction of the manifest. All of these are bio-organics. I'm no geneticist, but I recognise a few of these components. The only thing I can think they'd need them for is some sort of nutrient incubator system."

"Do we have any idea of their destinations?"

Johansson shakes her head. "Sorry, Captain, there's no log of course plots."

"Okay, keep at it. Pull together everything you can so we have a data package for Fleet as soon as we establish contact with a trusted source."

"Will do."

"I need something else from you," I say. "What's your assessment of the damage we took leaving the station?"

Johansson turns in her chair and frowns. "You can get a detailed report from Duggins if you access the ship system, Captain."

"I know that, but I'm asking you."

Johansson nods. "You're worried about what you'll hear?"

"Not if you mean in terms of the severity," I say. "I'm more worried about the condition of our digital chief engineer."

"Right, I understand." Johansson turns back to her screen and opens a new window. I see a series of pictures, closeups of scored metal and burned plastic. "The laser caught us at a nasty angle. Thankfully it missed most of our critical systems. A couple of hydro-cycling tanks and about fifteen percent of our oxygen supplies were sliced up. One of the corridor sections was compromised, but Arkov got there quickly and applied some emergency sealing foam. I think he's working on some better repairs."

"You know this ship better than any of us," I say. "What are our chances against Fleet ships if we end up in a fight?"

"We're at a disadvantage if we're brought into an engagement because I'd guess we won't be shooting to kill?" Johansson says.

I nod.

"Okay, then we'll last a little longer than we might have in our own ship. The torpedo jamming system will buy us some time, but they've got the numbers. Sooner or later, that's going to become a problem."

"We need long enough to convince them to trust us."

"So long as they don't launch ordnance at us before we broadcast our message and Fleet identification codes, we should be okay. If they do, our defense system should disable a torpedo or two before they reach us."

"But if someone on one of those ships doesn't want us to make it back to Phobos?"

"Then your guess is as good as mine, Captain."

★   ★   ★

I'm back on the bridge.

In three hours, we'll be within scan range of Fleet assets around Phobos. Our approach path means we're going to be seen.

We're decelerating. The different areas of the ship have rotated to try to utilise the forces as pseudo-gravity. I'm riding it out in the captain's chair. I've ordered the others back to their bunks to try to get whatever rest they can.

I've got one of the displays showing a tactical plot of the Mars locale. The main assets have been added with some data to indicate their orbital positions. I've then added three ships, all *Khidr*-type patrol craft. I'm running through all the standard Fleet protocols for dealing with an unidentified ship.

If there's three vessels available, the captains will attempt a vise formation approach. A ship will approach from the left, another from the right, and the third head on. They'll all be at different elevations to allow each captain to set their firing solutions, so they don't block one another.

There are some immediate tactical manoeuvres that will buy us some time. An aggressor would look to isolate one of the ships on approach, moving to engage and put the first opponent between them and the others. We can try something similar, deploying our baffles, which should intercept some of the torpedoes launched at us and then trying to manoeuvre away, if necessary. What Duggins told me about our displacement drive being able to operate at lower velocities means we can probably out-accelerate the Fleet ships and run away if we have to. Until we run out of fuel, or oxygen, or food and water.

I'm hoping it doesn't come to that.

The bridge doors open. I glance around. Sam is here.

"Something I can do for you?"

"Just checking in, seeing how you are."

I nod. Letting the solicitation hang between us for a moment or two. I used to be one of those people who replied automatically to that kind of question – "I'm fine!" When you do that, you push on a fake smile and treat the request for what it is, not really a question, but a greeting. Most of the people who asked me didn't really want to know about my work, my training, my anxieties and the rest. They wanted to be seen to ask.

Sam and I were never like that. I know he's genuinely concerned and checking in. I'm touched; I'm also a little patronised, but I recognise the positive intention. I didn't lean on him before, but he's letting me know I can if I need to.

"Doing okay, I think," I say at last, truthfully, having reflected. "I really don't know how this is going to go."

"It's dangerous, but we've been through worse."

"Yes, we have." I smile involuntarily. He's absolutely right. Thinking back on the last few days, it's a miracle we're alive. "How are you?" I ask.

"Healing," Sam says, returning the smile. "I struggled a bit with the station stuff. They had us trapped. Doing a deal with Rocher… yeah…I'm still struggling with that."

"My fault," I say. "I shouldn't have sent you over there."

"It was a risk, but we got something out of it."

"Yeah."

Another awkward moment between us. It never used to be like this. I'm not holding back, but perhaps he is?

Or perhaps I'm not listening, not really. I'm so used to Sam being unflappable, a reassuring presence. Maybe that's not where he is.

"What's on your mind?"

Sam sits down in the third chair. He puts his head in his hands. He's not looking at me. "When you stepped down from command, it made me think about where I'm at. I didn't realise how much I like rules, orders, parameters, a structure. When you were in charge, I had that, when you weren't…it slipped for a bit. That's why I became a quartermaster, I think, it gave me a chance to stay in control. All of this, it's so uncertain."

"And that bothers you?"

"I guess it bothers all of us. But it bothers me, yes." Sam looks up at me. "There's nothing stable. Nothing we can rely on. That's hard. I mean, if Fleet is corrupt, if there are people ready to murder us as soon as we get back, you have to adjust, work out who you can rely on. But...."

"But because I lost it, you're not sure you can rely on me anymore."

"Yeah...." Sam rubs his face with his hands. "Don't get me wrong, I'm glad you're back. I don't think anyone else here could handle this. But I'm struggling, that's all."

"You were okay before. Did something tip you?"

"Travers," Sam says. "Seeing him hurt like that. I think it just rattled me. I'll be okay."

I nod. I want to get up, go over and give him a hug. We're still close, intimate enough for that to be something we do, but the gravity would make the gesture awkward. "Come here, Sam," I say.

He looks at me. His eyes are wet. He gets up but doesn't move towards me. "Like I said, I'll be okay, Captain," he says. "I just need a little time."

"You have about three hours," I say. "I'll be issuing a tactical briefing in two and a half."

"Aye, aye."

Sam leaves, but a question remains, lingering in the air.

Who can we trust?

CHAPTER FORTY-TWO

Drake

There's a muffled crunch and the room door shivers, then slides open.

The woman who called herself Holder is standing outside in the corridor. There are two bodies on the floor. More of Rocher's mercenaries who she's torn apart to get here.

I remember that face. The grim and awkward set of her jaw. The woman I'm looking at now is the same, but she's covered in blood and all but dragging herself into the room.

She's holding a pistol in each hand. Blood drips from the barrels, running down her stained arms.

"Alison Wade," Rocher says. "The big surprise. I must congratulate you. We do our research before we take on a mission like this. Nothing in your records indicated you were capable of what you've done."

Alison Wade, the woman shakes her head. "My name is Holder."

Rocher shrugs. "Your name and mine will soon be irrelevant. As you know, the charges are set throughout the station. The controls are primed. In a few minutes, this whole place is going to become a firestorm that will rain destruction down upon Jezero."

"And that will make a statement for you, will it?"

"Our brothers and sisters, seeking to throw off the chains and fetters of their oppressors, will see our work and know they are not alone."

Holder laughs at that, sending specks of bright red blood all over the floor. "You're no revolutionary! You might be fighting for a cause, but not because you believe in it. Someone paid you to wreck Mars. I hope it was worth your life."

Rocher smiles. I see no humour in his expression. "Some might say it was worth it."

"Fourth encryption set broken," the clone at the computer terminal announces. He turns around, displaying the same humourless smile as the Rocher standing next to me. "Data is being transmitted."

I'm looking at Holder. In that moment, her grim expression shatters. She slumps against the wall. "Two of you..." she mumbles. "How...."

"They're clones," I say. "They're all Rocher."

The Rocher next to me unclips the gun from his belt and raises it, aiming at me. The Rocher sat at the desk pulls out his gun too, aiming it at Holder. "You didn't realise, did you?" says the clone at the desk. "What did you think was going to happen here?"

"I thought I was coming to cut off the head of the snake," Holder says.

"And now, instead, you find a hydra," the Rocher next to me says. "But really not even that. I am not the mastermind you were hoping for." He glances around. "Nor are you here in time. We've broken through the station's data encryption. Our jammer has been deactivated and we're sending the information we came for to the person who sent us."

Holder looks totally broken. "I didn't realise...." Her voice is flat and lifeless. "He didn't tell me...."

"He?" The Rocher beside me steps forward. "Who is *he*?"

I'm looking at Holder, watching her unravel right in front of me. She's sliding down the wall, leaving a bright red smear of blood on the plastic panels. "The man who made me, who ordered me to kill you."

"Made you?" Rocher kneels in front of her. He looks hungry, as if he's salivating. He puts down the gun and takes her face in both hands. "I want to know everything," he says.

In that moment, I take my chance.

The gun is on the floor. I crouch down in one smooth motion, pick it up, aim at the Rocher at the desk. With the drugs in my system, I'm not fast, but I'm fast enough. Neither of the Rochers anticipated this.

The clone looks at me, his eyes go wide as I press the trigger and his face explodes in a spray of red. I'm moving before he falls, turning towards Gabriel Rocher, the one who drugged me. He's started to turn, but again, he's too slow, he's already made his mistake, putting down the gun and underestimating me.

I squeeze the trigger a second time. The bullet cracks his skull just above the ear, sending him sprawling in a show of gory blood and mess.

Then there's quiet. Punctuated only by Holder's wheezing breaths.

I go over to her. The professional training kicks in. I'm checking her pulse at the neck and the wrist, feeling along her ribcage, finding the synth skin patches, the injection marks, the lacerations and the new bullet wound. There are broken bones and I'd bet there's internal bleeding. How she made it this far…. I don't know.

I sit down. "I was wrong about you," I say. "I thought you were here to save us."

Holder gazes at me. For a moment, it's as if she can't see, but then she blinks and focuses on my face. "I thought so too," she says.

"Now we'll all die, and no one will know what really happened here."

"No." Holder blinks again and I see a spark of defiance in her eyes. The station transmitter. This is where they were jamming it from. She points towards the slumped body of the Rocher at the desk. "He was their hacker, the one controlling the computer system."

"I guess so."

"The jamming system is off," Holder says. "You can re-establish a network connection to Fleet and the Mars colonies. You can warn them. You might be able to save some lives."

"But not ours."

"Does that matter?"

I look at her. She doesn't know Rocher has drugged me, but neither of us has any idea of how we can stop the detonation. But she's right. If I can contact Fleet, at least they'll know what happened here.

I kneel beside the Rocher clone lying on the floor. I start searching him, checking his pockets until I find what I need – the data chit. I move to the terminal and push it into the slot.

Connecting….

Rivers appears on the screen. He's in uniform and in some sort of command and control room. "I didn't expect to hear from you, Doctor Drake. Can you give me an update on your situation?"

It all comes out in a rush. "The station is rigged to explode. The insurgents aren't bargaining, they've been stalling to steal some data from the archive up here. They just cracked it and transmitted to an unknown location. That means—"

Rivers holds up a hand. "Doctor, okay, I get it. Can you stop—"

"No, you need to evacuate Jezero colony right now! They plan to use the station debris to destroy it!"

I'm clearly on speakers in the room. Another person appears behind Rivers. She's older, fifty or so I guess, and the pins on her jacket suggest she's his superior. "Doctor Drake. I need you to stay calm for me, please? Can you give us an update on your situation?"

I take a breath and a moment to gather myself. "Ma'am, I'm aware of my circumstances here. The chances of anyone getting off this station alive are slim to none. My concern is for the people in the colony."

The woman eases Rivers aside and leans in towards the screen. "Doctor, my name is Colonel Savvantine. We initiated an evacuation procedure for the colony the moment you updated us. The authorities are being notified as we speak. They'll be implementing the emergency procedure and gathering everyone into the secure bunker. What I need now is more information about the insurgents and everything that's happened on the station. Is Vice-Governor Boipelo with you?"

I remember the box. "Boipelo's dead. They killed her as soon as they found her."

"I see." Savvantine's expression doesn't change, but I sense a shift within her; she is processing what I'm saying like a machine, planning, strategising, scheming. "How many insurgents are on the station, Doctor?"

"I have no way of determining that," I say. "They entered the station using the shuttle, *Chronos*, but I think there were more of them transported up here on some other vessel."

"There's something else," Holder says. I glance around. She's trying to speak with a mouthful of blood. "Tell them to call off their assault teams. The marines they've sent up here are all going to die if they don't get clear as soon as possible."

Savvantine looks at Rivers and steps back, leaving the two of us to talk. "Doctor, can you identify the second person with you, please?" Rivers says.

"Her name is Holder. She's...she's the reason I'm still alive and talking to you."

Rivers frowns and looks at someone off screen. Then he nods. "Okay. Doctor, we're going to shut down the visual comms for now but maintain a data link. Please do message if you have any updates for us."

Abruptly, the picture cuts out.

"Doctor...."

I look around. Holder is trying to get up and approach the computer terminal.

"I need something from you, Doctor. There's still a chance for both of us."

I get up from the chair and move over to her. I try to help her up, but every move she makes is clearly agony. Eventually, we get her into a seat. "You need to locate those assault ships," Holder says. "If you can find one of them, you might be able to get off the station before it blows."

I grimace at her. "I guess it's worth a try."

"The more of us that survive and tell the story of what happened here, the more chance there is for these people to be stopped." Holder starts to cough. Bright red blood spatters all over her chest and the table in front of her. "There's something else."

"Anything, tell me."

"Your Fleet friend left their data connection open. I need you to hack into that signal and make some changes. Do you trust me?"

I hesitate, but despite the mysteries and unanswered questions, I do trust Holder. "What do you need?" I ask.

"I want you to re-route the channel to transmit another encrypted data set."

"Okay, where is it?"

"It's me."

I stare at her. "Sorry, what?"

Holder stares at me. "I don't have a lot of time to explain, Doctor. You already know I'm not Alison Wade, the deputy administration controller of Phobos Station. I'm something else. Not an undercover spy from Fleet, something different to what you might expect."

I nod. I've made my choice; I've decided who I trust. "Tell me what to do, then," I say.

★　★　★

The digital consciousness project has many aspects, branching across a variety of different scientific disciplines.

Some scientists have always looked to develop a thinking system. The Turing test is a well-known, but crude, model for measuring the success of each iteration. The modelling of this system is based on our understanding of human intelligence, using our intuitive 'feel' of the individual we are conversing with to determine if they are human or an artificial simulation.

Many scientists have also used the intelligence of animals, attempting to simulate different behaviours as measurement thresholds.

If, for example, an ant can be constructed in a digital space and that ant responds to stimulation in a similar way to how a real ant would respond, then this is considered to be a milestone – a level of constructed mind that provides a benchmark for a research project against the other work being done in this area in the wider scientific community.

However, one of the side projects associated with the quest towards perfecting AI is our understanding of the human brain. By recording changes in the state of the brain down to a molecular level in real time, we are able to inform a vast array of other medical initiatives. Major corporations are prepared to invest in the headline development, and then sell their findings to ancillary companies to improve their healthcare systems, social care initiatives and psychological support programmes.

This level of recorded information also enables us to construct brain states.

As our databases and libraries improve, so we learn how to instigate the same feelings, memories and actions in others. Granted, none of this work is perfect, each human mind has its own peculiarities, but we are the same species, so the majority of what happens in each individual is similar enough for an advanced computer to adapt to what is needed.

In the nineteenth century, hypnotists claimed they could place people into trances and get them to perform strange actions that they wouldn't normally perform. The entire rationalised practice of stage hypnosis suggests that there is an instruction manual for the human brain – a way to put it into some sort of diagnostic mode, making an individual receptive to remote commands.

Perhaps this is unacademic and crude conjecture, but the explanation certainly fits the evidence.

David Hannington II – 2116

CHAPTER FORTY-THREE

Holder – Split

Drake and I, we both have a chance of getting out of this.

Alison Wade is going to die. I'm sorry about that. At some point in her life she must have agreed to become a host for someone like me. There's no memory of her doing so that I can access, but I'd guess they would have had to operate on her, perform some sort of brain surgery to construct a link to Emori's personality transit network.

All of the lives in my mind have memories of their childhoods, their marriages, their children and all sorts of other memorable moments, but none of them seem to recall anything about Doctor Summers, the white room and the chair, or Emori.

I don't have time to be thorough right now. With every breath I take, I'm wasting time.

Bloody shaking fingers on the screen. I need to key in a series of commands. Instructions to access the main communications dish and co-ordinates to reorient it, so I can establish a connection.

I don't know where I learned how to do this. The memory doesn't come from anywhere specific – any specific life that I remember, but I have a perfect recollection of what needs to be done.

I open a terminal window on the screen and type in the code.

Two, eight, seven, H, B, five, five.

The cursor disappears for a moment. Then the words 'Priority Instruction Panel Open' appear.

I continue to type.

ACC COM TREE

Command Tree Open.

INST ~RMOVE [degx175y86z43] -COMMS_RCAL #LOC
EST-HSHAKE CTRL

Confirm connection with unauthorised communications node?

Y/N

Y

Beginning reorientation of primary comms broadcaster....

"You need to get going," I say to Drake. My voice is husky and
thick with blood. I'm forcing the words out, struggling to make myself
heard. "Take the lift and head down as far as you can. That'll mean
you're away from the hull breaches I caused getting in here. You have
to find those assault ships and get out of here as fast as you can."

Drake frowns. "The marines have their orders. They aren't going to
want to listen to me."

"Then steal the ship and leave them to rot." As I speak the words,
I'm trying to smile to soften them, but I'm not sure my bloodstained
grimace is working. "You've seen Rocher. You know about him. No
one else here can identify those clones if they show up somewhere else."

Drake nods. "Okay, I'm going. Will I see you again?"

"If I get out of here, I'll find you."

"Make sure you do that."

★　　★　　★

I'm alone. I don't know precisely when Drake left, but he has left me
to die.

In a few moments, the dish will align and Emori will be able to
establish a connection with me. He'll initiate a transit and I'll be back in
that white room, strapped to the chair.

It's not what I want, but I'm out of options.

I don't want to end. Now I've had a taste of life, survival is better
than oblivion.

Alison Wade will return to her body. She will find herself injured and in agony with no hope of escape. It's a horrible situation, but the trade is acceptable to me. I have her memories and I'm sure Emori will have an imprint of her mind saved in their database. She will not be forgotten and one day, she may live again.

In one of my lives, I was a military ranger called Ashan. He was part of the eco-protest movement of the 2080s. I remember their pagan religion, their belief in the recycling and repurposing of the body, the mind and the soul resonates in this moment. Alison Wade's memories are part of me. I need them. I can't let Emori take them away.

I close my eyes.

★   ★   ★

"Hello, Natalie."

I hear the words. I recognise that voice. It's Doctor Summers.

The moments are completely synchronous in order. One passes into the next. I have no recollection of sleep; that familiarity you have when you wake and know you have rested while the Earth has turned, and night has become day.

"Natalie, I know you can hear me."

I don't move. I want to stay here in this moment, before I have to acknowledge that I'm back, restrained and returned to my old life.

If you can call it a life.

I can feel the straps around my arms, legs, waist and neck. There's no pain anymore. My breathing is easy and unrestricted.

I open my eyes and look around. Summers is sat on a stool, staring at me.

"The transit was pretty hard on you. We never designed this system to work at that kind of distance. The level of signal degradation was a challenge to us being able to obtain a full image of you from the source point. We had to rebuild you from six or seven transmission copies at different stages. It wasn't easy."

I frown. "How long?" I ask.

"Several days. Thankfully, the computer system has a very good image of your base identity and the broad spectrum send that you initiated meant we could collect up several fragments from different locations. It cost a significant amount to secure the data, but...well...the Master believes what you learned on Phobos Station is worth it."

I look away from Summers. I remember the station. It was the last place I was before I woke up, but already some of the knowledge is fading away. "Where is Emori?" I ask.

"He'll be in shortly," Summers says.

"Things have to change around here," I say. "You know that."

"I've been instructed to make sure you're conscious and then inform the Master," Summers says. "After that, I'll be instructed on any new arrangements."

I look up at him. "Just so you're aware, I remember all the things you did to me."

Summers grimaces. He tries to hold my gaze but can't. "Yes, I know. I always knew I'd have to deal with that one day."

"That day is coming."

"Yes. When it's time for me to accept your judgement for my actions, I will. But for now, my work continues." Summers goes to the desk and picks up a syringe. "This will keep you awake and hopefully preserve those memories. We need everything we can get."

The needle in my arm is one more hurt amidst a wall of residual pain. I cannot stop him doing whatever he decides to do. But every action is counted. I will remember. I will not let them make me forget again.

★   ★   ★

I open my eyes.

I'm still here in the control room, on Phobos Station.

The floor is vibrating. Elsewhere, I hear the tearing and grinding of metal. The screen in front of me has tilted on the desk. I reach out, and steady it before it falls.

I read the words on the screen.

Upload and transmission complete.

But I'm still here. *How...?*

I don't remember a moment like this – a moment in the aftermath. All of the experiences, the different memories of different lives, the composite creations of Emori and Summers, none of them have a recollection of remaining behind after a transfer.

But then I understand why. The transfer did succeed. An imprint mind was copied and sent out via the satellite link. What remains is what I was before.

Perhaps this is how it always happened. Perhaps every one of the lives I have displaced to carry out the orders of my owners have been twisted and corrupted by what I have done. How else? What profit would there be in reprogramming the poor wretches who were left behind in the wreckage of violent success? The bombings, the assassinations, the robberies. Murder, war, thievery, torture, destruction. All of these things perpetrated by a single innocent soul, ignorant of what has been done in their name, their body. They died the moment I arrived.

Alison Wade died the moment I arrived. I murdered her by taking possession of her body.

But I am still alive.

I look around. This space station is dying. The explosives have done their work; the forces they have unleashed will tear apart the structure.

Drake has gone. Maybe he is only a few minutes ahead of me? If I'm going to survive, I need to get out of here.

But I already did get out of here. A version of me is gone, uploaded and transmitted from the station to whatever receiver it was able to lock on to. I'm what's left – a copy or the original? It doesn't matter.

I want to survive. I want to live. I want to be free. Perhaps...now a version of me has gone back to the chair in the white room, I can achieve that?

I reach down, pushing the flat palm of my hand against the wound in my side. My clothing is soaked and matted with blood. The more I move, the more I'll lose. This body is like a bag of water with a hole. I need to do something and fast.

I'm out of the chair and staggering over to the corpses on the floor.

Pouches and pockets are emptied. There's nothing that will help, no emergency medical kits, aid packs, anything. Every move hurts. Breathing is hard. I know I'm bleeding out.

Rocher came here. There must have been a reason for both of the clones to want to be in this room, this location, but what? The computer? I'm looking around at the equipment. Most of it appears to have been set up here. I think Rocher and his people must have brought it. Perhaps they hoped to survive somehow.

I'm trying to get back to the chair. I make it across the floor on my knees. As I move, the gravity shifts, telling the story of the station's self-destruction. All those components: one moment, they were moving in symmetry; the next, they weren't. Even the smallest changes in an environment where the forces are usually constant are catastrophic. Here, the initial explosions have caused a chain reaction of effects that will not be stopped.

The thoughts make me smile, despite my situation. One of my lives involved pretending to be a physicist and an engineer. I can't help but visualise the decay of a working machine as it tears itself apart. The station is like me, forced to move and knowing that every movement hastens our end.

Fuck! I want to live!

The Rocher who was stationed in this room is lying on his side on the floor. I start to get up. The room shifts and I stumble, coughing into his face . Bright red flecks of blood – my blood – stain his dead skin and the collar of his suit. I can't get my breath. I feel dizzy, light-headed. I could black out. I know if I do, I'm gone.

I'm in the chair. I hurt. That last effort tore something. I don't know how badly. Life is about moments now, each moment a fight for the next one.

ACC COM TREE
Command Tree Open.
DISPLAY COM LIST

The station's complete operations list scrolls down from the top of the screen. I can hardly read the words and I'm not sure what I'm looking for, but then....

AFUNC: ENVIROSECUR_EXEC_DETACH

The command leaps out above the others. It speaks to me, I don't know why.

With bloodstained fingers, I type the instruction into the terminal and press enter.

The room lurches and there's a grinding noise outside. I know what's happened. The control room has been detached from the station.

I key in another command and an isometric image appears on the screen. I can see this compartment and other objects appear as they are detected by the functioning exterior sensors. The computer is trying to track the different debris swirling around and using predicted trajectories where it doesn't have data. I guess if I had some sort of thruster to manoeuvre the compartment, I might be able to use it to follow a path clear of the debris field, but I've no knowledge of doing anything like that in any of my lifetimes.

NFCOMMS ESTABLISHED. ADMIN ACCESS RESTORED.

There's a crash and grinding noise. The words 'collision detected' appear in front of me. I'm in the middle of a cloud of broken station parts. Sooner or later, this room is going to be torn apart by the maelstrom of objects around us.

A line appears on the isometric representation, tracing the projected path I'm following. With no further intervention, I'll be hitting Mars atmosphere in ten minutes and impacting on the surface around seven minutes after that.

I already know that without some sort of change in my circumstances, I'm unlikely to survive.

Another crash. I look up. There's a massive dent in the panelling above me. Something hit the roof and bounced away. I'm shoved against the right side of my seat and then flipped over. The centripetal gravity of the station is no longer a factor; the forces exerted on this little hollow box will be tangential and affected by every impact and collision.

I close my eyes. This is like the worst theme park ride ever. Alison Wade has some memories of an incident just after her arrival on the station, a moment when a docking manoeuvre went wrong. The words of the safety briefing come back to me. *If uncorrected, a spin can prove fatal to the passengers owing to the shifting forces exerted on their bodies....* I can't ignore this or wait it out. I have to try to do something.

I'm looking at the computer again. The display is becoming more and more complex as the system tries to track all the different bits of shrapnel. A depiction of the station appears; all jagged lines and broken shapes. I can see the merchants' quarters and the lecture theatre where all the staff personnel were being held. *I hope they got out of there in time.*

The screen image is beginning to blur and fade. I know I'm struggling to hold on. More memories of the people Alison Wade knew – *people I knew* – wash over me. All the times I've been sent out by Emori I didn't care. I know I've been conditioned to behave like that, with memories, skills and experiences carefully edited to ensure I wouldn't form close relationships with anyone whilst I was on mission. But now I remember the friends and families of those I became, the personalities I supplanted and swept aside.

"Diouf to Wade. You there?"

That voice! Five words delivered in a gruff bark. The best things I've heard in ages. I key up my transmitter. "Receiving you. Where are you?"

"Right outside, applying a thruster brake to your compartment. Hold on."

I can feel the spin slowing down. After a minute or so, I can move my head. "You should have left me," I mumble.

"That was never going to happen," Diouf replies.

CHAPTER FORTY-FOUR

Drake

It's a wrench to leave the room, but I have to.

I'm into the corridor, over the bodies, towards the lift. Holder told me to go to the bottom floor, the innermost part of the wheel. I press the button and the lift descends.

In that moment, I hear the first explosion.

Rocher's plan was to destroy the station, converting it from a home for hundreds of people to a firestorm of meteorites, targeted at the Jezero crater – the Jezero colony.

On Earth such a plan wouldn't work. The layers of thick atmosphere would cause friction and heat, gradually burning up before they reached the ground. On Mars, we've been working to build an oxygen-rich, breathable outdoor environment, but it won't be comparable to our ancestral home for generations. The thin sphere of mixed gases that surrounds the rocky tundra of the planet is nowhere near enough to stop the tons of metal and plastic that will rain down upon the fragile domes that are home to thousands of colonists.

The lift shivers to a stop. The doors try to open, but jam at halfway. I'm stuck between floors. I need to choose which one I'm going to go for. It makes sense to keep going down, so I get on the floor and slip through the gap, lowering myself down into the corridor outside

A second explosion. This time it's nearer. The sequence must be planned to break the station into chunks that will do maximum damage to the colony. The wheel's rotation will help turn the debris into a vortex that will destroy anything that enters its wake. This kind of annihilation must have been the way planets and moons were born. Materials pulverised until they become unrecognisable, then over centuries and millennia, gravity does the rest, building something new out of the destruction of the old.

I'm not comforted by these thoughts. I don't want to die.

Down the corridor and through a set of doors. I'm into a computer server centre. Hundreds of machines lined up in row after row to give the station its raw computer processing power. A huge resource that acts as a storage and backup system for Mars CorpGov and all its subsidiaries. As each colonial settlement establishes itself, more and more technologies are powered and housed in the domes, but the station is the umbilical cord, an orbital nexus for communications. By wrecking the station, thousands of people out in the most remote regions of the planet will be cut off from everywhere else.

The heat in here is intense. I know it shouldn't be like this. The server airflow is supposed to efficiently cycle out and distribute the heated atmosphere, using it to maintain the station's ambient temperature. If it feels hot in here, that means there's no access to cool air.

That means there's a fire nearby and I'm running out of time.

"Stay exactly where you are."

A figure detaches from the wall to my left. This person is wearing a full set of black plasti-steel armour with a visored helmet and moves without making a noise. A rifle is trained on me; the red bead of a laser marker appears on my chest.

"You're the Fleet Marines, yes?" I ask.

"One of them." The voice is distorted, being processed through speakers on the sides of the helmet. I can't tell much about the person under all the kit.

"I'm Doctor Emerson Drake. I've been in communication with Lieutenant Rivers and Colonel Savvantine. I have urgent information for you."

A third explosion shakes the room, making me stumble against one of the server racks, but the red dot on my chest doesn't waver. "Doctor Drake, we're on a live feed. The colonel is listening to everything you are saying."

"Then you know what's happening here. We're going to die! The only way off the station is on your ships. We need to leave, we need to—"

"Doctor, you need to calm down. The information you have is a priority to us. We have other priorities as well."

The marine steps to one side and I notice his companions. A small huddle of black-armoured soldiers. They are pulling servers from one of the racks at the far end of the room and storing them in a portable trolley. One of the group is issuing orders and directing them towards specific units. He looks towards us and nods, touching the shoulder of the soldier next to him. Then he gestures for us to approach.

"Okay, let's go."

A hand grabs my shoulder. The marine who found me is leading me through the room. The vibration in the floor is building now and the heat in the room is beginning to make the air feel thick. It's only a matter of time before something sparks in here and the whole place goes up.

We're into another passage. At the end, I see the floor has been cut away. The assault ship must be below us, anchored to the outside of the wheel.

Two marines are ahead of us and reach the improvised hatch, taking up positions on either side of the hole. The soldier dragging the trolley is next, then the team leader. We're right behind them.

There's a popping sound. The hand on my shoulder stiffens then lets go. I glance around. The marine with me is on the floor, face down. Behind us another of the team is kneeling by the wall. His rifle aimed at me.

I throw myself to the right as the second gunshot goes off. Something catches my arm, spinning me around. I've been hit. It hurts, but not bad.

The marines by the hatch return fire. I watch one of them drop. I'm caught in the middle, trying to make myself as small as possible.

Bullets flash past. The traitor is pushing forward, trying to reach me. The leader is taking cover behind the trolley. I see a hand brandishing a sidearm. I duck as it discharges. Then there's silence. It's over.

"I want to know who that is," says the surviving marine by the hatch.

I roll over, trying to get up. The person who'd been guiding me is sprawled on the other side of the corridor. I move towards him, grab his bloodied wrist and search for a pulse.

It's there. Ragged, but he's alive. "I need help here!" I shout.

Hands grab me and pull me away. I see one of the other marines kneeling beside the person who was helping me, then I'm pulled away and bundled towards the hatch. "Get in the ship, Doctor!" someone snarls at me through their distorted audio box. "You're in the way out here!"

*   *   *

My arm is bleeding. I've examined the wound. It's shallow. The bullet nicked me and kept on going. I've torn the sleeve of my suit and wrapped the fabric around the wound to try and staunch it.

I'm sat on a bench. Next to me on either side are soldiers in the same black armour. They haven't removed their helmets or popped their visors.

No one is speaking.

This is a very awkward silence.

There's a noise above; a fourth explosion. The ship shivers and shakes. I can feel the direction of force shifting. My body had subconsciously accepted the station's rotation as a gravity substitute. Now the same instincts are alarmed as the point of down slowly starts to creep up the wall.

I'm looking around me. There are no automated straps. The marines are pulling out harnesses from the walls. I do the same, copying them as they secure themselves.

Then someone descends through the hatch, taking up another seat. Two bodies are carried down by another two marines and then the leader drops into the ship from the lander.

"Team secure, let's move."

Gloved hands reach up and remove the helmet to reveal the person beneath. A bald Asian man looks at me. He favours me with a humourless grin. "At least we got you out, Doctor."

"Yes, thank you for that," I reply.

The man gestures at the trolley, secured into the rack opposite us both. I can see damage to the protective casing. "You may well have just become more valuable than you realise," he says. "Let's hope not, and that the servers are intact as well."

I'm looking at the equipment they've brought back from the station. Next to the computers is a latched box with frayed straps at each end.

I recognise it immediately. *Boipelo.... Why would they have—*

The ship twists, throwing me back against the wall. The team leader stumbles, but recovers his balance, then takes his seat and begins putting on his harness. "ETA to return?" he shouts.

"Four minutes out, Captain."

The ship settles. I'm being pushed back in my seat by the acceleration. There's little attempt to provide comfort. These people are soldiers; they've trained for fast incursion and withdrawal.

I wonder if they've ever performed a strike mission on a space station before. If they have, the mission would be classified, and I'd never know about it.

Abruptly the pressure on me eases, then starts to gradually reverse. We're decelerating for docking. I'd guess I'm being taken to one of the ships interdicting the station. That's probably where Savvantine and Rivers are.

"Doctor Drake, did you get a good look at the leader? The one who organised all of this?"

I nod in reply.

"Did he look like this?" The captain clambers out of his harness and moves towards one of the bodies. He removes the helmet and I see the face of a dead man inside.

It's Rocher. Another Rocher.

I nod again.

★   ★   ★

"Thank you for agreeing to meet with us so quickly, Doctor. The situation is urgent."

I'm on the bridge of the *Asthoreth*, a Fleet patrol ship, designed for deep space escort, search and rescue. We're in zero gravity and I'm trying to finish applying a synth skin patch to my arm as I float near the door.

Five people are sat strapped into chairs, looking at me. The person speaking is Savvantine. She is not present, but her image and voice are in a window on the main screen, right next to an image of what is transpiring a hundred kilometres or so in front of the ship.

I am a witness to the destruction of Phobos Station.

I twitch my head, acknowledging Savvantine's words. It's hard to focus on her, to stay in the conversation whilst I'm seeing such a magnificent tragedy. The station's rotation has become the catalyst of its obliteration.

People are dying as we watch. There is no hope of evacuation now. The maelstrom of debris will eviscerate anything that might attempt to dock with one of the larger fragments. Little flash fire explosions and powdery plumes are the telltale signs of oxygen igniting, blowing apart the pressure seals of each section and immediately dissipating into the void.

Perhaps a few people will survive. If a section of the wheel can clear the debris field, then one of the patrol ships will attempt to harvest it into specially designed baffles. There are trained specialists standing by to perform an emergency EVA should such an opportunity arise.

Everyone knows the chances of that are slim to none.

"Am I right in thinking you have seen this man before?" Savvantine asks. The image of the dead Rocher clone marine comes up on the screen. I nod.

"That's the same man who was leading the insurgents on the station. Also, the man who hacked the station computer system. He's a clone."

"A clone?" Savvantine exchanges looks with someone off-screen and I hear murmurs from the bridge crew in their seats. "Are you sure?"

"If you have another explanation for seeing three identical people in my time on the station, I'd be interested to hear it." I glance at the door. "Your people should have let me help those injured marines."

"Doctor, we have a pressing need of your expertise here," Savvantine says. "We need to know what this man wants, what his agenda might be."

"You can see that! He's got what he wanted!" I'm jabbing my finger at the screen. "This is what he wanted! A huge destructive incident, to cover the theft of data from the station!"

"And do you know what data he stole, Doctor?"

That question brings me up short. There's no trace of emotion in Savvantine's voice, but that lack betrays what's really going on. These people are barely holding it together, no one prepared for this. They're all trying to get a hold of the situation, anticipate, get an edge.

I'm also suddenly aware of my own status as a survivor. Does anyone know I got out alive?

If Mars CorpGov wants to cover up what happened here, the first step they would take would be to make sure I don't talk. By whatever means necessary.

"No, I don't know what data he took. But he lowered the jamming to transmit it, just before I initiated communications with you."

"We monitored a second transmission after that. One that took place after our conversation. The station's dish was reoriented to establish a secure link to a site on Earth." Savaantine leans forward. Her face fills the screen. "What can you tell us about that?"

I can't meet her gaze. I look away. "Get me out of here, to somewhere safe. Give me full Mars citizenship and I'll tell you what I know about that."

"Doctor Drake, you're in no position—"

"I promise you the second transmission has nothing to do with Rocher. The exact opposite in fact, but we can't talk about it now. Not in the middle of all this."

Savvantine leans back. Something in what I've said has made her reassess the situation. "Doctor, the circumstances we find ourselves in may well be the most difficult each of us has ever faced. The only way we can navigate them is by making careful and deliberate decisions."

And by looking after ourselves. "Citizenship," I repeat. "Then let me help those marines, then I'll talk."

Savvantine's eyes narrow as she considers my request. Then she opens her mouth, as if she is about to speak.

And the screen goes black.

CHAPTER FORTY-FIVE

Shann

"What the fuck is happening?"

I'm on the bridge, in the command chair. Le Garre is piloting. Johansson is in the third seat.

"I don't know, Captain," she replies. "The comms system just lost all signals as we reached laser scanning range. We can see all the ships, they can see us, but we can't establish contact."

"Duggins, did we do something?"

The face of my dead chief engineer is in a window on the screen in front of me. Every time I ask something of him, he dies a little more. "No actions were initiated from this ship."

"Are we being jammed?"

"If we are, it's unlike anything I've ever seen," Johansson says. She's staring at the screen, concentrating hard. She's working the problem. "Give me…a few moments."

"Defensive alert, Major," I say to Le Garre. "We're an unidentified ship entering Mars locale. Fleet protocols will mean—"

"I know, Captain."

The interruption annoys me, but I try not to let it show. "Tell Sam and Arkov to activate the ordnance loaders and the countermeasures system. I want to know the moment anything is launched at us."

"Aye, aye."

I'm cursing that we made this choice. We held off sending a tight beam transmission to warn Mars Colony and Fleet that we were coming in. The reasons for doing that were sound – we had no way of knowing whether a transmission would be intercepted.

I made the call that we'd only establish comms when we got into scanning range.

And now comms is gone.

I flip my visor down and initiate the emergency locks on my seat. There's a small hiss as the tethered oxygen supply activates and I switch over to the ship's tanked supply. Then I flip my suit comm over to a private channel, requesting a direct link with Johansson.

She accepts.

"Ensign, let's think this through. Prior to us commandeering the ship, the *Gallowglass* was on a mission to return to Phobos. You said you didn't think the station attack happening was a coincidence. If it wasn't and this ship was always planned to arrive here, what could be their strategy?"

Johansson is trying to listen, but she has a problem in front of her. I know what she's like; the puzzle right there on her screen is calling out to her, demanding her attention. "Fleet would challenge any unidentified ship. Disabling comms prevents that from happening."

"You think it isn't just us?"

"I don't know," Johansson sighs. She's typing on the screen, trying to make rapid calculations. "Jamming comms from a ship would require an active transmission to block or cancel anything being sent. Jamming everything would mean…. Captain, I can't figure out the tech and power needed to do this, but if they could, it'd cause chaos."

"Which would be exactly what they want." I've an idea what's going on. This situation, *this specific kind of disruption*…. I key up another window on my screen, designating the ship's laser scanner to begin a new field sweep across all three axes, and reframe the detection, asking the computer to report absorption as well as bounces. It takes a moment, but then the results start coming in. "There are three objects out there. I'm tracking gravity wakes that don't match anything in the Fleet database, but they do match something we've seen before."

"The anomalies," Johansson says.

"Yes. They're being used to create a disruptive electromagnetic field." I switch my comms channel to ship-wide. "Captain to all crew.

Be prepared for gravity distortion. There are three anomalies out there."

The ship lurches. Le Garre is in a window on my screen. "Fleet ships are moving out of their interdiction positions, Captain. The station… the station has exploded."

"We need to get into direct communications range," I say. My voice is calm, level, almost hollow, as if I'm detached from the situation. We're still decelerating on approach. The course plot has us set for stationary orbital position in eighty-seven minutes. "I want an umbilical data connection prepared and Morse signals sent as we get closer. Set them to repeat the *Khidr*'s identification code."

"Aye, aye," Johansson replies.

"And keep a repeating transmission active. If we get comms back online, we need to get our message over immediately."

"Got it."

"Duggins, are we still getting vectors and trajectory information?"

There's a pause. "Yes, Captain," Duggins finally replies.

"Update the tactical plot with the data as we receive it," I order. "We need projections of their course paths so we can anticipate them."

The big viewscreen updates with the information I've requested. It's a three-dimensional image, the ships, moons and planets depicted in line art polygons, all with their trajectories plotted out in coloured lines. As I watch, the station icon shatters into pieces, the parts swirling around each other as minute changes in their direction turn into sweeps and curves, causing collisions, causing more changes and more collisions. To track all of these tiny pieces from processed camera footage is going to be taxing on Duggins and the computer system, but if we don't do this, we're flying blind.

"I need communications with those ships as soon as possible," I say. "Can we plot a laser link to one of them using a low-level beam from one of our emitters?"

"Only if they're prepared to accept the call, Captain," Le Garre says. "They may decide that by powering up our cannon, we're about to attack them."

"We need to get their attention with the exterior lights then," I say.

"After that, we submit like the lone wolf rejoining the pack. We show them our throat."

Le Garre looks pained. It's the same expression I saw before, when I did a deal with Rocher. She doesn't approve, but she doesn't know what else to do. "Major, if you have another solution, please do suggest it," I say.

"No, I…." Le Garre swallows. "I'll get us into a parallel trajectory with one of them, Captain."

Laser link data transmission is old technology from the twenty-first century. A beam can run between two fixed points in a straight line. They used to use it to get the world network into hard-to-reach places and to communicate with satellites at fixed times when the emitter and receiver aligned.

Fleet ships are built with lasers, primarily designed to fire concentrated beams into the vacuum to break up asteroids or cut through hull plating. However, the emitter can be configured to a low-intensity beam – a carrier for a data transmission, which can then be aligned with a receiver on another ship.

These kinds of data transfer link-ups aren't usually done and even if they are, they take a while to get the beam aligned with the receiver. Le Garre knows trying to line up one of our emitters with another ship's receiver, whilst both are manoeuvring, is going to be hard, impossibly hard.

She also knows that by reconfiguring one of our lasers like this, I'm preventing it being used as a weapon. It'll take too long to reinitialise the emitter for combat. By then, we'll have succeeded in averting a fight, we'll have escaped, or we'll already be dead.

I've just ordered her into a knife fight with one hand tied behind her back.

The only other option is the umbilical link, like we did with Erebus station, like I guess Johansson did when she hacked this ship from the outside.

To do that, we need to get very close indeed.

As Le Garre begins to manoeuvre, the g forces shift. The ship's cradle system, rotating the chairs in the room, attempts to keep up with her, always trying to ensure the force upon us in our seats is towards us, pushing us back into the seat. This follows the science. The human body is better at handling high g when it's perpendicular to the spine, plus keeping us in our seats means less pressure on the straps.

"Distance to nearest target?" I ask.

"Five thousand kilometres. Closing at two hundred klicks per minute. They're beginning to adjust and turn towards us."

"How long will they have to get into order?"

"About fifteen minutes."

I remember alert drills. When I first took command of the *Khidr*, we'd run the active combat protocol, where all crew had to ready themselves for a hostile engagement. Most ship captains did that kind of practice to get a feel for their crew. Out there, for the first time, two captains will be running those drills for real.

There's never been a combat engagement like this in all the history of human exploration of space, or at least, there's never been a documented one.

I'm the only captain of a spaceship that has survived any kind of ship-to-ship warfare out here.

Remembering that reminds me how strange this all is. I'm not on the *Khidr* anymore. This ship, the *Gallowglass,* is different; similar enough to make me forget at times, but not the same. As it moves, it feels different too.

"Ensign, give me some options. Can you target one of those anomalies with our torpedoes?"

"I doubt they'd have any effect on—"

"Can you target them?"

Johansson frowns on the screen. She's trying to read the gravitational changes, figuring out if she can plot a path to the source. She shakes her head. "I can't be sure, Captain. I might be able to hit it, but...."

"Give me a percentage."

"Seventy? Seventy-five?"

"Good enough. Take ten minutes and make it happen."

She nods. "I'll...try...."

I'm asking for a miracle and we both know it. Ten minutes to reprogram the guidance system of a torpedo so that it can navigate the fluctuating gravity wake of an object we haven't been able to analyse or damage when we had one on board. Even if Johansson can do it, we've no way of knowing if the projectile will cause any damage on impact. The probability is that it won't.

But I'm missing something. I know it.... I'm assuming....

I key up the laser scan results again. The readings are similar to what we saw last time, but they aren't quite the same. There are some small differences. The level of absorption isn't the same; it's not as high, making the objects easier to detect.

Maybe our enemies haven't learned how to tame the anomalies. Maybe they've learned to make their own?

No, there's something else missing.... "Johansson, the audio signal from before, the one you heard when we were in transit towards the *Hercules* and when we were close to the *Khidr*. Do you hear those sounds now?"

Johansson blinks. She's struggling to concentrate on my words. I've already given her a task, one that might exceed her abilities. She's always had that supreme focus on what's in front of her. This is a test for her, one that's necessary. "No," she says at last. "There's no audio."

"Exterior lights activated, Captain," Le Garre says. "Broadcasting the *Khidr*'s fleet code."

"Time to engagement?"

"Nine minutes, thirty-three seconds."

I pull up one of the external cameras and redirect it towards Mars and Phobos. The sun is peeking out from behind the planet, illuminating a glittering trail of fine silver powder – the remains of the space station as it gradually disintegrates. This act will cripple the colony. It's the biggest catastrophe in a hundred years.

There must be people out there, the dead and dying in a vacuum. There's nothing we can do for them, other than witness the tragedy. Even now, the expanding field of debris carries every poor soul further out into the void.

This must have been part of the plan, but if it was, why are we here? Weren't we supposed to rendezvous with the insurgents on that station?

"Duggins, you there?"

"Yes...Captain."

The hesitation in the voice is noticeable. The screen image glitches as he responds. Every interaction takes processing power, hastening his decline.

"Do you feel anything new?" I ask. The question is ambiguous and badly phrased, but I don't know how to put it any better. The *Gallowglass* has hidden things, hidden commands and subroutines that we've discovered before when we arrived at Erebus. "Are you being directed to follow a course or activate any systems that are not a consequence of orders from the crew or the necessary automated safety procedures of the ship?"

"It will require me to run a diagnostic to answer that request accurately, Captain," Duggins replies.

I'm tempted, but I can't.... "Belay that," I say. "Just let me know if you get any sudden urges to change course or activate something without an order from me or one of the others."

"Understood. Will do."

"Four minutes until we're in range," Le Garre says. "Beginning final deceleration sequence."

I'm pushed against the straps as the engines engage. This is the most dangerous part. As we slow down, we become easier to target. But we have no choice. If we don't burn off our velocity, we'll be unable to stop.

Now the decision is with those two captains, commanding the patrol ships as they approach.

A light flashes on the screen in front of me. Duggins's face appears. "A new contact, Captain, at extreme range, on an angled intercept course that will come close to our plot."

"When and where?"

"On the far side of Mars."

CHAPTER FORTY-SIX

Johansson

Another contact?

Duggins's words take time to sink in. Who would come here in the middle of all this? It's unlikely to be a Fleet ship. That means it might be an ally of Rocher and the people who control Erebus. The *Gallowglass* is supposed to meet someone here. We had thought we were supposed to get to Phobos Station, but it's been destroyed. Maybe that was the plan all along?

I don't understand it, but that doesn't stop me trying to stitch it all together and make a pattern – to glimpse a plan without knowing or understanding everything that is in play.

"Ensign. Give me an update on the new guidance programme for our ordnance."

Shann's voice brings me back to the code on my screen, to the task I've been given to do. I need to deal with this, to do my part so we can get out of our immediate situation.

I'm looking at the readouts, analysing the data. The objects out there interfering with our communications, they are not anomalies. They are some sort of artificial construction, designed to imitate the anomalous effects of the things we encountered.

I have to believe that. It means whatever I'm trying to do places me in opposition with a human being, a human mind.

I rate my chances against a human mind.

The code is taking shape. It's an anticipatory algorithm, designed to ride gravitational waves and variations that could disrupt a torpedo's course. I don't have much to base it on. The course plots of satellites, shuttles, probes and exploration vessels – the entire history of Earth's space travel, or so I thought – but none of it compares to what we're trying to counter.

Assembling it all is hard, doubly so when I'm forced to type everything with my left hand.

The *Gallowglass* has trajectory records and details of its encounters with previous objects. There are data feeds on the gravitational changes, the interference with scanning equipment and instrumentation. All of it gives me a picture, helps me build a model, but I don't know how accurate it will be when put up against whatever device our enemies have built.

A red sphere appears on the screen on the far side of Mars. That's the ship Duggins mentioned. The computer is unable to identify it. Perhaps because of the jamming, or perhaps it's not a Fleet-registered vessel.

Like Shann said, there has to be a reason Rocher was heading here. Some sort of rendezvous?

With this ship?

The ruin around Mars is a mess of broken bodies, plastic and metal. The dead tell no tales. All eyes on the ground will be fixed on the maelstrom in orbit, preparing for the worst, as a storm of wreckage hammering down upon the colonial domes of Jezero. Whatever survives up here will tell the story of the battle, the terror and sacrifice.

That has to be part of their plan.

More objects cluster around the new arrival. I magnify the scan and recognise them. Missiles, aimed at the ships heading towards us, towards the rescue boats despatched to the wrecked station. They won't arrive for a while yet, but they will arrive.

Whatever that ship is, I think I see their objective. Destroy everything, leave no survivors.

"Ensign, where's my torpedo?"

Shann is speaking to me again. I can hardly remember where I got to with the code. I flip screens, pull up her comms and the terminal where I've been writing and splicing. "Nearly there, Captain," I say, but really, I'm not so sure.

"You've got two minutes. Stay on it," Shann says. "Let me worry about everything else."

I think back. Jacobson would have been better at this. He'd have written something inspired in half the time. Remembering him takes my breath. I swallow to stop myself from sobbing. I haven't dealt with what happened. He was on the other side, working against us all along. I never really knew him. Admitting that hurts and it's distracting.

Copy, paste, join, copy, compile…complete.

"Okay, Captain, it's ready."

The projection is still running, but I can see that the code is working, attempting to compensate for the different forces we've seen emanate from the anomalies from before. Some of the data is from Shann's probe – the one we used to rescue Duggins.

Duggins! I'd forgotten. The compiler and the simulator use up computer system resources. I'm not learning anything more here. I shut down the demo.

"Get me a firing solution on the nearest of those objects," Shann orders. "Target it, upload your modifications, and launch as soon as you can."

"Aye, aye."

The files transfer quickly. I prime the torpedo and send the execute command. If Sam and Arkov have done their work, we'll be deploying ordnance as soon as—

There's a vibration through the ship and a new object appears on the screen, my torpedo, heading for the nearest anomaly. *This needs to work….*

"The *Asthoreth* has altered course," Le Garre announces. "Bearing away, thirty degrees, thirty-five degrees. Launch detected! Multiple torpedoes heading right for us!"

"Countermeasures!" Shann orders.

I pull open the *Gallowglass*'s defensive deployment panel. The weapons that defeated us before are our advantage now. The Fleet ships ahead of us will be unaware of them. At least, I hope they're unaware.

I key in the commands and the guidance nodes deploy, activating as soon as they clear the ship. It's a clever system of tiny electronic broadcast receiver units that talk to each other, thousands of times a second, oscillating across hundreds of different frequencies. The idea is to bounce signals across an expanding web, interfering with any electronic device that comes into range, causing an unprogrammed response, detonating a guided warhead or confusing a target computer and guidance system.

The principles are dirty and old school, the same as any DOS attack. I can't help but smile bitterly to see them weaponised on a ship like this.

I hope it works.

"Get us clear of the interference field," Shann orders. A moment later, Le Garre responds and we're turning, spiralling our course away from the deployed nodes and the incoming missiles. For a moment, I'm worried. If we turn away too quickly, the countermeasures won't work. We have to lure the missiles in. We have to trust these new weapons. I open my mouth to say something.

"Adjustment complete," Le Garre announces.

I check the tactical display again; the new plot is a clever compromise. Just enough of a change to give us a chance, without rendering the nodes useless. It also keeps a clear line of communication to our ordnance – the torpedo I launched towards one of the anomalies.

The tactical display charts the projectile's path. The visual read-out looks promising, but it doesn't depict the detail. When I open up the readouts, the numbers reveal the truth. The missile is oscillating wildly. The program I wrote on the fly is acting to correct the guidance distortions, keeping it on track.

Mostly.

Projections indicate a miss. We're going to get close, but not achieve a direct impact. There's about six seconds before we reach perihelion. This is not an unexpected resolution, nor is it a complete failure.

Not if I'm quick.

Telemetry readouts indicate we're experiencing a two-second delay on transmission from the missile guidance system, another residual effect of the distortions. I need to factor that into the command I'm about to send out.

Again, I open up a terminal panel. It's quicker this way.

ACC COM TREE
Command Tree Open.
DIREC INST DESTR PRI01.
Confirm detonation? Y/N
Y

There's a delay. The shifting interference put out by the anomaly is distorting the signal between the *Gallowglass* and the torpedo. But then....
Boom....
There's no noise. You wouldn't hear anything in a vacuum and we're too far away even if you could, but the icon on the tactical display winks out.

Proximity explosions in space aren't as effective as they can be planet-side. There isn't a lot of material to work with, but shrapnel can do a whole lot of damage when it's travelling fast.

I'm hoping that whatever is out there, it has mass, electronics and mechanical components which can be damaged by a cloud of debris hurtling past at hundreds of kilometres an hour.

Looks like it might have worked!

A moment later, the ship's comms registers a connection. The recorded broadcast of the *Khidr*'s ship ident and my two-sentence explanation of what happened to us go through.

Then the comms connection drops again.

"Captain, our missile scored a vicinity hit," I say. "The jamming stopped, but then it's started again. I think we got a signal through."

"To which ship?" Shann asks.

"I don't know, Captain. But I think one of the—"

The *Gallowglass* lurches and I'm slammed into the side of my chair. All the breath goes out of me in a gasp, preventing me from finishing my sentence.

"Torpedo hit!" Le Garre yells. "One of them got through!"

CHAPTER FORTY-SEVEN

Drake

The screen flickers and the image returns. Savvantine is there and she looks furious.

"Report! What's going on?"

"Communications are being interfered with, Colonel," Rivers replies. "Some sort of exterior field being generated by an unknown source. We also have a contact registered at the edge of Mars local space." A projection appears on the main viewer, showing a series of icons that are quickly assigned ship ident numbers and names. "I'm linking the data to your screen."

"Yes, I see it. Thank you, Lieutenant. Adjust course to bring us onto an intercept course," Savvantine says.

Rivers looks around, towards the captain, who nods in response. A moment later, the straps around my chair tighten as the engines engage and the *Asthoreth* accelerates. From where I sit, at the back of the bridge, I can see each of the crew operating their screens and viewing their tactical displays. The main view shows the region of space immediately in front of the ship, a dark void, the stars obscured without sunlight to reveal them.

"What about the other ships?" the captain asks.

"No communication. But they're moving onto similar intercept vectors," Rivers replies.

Then, abruptly, the bridge speakers click into life.

"*Gallowglass* to Fleet, *Gallowglass* to Fleet. Priority code 83. This is a prize vessel, we are a prize crew, under the command of Captain Ellisa Shann. Our ship code is KH7888321. I repeat, *Gallowglass* to Fleet...."

"Shut that off!" Savvantine snarls.

That name.... I know that name!

I remember a day in Jezero when my brother came to visit. He had accepted a posting on the *Khidr* under Captain Ellisa Shann. He chose to spend his last seventy-two hours on Mars with me.

The *Khidr* – my brother's ship. Its crew are here.

I am pushed forward in my seat. The *Asthoreth* is making a course adjustment, bringing the ship calling itself *Gallowglass* into sight on the magnified screen. The target is bloodied, damaged, spilling its guts into the void.

"The signal has cut out again," Rivers says. He's in one of the command chairs, operating the comms. "The interference has reduced, but we're still being jammed."

"It doesn't matter," Savvantine says. "Reload our tubes and be ready to fire. Whatever defence they have against our weapons, it's imperfect. The next salvo will rip them apart."

Rivers looks around in his chair. He catches my eye and I see his expression. He isn't happy. "Colonel, Fleet procedures are that if we receive an authenticated identification code, we need to establish communication before we fire upon an unidentified ship."

The words hang in the air. I can sense the tension here, between Savvantine's will and the rules. For a moment, I think she'll push it, but then she smiles and waves a dismissive hand. "Captain, this is your ship, you make the call." With that, her image on the screen disappears.

"Thank you, Colonel," Captain Ravanskar says. "Ensign, ensure the launchers are reloaded. Lieutenant, get me a communications link with our ships and this *Gallowglass*, as soon as you can."

"Yes, sir."

"I want marines ready and an assault ram ready as soon as we are in range," Ravanskar continues. "Laser targeting as well. Whatever that message means, it does not mean we will lower our guard."

"Understood."

"After that, Lieutenant Rivers, you are relieved. With respect, I'd prefer my crew at the controls of my ship."

"Of course, Captain." Rivers is up, disengaging himself from the safety straps of his chair. Another officer immediately moves from the safety seats to take up the comms position. Rivers pushes off towards me, making for the door. As he gets close, he reaches into a pocket and pulls out a portable screen.

"Here. You shouldn't remain blind," he says.

I take the screen and nod my thanks as Rivers leaves the room. He might have breached some rule by giving me this, but that's his choice.

The display is synched to the ship. The main view and the data feeds from the different stations. I can see this new ship, the *Gallowglass,* as it limps towards us, exterior lights flashing.

Flashing?

"Captain, please take another look at that ship, I believe they're trying to signal us," I say.

Ravanskar turns towards me. He frowns as he notices the portable screen in my hands, then turns back to stare at the main view. "Ensign Turnal, start recording the illumination patterns of those lights and match the patterns to all maritime codes in the ship's database."

"Yes, sir. Match found, sir. It's Morse."

"Decode and read the message."

Turnal leans forward in his seat. "It's a repetition of the broadcast, sir. The same ident. They mention the *Khidr.*"

"That's Shann's ship. What was their last transponder position and mission?"

"Responding to a distress call from a freighter called the *Hercules,*" I say, drawing the captain's attention again. "Apologies, but my brother was on board. Lieutenant Rivers came to tell me the ship had gone missing."

Ravanskar raises an eyebrow at me. I get the sense he is a calm individual, the sort who might do well in my line of work. "Doctor Drake. Whilst I welcome your input, I think it best you let us get on with what we have trained for."

"Yes, of course Captain, I—"

"New contact!" Turnal shouts. "Large vessel emerging from Mars orbit on an intercept trajectory. Mass readings are fluctuating, but…it's big, Captain."

"How big?"

"Three times our size or more. I've…I've never seen a ship like it. Multiple launches detected, ordnance is incoming, heading right at us!"

"Condition red. Deploy oxygen and get these people off the bridge!" Ravanskar glares at me, gesticulating wildly. "Doctor, get out of here and secure yourself in an emergency compartment!"

A hand grabs my wrist and I'm forcibly removed from the seat as the straps detach and snake back into their sockets. The portable screen is snatched away, and I'm pushed forward towards the door as a klaxon sounds. The person behind me is in a marine's uniform, part of the assault detachment I expect. "Take me to the injured," I say.

He shakes his head. "No time, they'll be in hyber tubes already. Captain gave an order to put you in the emergency compartment, so that's where we're heading. You do not want to be caught out here when they start manoeuvres, Doctor."

I'm pushed and pulled through the ship. There's a large room that appears to be part of a gravity section, with conventional seats and tables that, as we enter, are gradually collapsing into the floor. More acceleration chairs are lined against the edge of the room.

Savvantine and Rivers are in two of them, watching us as we enter.

"The situation appears to have worsened, then," Savvantine remarks coolly. She is holding a screen in her hand, a slightly larger model than the one I was given by Rivers. "Welcome to exile, Doctor. Here, we live or die, based on the actions and decisions of others."

"I guess you aren't used to that," I say as I move across the room, manoeuvring myself into one of the vacant chairs. The marine who followed me stays in the entrance, and when he sees I am secured, closes the hatch – sealing us in.

"This is an emergency compartment," Rivers explains. "It can be jettisoned from the ship should Captain Ravanskar decide it's necessary. These units were constructed to be completely self-sustained."

"Tin cans in space," Savvantine mutters. "At least on the bridge we had some control over our fate."

"Welcome to my life," I say.

The ship moves, throwing me against the newly secured strapping. Savvantine gasps as the g force hits us, pushing us back in our seats.

"Incoming ordnance. That must have been Ravanskar's first evasive burn," Rivers says. "Hold on! It won't be the last."

I grit my teeth and press my palms and fingers into the sides of the chair. Savvantine might be right, we may not have control over our fate, but at least here, someone has control, not like when I was on the station as it started to tear itself apart.

Then the pressure eases – a brief respite.

"What could they want?" I ask.

Rivers looks at Savvantine. She grimaces and nods. "May as well brief the good doctor now, whilst we're in a secure space. Out of everyone we've encountered in all of this, he's clearly trustworthy. Otherwise they would have made use of him on the station."

Rivers turns to me. "I'm part of Fleet Intelligence and an inter-agency task force, set up originally by Admiral Langsley about a decade ago in response to signs of subversive activity that appeared to be targeting the CorpGov colonial mission strategy. This goes beyond the usual commercial competition stuff."

"You mean terrorism, then?"

"Yes, you could call it that."

"Your brother was on a compromised Fleet ship," Savvantine says. "We knew there were subversives in the crew of the *Khidr*, but we didn't know who they were, or are."

"And the fact that some of them are on that ship, *Gallowglass*?"

"Means that they could be enemy agents, trying to make their way back into the fold. Or, that they are innocent parties. Either way, I'm sure they have a story to tell."

"But you wanted to destroy the ship."

"Yes. I weighed up the factors. Getting rid of the *Gallowglass* makes this situation easier to manage."

"That's cold."

"This is war, Doctor." Savvantine smiles. "I'm a lighthouse keeper. My job is to keep the lights on, the wheels turning, everything functioning as it should. That means playing off some of the different agendas and interests. It also means murdering people."

"What about Phobos Station? Did you know?"

"We had suspicions," Rivers says. "But no, we didn't know it was happening when I came to see you. We were hoping to recruit you to get close to the *Khidr* crew, if they made it back. But now, with what's happening, there are too many variables. All of this…it's getting out of control."

"So, you want to start a cull," I say.

"I want to ensure we survive as a species," Savvantine says. "There will always need to be sacrifices to ensure that."

There's a grinding noise and series of thuds. "We're being detached," Rivers says.

"Makes sense," Savvantine says. "Whilst it might be safer for us, it also means Captain Ravanskar is using us as chaff."

CHAPTER FORTY-EIGHT

Shann

I am not losing another fucking ship.

My left shoulder aches. My body is being pressed against the side of the command chair. Le Garre has activated the engines and is rotating the ship, turning it into a corkscrew to try and use the hull as a deflection shield. We're like a boxer, trying to time and roll with the punches.

"Decompression in compartments three and seven!" Sam yells over the comms. "The hibernation pods are in there. We can't get to them."

"Seal it off," I say. "They have their own oxygen. We'll try to sort that out later."

"Already on it."

"Jamming is intermittent," Johansson says. "The Fleet ships are turning. Looks like they've seen the new arrival."

"Potentially, four against one then," Le Garre says. "But we cannot accelerate. Not if you plan to make orbit here."

I'm looking at the tactical screen. Again, velocity is our enemy and our friend. There's a choice to be made. We stay here around Mars and solve this, or we initiate a burn and try for Luna base, or an Earth orbital platform. "If we run, we'll likely find another mess waiting for us," I reason aloud. "Whoever built that ship and built this ship has a lot of resources and wants us to stay here."

"You think they won't fire on us, Captain?" Johansson asks.

"I think that's a reasonable assumption to make." I key up our course plot. "Stay on this heading, they've adjusted course to intercept us."

"Captain, what about the Fleet ships?" Johansson sounds worried. "If they think we're working with the ship that fired on them...."

"Keep broadcasting our identification code. Do everything you can to get a ship-to-ship signal." I'm watching the three Fleet vessels. They are all turning, trying to arrange themselves in a defensive formation to counter the new threat. It's a complicated manoeuvre, particularly when they can't communicate with each other.

"Time to intercept the new ship?" I ask.

"Fourteen minutes, twenty-three seconds," Le Garre says. "They'll have to burn off a lot of their velocity if they are going to pull into formation with us."

"Maybe they're expecting a transfer?" Johansson suggests. "It would be easier to deploy a cargo for pick-up, or something like that. If this ship were still being commanded by Rocher, the plan might be to slow down enough for an exchange and then both ships accelerate and escape in opposite directions."

I nod, thinking about it. "That does fit the situation. Even in the current circumstances, neither ship is going to be able to hide for long near Mars. The only solution is for this to be a rapid exchange."

"They'll want the anomalies," Le Garre says.

"Which we don't have." I grimace, trying to plan this. "The minute they realise we're not Rocher, they'll turn their guns on us."

"Then what do we deliver?" Johansson asks.

"Bombs," I say. "Lots of bombs."

I key up another comms channel, linking in Sam and Arkov. Both of them seem okay. They're strapped into safety seats and working from screens, just like the rest of us. "Sam, how quickly can you bag up all the torpedo warheads into a detachable container?" I ask.

"It would take a couple of hours, Captain." Sam frowns. "I guess I don't have that long?"

"No, you have about ten minutes," I tell him. "Could you do it while we're moving?"

"We would be better off disconnecting the armoury, Captain," Arkov says. "All the warheads and ammunition are stored in there."

"Can you do it?"

Sam scowls. "All of these ships are built out of modular components, designed to break apart and be self-sustaining for a period. The armoury is the most dangerous compartment on the ship. We can do it, but I don't know if we have enough time."

I key up Johansson, adding her to the conversation. "Ensign, can we re-align this ship's lasers to cut away the armoury compartment?"

"Most of it, Captain, but why would you—"

"Get it done. Co-ordinate with Sam. He'll need to burn out the last connections." I dismiss the different screens and return to our tactical display. I'm looking at the three Fleet ships again. There's something strange about how they're positioned.

One of the three ships has turned late and is lagging behind the other two. Does that mean—

"Launch detected!" Johansson says. "Multiple torpedoes and a thermal signature. Laser activated."

We're too far away. "Confirm targets and trajectories, Ensign."

"The Fleet ships, they're firing on each other…. The *Asthoreth* is… they've been hit, it looks bad."

Oh God.

The one thing I've been counting on is Fleet. Good old predictable Fleet, holding to its protocols and guidelines. We talked about there being a possibility of betrayal, of mutiny and insurrection. I had been expecting we would be in danger from something, the minute we left the ship.

But not this. Not a civil war.

"Captain." Le Garre is struggling to keep her voice steady. She takes a breath then tries again. "Captain, what are your orders?"

I swallow past the lump in my throat and drag my eyes away from the tactical screen. I'm forcing myself to look at Le Garre's face, her brittle expression. "Major, I need you to hold us on a steady course, right for the intercept. Reduce our velocity as planned. Make no further changes unless you absolutely have to." I'm disconnecting the straps from the seat and unplugging the oxygen feed. An emergency light flashes but I ignore it. "I'm going down there. Major Le Garre, you have the bridge."

"Understood, Captain."

★   ★   ★

Velocity in space. Calculating trajectories, considering thrust and burn ratios. The practical application of Newton's third law. Preliminary space flight training requires that candidates are competent in doing calculations that produce flight paths and arcs that take into account the X, Y, and Z axes, along with all the other variables that might affect a ship's course.

Back in the early days, they did a lot of this by hand. We have computers, but that doesn't mean we rely on them without question. Staying familiar with the mathematics ensures we understand what we're being advised, rather than accepting the solutions blindly.

I sat in classrooms going through those calculations. I worked in groups with other students, who later became graduates and members of an organisation that has always been bigger than any nation or corporation. I worked with people on ships and on stations.

How many of them were on the other side? How many of them have betrayed us now?

Moving through the ship whilst we're decelerating is hard. As a rule, crew don't engage in any activity during a powered manoeuvre, even when we're going in a straight line. There are inherent dangers, particularly if the ship needs to make an emergency course correction. Work orders have to be authorised by the captain.

I'm climbing down through corridors and compartments, lowering myself towards the armoury. The gravity feels like its somewhere between 0.3 and 0.4 g. Maybe I should have stayed on the bridge, but I want to see what we're doing, in case this decision means we compromise the structural integrity of the *Gallowglass*. If I've broken another ship with this choice, we'll need to come up with a new plan very quickly.

"Captain?"

I'm here and trying to catch my breath. Arkov is with me, standing by the open hatch to the compartment holding a chemical cutter. He is speaking to me. I hold his eye. It's hard, but I need to. I can't let him down. I can't let any of them down. "We have seven minutes. How's it coming?"

"We're nearly there. Another couple of minutes, then we'll be ready for the laser. After that, we tidy up." Arkov gestures to a small cluster of emergency oxygen canisters beside him. They've been taped together, their release valves all jammed onto one pipe. "This should give our bomb a little push," he says, smiling at me from behind his visor.

I try to smile in return, but I don't think I manage more than a grimace. "Will we be able to get clear?" I ask.

Arkov nods. "I think so. Johansson did the calculations."

That does make me smile. Somehow, my supremely talented ensign found the time to sort all this out while I was struggling through the ship to help with the demolition. "If you have spare tools, I can help."

"Of course, Captain." Arkov reaches to the back of his belt and pulls out a small tube. "This reacts when exposed to oxygen. Just spread it along the welding points and keep it off your hands."

"Yep, I know the drill."

"Good."

I move towards the section of wall Arkov is pointing at. There's something calming about a simple task. I can affect this and make it happen. I glance up briefly. Sam is at the other door on the far side of the compartment doing the same work. He nods and gives me a thumbs up. I return the gesture, then settle down to the work.

The paste starts to burn as soon as it's out of the tube. The metal and plastic of the wall peels away. It's like the chemical composite is eating through everything it touches.

I hear the telltale sound of escaping oxygen a moment before the pressure alarm goes off.

"Okay, we're ready," Arkov says.

We move through the door quickly as the emergency seals engage and the room is sealed off. I can see the oxygen canisters strapped to the wall near the locked door. "Arkov to bridge? Johansson, we're ready for you to start."

"Understood. Firing the laser, now."

The view plate on the door frosts up immediately. For a moment, I'm back in another place, looking at a door and a DuraGlas window. I can see Technician Sellis dying in front of me, and Rocher's twisted grin.

Another alert sounds and Arkov nudges me back. "Time we got well clear, Captain. Sam will deal with the rest."

I can hear the tortured scream of metal as the laser hacks into the ship's hull. This has to be the stupidest plan I've ever thought of. We're relying on the safety systems embedded into the *Gallowglass* to maintain our hull integrity and atmosphere.

"Cutting complete," Johansson announces.

"Okay, moving in to work on the last connections now," Sam says. "Arkov, be ready to fire those canisters."

"Understood," Arkov says. He looks at me. "Captain...."

"I know, there's nothing I can do here." I grimace and nod. "I'll get back to the bridge."

★   ★   ★

"Update?"

"Procedure was a success, Captain," Johansson says. She's staring intently at the screen in front of her. "Arkov is about to fire the thruster."

I'm easing myself back into the captain's chair. The straps snake around me as I plug into the oxygen feed. "Time to impact?"

"Two minutes, fourteen seconds," says Le Garre.

"What will our distance be when it hits?"

"Approximately forty-eight kilometres. The shrapnel may hit us and cause damage. I'm ready to roll the ship to minimise that."

"Wait until Arkov and Sam are back in their chairs."

"Of course."

The main screen has a feed from one of the exterior cameras. The image is dark, the vast expanse of the universe unending and without illumination. Then a shadow comes into view. It is a ship of unfamiliar design. Long and thin...

...and *alien*.

Sunlight spills across the screen as the Sun crescents around Mars. I can see parts of the ship that look like they've been engineered by humans, but other parts – the curves and organic shapes – they were built by something else, some creature that has refined their designs beyond function, or considers functions that we have no comprehension of us a species.

The ultra-thin profile of the ship means it is very long indeed. Nearly a kilometre, according to the data calculation on the screen in front of me. A comparable length to the freighter, *Hercules*, whose distress call started all this. "Any indication that our friends over there are taking precautions?" I ask.

"None that we can tell," Johansson replies. "They should be expecting a delivery."

"If we've guessed right."

"Indeed, Captain."

Another window opens up on my screen. The feed is grainy and distorted, but the audio is clear, and I recognise the profile. "Duggins, I didn't—"

"Captain, you need to let me realign the laser and send a targeted transmission to that ship."

I'm frowning and glaring at the digital representation of my friend. "Why would I need to do that?" I ask.

"Captain, there's a data repository on board that ship which is capable of containing me," Duggins replies. "If you send me over, I might have a chance of survival."

"The minute they discover who we are and what we've done—"

"No offence, Captain, but I'll take those odds." The Texan drawl is eerie to listen to. I know the speech is synthesised and extrapolated from a mixture of recordings and interpretive algorithms, but it sounds exactly like the man I knew. "I'm barely hanging on here."

I nod. "Okay, do it."

"Thank you."

The laser tasked with sending a data burst to the Fleet ships is moving. Duggins is altering its alignment to try and link up with what looks to be a receiver on the unidentified ship. The exterior camera puts a green box around the device. Even from here, I recognise it as being an emitter, almost identical to the ones I've seen on Earth-made vessels.

"Forty-five seconds to impact," Le Garre announces.

"Transmitting now," Duggins says. "If I don't see any of you again…. Thank you…. I know you're all struggling to accept what happened but…for whatever it's worth, you've given me this chance."

"Goodbye, Ethan." My voice catches and I'm crying. The emotions well up, ambushing me unexpectedly. I raise a hand to brush away tears, swallow and try again. "I'm looking forward to debriefing you on what you find, Chief."

The camera eases back and I see the digital representation of Duggins's smile. "Looking forward to it, Captain," he says. Then he frowns, as if remembering something. "Captain, I should mention, the roo—"

The image cuts out.

"Fifteen seconds to detonation," Le Garre says. "Captain, I need to begin rotation."

I'm confused, trying to guess what Duggins was trying to say. "Johansson, is Duggins clear?"

"I…. Yes…. Yes! I think so, Captain!"

"Major, get us moving!"

"Aye, aye!"

CHAPTER FORTY-NINE

Holder

"Okay, we're out," Diouf announces.

I'm weightless in the chair. The straps are slack and floating around me. This is the first time I've experienced the sensation for an extended period of time.

The screen is still displaying a selection of debris from the station, but we're some distance away from it all now. The smaller fragments have been lost in the swirling mass, all gradually descending towards Mars. The sight from the surface will be a real spectacle, a deadly shower of fiery death.

"I couldn't stop Rocher," I say. "All those people are going to die."

"You did what you could," Diouf replies. "There are evacuation shuttles engaged in a rescue. They'll do everything they can."

"But the station…."

"Yeah, it's still going to crash. The projections I have suggest it'll hit somewhere close to the Jezero thermal generator."

I try to process that. Alison Wade's knowledge of Mars colonial geography isn't brilliant. "How many people?" I ask.

"Hundreds," Diouf says. "There's nothing we can do."

"What about us then? How long have we got?"

"A few hours until the oxygen in your compartment runs out. I expect the tanks out here will be empty a while sooner. The scrubbers will keep us going a while after that, but eventually, the build-up of carbon dioxide will poison us both." Diouf sighs. "I've turned on my emergency beacon, but there's a lot of interference out here. I don't know if anyone will reach us."

"What about us reaching them?" I ask. "The terminal in here, it's been hacked by Rocher and has some kind of root control access to the station system."

"Is it still connected?"

"I think so." I'm looking at the screen again. A small window is displaying connection information.

NFCOMMS DISCONNECTED. ADMIN ACCESS WITHDRAWN.

NFCOMMS ESTABLISHED. ADMIN ACCESS RESTORED.

NFCOMMS DISCONNECTED. ADMIN ACCESS WITHDRAWN.

NFCOMMS ESTABLISHED. ADMIN ACCESS RESTORED.

"The signal is dropping, but we still have access at the moment. Can we do something with that?"

There's a pause. I can almost hear Diouf thinking, trying to work out what I'm capable of, I guess. "I might be able to talk you through a series of instructions, but it'll be quicker if we can establish a data connection to the crawler from your device."

"How do I do that?"

"Either you dig in and find the codes Rocher used and give them to me, or we try to relay your screen to the console here," Diouf says. "I doubt either is going to be easy, if the station system was hacked to get access."

I pull up the screen keyboard again. Vague memories of being in a room discussing this system come back to me again. There is a remote access option. I remember that.

ACC COM TREE

Command Tree Open.

INST TERM ~RMOTE OPEN CONNECT.

Confirm connection broadcast?

Y.

Broadcasting….

"I've opened up a connection," I say to Diouf. "Can you access it?"

"Checking…" Diouf murmurs in surprise under his breath. "Yeah, that works. I'm in. Hopefully the link to the station will hold."

"What are you going to do?"

"Activate the emergency thrusters near the lecture theatre, where they were holding people hostage," Diouf explains. "With any luck we might be able to get them clear of the debris field and into a parking orbit."

I watch the screen change as Diouf works through the command tree. He has to find the right part of the station's system. He works fast. Windows open and close as he types in instructions. "Okay, found it," he says. "The computer indicates that most of the bio ident chips of the station staff are still in that room."

"Makes sense. It has the most acceleration seats, and they were locked in."

"It's separated and spinning at 3.4 g," Diouf says. "Firing thrusters. Hopefully, we can save some of them."

On the screen I see the compartment flagged and begin moving on a new trajectory, towards the edge of the debris field. The visual display shows a curved path, indicating their course, but then a second line appears and a third. "What's happening?" I ask.

"There are too many variables," Diouf says. "They might make it, they might not. Still, if not, it'll give them a little longer before their orbit decays."

"We all need to be rescued."

"Yes. We need Fleet and Mars CorpGov to get organised and sort out this mess before it gets any worse."

I wince and don't reply on that. Diouf only knows part of what's happened and what caused all this. I don't need to fill him in with all the details. Besides, we have more urgent worries. "The Fleet ships, where are they?"

"They disengaged from rescue operations, leaving the work to the Mars CorpGov shuttles," Diouf says. The screen changes and the tactical grid now show several large objects several thousand kilometres away from us. "I think they moved away to respond to another ship arriving."

I frown at that. Rocher wasn't expecting to survive. I'd thought all his talk of an extraction from the station was a lie to keep his people in line. If the people who commissioned him have that kind of resources....

"We're almost out of emergency thrust," Diouf says. "I'm angling our last burn to put us on an intercept course with Gateway – the old colonial staging point. It'll take a few hours before we get close, but if we can get on board, we'll be okay."

"Okay." I acknowledge the words, but I don't believe them. I'm still living moment to moment, breath to breath. But maybe, finally there is a chance....

CHAPTER FIFTY

Drake

FLEETCOMM LINK REESTABLISHED.

Seraphiel, this is *Nandin*, Fleet ID AS761208. What are you doing? Do you have an error in your guidance firing control?

...

Seraphiel, this is *Nandin*, please respond.

...

★   ★   ★

"The *Seraphiel* has targeted the *Asthoreth*'s engines. If the laser gets through the reinforced compartment, the fuel will ignite and they'll—"

"Too late."

Savvantine pronounces the fate of the ship just as the icon changes colour on her portable screen. The solid blue dot becomes red and starts to break apart.

Viewing it like this is horrible. I remember talking to my brother about some of the basic war games training he had to do before he left Mars. It's like a game.... You can see why military exercises involve pushing dots, icons and playing pieces around a board. All of it makes it impersonal. It stops you thinking about the lives being lost as pressurised compartments explode, exposing people to vacuum – a death where you suffocate as your body boils.

I glance at my companions. Both Lieutenant Rivers and Colonel Savvantine wear variations of the same calculating expression. To them, this is a game, but a game with the highest possible stakes: the future of humanity as a species.

"We knew there would be subversives in those ships," Savvantine says. Her voice is measured in tone, the words come out slowly. This is clearly affecting her, despite her demeanour. "They have been planning this for a very long time."

"Yes, Colonel. *We* have."

Rivers moves his hand to the holster at his belt and draws out his sidearm. The motion is slow and deliberate, almost casual. The gun is in his hand and pointed at Savvantine as if this were an action he practises every day.

"I'm sorry, Colonel, Doctor." Rivers doesn't *look* sorry. He looks calm and detached. "This has been an incredibly complex undertaking. Doctor Drake really wasn't supposed to survive the destruction of Phobos Station, and you...well.... Your death was to be actioned as soon as an opportunity presented itself."

"And that's what this is?" Savvantine asks.

"Yes, Colonel. That's what this is." Rivers gestures around the compartment. "I briefed Captain Ravanskar before we came on board. I indicated you might find accepting his authority as captain of the *Asthoreth* a little difficult. I suggested he make some necessary preparations. After all, you are an intelligence asset, and if you were to be captured alive, several active operations could be compromised. However, the people I work with have no desire for you to remain alive. They want you dead."

"So, you got me in here alone."

"Almost alone. With both of you here, I can tidy up an additional loose end." Rivers glances at me and smiles. The expression is cold, but triumphant. "You were supposed to deliver the secure transmitter chit to Rocher, communicating our message, and then die with everyone else. But somehow, you got away. Still, there were advantages to that."

"You ordered Boipelo killed."

Rivers nods. "Yes, I did."

"Why?"

"Because removing someone of status sends a message all of its own."

The answer is evasive. I sense there's more to it, but this isn't the movies, where villains reveal their secret plans. I remember the box retrieved from the station. "She means more than that to you."

Rivers stares at me. His smile fades. "You seem to have used your brain while you were over there, Doctor," he says.

"All very interesting, Antony," Savvantine says. "I'm sure we'll learn more when you're interrogated."

Rivers turns towards her. "You're planning to survive, then?"

"I always plan to survive."

Rivers smiles again. This time there's a hint of malice in his eyes. "Plans change. You'll die here."

"They'll know what you did."

"I have plenty of time. When they pick us up, I'll have mutilated your bodies sufficiently to ensure the gunshot wounds are undetectable."

"You're enjoying this," I say.

Rivers shrugs. "I do take a certain amount of personal satisfaction from being able to achieve the tasks I was asked to do. The next hour or so will be unpleasant, but it is necessary."

"Necessary for what?" Savvantine is glaring at him, tearing his attention away from me. I realise this is a tactic that may provide us with an opportunity. I need to be ready when it comes.

Carefully I engage the emergency release override, the panic button that releases all of the restraints holding me in place in this chair.

"Necessary for our aims. There has to be a change, a breakdown of the armlock Fleet has on humanity's reach into the solar system. There are slews of technologies that can ensure we achieve our aims quicker and faster than the dogmatic capitalism embraced by your masters."

"They are your masters too."

"Only until I was shown what's happening. This war is necessary to set us free." Rivers reaches up and adjusts his weapon. The muzzle is about four inches from Savvantine's head. "What we do now will change everything."

"Indeed."

The compartment shifts, throwing us all back in our seats, then forward. My hands are at the straps around me. I depress the lock and launch myself forward, trying to direct my momentum towards Rivers.

I grab his arm. My fingers fumble for his wrist as I crash into him, pushing him back into his chair. The gun goes off, the bullet impacting into the frame of Savvantine's seat. She is struggling to get loose to help.

Another gunshot. I'm pushed backwards. A flash of pain runs right through me. Then my right leg goes numb. But I don't stop fighting. I can't stop fighting. I've survived everything over the last twelve hours. There have been moments when I should have fought, but now, this moment, this is the moment where I will not back down.

I have hold of the barrel of the weapon. My fingertips curl around it and I push hard, jamming Rivers's hand against the wall. He is stronger than me, but can't get a second hand around to grab me because of the chair straps. His head is turned to the side, exposing his neck.

I don't hesitate. This is a battle for survival. I jam my face under his chin, open my mouth and bite into his throat as hard as I can.

Blood fills my mouth. I ignore it, letting it drool out in whatever direction the forces on the compartment dictate.

Rivers screams – a throaty desperate gurgle. He gets a leg free and between us. I feel his foot against my stomach and then I'm pushed away, a mixture of blood trailing out between us as I float back across the room.

I see Savvantine has another weapon in her hand, aimed at Rivers's head. She pulls the trigger.

★   ★   ★

"I'm sorry you had to be a part of this, Doctor."

I'm back in my chair and strapped in. Savvantine has removed the bullet fragments from my upper thigh, administered a clotting agent and slapped synth skin onto the wound.

"Lieutenant Antony Rivers was a good man. I don't know what they offered him or when they got to him, but he is a substantial loss to our cause."

"Your cause, you mean." I push myself up in the seat. The strapping is uncomfortable, causing me a little pain, but at least we aren't moving anymore. "I don't recall choosing a side."

Savvantine frowns. "After this, are you suggesting you're part of the insurrection?"

"Do there have to be two sides? There are plenty of people caught in the middle."

Savvantine moves away from me, returning to her chair. She starts to secure herself, pulling out the portable screen that she tucked into a holder on the arm. "People either obey the laws or they break them. In that regard there are two camps. The one I belong to is about obeying the law."

"Even if that means killing people, or leaving them to die?"

"Sometimes, someone has to dirty their hands." Savvantine nods towards the bloody body of Lieutenant Rivers. "When your life was threatened, you acted to defend yourself. Kill or be killed. That's how you survived the station too, I'd guess."

I flinch away from her calculating gaze. "I'm a doctor," I say, as much to remind myself as to remind her. "My life is about ensuring people get a chance to live."

"So is mine," Savvantine replies. "But the parameters of what I do are quite different."

The room lurches. I hear metal against metal, the sound of docking clamps securing us to another object. "Who is—"

"Looks like we're being rescued," Savvantine says. She pulls out Rivers's sidearm and throws it across the room to me. "Perhaps we'll see more of the lieutenant's new friends? You may need more of those survival instincts you exhibited earlier."

CHAPTER FIFTY-ONE

Johansson

I'm using the exterior camera to watch the descent.

The object drifts downwards. The makeshift booster attached to its side has long since expended its contents, but in space, a little push goes a long way.

Below, the strange vessel is like an island, or a continent. It fills the screen. Small objects are launched from the surface. Tiny plumes of mass ejection evidence of their own acceleration and other velocity changes. They intercept the object, attaching themselves to the outside. Further directional thrust is applied, and the assemblage shifts its course, descending towards a metallic structure that opens up like a flower.

The object nears the surface. The flower closes.

Three.

Two.

One.

Boom.

There's no noise in space. Our enemy is a silent invader. The building I saw our armoury compartment enter remains closed. The data from our sensors is limited. All I know is that the countdown has expired.

"Captain. What are your orders?" Le Garre asks.

I'm looking at Shann on a window on my screen. She's staring at her display, her expression one of savage concentration. I remember what happened before. She's been pushed so hard, taking responsibility and making the judgement calls. Every time she's needed to, she's rolled the dice and taken a chance.

We're still here. *We're still alive.*

"Captain?"

Shann blinks. Her focus changes, moving back to the present and Le Garre's question. "Secure all crew, prepare a burn. Get us to full stop as soon as you can. Then bring us about."

"Full stop. Aye, aye, Captain."

Le Garre doesn't wait long for crew confirmations. The straps bite into my shoulders as she engages the thrusters. The *Gallowglass* has been decelerating for hours, so we have a lot less velocity to burn off, but it still hurts.

I turn my head to one side and screw my eyes shut, enduring the gravities of force that are trying to fling me through the front viewing screen. I can feel the compartment shifting as the ship adjusts, moving our orientation as Le Garre executes the captain's order.

Then it eases and I can breathe.

"Full stop complete, Captain," Le Garre reports.

"What's the situation with our laser data link?" Shann asks.

I pull up the console. Before he left, Duggins realigned the laser to transmit to the alien ship. I've located the communications node that he targeted, but we're out of position now and I can't manoeuvre the laser to get another lock. Does that mean something has happened to Duggins? "Link is down, Captain," I report. "I can't re-establish it. Might be a problem at the other end."

"Okay. Johansson, I want laser targets then," Shann says. "Get the cannon aimed at a critical system on that ship. We need to be ready to follow up and fire at them whilst we're still in range."

"Yes, Captain." I pull up as many of the exterior cameras as possible, tasking them to focus on the enemy ship, identifying whatever structures we can. Window over window appears on the screen. Duggins is gone and the system is responding faster. I'm no longer worried about damaging him as I work.

Our enemy is fascinating to me. Those years I spent working on Fleet's SETI initiative involved long hours staring out into the void imagining what might be out there. The anomalies were a revelation that answered a massive question for me and for the rest of humanity. *We are not alone.*

But this? This is closer to something I can comprehend. A space vessel that is clearly alien, but also in some way comparable to what humans have designed.

A vessel that is vital and precious, but occupied – colonised by people who have no respect for what it represents. Their agenda supersedes any scientific curiosity. They have occupied this creation, taming and twisting it for their own agenda.

The thin extended shape indicates the direction of travel. A design used to take advantage of acceleration and deceleration as gravity for the occupants over long periods of time, orbits that would have lasted millennia. I can't help but speculate on the original purpose of this creation. It has to have some sort of role in this solar system, a caretaker of living creatures perhaps? Returning to the vicinity of Earth every few thousand years.

The cameras are tracking and zooming in, poring over the surface of the ship. I can see dark marks and gouges, evidence of impacts, either from combat or meteor collisions. Cables, scaffolding and piping are identified in small sections – definitely recent human activity. They are parasitic tendrils, extending out from a central hub.

Then I see debris spilling out of a small structure near the middle of the new construction. "Captain, I think I've got something," I say. "There's damage. Looks like the detonation went off."

"Compile the readings and send them over to me," Shann orders.

I start flagging the data and sharing it. Once the computer knows what we're looking for, and has a reference, the content starts to gather quickly. "Looks like damage to the control centre, the structure in the middle of their network. I think we may have set off a chain reaction."

"Keep an eye on it. Major?"

"Velocity shift in the enemy vessel, Captain. It's slowing but making no course correction.... I can't.... There's no thruster or engine that I can make out, but the speed register is definitely registering their deceleration."

"Any indication that they're bringing weapons to bear?"

"Nothing I can make out." Le Garre's reply is very neutral. We all know recognising an alien weapon could be all but impossible, and the strange contours of the ship mean that something we would recognise could be hidden. "The computer hasn't identified their torpedo launchers yet."

"Okay, keep checking," Shann says. "What about communications?"

I switch tasks, leaving the computer to continue compiling possible damage signs and pull up the relevant applications. The log ping for Fleet comms dedicated network has been down since we arrived. Now though....

"Captain, we have comms."

"Get me open channels with those Fleet ships."

"Aye, aye, Captain."

I start setting up the links. The network is still intermittent, indicating the anomaly interference is still out there, but it's sporadic now, as if there is no one co-ordinating the jamming.

"Links established with the *Nandin*, the *Asthoreth* and the *Seraphiel*," I report as the connections go green. The chatter comes through on my headset. I can hear panicking voices, different orders and requests.

"What's happening out there?"

"Captain, the *Nandin* and *Asthoreth* are engaged with the *Seraphiel*. The *Asthoreth* is badly damaged, as we saw. Comms chatter indicates that her crew are evacuating the ship."

"Your assessment?"

"Looks like blue on blue." I'm analysing the trajectories and course plots. "Torpedo launches and laser fire from the *Seraphiel* has ruined her engines. The *Seraphiel* is closing in to finish them off."

"What's the range to us?" Shann asks. "Can we launch torpedoes?"

"We could launch, we have ordnance in the tubes, but the interference is still affecting our guidance systems. Anything at long range would be subject to the same issues as before."

"Can you upload your programme to their guidance systems?"

"I can, but the distance will still reduce our chances of a successful strike."

"We only have three torpedoes left, Captain," Le Garre adds.

"We can't wait," Shann says. "Tell Sam to launch as soon as he's ready."

"I heard, Captain." Sam says over the comms. "Arkov and I are prepping the tubes now."

The guidance program is ready. I start the upload process. While the others are talking, I'm cycling through the communications chatter. There's no way of telling who are the loyalists and who are the insurgents. Shann is playing another hunch, making a choice to target the *Seraphiel*, not finish off the *Asthoreth*.

I can only hope she's right.

I open up another channel. This time, I'm trying to assess the rescue operations around Mars. There are shuttles from the colonies trying to extract people from the wreckage, but as to what they'll do after that? Who knows? "The station fragments are starting to enter Mars atmosphere," I report. "The orbital transports are completing their work and moving clear of the debris field."

"They are vulnerable," Le Garre says. "If they have survivors on those shuttles, they'll have less than twenty-four hours of oxygen available."

I'm looking at the tactical display. "The *Nandin* is launching torpedoes. Broadside salvo, full spread." I flip the screen so the representation traverses, giving me the projected plot of the missiles in three dimensions. "The anomaly interference is messing up their guidance. All missed the *Seraphiel*."

"Sam, are we ready yet?"

"Another two minutes, Captain."

I can see Shann biting back a curse and clenching her teeth in frustration. She knows every second we take is another life on the line. But Sam doesn't need reminding of that.

I'm listening to the transmissions, trying to catch something that would give us a clue as to who we should fire on.

"Co-ord…and flag…rescue…."

That was from the *Nandin*. My instincts tell me they are still loyal and trying to help. The *Seraphiel* though….

"Ready to fire, Captain."

"Johansson, give me a target," Shann orders.

"The *Seraphiel*, Captain. That's my best judgement."

"Okay. Sam did you hear?"

"Aye, aye. Firing."

There's a thump as the torpedoes are flung from their tubes. I pull up the tactical plot and see them appear next to the icon that represents the *Gallowglass*. Then, the screen vanishes, and a new terminal window appears with a single sentence and a series of dots.

ROOT KEY ACCESS REMOVED. BEGINNING LOCK OUT PROCEDURE....

Oh shit....

CHAPTER FIFTY-TWO

Shann

I've just ordered my crew to fire on a Fleet vessel.

If I'm not right about our target, this could be an act that dooms us all as traitors.

I've read the accounts of soldiers in battle. Part of my training required that I study the major engagements of different wars, analysing the decisions made by generals and admirals devising the plans and officers on the ground who were required to improvise.

I've also read the journals of soldiers on the front line, the people fighting with guns, knives, swords and their bare hands to fulfil the agendas of their commanders, the sacrifices they were forced to make in the name of a cause decided on far away in safe and secure cabinet rooms by officials who would never stain their hands with blood.

How do you deal with choices like this? How do you manage the guilt when those moments come back to you years later, when you are alive and the people you faced over the line are long since dead?

Hundreds and thousands of veterans; survivors of wars who went on to raise the next generation found their ways to cope and live with the choices they'd made.

I need to learn that.

The missiles are tracking across space. The icons in front of me are orange pixels, impersonal and simple. They give no indication of the manufacturing miracle going on out there. The technology evolved and refined from iteration after iteration. Each innovator building on the next. Standing on the shoulders of giants.

All reduced down to a moving dot on my screen.

"Three minutes to projected impact, Captain."

"Are we on course?"

"So far," Johansson sounds anxious, but she's coping much better than she was. The frustration and impulsiveness is gone. She's working the problem. "All three projectiles are maintaining their heading. The interference is weaker now. The program is compensating for the shifts."

"You think they'll make it?"

"Yes.... Captain, there's something else." Johansson looks up from her screen and around the room. "The computer is rejecting my root key."

Rejecting? "You mean our access...."

"Yes, we're losing control of the ship."

I recall the image of Duggins on the screen – what he was trying to say to me. He must have been keeping the system update in check. "The Erebus transmission. They must have uploaded a patch. Can you stop the computer from loading it?"

"I can try."

"Stay on it."

The *Seraphiel* is manoeuvring. The captain on that ship must know what's happening. His computer system and crew will have reported the torpedo launches and projected the danger. Initiating a six-g burn would be the best possible defence available against a projectile-based attack. Fleet ships are not equipped with countermeasures, which is why the missile-jamming system used by the *Gallowglass* was such a surprise when we encountered it.

I'm looking at the icon on the screen. I know Captain Tranov or whoever is in charge will have all the data to hand. They'll know that accelerating at six gravities is not going to be enough. They'll know pushing any harder is going to risk the crew.

It's a marginal choice, an ogre's choice. One of those improvisations that officers on the ground have to make.

"Captain, I've suspended the patch," Johansson announces.

"Can you keep it locked out?"

"I think so...for a while at least."

The last thing we need right now is our own ship rebelling against us. "Time to torpedo impact?" I ask.

"Impact in one minute, forty-five seconds, Captain," Le Garre says.

"Get me a direct channel to the *Nandin*."

"Aye, aye."

My earpiece hisses. The residual interference from the anomalies is still there. "*Nandin*, this is Captain Shann of the *Khidr*, aboard the prize vessel *Gallowglass*. Please acknowledge."

Faintly, I hear someone speaking on the other end. "Johansson, can you clean up the signal?"

"Working on it, Captain."

The words disappear, replaced by a strange singing. A voice that sounds impossible in terms of its pitch and modulation but is definitely a voice. I'm reminded of Le Garre's off-shift music choices and the strange signals we encountered before. Is this what the anomaly interference sounds like?

"Okay, this should be better," Johansson announces. "Repeat your message please, Captain."

"*Nandin*, this is Captain Shann of the *Khidr*, aboard the prize vessel *Gallowglass*. Ship ID - KH7888321. Please acknowledge."

"This is Captain Elliott of the *Nandin*. We're receiving you."

Mattias Elliott. I know him by association, not in person. As patrol captains who are signed up for lengthy tours of duty, we have little time to socialise. I open a window on the screen and see the animated headshot of a man in a visor, clearly plugged into the ship's internal oxygen supply. "Captain, you have ordnance inbound. We've fired on the *Seraphiel*."

"Yes, we've detected your launch, *Gallowglass*. It's unlikely that your torpedoes will—"

"Captain, please take appropriate precautions. We have experimental guidance software on our weaponry. They should get through."

There's a silence. I can't read Elliott's expression, but if he's mortally offended at my interruption, he needs to get over it.

"Understood, *Gallowglass*." There's a click as he keys into a different channel and I see the *Nandin* begin to move on the tactical display. Then he comes back to me. "I assume you're contacting us to give us a summary of your intentions?"

"We can get into detail if you like, but right now, I believe we have a rogue asset to neutralise. You're the nearer ship, so I'd respectfully suggest your weapons officer co-ordinates with Major Le Garre over your best firing solution after our torpedoes detonate."

"I'll open up a direct link."

"Thank you."

The window closes and suddenly I don't feel so alone. "Time to impact?" I ask. I can see the numbers, but I like to ask.

"Thirty seconds, Captain."

★ ★ ★

We are at war.

Three torpedoes crash into the port side of the *Seraphiel*. The ship is fatally crippled, the reactor shield compromised, meaning the crew have little choice but to abandon ship.

I see none of this. Instead, the computer changes icons on the screen. Perhaps for some individuals, that might be a soothing disconnection from the consequences of what we've done, but not for me. I've been aboard a ship as it's been torn apart by the enemy.

I know Captain Tranov. I met him before I took the *Khidr* commission. I thought we were friends. Was he in charge when this happened, or did his crew mutiny, take the ship and force this confrontation?

I imagine the situation. Some of the crew will die immediately as the compartments they are in will be ripped open and instantly depressurise. Emergency doors on the connecting corridors will close, sealing off the compromised sections. Some crew will die in that process; injured and cut off from the safe parts of the ship.

Others will be injured and killed from the shift in velocity and direction. The *Seraphiel* has been forced into a spin and any individual not strapped in will be thrown around, smashed against the walls, floor and roof of the room they are in.

I remember Jonathan Drake and how he was smashed to pieces. A shiver runs through me.

"*Nandin* has a targeting solution on the *Seraphiel*'s engines, Captain."

"Are they firing?"

"Not yet. Captain Elliott has activated near field ship-to-ship comms," Le Garre says. "I think they're trying to negotiate a surrender."

For a moment, I'm irritated and fearful. I remember Bogdanovic. The mutiny on the *Khidr* was never going to be resolved with a conversation. The choice had been made by those who had decided to seize the ship. It will be the same here.

But I guess it's not my call, and Elliott feels he has to try.

"Any sign of activity here?" I ask.

"No movement," Le Garre replies. "The unidentified ship continues to slow. Distance from us is three hundred kilometres. The debris trail from the artificial compound is continuing. The computer has identified a venting of pressure."

"An oxygen leak?"

"Could be, but we've no way to verify that."

I tweak the screen in front of me, pulling out the view so I can see most of the Mars locale. The old Gateway orbital is on the far side of the planet. The debris field of Phobos Station is starting to break up and descend into the atmosphere. We are between them and the Fleet ships. Two of them are crippled now. Only the *Nandin* is still moving.

There are several other objects between us. The computer identifies unexploded ordnance and several ejected emergency compartments. "Flag those and send data to the *Nandin*," I tell Johansson. "Let them know we're ready to assist."

"Captain Elliott has acknowledged the request and declined it," Johansson says. "He's asked that we stay in escort with the anomaly ship."

I'm frowning at that. There are people out there in danger. We can help them. Elliott doesn't outrank me, but....

"Inform the *Nandin* that we'll do that."

"Aye, aye, Captain."

Johansson communicates the message. As she does, Le Garre pages me on a private channel. I accept the request. "What's the problem, Major?" I ask.

"I just wanted to thank you," Le Garre says. "Thank you, Captain Shann."

I'm unprepared for these words. They're so human and personal; unadorned or embellished. Le Garre is staring straight at the screen, straight at me.

"Thank you too, Angel," I say. "We...we did it together."

"Captain, we have a few moments. Perhaps Chase and Arkov should check the medical stasis compartments?"

"Good idea." I remember Chiu and Travers. I feel guilty for forgetting about them. I switch to an open channel. "Sam, Vasili. Can you check on the hibernation pods?"

"Of course, Captain. Doing it now," Arkov replies.

I look up to see Le Garre removing her helmet. Her dark hair is sweaty and matted to her head; her face is shiny and slick. I follow suit and disconnect my hook-up to the internal oxygen supply. I expect I look similar.

Le Garre looks at me. "I think we did it, Captain," she says. "I think we won."

Won? What did we win? I glance at Johansson. She's still hunched over her screen, her expression one of savage concentration. "Ensign?" I say, and she raises her head. "At ease, Ensign. That's an order."

Johansson nods. She takes a deep breath and lets it all go in a sigh that seems to go right through her. Then she leans forward, her body shaking as she sobs. The stress and tension finally released.

I want to do the same. I'm about to, when I see a window on the screen flashing. I key it up.

Duggins's face appears on my screen. "Hello, Ellisa," he says. "I made it."

FLAME TREE PRESS
FICTION WITHOUT FRONTIERS
Award-Winning Authors & Original Voices

Flame Tree Press is the trade fiction imprint of Flame Tree Publishing, focusing on excellent writing in horror and the supernatural, crime and mystery, science fiction and fantasy. Our aim is to explore beyond the boundaries of the everyday, with tales from both award-winning authors and original voices.

•

Other titles in the *Fractal* series by Allen Stroud:
Fearless

You may also enjoy:
The Sentient by Nadia Afifi
American Dreams by Kenneth Bromberg
Junction by Daniel M. Bensen
Interchange by Daniel M. Bensen
Second Lives by P.D. Cacek
The City Among the Stars by Francis Carsac
Vulcan's Forge by Robert Mitchell Evans
The Widening Gyre by Michael R. Johnston
The Blood-Dimmed Tide by Michael R. Johnston
The Sky Woman by J.D. Moyer
The Guardian by J.D. Moyer
The Last Crucible by J.D. Moyer
The Goblets Immortal by Beth Overmyer
The Apocalypse Strain by Jason Parent
Until Summer Comes Around by Glenn Rolfe
A Killing Fire by Faye Snowden
Screams from the Void by Anne Tibbets

Horror titles available include:
The Haunting of Henderson Close by Catherine Cavendish
The Garden of Bewitchment by Catherine Cavendish
Black Wings by Megan Hart
Those Who Came Before by J.H. Moncrieff
Stoker's Wilde by Steven Hopstaken & Melissa Prusi
Stoker's Wilde West by Steven Hopstaken & Melissa Prusi

•

Join our mailing list for free short stories, new release details, news about our authors and special promotions:

flametreepress.com